PROMOTED TO THE ITALIAN'S FIANCÉE

CATHY WILLIAMS

PREGNANT WITH HIS MAJESTY'S HEIR

ANNIE WEST

MILLS & BOON

First Published in Great Britain 2021
by Mills & Boon, an imprint of HarperCollins*Publishers*
1 London Bridge Street, London, SE1 9GF

Promoted to the Italian's Fiancée © 2021 Cathy Williams

Pregnant with His Majesty's Heir © 2021 Annie West

ISBN: 978-0-263-28242-9

Printed and bound in Great Britain
by CPI Group (UK) Ltd, Croydon, CR0 4YY

PROMOTED TO THE ITALIAN'S FIANCÉE

CATHY WILLIAMS

To my inspirational partner David
and my glorious daughters

CHAPTER ONE

'I'VE HAD A personal invitation.'

Evelyn Scott pushed the handwritten note across the kitchen table to Izzy. The salad the elderly woman had prepared earlier, using produce from the vegetable patch at the end of her garden, had been eaten, the home-made lemonade drunk and outside a burning orange sky signalled the arrival of dusk.

Here in Napa Valley, the horizons seemed limitless and the vast expanse of sky was a canvas upon which every shade of colour begged to be painted, depending on the time of the day and the vagaries of the weather. Izzy could have lain on her back in a field for hours, just appreciating its spectacular, ever-changing beauty.

'A personal invitation?' She reached forward to take the note and realised that, while they had been lazily conversing for the past hour and a half, while the older woman had listened and responded to everything Izzy had had to report, she had been busily hiding the fact that she was worried sick. And Izzy knew the source of that worry.

She read the note.

It was written on a piece of heavy, cream parchment paper, the sort of paper she associated with aggressive bankers calling in loans or hard-nosed lawyers threatening jail.

The writing confirmed that first impression. Long, determined strokes issued an invitation to tea, during which the sale of the cottage could be discussed 'face to face'. The invitation looked more like a summons.

'It's the first time I've been approached by the man himself.' Evelyn rose to her feet and began clearing the plates and glasses, waving aside Izzy's offer to help. 'You don't need to concern yourself with an old woman's problems. That's not why you came here in the first place.'

'Evelyn, your problem is my problem.'

It still felt weird after nearly a month to call the older woman 'Evelyn' instead of Nanny Scott, which was always how her mother had referred to her. To this day, Izzy had vivid memories of sitting in her mother's bedroom, watching as Beverley Stowe brushed her hair and dabbed on lipstick, smacking her lips together to distribute the colour evenly, inspecting her face from every angle as she chatted away. Izzy had listened avidly. She'd thought her mother to be the most beautiful woman in the world and she had drunk in every single thing that had passed her lips with the fervent adoration only a child was capable of.

There had been a thousand tales about Nanny Scott. Izzy had met Evelyn Scott for the first time on her one and only trip to California when she'd been nine, a year before her mum and dad had died in a plane crash. That holiday was etched in her mind because holidays with her parents had been few and far between. She could still relive the high-wire excitement of being with her parents for that heady, hot, lazy month in summer as though it had happened yesterday and not thirteen long years ago.

So now, sitting here, seeing the worry on Evelyn's face, Izzy felt anger surge inside her at the preposterous and intimidating antics of the billionaire who wanted to buy the cottage out from under the seventy-nine-year-old woman's feet, and to heck with what happened to her after that. He had sent his minions, but the message had not been delivered to his satisfaction, so here he was, knife at the ready to cut an old woman loose for the sake of money.

'No,' Evelyn said firmly. She placed a plate of home-made pumpkin pie in front of Izzy and sat back. 'You have enough on your plate without all of this nonsense. No one can force me to do anything.'

'My plate is looking very clean and empty at the moment,' Izzy returned.

'So you finally took my advice and picked that phone up and spoke to your brother?' Evelyn's brown eyes sparked with lively interest, her own problems temporarily set aside. 'I knew there was something you wanted to tell me. An old woman can sense these things.'

Izzy reflected that *this* was exactly why she had no intention of returning to Hawaii until she had sorted out the situation here. No, she wasn't obliged to, but where did decency and a sense of fair play go if you only did what was right because you were obliged to?

Izzy had fled Hawaii after her heart had been broken. And she had fled to the place where her mother had grown up, feeling an overpowering need somehow to *be close* to her mum in the wake of her disastrous affair with Jefferson.

The yearning just to *feel* that the spirit of her mother

was close by had been silly, childish and irrational, but it had also been overwhelming enough for her to heed its insistence.

She'd rooted out the tin that was stuffed with old photos, postcards and pretty much everything she had gathered over the years before her parents had died. She had pored over faded photos of the sprawling ranch where her mother had spent her childhood before she had left home at eighteen and begun a second life in England. She had squinted at pictures of Nanny Scott, the grandparents she had only met once and all the pretty young people who had crowded her mother's teenage years. And then, heart swollen with sadness, whimsy and nostalgia, she had dumped all her responsibilities at the hotel where she had been working and quite simply *fled*.

Of course, she'd felt guilty at leaving her brother in the lurch, but she had made sure that everything was up to date, and she'd known that Nat would be able to take over temporarily. She'd also known that Max would descend and everything would be sorted because that was what he did. He wielded a rod of iron, gave commands, issued orders and *things got done*.

She'd felt far too bruised for any residual guilt about running away to anchor her in a place she no longer wanted to be, doing a job she hadn't the heart to do, however privileged she might be to have had it in the first place.

It was as if her wounded heart had made her face all those long years of living in a wilderness, learning how to manage a life without the love and input of parents, watching and envying her friends and the relationships they had with their parents.

So often her youthful heart had twisted when friends had moaned, because at least they'd had a mum and dad to moan about. Max and James had both done their best for her but there'd been only so much her brothers were capable of doing. She had stared deep into the void left by her parents' death and, in the wake of Jefferson and her bitter disillusionment, had been driven to confront it, to search for that missing *something*, which foolishly she had thought she might find if she went back to where her mother had lived.

She'd known that the big house, as her mother had called it, had long been sold, along with the vineyards. She hadn't gone there expecting to walk into her mother's childhood home. But just *being* in the area was soothing and she had been over the moon to find that Evelyn was still there when she had visited the cottage.

She'd half-expected her brother to ferret her out. He had sufficient clout to get someone to locate her within seconds, but he hadn't, and it had given her a chance to really connect with Evelyn. And, over a couple of weeks, she'd heard about the problems she was having, trying to hang onto the cottage in the face of ever-insistent demands that she sell to the guy who had bought the big house, and the even bigger house that adjoined it, so that two medium-sized vineyards could be turned into one enormous one. Another greedy developer with no scruples.

Evelyn had also been there to hear about *her* troubles and she had no intention of abandoning the older woman now, in her hour of need.

Not if she could help it.

'Well?' Evelyn pressed. 'I'm tired of thinking about my dreadful woes. Tell me some good news. And I know you've got good news! I may be old but my eyes are in perfect working condition. What did that brother of yours have to say? Gosh, my dear, I wish I had had the opportunity to meet all of you so that I could put faces to the names. I wish I knew what James and Max looked like in the flesh, and not just in those pictures you showed me on your phone.'

Izzy surfaced from her thoughts. Obligingly, she told Evelyn about her phone call, which she had been hugging to herself for the past few hours. Yes, she had spoken to Max, after a lot of procrastination. He hadn't hunted her down he had listened to Mia, thank God, and had chosen to hang back but, even so, he would only have done so reluctantly.

Izzy had been terrified when she'd made that call to tell him that there was a chance she would be staying on in California because of a muddle with Evelyn's accommodation.

She had worried that he would be fuming. Silently, aggressively, *scarily* fuming. She'd expected him to order her back and had been geared for an argument. But he'd been great. He'd told her he'd been touring the islands, much to her amazement, because she couldn't remember her brother *ever* doing *anything* that didn't involve an office, a computer and an army of yes-men lining up to do as told. And he'd assured her that everything was covered. Had told her that when she did return they would talk about what she wanted to do instead of what he wanted her to do.

Rather than ask *Who? What? Why?* and *When?*, and risk a change of heart, she had rung off and counted her blessings.

She reached for the note again and gazed at it before looking at Evelyn.

'You won't be going to have tea with that guy,' she said quietly but firmly. She reached across the table and held the older woman's hands between hers. Evelyn was as thin as a bird and Izzy could feel the bulge of her veins under her transparently pale skin. She was strong enough, and got a lot of exercise tending to her garden, but it still felt as though a puff of wind might blow her away.

'I've got to get it out of the way.' Evelyn sighed.

'No,' Izzy said. '*You* don't. *I* do.'

Gabriel Ricci looked at his watch and frowned because the woman was running late.

He had issued the invitation for five-thirty. He'd figured that that would be roughly when someone in her late seventies would probably be sitting down for a cup of tea, coffee or hot chocolate and a slice of cake, having had an afternoon nap of some sort. It was an assumption made on absolutely no concrete evidence because he hadn't actually had a cup of tea with anyone elderly at five-thirty in the afternoon in his life before.

Five-thirty was the very peak of his working day. Cups of tea and slices of cake were the last things on his mind. However, needs must. But it was still irritating to find himself waiting, because he had reached a position of such power and influence in his life that he usually never had to wait for anyone any more. He beckoned, and they duly appeared exactly when they were meant to.

How life had changed, he reflected idly. He looked around the stunning sitting room with its pale colours, lavish artwork and its view of acres upon acres of vine-yards outside, rows upon rows in perfect symmetry, marching in exquisite formation towards the horizon.

He could still remember the cramped house he had grown up in—the dingy paintwork, the meagre patch of grass outside that had had to multi-function as back garden, vegetable plot and place to hang the washing on those hot summer days in Brooklyn. He and his parents had lived cheek to jowl with their neighbours, and life had been crowded and chaotic. It was a place where the toughest rose to the surface and the weakest were either to be protected or allowed to sink to the bottom.

Against this backdrop, his devoted parents had managed to nurture the importance of education and the need to get out or go under. There were many times when Gabriel had resented the repeated mantra to 'study hard and make something of yourself'. Because slacking off and having fun had been an irresistible temptation, especially when he'd known that he could have been the leader of the pack with the snap of a finger. He was big, he was street-sharp and he was fearless. But the mantra had sunk in and he had had too much love and respect for his hard-working Italian parents to walk away from their teachings.

He'd studied. He'd worked hard. He'd ended up at MIT studying engineering, and after that at Harvard, doing a PhD in business. He hadn't set his sights on climbing the ladder. Climbing wasn't going to do. He'd set his eyes on soaring to the very top of the ladder. Soaring was something he was in favour of. He wasn't going to replicate his father's life, taking orders from people dumber than him but with money, lineage and connections. He'd raced to the top of the food chain and savoured the freedom and respect that came with great wealth and even greater power.

He had politely turned away all the lucrative offers from the giants and instead, unannounced, had headed straight through the front door of a small, family-run investment company that was slowly being ground into the dust by the big boys in the business.

Sitting here now, Gabriel could still smile at the memory of that small company, with whom he still kept in close contact, because that had been his springboard and he had chosen wisely. He had catapulted them out of gridlock, got them back on the race track and had seen them steer a course through the minefield of threatening competition all around them. When they'd sold the company two years after he'd joined, they'd made millions and Gabriel had made even more.

The rest... Well, he was feared now. He had long ago said goodbye to that street-fighting Brooklyn boy who had never quite belonged because he'd been too ambitious, too smart, too focused on finding a way out. Life hadn't been easy in the years since but it had been good, at least financially—better than good.

Good enough not to sit here, at nearly six in the evening, waiting for the Scott woman to show up.

He was standing up, impatiently moving to pace the room, when the door to the sitting room was pushed open and he looked round, seeing first Marie, his housekeeper, and then immediately behind her...

Gabriel stopped dead in his tracks.

He'd been expecting a woman in her late seventies. He'd known what she looked like. He'd had a photo of her emailed to him prior to this meeting.

Instead, he was looking at a young woman, as slender as a reed with silvery white-blonde hair that tumbled in curls past her shoulders and down her back. Her skin was satin-smooth and her eyes cornflower blue—as clear as crystal.

She was dressed in dungarees and one of the straps had slipped off her shoulder, revealing a cream vest underneath and the shadowy curve of a small breast.

He was annoyed at the sudden lapse of self-control but, even as he stifled it, he could still feel the stirring of his libido and the uninvited, utterly misplaced notion that this sort of immediate, knee-jerk physical reaction was just not him—and *that* annoyed him even more.

He abruptly broke the silence while moving forward. 'And you are?'

His voice was cool and soft, and feathered down Izzy's spine like the promise of danger.

What had she been expecting? Not this.

The house she had approached only distantly resembled the much smaller place her grandparents had owned, the one captured in that handful of faded photographs Izzy had lovingly stashed. It had clearly been extended over the years and was now the fitting palace of a billionaire, although she wasn't quite certain how long the guy had owned it. According to Evelyn, it had been bought and sold twice and, she had confided the evening before, he was the last buyer and recently on the scene. He'd done all the renovations, though, and Evelyn knew that because she had seen those very renovations in progress over the better part of a year, during which time the vineyards continued to be maintained to the very highest standard.

Yet she had still been impressed by the scale of the

place. It was vast. A vast white mansion fronted by a courtyard that could have housed a hundred cars with room to spare.

She'd stared but was undaunted. She was familiar with staggering wealth. She knew what it could and couldn't buy, and a seventy-nine-year-old woman was not one of those things on the table for sale, and she intended to make that very clear.

She'd been shown in by a young girl with a cheerful demeanour and not many words, and she'd been feeling pleasantly bolshie until now. Until she stood in this exquisite sitting room, with the door quietly shutting behind her, staring at the most beautiful man she had ever seen in her life.

He was tall, a few inches over six feet, with a body that was lean and muscular, as sinewy as an athlete's. He was wearing a short-sleeved white polo shirt and dark trousers that rode just low enough on his lean hips to emphasise the taut narrowing of his waist and the length of his legs. His dark hair was slightly too long, curling against the collar of his polo shirt, and he had lashes to die for, lush and dark, shielding eyes that were as cool as black ice. And he was burnished bronze, exotically stunning.

He took her breath away and the confidence with which she had sauntered into the house evaporated as fast as dew on a summer's morning.

'Well?'

Izzy discovered that her mouth was dry and she averted her eyes because the temptation to stare was overwhelming. Unfortunately, eyes averted, she could still see the image of him in her head, so drop-dead gorgeous with olive skin, eyes as dark as midnight and features that were so perfectly chiselled that for a second you could almost overlook the glacial lack of welcome in his expression.

Not for long, though, as his coldly delivered question snapped her right back down to earth with a bump.

'Izzy Stowe,' she said abruptly. He strolled towards her and she backed away a couple of inches and folded her arms in a gesture that was semi-belligerent, semi-defensive.

'And you are standing in my living room because...?'

'You sent a note to Evelyn Scott. You wanted to discuss the business of bullying her into selling the cottage.' Defiant words, she thought, which was precisely the opposite of how she was feeling. Intimidated, was more like it. She shuddered to think how Evelyn would have coped. Evelyn was lively, but she was older, and might have been easily cowed by this kind of man. Frankly, who wouldn't? He looked the sort who'd had dungeons constructed for anyone who dared get in his way.

'I have no desire to talk to anyone but Mrs Scott. The door is behind you, Miss Stowe.'

With great effort, Izzy stayed her ground.

How rude! But why should she be surprised? Anyone who was happy to use bully-boy tactics on an old woman wasn't exactly going to be the sort who prioritised good manners and common courtesy, was he?

'Evelyn has given me full permission to deal with this situation.' She remained where she was but she badly wanted to turn tail and flee.

'Your qualifications being...?'

'We're old friends and I want to look out for her.'

'Isn't she capable of looking out for herself? She

seemed very determined in her replies to my legal team when they've been in contact with her.'

'Would you mind if I sit?' Izzy noted his hesitation and knew that he was weighing up his options. He was a busy man, she guessed, with limited time to spare running round for an elusive old woman. Another day waiting for a meeting would be an unnecessary delay and maybe he was weighing up the odds of the result being exactly the same—no Evelyn but *her* again.

He nodded curtly to one of the chairs and Izzy tentatively inched towards it and sat. Immediately she felt at a disadvantage, because he continued to tower over her, but her legs had been wobbly.

'Speak.'

One word delivered as he continued to stand over her, staring down through narrowed eyes.

Izzy noted that the invitation to take tea had obviously been rescinded now that she had been the one to show up rather than Evelyn. He hadn't even offered her a glass of water and he showed zero signs of remedying the oversight.

'Would you mind sitting?' she asked. 'I don't want to have this conversation craning my neck.'

She half-expected him to ignore her but instead he dragged a footstool over and positioned it directly in front of her so that she had no option but to look at him. Up close like this, he was even more forbidding, because he was so much closer—close enough for her to breathe in the warm, woody scent of whatever aftershave he was wearing, and definitely close enough to see the unforgiving coldness in his dark eyes.

'Evelyn has confided in me about her situation.' Izzy kept her voice even and calm. His eyes were sooty-black and scarily watchful, and she could sense her every word being carefully dissected and meticulously inspected from every angle. She shivered.

'Are you related to Mrs Scott?'

'*Miss* Scott. Evelyn never married.'

'That's of little relevance to this situation.'

'Is it, Mr Ricci?' Izzy asked quietly. 'That cottage is where Evelyn's lived most of her adult life. Well over five decades. It's all she's ever known. She has no husband, no partner and no children. Do you really think she's going to jump for joy at the thought of leaving the one place in the world that represents stability for her? Furthermore, she has all her friends within driving distance, and all her social meetings happen in the town. Yet you want to drive her away from the one place she's ever called home.'

'That's a very rousing speech, Miss Stowe, but I don't care for the emotive vocabulary. I have not been using bullying tactics and my desire is not to *drive* anyone anywhere. Nor, for that matter, is it any of my concern whether the woman never chose to get married.'

'You want to buy her cottage!'

'At a price that's way over the market odds.'

'There's no price high enough to dislodge someone from the only place they know as home.'

'I beg to differ.'

Without warning, he vaulted upright, and Izzy followed his unhurried progress to a buzzer on the wall. Within seconds, the very same young lady who had shown her to the sitting room was knocking on the door.

'Something to drink, Miss Stowe? Before I persuade you that it would be in Miss Scott's best interests to take the offer I'm making and run with it.'

The sheer arrogance of the man was mind-blowing, Izzy thought. He was prepared to hear her out but it was clear that his mind was already made up. As Evelyn had pointed out, though, no one could force her hand. He'd probably figured he'd be onto a winner by confronting Evelyn face to face, oozing menace, muttering veiled threats and then just waiting for her to crumble in fear.

Gabriel Ricci, Izzy concluded, was everything she disliked in a person. He was rude, ruthless, arrogant and utterly incapable of seeing anyone's agenda but his own.

She was guiltily aware that in many respects he reminded her of Max, although her brother had very logical reasons for being the way he was.

When she'd been much younger—too young after the death of their parents really to understand the complexities of the situation—she had absolutely *hated* her older brother for his inflexible, disciplinarian approach. He had overseen everything she'd done with a baleful and unforgiving eye, forcing her to toe the line, refusing her all the little liberties her friends had enjoyed. Permission had had to be granted for the smallest of excursions and, as she had become a teenager, he had become stricter yet.

Only when James had sat her down one afternoon, and gently tried to explain why Max felt driven to protect her, had she come close to understanding those heavy-handed tactics. He had taken over as the head of the household and it had fallen to him to make sure as little changed as humanly possible for both James and her. It had fallen to him to run the company until James had been able to step up to the plate and help, which he had. So he had ruled with a rod of steel, and it was only recently that she wondered what had been lost for him in the process.

But what was *this* man's excuse for being a complete bastard?

He clearly wasn't in the business of trying to buy the cottage because he cared about the fate of the occupant. This was the first time he had even deigned to make personal contact with Evelyn. Prior to that, he had handed the messy business to one of his underlings to sort out.

'I'll have a glass of water,' she said coolly and he shrugged and turned to the young girl.

'A glass of water,' he said. 'Snd a bottle of Cabernet Sauvignon—with two glasses.'

'I won't be drinking any wine,' Izzy informed him abruptly. 'I'm not here to have drinks, Mr Ricci. I'm here to tell you that Evelyn won't be selling the cottage and, if you don't stop pestering her, I'll have no option but to get in touch with a lawyer.'

'This particular Cabernet is extremely good. Powerful yet elegant, and one hundred percent sustainable.'

'Have you heard a word I've just said?' She fell into temporary seething silence until the housekeeper returned with drinks as requested, carefully pouring Gabriel a glass and handing Izzy the water she had asked for.

She could barely contain her anger at his indifference to what she had to say.

'Well?' she snapped, as he took his time appreciating the wine.

'This is my first foray into the wine business,' he informed her, swirling his glass and then taking a sip as he coolly looked at her over the rim of the glass. He sauntered to the window and gazed out for a few seconds before turning to look at her.

Izzy said nothing, skewered into silence. Buried under her fury and feeling of impotence was the reluctant recognition that there was something mesmerising about the man. Her mouth wanted to hang open and she desperately had to make an effort to cling to her self-control because she knew with unerring gut instinct, if he sensed *any* weakness, he would take advantage of it with the ruthless speed of a born predator.

'I like this part of the valley and I like the size of the vineyards. Combined with the neighbouring estate, I have extremely promising acreage.' He paused to have another mouthful of wine and then he strolled back to where he had been sitting. This time, he leaned towards her, filling the space between them with such suffocating force that Izzy automatically slightly leaned back. A glass of water gave absolutely no Dutch courage.

'Here's the thing,' he said softly. 'Your friend is sitting on a patch of land that is in the midst of my vineyards. It is an oasis, I am sure, at this very point in time. However, should Miss Scott fail to sell, I have every intention of buying the land that abuts her oasis. I intend to keep this house for myself, my personal estate whether I am occupying it or not, but I will require suitable accommodation for the man who will effectively be running the show, and his staff. It will be a business of no small scale.

'There will, first of all, be the chaos of a compound being built. Your friend, I fear, will find herself surrounded by the bustle of people coming and going. It will no longer be quite the oasis it currently is. In due course, I intend to extend further and have a boutique hotel on the grounds for a handful of wine connoisseurs who want to sample the workings of the vineyard first-hand, taste the wines, watch the process from grape to barrel.' He shrugged elegantly. 'This, I fear, is the way of the world. Nothing ever stays the same.'

Izzy gaped, fascinated despite herself at the picture being painted before her dismayed eyes. Every word he said left her in no doubt that life as Evelyn knew it would change immeasurably. Perhaps not with the purchase of the vineyards, although all that increased production would surely ramp up activity, but should he buy the land around her then she would no longer have any peace.

'I have offered Miss Scott a remarkable deal,' Gabriel continued, while Izzy mentally grappled with how *a remarkable deal* could incorporate ruining someone's life. 'I will personally see to it that she has whatever other house she desires in Napa. Her friends are here? She could be closer to them. Furthermore, I will ensure that whatever house she wants is done to the standard she requires, and has as much or as little land as she deems necessary so that she can continue to fulfil her gardening exploits to her heart's content.'

'But it won't be her *home*,' Izzy whispered, fighting off the temptation to be lulled into giving his offer house room despite herself.

'A home is a moveable feast, Miss Stowe. Should she turn down my offer, I will not pursue the matter, but she could very well find that selling the property at a later date, on the open market, might not get her a quarter of what she would get right now from me. Who would want to buy a dated cottage surrounded by someone else's land and subject to all the disagreeable bustle that a full-scale business might entail? I certainly wouldn't, should she contemplate selling to me at a later date when disillusionment has had time to set in.'

He sat back and tilted his head to one side. 'I should stress that this is a one-time opportunity, Miss Stowe. Convey that message to her. I intend to be here for another fortnight but I will want your friend's decision by the end of the week. I will begin talks with Ferguson about buying his land at that point and, once that's been set in motion, this offer will no longer be available.'

This was her cue to leave. She could read it in his expression. He'd allowed her to have her little moment but he'd known that his powerful argument would throw her, as it had.

'I'm not scared of your threats, Mr Ricci.' She rose to her feet to find that her legs still felt wobbly.

'I seldom threaten. I find it's a tactic that pays few dividends.'

Izzy stared at him. He was so ridiculously beautiful, and yet he chilled her to the bone, because there was nothing there that was warm or even *human*.

The tense silence was broken by the sound of racing feet, and then the door to the sitting room was flung open and there, standing in the doorway, was a child.

CHAPTER TWO

'ROSA!'

Gabriel registered his daughter's breathless presence in the doorway at roughly the same time as he clocked the astonished expression on Izzy's face. Both were a source of annoyance, in varying degrees and for different reasons.

His daughter, because she should be getting ready to wind down and go to bed.

What the hell was that dragon of her nanny doing? She was paid handsomely to make sure that his daughter's routine went unchanged, even though Rosa wasn't at her mother's house in New York. She wouldn't be slacking off. She might not be top of his Christmas card list but she was completely trustworthy when it came to his daughter...so what the heck was this all about?

And Izzy, because her presence under his roof had nothing to do with the personal side of his life. She was there to nit-pick over the business with the cottage, and in Gabriel's world business was never allowed to push past any unopened doors. Rosa was his six-year-old daughter and he didn't need the woman's curiosity clouding the issue of why she was sitting in his living room.

And curious she was. Her aquamarine eyes were ablaze with curiosity and surprise.

'What are you doing down here?' Gabriel covered ground fast and now scooped up his daughter, who wrapped her legs around his waist while peering animatedly over his shoulder to where Izzy continued to stare with undisguised interest.

'Who's she?' Rosa piped up by way of reply.

Gabriel frowned because he wasn't inclined to get into a conversation about Izzy.

'*She*...is about to leave,' he said, heaving his daughter back to the ground and holding out his hand for her to take, which she did, while craning back to inspect Izzy. 'And where is Bella?'

It never failed to amaze him that a name that translated as 'beautiful' could apply to someone as ferociously unappealing as his daughter's nanny.

Bella Esposito was in her mid-sixties and had been Rosa's nanny for the past three years. A retired deputy head at an all girls' school in downtown Manhattan, she had been brought on board by his ex-wife Bianca, and had approached the position with the zeal of a despot accustomed to being obeyed.

'She is the only one I would consider for the job,' Bianca had announced, at the time having dismissed the previous nanny with five minutes' notice because she had failed to take the job as seriously as she should have. 'She's related and I trust her completely. Young girls do not have the required approach to discipline that Rosa needs!'

Bella was a cousin of a cousin of an aunt and, when it came to discipline, she had a first-class degree in instilling it.

There were strict rules to cover all occasions. Orders were barked, bedtimes were obeyed to the very second, snacks were banned and leisure activities were supervised with rigour.

Gabriel privately loathed the woman but what could he do? Aside from the fact that he worked so, as now, the time Rosa spent with him required the presence of a nanny, he was also in the position of having his hands tied.

Bianca would have enjoyed nothing better than making life difficult for him. Quibble over the nanny, and she would conspire to withhold his daughter from him, whatever the distribution of custody. As it stood, she was prone to changing dates with next to no notice and threatening to return to court for full custody if he complained. Would she? It was a risk he had no intention of taking, and neither was he prepared to antagonise his ex to the point where the axe of retaliation might fall upon his daughter's unsuspecting head.

He had bitten down the urge to wield his influence so many times that he had lost count.

Right now, Rosa was with him for three weeks of her summer holiday, and on the horizon lay a fight that he could only contemplate with growing horror. Bianca, she had informed him only a fortnight ago, was intent on returning to Italy. Her mother needed her, she had piously declared, which was nothing short of a joke, considering she and her mother were as close as two combatants in a boxing ring.

Was she angling for yet more money? Or was she being serious? She didn't stand a chance in hell of removing his daughter from his orbit, surely, but he wasn't willing to take any chances. He would have to hang back, however much it enraged him, and use persuasion to woo her away from the idea of leaving New York.

Truthfully, he worked long hours and led a lifestyle that was not ideally suited to parenting a six-year-old child, even though all that work was fuelled by his driving need to make sure that his daughter got the very best. Every hour he worked was to give her everything he possibly could.

He did his utmost when Rosa was with him but sometimes deals could not be ignored and his ex-wife knew that all too well. As she knew about his love life. Who didn't? He had been snapped on more than one occasion with some passing beauty on his arm gazing up adoringly, little knowing that she would soon join her predecessors as footnotes in his love life.

And on top of that...

Gabriel was at the very pinnacle of the pecking order. In the world of business, he ruled the roost, with fingers in many pies. He was the darling of the *Financial Times* and a past pin-up on magazines, from business to gossip.

He had got to that position by dint of sacrifice but he was very well aware that deep down, buried under the self-assurance that was so much a part and parcel of his powerful personality, lay uneasy guilt.

He'd been married at twenty-six and divorced by thirty. Bianca had been descended from Italian royalty, and a far cry from people of his own background, which had been rooted in poverty. She had been flamboyant, beautiful, and demanding of attention. But he had put work first. Where she had wanted parties and social events and opportunities to parade her voluptuous beauty, he had given her diamonds and pearls and turned his back on her needs. He had done what he had always done best and focused on his empire, leaving her to drift into the arms of another man.

Who could blame her? was the thought that sometimes kept him awake in the early hours of the morning. The tough Brooklyn kid who had seen work as his passport to freedom had proved more resilient than the wealthy, urbane empire builder she had fallen for and signed up to.

Worse was the realisation that he had been *relieved* that the marriage had crashed and burned, and the realisation that he had found her intensely annoying almost from day one.

But he refused to allow his daughter to become a casualty of the divorce, so he played by the rules set out for him, driven by guilt and uncertain how far he could push his luck, given his lifestyle, which would never change.

It was a mess.

Even more of a mess now.

He surfaced to hear his daughter whispering that Nanny Bella wasn't feeling very well.

Gabriel stilled. He half-turned and shot a sideways look at Izzy, who appeared to be consumed with interest in a business magazine that had been lying on the walnut table in front of the sofa, studiously ignoring the drama being played out, despite her initial curiosity.

'Ill?' Was there a germ on this planet equipped to get past the woman's suit of armour? he wondered.

Yet, illness or not, where the hell was she? This was the first time Rosa had ever ventured out of her bedroom while Bella was on officious duty.

He hesitated, torn between releasing his iron control

over his private life and asking Izzy to keep an eye on
Rosa and carrying his impressionable daughter up with
him to find out what was going on.

'Would you mind…?' He led Rosa across the room
and paused as Izzy looked up at him. 'My daughter…'
he said heavily, raking his fingers through his dark
hair and briefly glancing away. 'Some situation with
her nanny…'

'I'm Rosa,' Rosa helpfully piped up, stretching out
her hand. 'Who are you?'

'I'm Izzy.'

'I love your hair.'

Izzy smiled and met Gabriel's midnight-black eyes. 'It's
fine. I'll stay here with your daughter if you want to go
and see what's happened to the nanny.'

He didn't want to do that. Izzy could see reluctance
stamped all over his lean, dark face. He hadn't expected
his daughter to barge in just when he'd been about to
send her on her way, and he certainly hadn't expected
to end up having to leave her in the room while he went
to find out what was going on with the errant nanny
in his employ.

He'd been put in an unenviable position. Izzy suspected that he was the sort of guy who was in love with
self-control, so being put in unenviable positions would
be very low down the list of things he appreciated.

She couldn't help but feel an uncharitable twinge
of satisfaction that he had been temporarily waylaid.

It had taken every ounce of willpower to try and
bury herself in the boring business magazine lying on
the table in front of her. She had picked it up because
her innate politeness had forbidden her from ogling the

beautiful child who had entered the room with too much overt curiosity, or marvelling that a man who was made of ice could actually be a dad, and a very affectionate and loving one from the looks of it.

The cardboard cut-out, one-dimensional picture she had had in her head no longer seemed quite so straight-forward.

'What are you doing here?'

Izzy grinned, liking Rosa's precociousness. She was a stunning child, with long, dark hair tucked behind her ears, an olive complexion and huge, dark eyes. She was in her pyjamas, which involved a lot of coloured dinosaurs clamouring over highly patterned terrain. Izzy approved. In her hand were a few sheets of paper.

'What have you got here?' Izzy asked, with interest.

'Drawings. For Dad.' She held them out and Izzy spent a few minutes admiring the art work and making the right appreciative noises while with one ear she listened out for returning footsteps on the wooden floor.

'Are you here for the weekend?' She smiled and reached for the crayon in Rosa's hand without thinking.

'Three weeks. Mom's gone to the house in Tuscany and Dad's got me while she's away.' She shrugged. 'It's his turn. I prefer being with dad anyway, even if he's at work a lot.'

'And Bella is the girl who looks after you?'

None of my business, Izzy was thinking as her hand skimmed absently on the blank space on the paper, doodling one of the dinosaurs on Rosa's pyjamas, giving it expression, movement and an outfit. *I'm here to do a job, to sort out Evelyn. This man is unscrupulous and the last thing I need is to get involved in his family dynamic...*

'Bella isn't *a girl*,' Rosa said scornfully. 'She's a witch and I hate her. Wow. I love that drawing! Can you do another?' Just like that she had switched from loathing for the nanny to excitable admiration at what Izzy had done. But Izzy had no time to reply because the door was pushed open and this time standing in the doorway, just as Rosa had stood in the doorway a short while ago, was Gabriel, devoid of the cool composure she had seen in him before.

'Bella's collapsed,' he said abruptly. He looked at Rosa. 'I could call an ambulance out, but by the time it got here it would probably be faster for me to drive her to the hospital.'

'What's wrong?' Izzy leapt to her feet in consternation.

'My guess would be appendicitis, judging from what she's managed to say…and possibly a ruptured one. I have to go. Rosa…' He raked frustrated fingers through his dark hair, his body restless with tension and urgency. 'A hospital is not a suitable place. I will have to talk to doctors…'

'I can come.' The offer was out there before Izzy could think about it. She saw the struggle on his face, but time was of the essence, and he nodded.

'It would help. I will be down in a few minutes. If you wouldn't mind meeting me with Rosa by the front door…we need to move at speed.'

Izzy did as she was told, barely thinking as she hurried to the front door with Rosa, grabbing the crayons and paper and stuffing them into her bag, because she would have to occupy the child while her father did what he needed to do.

He could have left Rosa behind with her, but of course why would he? He didn't know her from Adam.

How ironic that Izzy had come out here to try and imbibe the spirit of her mother, find solace in her memory in the wake of her broken heart, yet in the very house in which Beverley Stowe had grown up she felt nothing but Gabriel's overwhelming personality. Now here she was, swept along on a wave of unexpected circumstances, and whimsy could not have been further from her mind. She could have dug her heels in and left him to his own devices, to sort out an ill nanny with his daughter in tow, but that option had not even occurred to Izzy.

She was barely aware of the drive to hospital. Rosa clung to her in the back seat of the black four-by-four, scared and silenced by the tension. In the front, Bella moaned while Gabriel drove fast, his body language signalling complete focus on what was going on. As soon as they made it to hospital, he turned to Izzy and, in between giving orders for a wheelchair to be brought for Bella, said that he would meet her as soon as he could in the reception area. He hugged Rosa, stooping to murmur a few reassuring words, and disentangled her even as he glanced up to where Izzy was staring down at them.

'Thank you,' he said gruffly.

Then he vanished behind the rush of people sweeping Bella away.

Izzy had never babysat anyone before in her life. Her dealings with young kids had largely been confined to meeting some of her friend Mia's nephews and nieces now and again. Now, though, something fired up inside her as she held the little girl's hand and hunted down the reception area, which was half-empty.

She felt a rush of emotion because she could *feel* Rosa's confusion. Being deprived of her dad frightened her, even for this short space of time, and Izzy could understand that fear. Heck, hadn't she spent so much of her life experiencing something very like it?

She chatted all the while until she felt Rosa relax, her voice calm and soothing. She spent the next hour or so entertaining her by drawing whatever she wanted until, at a little after nine, Rosa fell asleep without warning and with the innocence of a child, her head resting on Izzy's shoulder, her small body softening into slumber.

Izzy breathed in Rosa's child smell, rested her head on hers and thought about her own childhood, but not in a way that was maudlin or self-pitying. She thought of her loneliness after her parents had died and the way she had hugged it to herself because there'd been only so much her brothers could do to alleviate it. She thought of Jefferson and wondered whether she'd been so desperate to *love* and to *be loved* that she had overlooked all the signs of a person who had never been right for her.

She mused about this quest of hers in Napa Valley, hoping for memories to be the balm that might heal her heart. She knew, in an accepting rush, that the only person who could help her deal with her broken heart was herself. Unlike Rosa, she wasn't a child any longer.

It was after ten and she had drifted off to sleep by the time Gabriel returned, gently nudging her back to consciousness.

Izzy blinked, stifled a yawn and eased Rosa off her so that she could straighten.

He looked exhausted and, for the first time since she had met him, practically human.

'Have you…? Is everything okay?'

'Thank you for staying here with Rosa. I appreciate it.' He lifted Rosa, who remained asleep, and nestled her against him, waiting for Izzy so that they could leave, briefly explaining what had happened as they walked towards his car, which mysteriously was waiting for them. He must have ordered someone to bring it to the front of the building.

'I should be heading back.' Izzy hesitated and glanced over at him. The breath caught in her throat. He was so extravagantly beautiful, she thought distractedly, especially right now with Rosa curled into him. She had managed a brief, whispered chat to Evelyn while Rosa had been asleep against her, and had detected the anxiety in her voice when she had asked how the meeting had gone. Izzy hadn't had the heart to tell her that it hadn't quite gone according to plan. The man who wanted to buy her out had no intention of being Mr Nice Guy, whatever the circumstances.

It was easy to start feeling gooey and soppy, because there was something so touching about a dad and his kid, but that was irrelevant. Just because a sudden emergency had blown his cool for a couple of hours didn't mean that he had suddenly had a personality transplant.

'You haven't eaten.'

'I'm fine.' She blushed and looked away but he was already opening the door for her, having settled Rosa in the back seat.

'How has Rosa been?'

Izzy hesitated and then dropped into the passenger seat, waiting until the car roared into life before talking.

He wanted to find out about his daughter and that was only to be expected. He would want to know whether she'd been upset or in any way traumatised by the sudden tempest that had blown up.

They maintained a truce for the duration of the drive back to his mansion as Izzy told him what she and Rosa had done whilst they'd waited for him to sort out the situation. And, once inside, the thought of digging her heels in and refusing the food on offer seemed a huge effort. She was tired, she was hungry and anyway, having done him this favour, maybe he would be more amenable to listening and really taking on board what she had to say about Evelyn.

She wasn't *socialising* with the man, nor was she going to be swayed because she'd glimpsed a side to him that wasn't entirely objectionable. It made sense to be here, she thought, having been left in the kitchen while he disappeared to settle Rosa, because their conversation wasn't over and this might just be the perfect time to reintroduce it. She perked up just thinking about it.

She waited at the kitchen table and stiffened, immediately nervous, as he breezed back in and began fumbling through the fridge and in cupboards, extracting items of food at random. Bread, cheese, tomatoes and various other items wrapped in deli containers were piled onto the counter.

Did he even know the layout of his own kitchen? Izzy wondered as he continued to open and shut drawers, finally locating cutlery and a couple of wine glasses.

'No, thank you.' She covered the glass with her hand. 'I really can't hang around.'

Gabriel shrugged and began slicing the bread into uneven wedges.

'Join me, or are you in too much of a rush to escape even though you're hungry?'

'I only came here because you wanted to know how Rosa was, Mr Ricci, and it was only fair that I reassured you that she was fine. I haven't changed my stance about you and about trying to convince you that what you're doing to Evelyn is a terrible idea.'

'You've met my daughter. I think it's appropriate that we drop the formal address. My name is Gabriel. So feel free to call me Gabriel and I'll call you Izzy. Rosa likes you. She woke up just long enough to tell me that as I was settling her.'

Izzy bristled because she was sitting here, intent on not relaxing into chit chat, but he was tucking into the food without restraint and taking the conversation away from the cottage.

She wasn't going to let him think that he had wrapped it all up in a five-minute warning talk, and that once she'd gone he'd be able to wash his hands of her.

'She's very engaging.'

'I'm not sure Bella would agree with you,' Gabriel said wryly. 'But, in fairness, she hasn't made life particularly easy for her nanny. Drop the pride and eat some of this food, Izzy. It's not much but you must be starving.'

'I'm good, thank you, Mr… *Gabriel*. I just don't want you to think that everything's forgotten, that the business with the nanny has overtaken the reason I came here to see you in the first place. I don't want you to imagine that you can threaten me into retreat.'

'Pick your battles,' he returned softly, glancing at her. 'You're not going to win this one.' He nodded at the food and she ignored him. Her taxi would arrive soon enough—she had taken a couple of seconds to order one—but where did they go from here?

'Would you at least come to the cottage?' she ventured, because if she left without any follow up in place she felt the next correspondence, should Evelyn fail to accept his offer, would be something informing her that he had begun the process of buying the rest of the acreage around the cottage and to expect the builders soon.

'Why would I do that?'

Their eyes met, bright blue colliding with darkest black, and again she felt a shiver of awareness, a hint of danger that went beyond anything to do with the cottage and the silken threats of what he could do. It was a hint of danger that confused and panicked her. She was too *aware* of him. When his eyes rested on her, she felt a lot more than just angry. She felt...*unsettled*, as though a part of her *enjoyed* whatever weird, incomprehensible sensations he managed to stir deep inside.

He unsettled her on a physical level, and she hated that, because it was distracting and bewildering. Jefferson had left her disillusioned with her first foray into the business of a relationship. She'd been badly let down. She'd fled, disappointed and embittered by her experience, so why was she finding her eyes drawn to this man?

'Perhaps if you met Evelyn...'

'I would have...' he relaxed back to look at her coolly '...had you not decided to jump to her rescue and represent her in her absence. What is your relationship with her, anyway? I don't believe you said.'

'I believe I did,' Izzy returned. 'Friend.' Should she tell him about her connection to the house? What would be the point? It was hardly as though the house had awakened anything inside her at all. Aside from knowing that her mother had been brought up there, it could just have been any mansion. Too much had changed from those wistful photos her mother had taken all those years ago.

While the cottage—and Evelyn—had both stirred feelings inside her, taking her back to the past and helping her recall her mother. Was that why she felt so strongly about protecting it? About not seeing it turned into something for someone else, expanded into a compound to house strangers, which would probably involve it being razed to the ground and replaced with something cold, anodyne and functional?

'You're here on holiday…' He inclined his head and his expression was both lazy and shrewdly calculating at the same time. 'And a long way from home, judging from your accent. Did you just decide to pay Miss Scott a visit out of the blue—since you insist on talking about this?'

She took a deep breath. 'Why all the questions? It doesn't matter why I'm here, does it?' She paused. 'I'd really appreciate it if you did come to the cottage and did meet Evelyn,' she said quietly. 'It might make you change your mind.'

Gabriel's eyebrows shot up. 'I assure you, Izzy, that I'm not a man who ever changes direction.'

'That's not something to brag about,' Izzy muttered.

She had spent so much of her life doing what Max told her to do: working hard to get good grades at school, studying for a degree she had minimal interest in because it made sense and would establish a clear career path, avoiding all the complications of fun relationships with boys because it had been important not to be distracted. She had finally taken a stand in throwing out Max's ideas for the hotel and imposing her own. She had found her voice, taken a deep breath and decided to use it.

So what if her stand had been a bit shaky? She had kept her plans for the hotel under wraps, trying to work out how she could break it to her brother that she didn't agree with his vision when she should have just *told* him.

Then, riding a wave of independence, she had flung herself into an ill-fated love affair, only to take the coward's way out when it had crashed and burned and disappear in search of something she now knew she would never find because her mother was in her heart and not in a pile of bricks and mortar...

But it had still been a stand. She had still dug her heels in with Max instead of dutifully settling into the career he had carved out for her...and he respected her for it! Wonder of wonders, he'd actually said so when they'd talked at last, on the phone. And she had still broken through the ever-increasing burden of her lack of love-life and so what if she'd made a mistake?

Both events had given her a huge morale boost and the courage now not to flinch in the face of a man who was clearly accustomed to getting his own way.

'Come again?'

'I said...' Izzy looked at him with challenging eyes '...that it's not cool to be inflexible.'

Gabriel was incredulous.

He was exhausted. It had been a long evening. He had used all the authority at his disposal to ensure the very top consultant was involved in making sure Bella got the best possible medical attention. As he'd thought, it was a ruptured appendix, and her recovery would be at least a week, possibly more.

He had phoned Bianca to explain the situation and discovered, to his surprise, that she had taken herself off to the Tuscan villa that had been part of her divorce package, revitalising his uneasy suspicions that threats about her absconding to Italy with his daughter hovered on the horizon as a dangerous possibility. He hadn't been able to picture the Italian beauty suddenly turning into Florence Nightingale to care for a mother she had never had time for, but Donata Mancini lived in the Tuscan hills, so why else would his ex be there now?

Unsurprisingly, he had had to deal with Bianca's evident pleasure that he had found himself without a nanny. She had only just stopped short of crowing that he could now see for himself what full-time parenting looked like. Not that she had a clue herself, he'd been tempted to say, bearing in mind her life of pampered luxury in which, if his daughter was to be believed, bonding times with Rosa involved joint manicures at her beauty salon—an experience Rosa described with horror.

Bianca had mournfully told him about her mother's failing health and how much she was needed in Tuscany but, she had hinted nastily, perhaps it would stand in his favour if he actually proved that he could manage single-handedly with Rosa and put some of his precious work to one side *for a change.*

The last thing he needed was this conversation with Izzy. The fact that he couldn't look at the stubborn little blonde sitting in front of him without his body hiving

off at a tangent was a sensation he found intensely irritating, a distraction he could do without.

It was infuriating enough that one very important
area of his life could not be controlled, that no amount
of power, money or influence could bring about the
conclusion he wanted when it came to his daughter.
He really didn't need for any more areas of his life to
go off-piste.

And yet…

There was something about the blonde that made him
stop dead in his tracks, even though she was the most
argumentative and irritating woman he had ever met.

'You really think that insulting me is going to encourage me to meet you halfway on this?' Gabriel
drawled. He shoved the plate to one side, pushed his
chair away from the table and angled his long body so
that he could stretch his legs out.

Each small, economical movement made for compul-
sive viewing.

'I wasn't insulting you, but I think it's a good thing
if someone can see all points of view and…er…give
other people a chance to speak their mind and make a
case for what they want. I mean…' she looked around
her at the impressive paintings hanging on the walls, the
pale, expensive furniture and the faded, silken elegance
of the Persian rug on the wooden floor '… I *know* you
probably don't want to be having this conversation but
do you *really* need to add to your wealth?'

There was genuine curiosity in her question because,
although she had had a comfortable lifestyle, thanks to
her brothers and her privileged background, she had
never really understood other people's fixation with

money. In fact, if anything, money had brought its own problems. Because how could you ever tell whether the people who pursued you wanted you for your money or for who you were?

Her assumption was that Gabriel came from money. He carried himself like someone born into great wealth. He had that mantle of self-confidence, that assumption of obedience that spoke of an elevated background.

For Izzy, it was a turn-off.

Gabriel said with amazement, 'Are you preaching to me about my life choices? And, yes, I really would rather *not* be having this conversation.'

Izzy decided to ignore that particular segment of what he had said. 'I suppose when you've been born into a rich background it's really tough to try and see how people feel and think who come from the opposite side of the tracks…' She pensively looked off into the distance, then frowned at her mobile phone, because the taxi was taking longer than she'd expected.

'You are an extremely challenging woman.' Gabriel gritted his teeth.

Izzy half-opened her mouth to tell him that *he* was equally challenging, and then blushed a bright red, because from the expression on his face he seemed to know exactly what was going through her head.

Her phone buzzed. The taxi had finally arrived and she leapt to her feet, relieved to be going. She would have to think about how best to make her case one more time because the man was intransigent.

Her high hopes were currently at rock bottom. If he couldn't be persuaded into seeing what the consequences of his actions would involve for Evelyn with his own eyes, then she would simply have to help the older woman adjust to a lifestyle she hadn't banked on at her age.

She was very much aware of him walking her to the front door. He emanated a powerful masculine pull that made the hairs on the back of her neck stand on end and gave her goose bumps. He was good-looking, she thought, but that wasn't it. She wasn't that shallow. Jefferson had been good-looking, in a different type of way. Blond hair and green eyes. Surfer looks. But he had been funny and free-spirited, and that was what she had been attracted to in him.

This man gave her goose bumps because of that aura of threat he wore. He would give anyone goose bumps. A charging army would stop dead in their tracks. The fact that he was drop-dead gorgeous was just a peripheral distraction.

'How long are you planning to stay in the area?'

The deep timbre of his voice interrupted the feverish train of her thoughts and she slid a sideways glance at him from under her lashes.

'I'd planned on staying…seeing this through…helping Evelyn…'

'Don't you have a job to get back to? Family? A significant other?'

'I…' She glared at him. He made her life sound bare and empty, standing there leaning against the door, watching her with lazy interest. She was only twenty-two, yet she knew that she had few friends, definitely no significant other and that there had never been any significant other until Jefferson, not even an adolescent first love. She'd launched herself into a relationship with Jefferson, high on a sense of freedom, in love with the idea of being in love—and here she was, still a virgin, because nothing had worked out. She wondered, somewhere deep down, whether anything ever would. Who knew? What she *did* know was that Jefferson had put doubts in her head that had not been there before. 'My taxi's here,' she said coolly.

'It'll wait.'

'Really?'

'Really. No one would dare pull up to this house and leave without my permission. I'm guessing that your flexibility on the lifestyle front answers my question.' He pushed himself away from the door and looked down at her for a few seconds. 'You want me to have the face-to-face conversation I had intended to have with your friend?'

Izzy shot him a hopeful glance and immediately felt a little unsteady on her feet. His lazy, veiled stare pinned her to the spot and sucked the breath out of her.

'You know I do.' She was aiming for cool, composed and a little sarcastic. Instead, she sounded breathless and flustered.

'Tomorrow. I'll come across to the cottage.'

'You know how to get there?'

'I have a lot of land, but I think I can work out the route to the gingerbread house without a trail of breadcrumbs guiding me.'

'There's no need to be sarcastic,' Izzy muttered. She tore her eyes away and looked down at her feet. When she next looked up, it was to find him staring at her in a way which made her feel giddy. 'What time can Evelyn expect you to come?'

'Both of you,' Gabriel told her smoothly. 'I want you there as well—not that I'm sure I have to say that, considering you've volunteered for guardian angel duty.'

He opened the door for her, letting in a waft of warm, evening breeze. 'I'll be over at six.'

Izzy backed out of the door and nodded. Tomorrow. Six. It was good news. He wouldn't be acquiescing if he was *completely* against the idea of letting Evelyn stay put.

And once they had sorted it out, whatever the conclusion, she would hang around for another week maybe— make sure Evelyn was fine—and then return to Hawaii.

And the weird, unsettled feeling afflicting her would, thankfully, be gone.

CHAPTER THREE

IT WAS VERY different here, Gabriel thought as he paused to look at the cottage tucked away amidst the trees. Where his mansion looked out to a sea of vines undulating towards a distant horizon, here, tucked away from the vineyards, the trees had been allowed to grow unchecked. It was the difference between order and a certain pleasing wildness. Flowers bloomed and the fading sun glinted through the trees, casting shadows in the undergrowth.

Gabriel had not ventured out here at all. He'd had no interest in it. His focus had been exclusively on the vineyards. He'd known about the cottage, and of course on the few occasions when he'd made the trip to the house he had glanced towards the sprawling, endless wooded area at the back and admired the contrast in scenery. That had been roughly the extent of it, though.

Had he not decided to extend his acreage, he would not have been overly concerned about the cottage. It was a gap in his holdings, but he could afford gaps. Who cared whether an elderly lady owned a tiny bit of neighbouring land? Doubtless, the previous owners had never anticipated extending their holdings, so the cottage in its little plot, situated in the furthest reaches and well out of sight, would never have proved bothersome.

It certainly wouldn't have been to Gabriel had he not been more ambitious in wanting to expand the winery. Not only would it provide jobs in the community—which was something that had clearly not occurred to Izzy in her heated rush to overturn his plans—but it would also be another step in that onward march away from the blistering poverty of his childhood.

So, alas, needs must.

Still, he could see what Izzy had been talking about. The cottage was very sweet. White picket fence, winding path to front door, faded red roof. It was fairy-tale stuff and, holding his hand, Rosa was clearly of the same opinion.

In fact, she had been enchanted by the woods ever since they had set off in search of the cottage. She had talked non-stop. She wanted to do some tree-climbing, she told him. Could she explore the woods on her own? She was bored staying in all the time. Could he come swim in the pool with her? Go to the shops with her? Play her computer game with her?

Right now she was hopping from one foot to the other, bristling with excitement. She ran towards the cottage, a slight, tanned kid in a scrappy T-shirt and a pair of denim shorts and some trainers, because she hated dresses or anything girly.

Gabriel followed.

His work load was intense. Things were happening with a couple of massive deals on the other side of the pond. His instinct was simply to get an agency to find someone who could temporarily cover Bella's absence, but his ex-wife's nasty jibes about his preoccupation with work had struck a chord. He was gearing up to an almighty battle with Bianca in trying to prevent her from absconding to Italy with Rosa.

Gabriel hadn't been born yesterday. For all his staggering wealth, he knew that in a court of law a mother would take precedence, especially if it could be proved that the father was consumed with work to the exclusion of everything else. Never mind the fact that Rosa, his number-one priority, the only female in his life to hold his heart, was the *very* reason he put in the hours. He had thrown money at Bianca following their divorce. She wanted for nothing, yet she remained embittered enough to paint him in the darkest of lights.

There was nothing more dangerous than a woman scorned. Gabriel had long concluded that Bianca's pride had taken a beating. She had been the high-born Italian beauty of impeccable lineage. Her mother was a dowager with far-reaching influence, even though the woman was now nearly seventy.

He, on the other hand, had been the poor kid made good. His parents had been in service and had lived in near penury. Bianca had been born and raised to be worshipped, yet he had failed to pander to her demands, had ignored her, had failed to be jealous of her increasing need to flirt with other men. He had committed the gravest of sins by not treating her as number one and the fact that he was 'just an upstart', as she had screamed at one point, had been the final humiliation for her.

The truth was that he had married in haste because she had become pregnant, a mistake he blamed himself for, even though he later discovered that she had deliberately stopped taking the pill. He had not loved her, not been in love with her. He had, in the end, been indifferent and she had increasingly recognised that and hated him for it.

Gabriel had no intention of allowing his vindictive ex-wife to remove his daughter from his orbit, not least because it would be easy for her to make Rosa pay for *his* sins. That unplanned pregnancy had endowed him with the most precious gift of his life and he had no intention of allowing Rosa to be taken to Tuscany and out of his jurisdiction. Not if he could help it.

And there was something else. Gabriel was aware that his focus should be entirely on Rosa. He knew all about the importance of family life. He had grown up with devoted parents who had bent over backwards for him. He was divorced but suddenly it felt as though he was being driven down a different road from the one he had spent the past few years walking.

Perhaps it was the removal of a nanny. Without Bella around, he would have to confront his own limitations. Maybe the escalating situation with his ex had also rammed home that single-handedly running an empire did not make for perfect parenting. Or maybe it was being here, under a vast and serene sky. Life here was so very different from the cut and thrust, his fast-paced life in New York, where slowing down for five minutes was a luxury he seldom enjoyed.

What had been planned as a functional visit to conclude the business of the cottage, which his people had been unable to do, had turned into…

Something quite unexpected.

And just like that he thought of Izzy—her long, curling white-blonde hair, the argumentative pout of her mouth, the fiery glare of those aquamarine eyes.

Unexpected indeed, Gabriel thought.

Ever one to find solutions to problems and to seize opportunities as they came his way, Gabriel began quickly walking towards the cottage, his mind engaged on a tangent hitherto not considered. Rosa was waiting impatiently and he smiled.

'I love this!'

She was grinning like a Cheshire cat and Gabriel grinned back at her.

'Who knows?' he murmured, squatting so that he was on eye level with her. 'Maybe you'll see a lot more of this enchanted place than I thought...'

With all the doors open, Izzy heard the sound of the knocker loud and clear, even though she and Evelyn were sitting outside in the back garden enjoying the last of the sunshine before it dipped away into night.

She'd explained the outcome of her meeting with Gabriel. She had actually referred to it as a 'meeting', making sure that everything was kept on a purely business level. This, in an effort to dispel some of the disconcerting effect he had on her.

She'd made sure to stress that nothing had been decided but during the course of the afternoon, as they had had tea and waited for Gabriel to show up, she had realised with a sinking heart that the older woman's hopes had been raised to an unrealistic level.

'I can't wait to show him my garden, dear,' Evelyn had told her excitedly. 'He'll want to see that this patch of land is not and never will be a blot on the landscape! You know how much I love this house and this oasis, dear. I feel that once he sees that for himself, he'll realise that there's no need to gobble up my house and land! He'll realise that we can be perfect neighbours.

I may be elderly but I'm fit as a fiddle and well able to look after my little patch!'

'He'll be in no doubt about that,' Izzy had said, tentatively repeating what she had now said half a dozen times about *taking nothing for granted.*

'He strikes me as a pretty ruthless kind of guy,' she had felt constrained to point out, as they'd made their way back into the house. 'Not a very pleasant man *at all.*' She had thought of all six-foot-something of smouldering masculine beauty and had shivered.

Now, as she pulled open the front door, Izzy hoped that Evelyn had listened to her and heard what she had tried to say.

She was prepped to hiss a warning to him that he should be *gentle* with Evelyn, because she wasn't as robust as she looked, but was immediately thrown off-course by the sight of Rosa, who smiled with pure joy as she looked up at her.

'Can you take me out to the back?' she asked, dropping Gabriel's hand and stepping forward towards Izzy. 'Is there an apple tree? Can you draw some more stuff for me? I should have brought my drawing pad.' She looked crestfallen. 'Dad, can we go back so that—'

'It's okay.' Izzy smiled. The dad might set her teeth on edge but his daughter was a poppet, she thought. She sneaked a glance towards Gabriel to find him looking thoughtfully at her. She hurriedly looked away and stooped down. 'I'm pretty sure I can rustle up some paper,' she said. 'And of course there's an apple tree! What cottage *doesn't* have an apple tree? And lots of plants and flowers and herbs and vegetables. I'll draw some cartoon pictures of them, if you like. You pick the vegetable and I'll turn it into whatever you want.'

'Excellent plan.'

Izzy glanced up at Gabriel's deep voice to find him stepping around her into the house and introducing himself to Evelyn. Gone was the cool, unyielding face he had shown Izzy. In its place was a smile of such easy charm that she had to blink to make sure her eyes weren't playing tricks on her.

They weren't. The tenor of his voice matched the twinkle in his dark eyes as he began chatting to Evelyn.

'What a stunning location... The cottage is charming... Tell me about all those photos... Yes, I'm sure the garden is as beautiful as the cottage...'

He now turned to Izzy, his smile still in place, although the expression in his eyes informed her that he wasn't about to brook any staging of a protest at this point.

'Why don't you take charge of Rosa for a while? Give me an opportunity to talk to Evelyn in private.'

Evelyn, Izzy noted with dismay, seemed to be lapping up Gabriel's superficial charm. Her eyes were bright, her smile was broad and she was positively blushing with pleasure as he continued to lay it on thick, chatting winningly while managing to propel her back into the house and out in the direction of the garden.

Evelyn was bustling towards the kitchen, chirpily telling him about some home-made lemonade and carrot cake. Izzy tried to catch his eye but he was having none of it, instead choosing to give his daughter the go-ahead to explore outside for as long as she wanted.

'Absolutely no hurry.' He finally looked at Izzy as he vaulted upright, so shockingly sexy in some faded jeans and a black polo shirt that he took her breath away.

Izzy scowled, deprived of any opportunity to tell him

what he should and shouldn't say to Evelyn, because there was no way she would allow him to offend the older woman in any way. Rosa was impatiently waiting to go outside and, as far as chaperones went, she was the best he could have hoped for, silencing all the warning protests bubbling up inside Izzy. When he grinned with slow, lazy deliberation, she realised that he knew exactly what was going through her head.

But what could she say when Rosa looked up between them, keen to play explorer out in the garden?

For the next hour and a half, while Gabriel was closeted away in the cosy sitting room with Evelyn, Izzy entertained his daughter. Which was not hard work, she had to admit because, the better acquainted she got with the child, the more she appreciated just how smart and curious the little girl was.

Notwithstanding, half of her was preoccupied with what Gabriel and Evelyn could possibly be talking about for such a long time. She was far from reassured when, having retreated to the kitchen table with Rosa so that part two of the entertainment programme—drawing—could be completed, she heard the sitting-room door open and within minutes Evelyn was framed in the doorway, beaming.

Gabriel towered behind her, his face revealing nothing at all.

'Time to go, Rosa.'

Rosa debated for a couple of seconds whether she was ready to leave, but then reluctantly began gathering up the sheets of paper while Izzy stood up, stretched and likewise mentally debated what she should do now.

She was spared the decision making when Gabriel

said in the sort of voice that assumed compliance, 'Why don't you accompany me back to the house, Izzy? You and I can have a chat.'

'Evelyn and I might…want to catch up…' Izzy glanced at Evelyn, who *winked*.

'You run along with Gabriel, dear, and we can talk tomorrow.'

As Rosa began clattering with the pencils Izzy had managed to locate in a kitchen drawer, and shuffling the bits of paper so that she could show them to Gabriel, Evelyn took Izzy to one side and said *sotto voce*, 'What a *lovely* man, dear. I don't know why I got myself so worked up about this whole thing. He seems very *understanding*.'

'Evelyn…'

'Now hush, dear. I know you went through that rough time, but not all men are the same, and Gabriel has been more than sympathetic to what I've been going through. The worry…' She shook her head and Izzy saw tears of relief in the older woman's eyes.

She groaned inwardly because the person Evelyn was describing bore no resemblance to the person Izzy had met yesterday, and Izzy was willing to bet that her version was much closer to the truth.

But she refrained from saying anything because she couldn't bear to see the optimistic light in Evelyn's eyes snuffed out.

She also refrained from saying anything as they walked back to the big house. The evening had brought a coolness to the air and, in her T-shirt and short skirt, Izzy felt a relief when that massive front door was pushed open and she stepped past Gabriel into the warmth.

He wanted to chat. It felt ominous, even though there was nothing in his demeanour to indicate any such thing.

'I'll settle Rosa.' He turned to her, addressing her directly for the first time since leaving the cottage. 'Why don't you wait for me in the kitchen? Help yourself to anything you like. This is wine-growing country. It would be a shame not to have a glass. There is some excellent Chardonnay in the fridge.'

He swung round before she could inform him that she had no intention of having anything to drink, repeating the mantra of the day before.

But once in the kitchen Izzy decided that a glass wouldn't do any harm. Indeed, she felt it might numb her senses to his overpowering appeal and the threat it posed to her attempts at composure.

She was rigid with tension by the time he strolled into the kitchen.

'You were with Evelyn a long time.' She said what had been feverishly playing on her mind ever since they had begun walking back to his house. With Rosa between them chatting non-stop, there had been no opportunity to find out what he and the older woman had discussed and all Izzy's worries had had ample time to bloom.

Gabriel shot her a veiled look but didn't say anything, preferring to help himself to a glass of wine, the same wine now in front of Izzy, as yet untouched.

He took his time before he replied, leaving her to stew for a few minutes, then sat down opposite her, his head tilted to one side, as though considering what he should say next and how.

'There was a lot to talk about,' Gabriel concurred.

'It was a mistake to delegate this situation to one of my employees. I'm big enough to recognise that I should have sorted this business out myself. I made a mistake sending in the boys to do a man's job.' He shrugged and sipped his wine while he continued to look at her over the rim of his glass.

'And has it been sorted?' The million-dollar question, which was answered in full when he remained noticeably silent in response. 'Evelyn is over the moon!' Izzy exploded angrily. How could he just *sit there*, having met Evelyn, having seen with his own eyes how emotionally dependent she was on the only place she had ever really called home? 'She really thinks that she's going to be allowed to get on with her life in the cottage! She really thinks that you're one of the good guys.'

'And you've already made your mind up that I'm not.'

'Why did you encourage her to think that everything was going to be all right if you had no intention of…of…?'

'You're looking at this through the wrong set of lenses.'

'I'm leaving!'

'No,' Gabriel said shortly. 'You're not. Sit back down, finish the glass of wine and we can discuss this thorny situation.'

'You can't tell me what to do!'

'No. I can't. What I *can* say, however, is that the option I am presenting makes sense and is the right course of action given the circumstances. I am far from being a monster, which you would see if you would just drop the emotionalism for five seconds.' Their eyes tangled and Izzy shot him a scorching look from under her lashes.

'Some things can't just be looked at with pure common sense. Some things are *invested* with emotion. It's just that *you*,' she returned without blinking an eye, 'Can't see that because *you* are as cold as ice!'

'Not always...' Gabriel murmured. Their eyes tangled and just like that the atmosphere between them shifted. Hot colour rose to her cheeks and suddenly the room felt way too stifling and way too small, the walls closing in as he continued to look at her with lazy, hooded eyes. She was clutching the sides of her chair so that her knuckles were white and leaning ever so slightly forward, unable to drag her gaze away from his lean, darkly handsome face.

He was the first to break eye contact. 'It's not a simple case of black and white.' He raked his fingers through his hair and sighed impatiently. 'I'm not a charitable organisation, neither am I Father Christmas. I don't intend to reside here permanently, nor am I qualified to manage these vineyards the way they deserve to be managed. The guy currently in charge here is renting a lodge in the town. Not ideal. He needs help. The staff, too, will have to be accommodated some distance away, simply because the cottage is out of bounds as a housing compound.'

'If you're not going to be here, why can't you use this place for them? It's big enough.'

'Not the point. I want to increase production and I'll need to buy up what's beyond the cottage. There will be infringement to a large degree on your friend's privacy.'

'And you explained all of that to her?'

'I...tried,' Gabriel said heavily.

'Well,' Izzy couldn't resist sniping with heavy sarcasm, 'You obviously failed, because Evelyn thinks it's all over bar the shouting, that she's going to be safe where she is.'

'What is her story? Why has she never thought of moving? She's on her own. Surely it's lonely being stuck out here? Wouldn't she rather be close to her friends? Her…whatever it is she does to occupy her time? Leisure activities? I know she devotes a considerable amount of time to her vegetables and the garden, and it seems she's an active member of the local gardening society, but are there other hobbies she would want to pursue that require her to be closer to the centre of the town?'

'Evelyn is…' Izzy breathed in deeply. 'Her entire life was devoted to the family she used to work for. They lived in this house, you see, and they actually bequeathed her the cottage because she was more than just a nanny. She was a family friend.'

'What family?' He frowned. 'I had no idea the family I bought this place from had children. Or a nanny.'

'I believe the place was bought and sold a couple of times before it became yours.'

Silence fell. Izzy fiddled with the stem of the glass and then nervously swallowed far too much of the golden wine and winced.

Gabriel looked at her, eyes narrowed, without saying a word. Her tone of voice. Her face, that delicate blush…

Had he ever met any woman whose face revealed so much? She was feisty and spirited and wasn't afraid of speaking her mind, but there was also a blushing ingenuousness about her that fascinated him.

Right now, her expressive face was leading him to conclusions that all seemed to tie together and make sense of her presence in the area, as they did her determination to defend Evelyn against the Big Bad Wolf.

'This family you're talking about…' He reached forward, elbow on the table, and gently hooked his finger under her chin so that she was looking at him. On the periphery of his mind, he was aware that her skin was very soft and satiny smooth, and he had to resist the urge to cup the side of her face with his hand, to stroke her cheek, to touch her lips with his thumb. He dropped his hand and sat back.

Izzy looked away and then twirled her hair in her hands, sifting her fingers through its length.

'Evelyn used to work for my grandparents. It's no big secret. She was my mother's nanny and remained with the family until the day they sold the place and moved away when my grandfather became ill. They needed somewhere smaller. They wanted to take Evelyn with them, but she wanted to remain in the area, and so they gave her the cottage and the land around it as a measure of thanking her for her service over the years.'

'Your family used to live here?'

'It's no big deal, like I said.'

No big deal? Gabriel thought. He had built an image in his head of fetching innocence, an ingenuousness that was refreshing. But of course, he'd been wildly off-target. If her grandparents had owned this property and the vineyards that went with it, they would not have been scraping the barrel to find food. He might have extended the original property and dragged it out of disrepair, because the years and the people before him had been unable to keep the place going, but even so…

The ethereal blonde with the big blue eyes was a trust-fund kid, and didn't he know all about trust-fund kids? You couldn't trust them as far as you could throw them because the assumption that they would get what they wanted was woven into their DNA. His ex had taught him a lot when it came to that particular subject. He might not have been the perfect husband, but she'd been able to trust him, and he'd mistakenly thought the same until she'd let him down in the biggest way possible. So, rich kids? Thanks, but no thanks.

Yet he had to concede that his daughter had taken a liking to this woman. In fact, Rosa had been unable to talk about anything else but the cottage, the apple tree and the blonde's amazing talent at drawing.

'My mother was an only child,' Izzy volunteered reluctantly. 'She talked a lot about Nanny Scott.'

'*Talked* about?'

'My mother died twelve years ago,' Izzy said shortly. 'I was ten at the time.'

'Twelve years ago,' he murmured. 'You were only a child. I'm sorry.'

She nodded and lowered her eyes.

In the brief, intervening silence, Gabriel couldn't help but marvel that his usually impeccable judgement had been flawed in this instance.

His own bitter experience of what a woman born into money could be like had been a deep learning curve. Wealthy men were often suspicious of gold-diggers, but as far as Gabriel was concerned with a gold-digger you knew where you stood. You had money, they wanted it and, if you chose to comply, then you did so with eyes wide open. But rich young things came with all sorts of hidden dangers and, whilst the rational part of him could concede that, rich or poor, no two people were ever the same, he still responded to trust-fund babes with a primal, gut reaction that had its roots in his own bitter, personal experience.

'So your purpose in coming here was to…?'

'See where my mum grew up.'

'And you decided to go one step further and fight Evelyn's corner when she told you about the cottage. Did you think that you would have a chat with me and I'd concede defeat?' He wondered whether a privileged background had inured her against failure. In his steady climb up the greasy pole, it had become apparent that there was a yawning gap between the way those born into money approached life and those who had grown up without it.

Moneyed people, whether they deserved it or not, whether they were clever or not or gifted or not, assumed that success was their due.

He watched her narrowly, making assumptions now that had not been made before.

'No, of course not.'

'Here's the thing.' He leaned forward and looked at her seriously. 'I am prepared to at least review the situation.'

'Really?'

'I hadn't expected to find myself persuaded into thinking any more deeply about your friend and her living here next to my land, but she is clearly dependent on the cottage because, as you have explained, it has been her home for very many years…'

'And of course,' Izzy jumped in with enthusiasm, 'The older you get, the more stuck in your ways you become and the less willing you are to have any kind of change in your life.'

'That's as may be.' Gabriel had listened and taken

on board what the older woman had had to say, but he had manoeuvred the conversation to exploring various options should they arise. He had encouraged her to talk about her friends in the town, and had made sure to point out how vital it was for people to have friends or family close by when old age began setting in. While she had waxed lyrical about the garden, and the joys of growing her own vegetables, he had quietly inserted the suggestion that some other properties came with outside space crying out for someone with green fingers, that the garden she maintained did not necessarily have to be the last one she ever maintained.

Far from threatening, he had charmed and had left her with things to think about. He had planted seeds. As a talented gardener, he felt that she would appreciate the effort.

Gabriel had no intention of abandoning his plans but, for once, he was not going to go for the jugular. He'd liked the woman. He would gently guide her in the direction he wished her to take and he had no hesitation that she would go exactly where directed.

But before he got there…

'I have a proposition for you,' he said, relaxing and watching Izzy closely.

'What is it?'

'You're hell-bent on saving your friend from the horror of having to sell the cottage for an unbelievably and unrealistically generous sum of money.' He watched as predictably she stiffened, sitting up straighter, her mouth pursing in immediate rejection of what he had said. And what a very nice mouth she had, Gabriel thought absently. Spoiled brat she undoubtedly was, despite outward appearances, but what an extremely fetching and addictively watchable spoiled brat.

Izzy opened her mouth to argue and he stifled the protest on her lips with a dismissive wave of his hand.

'I'm in no mood to start a pointless debate about whether my offer is generous or not. Back to my proposition.'

'You're so arrogant,' Izzy said.

'I know. You'd be amazed at how few women have ever complained about that trait before.'

'And conceited.'

'The two often go hand in hand.' He reluctantly smiled. Spoiled brat or not, no one had entertained him quite as much in recent times. 'I'm prepared to, at least, consider your friend's dilemma but in return you have to do something for me.'

'What?' Izzy asked cautiously.

'I'm here without a nanny and there are times when it is impossible for me to focus entirely on entertaining Rosa because I have work to do.'

'You want me to babysit her now and again?'

'Rather more than that. I want you to take over where Bella left off. There's no chance she'll be out of hospital any time soon and if I am to stay here, mulling things over about the cottage, possibly having further chats with Evelyn…'

'Provided I look after Rosa because you can't see your way to having a couple of weeks away from your work…'

Gabriel frowned but decided not to take issue with that blatantly provocative remark. 'You would have to live in. It's more convenient, especially if I need to return to New York for anything. I would need you to be on hand.'

'In other words,' Izzy said slowly, 'You're blackmailing me. You'll think about backing off if I help you out with Rosa. Why don't you just hire someone for a week or so?'

Gabriel thought of Bianca and the open airwaves between Bella and her. The last thing he needed was to give his ex-wife ammunition that she would cheerfully use against him in a court of law.

Izzy was not a nanny. She was a friend helping out now and again.

'My daughter is really taken with you,' Gabriel said truthfully. 'I very much doubt that any nanny would be able to slide seamlessly into Rosa's life for such a short space of time, whereas you...' She wasn't qualified, yet there was something about her he instinctively trusted, and the fact that his daughter was bowled over by her spoke volumes. She had a certain sweetness in her that was at odds with her wealthy background and he was willing to concede that she might not quite fit the one-dimensional mould he had been quite happy to slot her into.

'I... I might have other things to do... Plans for filling my time while I'm here...'

'No, you don't. A person with plans doesn't decide to remain in one place on a whim.'

'Don't tell me what I might or might not have planned!'

'It's a simple question, Izzy, a simple deal. Do you take it or not?'

CHAPTER FOUR

IZZY ARRIVED THE following morning with all her clothes stuffed into the Louis Vuitton suitcase she had brought along with her when she had fled Hawaii.

The mansion looked all the more imposing now that she was going to be moving in. When Gabriel had first put his proposition forward, just for a second Izzy had thought that he had been kidding. She'd clocked quickly enough that he was deadly serious.

He had laid it on thick with the charm for Evelyn's benefit and the older woman had fallen for it hook, line and sinker.

She had misguidedly believed that his easy manner, that way he had of looking as though he was really listening and utterly focused, meant that he was going to allow her to stay where she was without forcing her out by fair means or foul. He had been soothing and reassuring and she taken the wrong message from his demeanour.

Izzy had arrived at an altogether different interpretation of events and one she knew to be far closer to reality.

He was fattening Evelyn up for the kill. Let her bask in the contentment of thinking she was safe, and the second he told her what life would look like when the tractors moved in she would have no fight left and would collapse without a struggle.

That said…there was the slimmest chance that she was wrong, the vaguest possibility that he really was going to consider his options. So she felt that she could not reject his offer out of hand. Maybe, living under the same roof, she might even be able to employ some powers of persuasion to make him see sense, to steer him away from pursuing yet another unnecessary addition to his portfolio.

Now, as she rang the doorbell, she felt her stomach muscles tighten at the prospect of living with the man, sharing space with him, being *swamped* twenty-four-seven by his suffocating personality.

Izzy was banking down a rising tide of belated panic when the front door was pulled open, but thankfully not by Gabriel. Marie, the young housekeeper, had a tea towel slung over her shoulder and her hair was pulled back with a scarf. She was pink faced but smiling, and behind her Rosa was hopping from one foot to the other.

'She's been waiting for the past hour,' Marie confided. 'I could barely get the cleaning done because she's been tagging along behind me telling me about all the stuff you two are going to be doing.'

'Well, I'll have to get rid of this bag first…' Izzy smiled at Rosa, who immediately took charge as only a child can do. She flew up the stairs, breathlessly pointing out things along the way, and the question uppermost in Izzy's head concerning the whereabouts of Gabriel was lost in the excitement of her arrival.

She relaxed, the panic subsided and the day progressed, filled with an agenda of fast-paced activities inspired by an active and enthusiastic six-year-old with reserves of energy that beggared belief.

Izzy had almost forgotten her dread of being in the same house as Gabriel until, at a little after six and after an enjoyable visit to the cottage—where Evelyn had come alive in Rosa's company—they both wearily returned to the house to find Gabriel in the kitchen, drink in one hand, waiting for them.

In low-slung, faded jeans, a white T-shirt and bare feet, he looked sinfully sexy and horribly tempting, and Izzy stopped dead in her tracks as her mouth dried and her brain fogged over.

Their eyes met over Rosa's head and he raised his eyebrows, which brought her sharply back down to earth.

'I must just get changed.' She did a sweeping gesture to encompass her khaki shorts and T-shirt. 'I'll leave you two to catch up on the day.'

She fled, straight up to the room she had been assigned.

Her heart was beating like a sledgehammer. She stared out of the window, gathering her composure. It was a peaceful sight. Manicured grounds, an infinity pool and the sweeping expanse of vineyards in the distance all set under a vast sky. There was a feel of cowboy territory, with the purple haze of the mountains far away on the horizon. She looked away and headed for the *en suite*.

This, she told herself, was not going to do. She was not going to let herself get flustered every time she laid eyes on the man. She was not going to let him see the sort of unwelcome effect he had on her. She'd committed to this job, though it couldn't be called a job, because when he'd offered to pay her she'd firmly refused. She wasn't going to be undermined by a swirl of emotion that had no place inside her.

She was going to stop noticing the way he looked if it killed her. The truth was, she was emphatically *not* attracted to men like Gabriel Ricci. He wasn't easygoing and he wasn't fun-loving. He was yet another example of a rich financier who put money above everything else. Never having been allowed to be a rebel, part of her knew that her aversion to ambitious, ruthless workaholics was her way of sticking two fingers up at her domineering older brother and the way he had controlled her life.

The best thing she could do would be to ignore Gabriel's impact and instead focus on trying to get him to change his mind about the cottage. He'd told her that he was a guy who never changed direction but even the most unlikely people changed direction.

Look at Max! Who would ever have thought that her work-orientated, driven older brother, so accustomed to running her life, would have found it in himself to understand where she'd been coming from with the hotel? Would have sympathised with the whole Jefferson saga and held off on ferrying her back to Hawaii to pick up where she had left off? Just went to show that there was no such thing as someone never changing direction. Given the circumstances with Evelyn, it was a fortifying conclusion.

Izzy returned to the kitchen, freshly showered and in soft grey trousers and a loose, pale-grey T-shirt. She had tied her hair back into a braid, but her hair was so curly that it refused to obey the rules, and she knew that the neat look she was aiming for was a borderline failure.

Gabriel was nowhere to be seen, and for a hopeful moment she wondered whether he had taken himself back off to work. But, just as she was about to start exploring the kitchen with relative confidence that she wouldn't be interrupted, she heard footsteps and then there he was, framed in the doorway, still in those faded jeans and that white T-shirt, still barefoot.

She could feel every muscle in her body tense and she had to make an effort to breathe evenly.

'Is…is Rosa asleep?'

'At last. She was very over-excited.' He strolled towards the fridge, took out a bottle of water and drank from it, before turning to her.

'I…er…' Izzy was uncertain as to how this time of the evening would evolve. 'If you don't mind, I'll just head upstairs…'

'Marie prepares food every day while we're in residence. Join me.'

'I don't mind taking my food upstairs. I'm not sure how you spend the evenings once Rosa is asleep, but I wouldn't want to interrupt your pattern.'

Izzy knew that this was precisely how she should *not* be acting but he made her so jittery that she couldn't think straight in his presence. Yet she needed to. She needed to hammer home her point of view or else why was she here? She couldn't afford to dither and hope that he did the right thing off his own bat. She took a deep breath and risked a smile. 'Except I would say that your pattern's probably really disrupted already with Rosa's nanny lying on a hospital bed. Can I ask something?'

She watched as he peered inside the frying pan, tidily covered on the stove, and then the fridge, from which he retrieved a perfectly prepared salad under cling film.

He fetched plates from a cupboard. He still hadn't said anything although, once plates wer on the table, along with the opened bottle of wine, he quirked an eyebrow and said wryly, 'Could I stop you?'

'Why do you employ a nanny that your daughter dislikes?'

'Is that what Rosa has told you?'

Izzy nodded. This was really none of her business because whether Rosa liked her nanny or not was beside the point. The woman would recover, return to work and Izzy would be off, whether she succeeded in changing Gabriel's mind or not. They were all ships passing in the night so curiosity was a waste of time.

Still…the more she saw of the little girl, the more she liked her, and she was deeply curious as to the strange set-up with Bella.

And, if she were to be completely honest with herself, the distant set-up Rosa had with her mother—who, from all accounts, spent an awful lot of time socialising, shopping and pampering herself—concerned her. Izzy vaguely knew, from conversations with James over the years, that her own mother had been absent for much of her brothers' formative years—having dispatched both James and Max to boarding schools practically from the time they'd taken their first steps—but for her, things had been different.

Her memories were much rosier. Her mother had treated her like a doll, dressing her up and letting her experiment with her make-up, shoes and clothes. Izzy had known that her parents were both away a lot, compared to the parents of all her friends, but when they'd been around her mother had delighted in doing all sorts of mother-and-daughter things with her.

'I adore having a little girl,' she had once sighed, when Izzy had been turning eight, and that passing comment had thrilled her to the bone.

And then, in a heartbeat, both her parents were gone and she was left with a great empty space inside her, even though people had rallied around. And of course both her brothers had taken her under their wing and done their utmost to numb the shock and pain. That great, empty space had never really been filled. It had sat right alongside her every step of the way as she had moved from childhood into adolescence and then into adulthood.

Izzy thought it sad that Rosa's passing remarks about her mother were so lacking in affection. Of course, she knew that it might just be the nonchalance of a child, but there were so few stories she shared that seemed special. And could she actually be telling the truth when she'd flippantly let slip that she was taken out of school quite often and taught by Bella on the move, to accommodate her mother's love of travelling to far-flung places?

With a grim nanny in the equation, however competent she might technically be, it all seemed desperately sad.

'It's none of my business,' she said when he failed to answer. 'Whatever Marie has cooked, it smells delicious. Is this your routine when you're here? She cooks for you and you have your dinner on your own?'

'It's my routine wherever in the world I happen to be,' Gabriel responded drily. 'Unless, which is more often the case, I go out to eat.'

He looked at her with a hooded expression. This was a novel experience for him and normal rules did not apply.

What else had Rosa said to her? He was well aware that Izzy was here under duress and nursing some notion that he might be prepared to back down on his plans for the cottage.

He wasn't concerned about using her. He had met very many rich young things, and the one thing he knew for sure about all of them was that they were hard as nails. Whatever the guise. Wealth created a veneer, made you think that you could take what you wanted without conscience. Izzy might appear to be as pure as the driven snow but he would bet his life that she was tough as old boots. She probably thought that she could change his mind because she would have been conditioned to expect to get her own way in most situations. The overriding power of his past experience was a force that locked the door on trust.

His eyes drifted to her full pink mouth, that tangle of blonde hair and the pure cornflower blue of her big, wide eyes. Sexy as hell, he thought, and no doubt as experienced as any woman he had ever slept with, even though she might not give off the same vibes.

Just thinking about her in that way sent a rush of hot blood straight down to his groin and he shifted uncomfortably, turning away for a moment to busy himself doing something with whatever Marie had cooked—some kind of chicken dish. He was back to his usual cool when he strolled to the table, waving down her offer to help as he deposited the salad, cutlery and then the pan, not bothering to decant its contents.

Gabriel had suspected for some time that Bianca played fast and loose with the parenting process, although there was no way he would ever put his daughter in the position of having to provide answers to his questions.

His ex-wife was very good when it came to laying down ground rules, only to break them. She was very good when it came to blatantly defying the court order on shared custody, just keeping on the right side of his tipping point. She knew how to use his workaholic's schedule against him, just as she knew that the women he dated, the relationships that never matured into anything permanent, put him at a distinct disadvantage when it came to fighting her in a court of law for more custody of Rosa. She knew his weaknesses and she knew how to exploit them. And Bella could always be relied upon to ferry news back to her.

He looked under his lashes at the blonde helping herself to what seemed a vast amount of food for someone who weighed nothing. Momentarily distracted, he watched as she heaped her plate, before raising apologetic eyes to him.

'I'm hungrier than I thought,' she muttered.

'A woman with a hearty appetite. That's a first for me. Tell me what you did today with Rosa.'

Gabriel listened intently while she went through the events of her day with his daughter. He relaxed because, although he only had a scant idea of what life might be like for Rosa with his ex-wife, he knew what it was like with Bella and it warmed him to hear an account of what had been quite a different day for his daughter with Izzy.

His jaw hardened. He had been patient for a very long time with Bianca. Now he had the scent of payback in the air because, if his ex could play dirty, then he could return the favour if there was any suspicion that her parenting was below par.

The information he would never have prised from his daughter now hovered tantalisingly within reach because it was apparent that Rosa was building a close and confiding relationship with the woman opposite him tucking into her food with gusto. He thought that his daughter, like any other child her age, would be good at unconditionally giving affection to someone they immediately took a liking to.

'You asked about Bella,' he introduced when there was a lull in the conversation.

Dinner at an end, he pushed aside his plate, shoved back his chair and relaxed, linking his fingers on his stomach and watching her with lazy interest.

She looked so damned *fresh*. She looked like what he had first thought her to be—someone without the tiresome airs and graces that came with privilege… someone not yet cynical enough to think that money bought everything. He dropped his eyes and recalled the very expensive Louis Vuitton case that had accompanied her into his house. He had glimpsed her earlier from the window of the room he currently used as his office as she had stepped out of her taxi.

'You don't have to answer,' Izzy shrugged once again, and regretfully closed her knife and fork.

'Bella is a relative of my ex-wife,' Gabriel expanded, ignoring the uneasy tug inside him at this innocuous exchange of information. So unaccustomed was he to sharing any aspect of his private life with anyone, the admission felt oddly disconcerting. It felt like a tacit admission of *trust*, and yet it surely couldn't be? Trust was something that had been taken from him through those bitter years when he had discovered just how fragile it was.

'So I guess you had to employ her if your...ex-wife... asked,' Izzy mused sympathetically. 'It's tempting to give jobs to people you're related to.'

'I wouldn't have, given half a chance,' Gabriel grated. 'But unfortunately my ex-wife can be vindictive and is fond of playing games.' He looked away briefly. 'Including those that use Rosa as a pawn.'

'I'm sorry,' Izzy said, aghast and not hiding it. She felt a warm, protective rush towards her little charge and knew that it was because there was a meeting of mutual ground here. A daughter without her mother, whatever the reasons behind it might be, was a child set up to experience loss. She should know.

'Don't be. As you've said, this is hardly your concern.' He stood up and stretched before removing the crockery to the sink, where he proceeded haphazardly to stack the lot at the side. 'Bella's methods are draconian when applied to a six-year-old, which is why Rosa is so rebellious. She may do everything by the book but, when it comes to kids, that's not always the right way.'

'Couldn't you talk to your wife, your *ex*-wife, about that? It doesn't matter how vindictive she is, surely the main thing is Rosa's happiness?'

'In an ideal world, I would.' Gabriel said wryly. 'Unfortunately, the world is rarely ideal. I am just pleased that my daughter is having fun with you.'

'I'm not engaging her in any educational activities, though...'

'You mean like Bella?'

'There is a timetable from the sounds of it, and quite

a gruelling one. No subject is left unexplored, even during the holidays.' She relaxed and grinned. That glass of wine had taken the edge off her nervous tension, as had the fact that they were on neutral territory, discussing something other than the contentious issue of the cottage. 'I guess I would be able to do homework with her, but I wouldn't enjoy it. I did business studies at university but…'

Gabriel tilted his head to one side. 'But…?'

'But it was the wrong choice,' Izzy mumbled.

'Why?'

Izzy shrugged and swept her hair over one shoulder, a nervous gesture, because she needed to do something with her hands. 'I'm happy to keep to my side of the bargain.' She changed the subject. 'But will you really consider backing down on the business with the cottage? At least try and stand back and see it from a different perspective?'

'Of course,' Gabriel lied magnanimously.

Her non-answer to his question intrigued him. It was easy to pigeonhole rich young women because he personally had had a great deal of experience with them. Hell, he'd made the colossal mistake of marrying one of them!

Rich young women, he had found over the years, enjoyed talking about themselves and were always happy to fill in the blanks with minimum encouragement from him.

He had no problem with that. Bianca had put him off the institution of marriage for good. The experience had also taught him something very valuable about himself: he would always put work ahead of everyone and everything, with the exception of his daughter. Even so, with some guilt he knew that there was more he could do with her.

But for women? They would always take a back seat. He had grown up on the wrong side of the tracks and knew, from experience, just how tough life could be when you could barely afford to put food on your plate. His parents had worked their fingers to the bone, had done their best for him, but still they had been suffocated by a society that only recognised people with money. Their ambition had been to give him the opportunity to escape the trap into which they had been born and there was no way he had ever had any intention of disappointing on that front.

Poverty and scraping by? Bowing and taking orders from someone else who happened to have money even if they weren't any smarter? No way. Somewhere along the line, Gabriel knew that he had traded emotions for hard-headed ambition and he was not regretful about the trade-off.

It just meant that he knew exactly where women slotted into his life, and it had to be said that the hard-nosed rich young things he dated suited him. He wasn't in the market for emotional attachment but he was more than happy to show them a good time. When he thought of those other women out there, the sort of women he knew his parents desperately hoped he would meet, he felt a shiver run down his spine. Those women—with high hopes and expectations, vulnerable and waiting to be hurt, trusting and keen for their happy-ever-afters with a domesticated husband and kids running around—were women to be avoided at all costs. He just didn't have

what it took to give any of that to them and he was brutally realistic about those shortcomings.

The doe-eyed beauty with the rich parents intrigued
him and against all odds she stirred a certain amount of
curiosity just because she was different from the pack,
even though she did, indeed, come from the same stable.

And if he gained her trust…if she chose to confide
in him any shortcomings that might be mentioned in
connection with his ex-wife…then who was he not to
use that information to his advantage?

It would certainly make a change, bearing in mind
he had been on the back foot with Bianca ever since
their acrimonious divorce.

'I've spoken to the hospital,' he said smoothly. 'They
anticipate at least two weeks. It would seem that Bella
has some underlying health issues that might hamper
a speedy recovery.'

'Two weeks?'

'Of course, I can't tie you to a post and make you
stay…but you have to appreciate that such a major re-
think isn't something that can be effected in a handful
of days. A considerable amount of money is involved,
not to mention the man hours that have gone into re-
searching the feasibility of such a massive addition to
the vineyards I currently own.'

Izzy lowered her eyes then looked at him. 'Two
weeks,' she said. 'At the end of that, if you're still *considering the options*, then I'll know that you have no
intention of changing your plans.'

Three days after Izzy had moved in, Evelyn had wor-
riedly told her that she was sure she had spotted someone *out there* doing *something*.

'I thought everything was going to be all right,' she had said anxiously. It had surprised Izzy that, even though doubts were beginning to form in the older woman's head, she still insisted on clinging to the false belief that Gabriel—*such a lovely man*—wouldn't do anything underhand.

That very evening—after she had had her shower and delivered Rosa to her father for what had become an evening ritual, whereby he bonded with his daughter for an hour or so before she went to bed—Izzy headed to the kitchen to wait for him.

Disconcertingly, this too had become something of a ritual. How? She had braced herself for awkward encounters where she either avoided him or else tried to pin him down to make some kind of decision. Instead, she had been lulled into conversing about what she and Rosa had done during the day. He asked so many questions and, after a glass of wine, which was something else she had become accustomed to, she found that chatting to him and answering those questions eclipsed all her good intentions when it came to pressing him for an answer about the cottage.

She was uneasily aware that she was probably being used because he needed someone on tap for Rosa while he was working during the day, and he was right—a temporary nanny would have taken far too much breaking in for such a short period of time.

She grew fonder of the child by the day but she was shrewd enough to know that her adorable little charge was precociously clever and very much had a mind of her own.

Izzy had rehearsed her line of attack and, the minute he entered the kitchen, she said without beating around the bush, 'Evelyn said that she saw someone in the neighbouring vineyards and he seemed to be someone official.'

She gritted her teeth together, impatiently waiting for him to reply, watching as he peered into the oven to see what was there. Not for the first time, she marvelled at just how lacking in interest he seemed to be when it came to cooking for himself.

'Well?' she asked, resisting the urge to snap.

'Things that have been set in motion,' Gabriel countered smoothly as he strolled towards the kitchen table and sat down next to her, swivelling the chair so that he was facing her directly, 'Are continuing at the moment. Various experts were booked to inspect the vineyards I planned on buying quite some time ago. I'm sorry to disappoint you, but I don't intend to issue full-scale cancellation orders on the off chance that I may not go ahead with the project.'

'I'll convey the message to Evelyn,' Izzy said stiffly. 'I'm sure she'll be over the moon that the trust she had in you was completely misplaced. I've suddenly lost my appetite. I think I'll retire for the evening now.'

'Any messages about what I do with my land or any land I might be considering buying,' Gabriel informed her with steely determination, 'Will be conveyed by me.'

'What difference does it make?' Izzy tilted her chin at a belligerent angle and glared.

'You're very used to getting what you want in life, aren't you?' he returned softly.

Izzy floundered. This was a question she had not been expecting and the way in which it was delivered, coolly and with derision, sent a shiver racing down her spine.

'What makes you say that?'

'Izzy, you're a rich young woman, and I'll wager that you assumed, deep down, that you would get what you wanted, and what you wanted was for me to back-pedal on this deal whatever the financial fallout for me.'

'That's not true!' Tears pricked the back of her eyes and she felt herself break out in a light film of nervous perspiration. 'How dare you pretend to know what sort of person I am?'

'I am an excellent judge of people,' Gabriel countered without batting an eye. 'Of course, I might be wrong...' He shrugged his broad shoulders with just the sort of dismissive nonchalance that left Izzy in no doubt that he believed himself to be absolutely right.

'Well, you *are* wrong.' She stood up, flinging the chair back, her cheeks bright-red with defiance. 'I have *never* gone through life expecting *anything*!' She spun round on her heels and headed for the door, but then she stopped, her breath coming in fast bursts. He wasn't stopping her, and yet her feet refused to propel her out of the kitchen, because this was a conversation that seemed to need an ending. She could *feel* him behind her and her breathing quickened.

He could be...so...*arrogant* and yet she was ashamed to admit that she had been charmed by him over the past few days, had dropped her defences and fallen under some kind of crazy spell.

More fool her.

'Haven't you?'

Izzy slowly turned round and pressed herself against the door in a desperate effort at distancing him, although he was so close... Her throat tightened in an instant, horrifying response to his proximity.

With devastating clarity, she realised that she had spent the past few evenings not just relaxing in his company, not just dropping the antagonism that she had originally felt for him, but somehow *enjoying* the illicit thrill of being with him.

She had told herself that, whatever her physical attraction, he just wasn't her type. Yet her disobedient eyes had strayed, and so had her mind. He was *exciting* and she had enjoyed the excitement. She had never felt anything like it in her life before, and that frightened her.

How could she feel like this for someone who was such an adversary? Where had her sense of judgement gone? Her brief, unhappy fling with Jefferson now felt indifferent and irrelevant. How on earth had she been upset enough to flee? And where had gone all those valuable lessons she had thought she'd learnt?

Panicked at thoughts piling up inside her, she feverishly concluded that her lack of experience had left her at the mercy of a man like Gabriel Ricci. She was also vulnerable after Jefferson, her bruised heart seeking affirmation that life carried on, whatever.

The power of his personality and the wild sexiness of his overpowering masculinity had wiped out all the caution she knew should have been in place.

Her heart was hammering and she was conscious of her nipples pushing against her T-shirt, unconstrained by a bra. Between her thighs, she could feel her arousal spreading.

'You...you don't know the first thing about me.' She breathed shakily, her blue eyes enormous. 'You think you do because I happen to come from a privileged background.' Her nostrils flared as she breathed him in. Was it her imagination, or had he closed the gap between them by a couple of inches?

'Why don't you tell me where I've gone wrong?' Gabriel murmured roughly, leaning down, his dark eyes scanning her face. 'I know that you're sexy as hell,' he growled. 'Rich, young and temptation on legs. All adds up to someone assuming that she can get exactly what she wants.'

Sexy as hell? Temptation on legs? He hadn't exactly given any indication that he might be thinking anything along those lines since she had entered his house.

Izzy felt giddy. She thought of him looking at her and thinking those things, and it was such an incredible turn-on that she had to bite down on a whimper rising up her throat.

'You think I'm *sexy*?' she heard herself ask, even as she realised that that was the very last thing she wanted to leave her lips. She was driven to look at him, and the hot flare in his eyes answered her question.

She licked her lips. They felt so dry. The breath stuck in her throat and she could hear her own shallow breathing. Her hands were pressed tightly behind her back.

And, in that moment, everything stood still as he lowered his head and kissed her.

Long, slow and easy—it was a kiss that was as heady as a drug, and the feel of his tongue against hers sent a wave of red-hot lust through her.

She freed her hands and linked her fingers behind his neck. She wanted him so badly…just for a minute. It was all wrong, of course it was, but…

Izzy closed her eyes and lost herself in that kiss.

CHAPTER FIVE

HE WAS THE first to pull away.

What the *hell*?

Gabriel raked his fingers through his hair, angry with himself, not so much for kissing her but for his lack of self-control. He hadn't meant to touch but he'd looked at her—looked at those sulky, full lips, the unruly chaos of her blonde hair and the narrowed brilliant cornflower blue of her eyes—and his body had just decided to do its own thing.

Never before had that happened to him. His supersonic rags-to-riches climb had driven out every single urge that could not be contained. In his life, there had been room only for ambition and he had willingly accepted that. Women were a pleasant distraction but never the main event. The main event had always been to reach such heady heights of power that he became untouchable.

It was what had brought Bianca to him. They had met at a wildly extravagant party held on a private island in the Caribbean. She had been there as a friend of the family. He had been there because the man who owned the island wanted to schmooze him into doing a deal with one of his subsidiary companies, a loss-making cargo airline business. Gabriel had been there for exactly two days, just long enough to get the information he wanted, but not so long that he would actually have to circulate with a bunch of people he was programmed to dislike. Rich, idle, beautiful.

Surrounded by barely clad young women, Bianca had stood out because of her raven-haired, voluptuous beauty, and the fact that he could communicate with her in Italian had relieved some of his boredom at being stuck on the island. It had amused him to realise that he recognised her name, which was synonymous with Italian royalty. It amused him even further to think that the woman with the impeccable lineage hung onto his every word, pleased as punch that she had managed to capture the interest of the one man there all the foot-loose and fancy-free singletons wanted.

Obscenely rich, good-looking, ridiculously power-ful. Worked wonders!

Had he been just another poor Italian guy trying to eke out a living in the back streets of New York, the story would have been quite different. He had played with her on that island and then he had allowed himself to be coaxed into a relationship. She had followed him back to Manhattan and, when she had announced her pregnancy a handful of weeks later, there had been no option but marriage.

It had not been a cause for celebration but neither had it been a reason for despair. He hadn't figured on marriage yet, nor had he had any cravings to hear the pitter-patter of tiny feet, but with a *fait accompli* on his hands he had acknowledged that the security of his parents' relationship was something to aspire to rather than shun. They had always been there for one another and for him. Rather than succumb to the voice of doubt in his head, he had determined to make the best of the situation.

His parents had had massive reservations about Bianca and the wedding had been nothing short of a disaster, with her distinguished family members and rich, braying friends more or less side-lining his side of the family and his friends, all of whom he had invited in great numbers. Hell, he wasn't ashamed of his past, and people could take it or leave it as far as he was concerned.

But, given that dynamic, he should have predicted the fall of his marriage. He'd returned to his brutal work schedule, misreading—or perhaps, he'd thought afterwards, deliberately ignoring—the demands being made on his time with ever-increasing intensity. The drive to succeed was too ingrained to ignore.

Within weeks of Rosa being born, it had been evident that the union wasn't working, and really, it had just been a matter of time before a beautiful woman fine-tuned to expect male adoration found it in another man.

Gabriel had learnt many lessons from that experience, not least that he knew where he stood in the cut-throat world of making money, but when it came to women...? Well, in his world, trust in women was a commodity in very short supply.

Never again would he make the mistake of entering into any kind of relationship unless the rules of the game he was interested in playing were made crystal-clear. At all times, he would have complete control over his emotions.

As far as he was concerned, he'd tried longevity, and he wasn't cut out for it.

He had his daughter and that was all that mattered.

So now, here, to end up kissing some woman he'd

known for five minutes *because he hadn't been able to help himself* struck him as a full-on admission of weakness.

The fact that this particular woman belonged to the same kind of world from which his dearly beloved ex came stuck in his craw even more.

'That shouldn't have happened,' he rasped, scowling. 'Accept my apologies.'

It infuriated him that his libido was still in full throttle, red-hot and pulsing as he watched her wipe the back of her hand across her mouth.

Her scowl matched his, and for a second he was wrong-footed by that reaction, because given the circumstances most women would have been trying to find a way towards a repeat performance.

She'd folded her arms and was now staring at him with open hostility. 'No, it damn well shouldn't!'

'In which case, why did you enjoy it so much?' he asked and was gratified by the slow burn of colour in her cheeks.

'I did not *enjoy* it! You took me by surprise.'

He'd taken himself by surprise too.

'It won't happen again. Look…' He shook his head, but he could still feel the urgent throb between his legs telling him that, whatever he happened to be saying, his body was contradicting every word. 'I'll be going to Chicago tomorrow. Staying overnight on business. Let's forget about what just happened and get back to square one.'

Izzy continued to glare.

Her whole body was on fire, as if a match had been struck. He'd kissed her and she'd gone up in flames like a heady teenager instead of a woman recovering from a broken affair. She should have pushed him away. She should have remembered that she was going to be careful when it came to involvement with the opposite sex. At the very least, she should have recalled just how much she disapproved of him and his tactics with the cottage.

Was she so stupid that she was going to allow him to charm her, the way he had charmed Evelyn?

When the much-maligned nanny Bella left the sick bed and headed back to the call of duty, would Izzy cheerfully be dispatched, knowing that all she'd managed to achieve was to make his life easier by babysitting his daughter so that he could work, because he had charmed her into silence?

She was red-faced with mortification.

'I don't think that this arrangement is going to work,' she said with staccato jerkiness in her voice. She'd taken a few prudent steps back but those flames were taking their time dying down.

'Why not?'

'Because I… It would be uncomfortable…after this. It's not something that's going to just disappear because you say so…' After that kiss, how on earth would she be able to look at him without instant recall? How would she be able to fight the treacherous thought that one kiss wasn't enough?

'It would be only as uncomfortable as we allow it to be,' he said tersely. 'If you really don't think you'd be able to face me after this, then I can't stop you from leaving. But here's something to think about: maybe you wouldn't be able to face me for a completely different reason. Maybe you wouldn't be able to face me without wanting a repeat performance.' He looked at her in darkly brooding silence for a couple of tense seconds, then he brushed past her and began heading towards the commanding staircase that divided the sprawling mansion.

After a few seconds, Izzy sprinted behind him, heart hammering inside her. This was not how this conversation should end. This was not where this devastating kiss should take them, towards unresolved conclusions and angry exchanges. She reached out, tugged the sleeve of his shirt and he slowly turned around.

'It was just a kiss. You're right. Why should either of us feel uncomfortable?' She stumbled over her words and lowered her eyes. Standing on the step above, he absolutely towered over her, and she had to crane her neck just to meet his eyes.

He wasn't going to make this any easier for her, and she couldn't blame him, but he had said what he'd said, and she had to clear the air without her emotions getting the better of her and dictating her behaviour.

The silence lengthened. 'Things happen and…'

'And…?' he said softly, eyebrows raised, eyes still cool.

'I *don't* want a repeat performance, but even if I did,' Izzy admitted with grudging honesty, 'There's no way you should think that I would do anything about it. I… guess I overreacted because…' Her breath hitched in her throat and her voice tapered off into silence.

'You don't have to say anything more on the subject. You can keep the back story to yourself.' But when their eyes met she felt she could see curiosity in his. Or was that her imagination? The moment felt strangely intimate and for a few seconds she had the giddy sensation of standing on the threshold of something, although she had no idea where that sensation was coming from.

'I… When I came here, I was recovering from… Well, I was going out with a guy, Jefferson, who wasn't the person I thought he was.' She looked at him and smiled sheepishly. 'Sorry. You're not interested in a back story, and I don't know why I'm telling you any of this anyway. It's not your business. I just came after you because I don't want to leave either you or Rosa in the lurch, and I won't let what happened drive my behaviour. You took me by surprise, but I took myself by surprise even more, because I thought I was too hurt to respond the way I did…back there…to you…'

She began to turn away but paused when he said in a roughened undertone, 'I don't know about you, but I could do with a cup of coffee.'

No way… You've said what you wanted to say, now you can coolly and calmly go to bed, knowing you've set the record straight. There was no need for you to start babbling on about your private life because he isn't interested. He just feels a little sorry for you, and probably wants to make sure oil has been poured over every bit of troubled water. After all, he still wants you to look after his daughter…

'Okay.'

This time, he settled her into an oak-panelled sitting room that overlooked the pool at the back. Outside lights just about illuminated the still, dark water. The waving trees were dark shadows and the expanse of the vineyard was silent and orderly.

He reappeared with two cups of coffee, handed one to her and then pulled a chair over so that he was sitting right in front of her.

'You were saying?'

'I was babbling.'

'What happened?'

'It's all very boring,' Izzy mumbled. Why suddenly become coy? She'd invited this conversation by divulging details about herself he hadn't asked for. 'I came over to the States to take up a job setting up a hotel in Hawaii, and while I was there I stupidly got involved with a guy.'

'Why stupidly?'

'Please don't think that you have to be polite and listen to this,' she said, but she couldn't work out why she was willing to continue. Was it because something in those dark, dark eyes invited confidences? The same something that had made her talk far too much since she'd been here? Or was it because a part of her wanted to find out what a man made of the situation? It was okay to confide in your girlfriends, and Mia had been so sympathetic, but girlfriends took your side, and maybe she was curious to see what a man's response would be. Men, in her opinion, were always so…practical and prosaic, and this particular specimen took practical to the extreme.

She was so wet behind the ears. Had she dived into something with Jefferson without judging the depth of the water first? Expected more than could be delivered? Of course she had.

But…and here was the thing…she wondered if maybe she had made some fundamental error of judgement that only a man would be able to spot.

She was uneasily aware that there might be another reason why she was sitting here.

She liked being in his company. He excited her and excitement could be addictive. Her lips were still burning from that kiss, and all of that gave an edge to being here with him that made her blood run hot.

'I never do anything out of politeness,' he said matter-of-factly. 'Tell me what happened. I'm interested.'

'I didn't know anyone when I came over here,' Izzy offered in a halting voice. 'I was fresh out of university and this was my first job.' Why tell him that it had been an arranged one? She already knew what he thought about her and her moneyed background. No need to remind him of it. 'I didn't know anyone. I made friends with this lovely girl, Mia, who took me under her wing and introduced me to all sorts of people. She's into surfing in a big way and that's where I met Jefferson.'

'Jefferson. … Let me guess…a fellow surfer? Content to trawl the beaches and avoid the responsibility of actually holding down a job? I could probably describe him as well. Tall and blond. Long hair, I'll bet, and an easygoing manner.'

'More or less,' Izzy admitted.

'I'm guessing he saw you coming a mile off.'

'What do you mean?'

'That type isn't confined to somewhere like Hawaii. Stick a pin on any map where's there's a beach crowd in a well-to-do area, and you'll find a Jefferson waiting to meet someone who can fund his lazy life choices. They're the ones who hold down casual jobs that just about cover the bills, but most of their time is spent eyeing up prospective donors willing to contribute to the cause of promoting their lifestyle.'

'He was fun,' Izzy said half-heartedly, cringing at the ease with which Gabriel had read the situation.

'I'm sure.'

'He made me feel free.'

'And explain how you were trapped before, Izzy.'

'I know you think that I'm a spoiled, privileged brat who's accustomed to getting her own way, but my life hasn't been as straightforward as you think.'

Her clear blue eyes defiantly dared him to challenge her, and accordingly he tilted his head to one side and looked at her in silence.

How could this man manage to get on her nerves, encourage her to open up *and* turn her on *all at the same time*?

'I don't have to explain myself to you.' She backed off from completely succumbing to whatever pull he had over her, tried to shake herself free of the spell he was weaving.

'Quite true.' He paused. 'Did the man eventually ask you for money? You're right, you don't have to explain yourself to me, but I can tell from the expression on your face that I've hit the nail on the head. Trust me, you had a lucky escape.' He drained the remainder of his coffee and looked at her with brooding, veiled eyes.

Gabriel didn't do back stories and, as much as he was tempted to quiz her, he wasn't going to break habits of a lifetime. Doubtless, hers would be a tale of the poor little rich girl, lonely and misunderstood in her gilded cage.

He'd heard a number of similar tales over the years. Privileged backgrounds seemed to breed a disproportionate lot of angst in a certain type of woman.

He wasn't sure why he was so curious about this particular one but he wasn't going to explore the reasons. She'd slept with some man who ended up wanting to fleece her and she'd run away from whatever job she had because she couldn't deal with it. Experiences like that toughened up a person and it would toughen her up even though, right now, she looked immensely frail and vulnerable, with those delicately flushed cheeks and that hurt, defensive expression in her big, blue eyes.

He wondered whether that side of her was what his daughter found so appealing—the side that was strangely childlike, even though she could be as fierce and frankly more outspoken than most of the women he had surrounded himself with after his divorce.

He continued to look thoughtfully at Izzy, his thoughts cloaked by dark eyes that were adept at expressing as much or as little as he thought appropriate. Right now, he had no intention of expressing an iota of what was going through his head.

Izzy and Rosa had bonded and from that bond could come some very useful information. Slowly but surely, he was beginning to flesh out the bigger story of what life for his daughter was like with Bianca.

He had never wanted to play dirty, and had refrained from doing anything that conceivably could jeopardise his relationship with Rosa, but with the threat of having to fight to keep his daughter in the country the tides were beginning to turn.

If information could land in his lap without him having to do anything that involved Rosa feeling that she might be taking sides, then who was he to walk away from it?

And if that information could come via Izzy, with her clear, blue eyes and halting shyness, then why not encourage that conduit?

Solution-based as he was, Gabriel saw nothing wrong with his tactics. He would encourage confidences. Why not? He would see how things played out between them.

Certainly that kiss advertised a chemistry that sparked, and so what if he used that chemistry to get to where he wanted to go? No hardship there. They were two adults. One thing might very well lead to another, and pillow talk could prove very rewarding.

He thought of that one thing leading to another and felt himself involuntarily harden in immediate and pleasurable response.

'I know that,' Izzy confided in a broken, halting voice. 'Not that it felt much like a lucky escape at the time.' No, it was devastating to realise that she had been wanted for what she had and not who she was.

'A broken heart,' Gabriel inserted, 'is never easy to deal with.'

'And you should know, I guess.' Izzy shot him a sympathetic look. 'Considering you're divorced. I'll bet you've suffered a lot more than I have.'

Gabriel stiffened, automatically primed to repulse any attempt by anyone to ask about his private life. He didn't deal in explanations and he had never met any woman who dared encroach beyond the No Trespass signs which were always glaringly in place.

But a bigger picture was taking shape, stampeding over the ridiculous tightness in his chest at her story, and he knew that letting his guard down for once in his life would be a small price to pay.

He nodded curtly. 'Divorce is never pleasant,' he muttered.

'No, I can't imagine it is,' Izzy murmured. 'I'm sorry for you that it seems to have ended on such an acrimonious note, but I guess love and hate are just opposite sides of the same coin.'

Gabriel grunted.

'You don't want to talk about it.'

'Nothing to talk about,' he said and shifted, veiling his expression further. 'I prefer not to dwell on what's gone. Always more profitable living in the present and looking towards the future.'

'That's exactly what I came here to do,' Izzy admitted, sounding rueful.

'Until you became embroiled in the saga of the cottage and your mother's nanny…'

'Until that happened.' Izzy lowered her eyes and Gabriel could see the steady pulse in her neck, the gentle flush creeping into her cheeks. With some sixth sense he knew that she was torn between wanting to pursue a conversation about the cottage and not wanting to break the tremulous accord between them.

She looked up. For a split second their eyes met and held, and he smiled. There was a reason why she didn't want to ruin the electricity that had sprung up between them, and he had to concede that she wasn't on her own here. He was enjoying this sizzle of excitement, an undercurrent of tantalising, shimmering possibilities. That kiss had opened a Pandora's box and he, for one, had no intention of trying to shut it.

But neither was he going to make a play for her. He would let her come to him.

Was he using her? Maybe, but wouldn't she likewise be using him if they did what their bodies were clearly urging them to do?

She'd been hurt by some man she'd met on a beach. Subconsciously, she wanted to be pieced back together. He could sense that from the little she had told him.

And, if he offered himself to be that helping hand for the job, then wouldn't he be doing her a favour?

Wasn't it, really, a mutually beneficial situation? Yes. It was.

'It's late,' he murmured, fluidly rising to his feet and waiting for her to follow suit, watching as she scrambled up. He moved closer to her whilst maintaining a respectable distance and murmured sincerely, 'And again, that kiss…not planned. It's not like me to…' He hesitated and then continued absolutely truthfully, 'To allow my attraction to any woman get the better of me. But on this occasion, I lost the battle. You were beyond temptation.'

He drew back and began heading towards the door, very much aware of her alongside him, so slender, seemingly so fragile and, oh, so tempting. He turned and gave her a mock-salute.

'I'm going to head to my office. I'll have time to say goodbye to Rosa before I leave for Chicago, and I'll see you when I get back day after tomorrow.' He paused and crossed another of his self-imposed boundaries. 'I'll let you have my personal line. You'll be able to get through to me any time you want.'

'We'll be fine.' Izzy smiled reassuringly.

'I know you will, and I can't wait to see you when I return.'

He called. Of course, Izzy should have known that he would want to talk to her to find out how Rosa was doing, but she was still flustered when he phoned that first time, pretty much as soon as he landed in Chicago. The dark timbre of his voice sent shivers racing up and down her spine.

It brought to mind the devastating impact of his kiss, the way his mouth on hers had made her feel. It also brought to mind what he had said. He had put his cards on the table, told her that he was attracted to her and then he had walked away, leaving her thoughts in a jumble.

He didn't pursue the conversation or make any suggestive remarks when he spoke to her on the phone. The fact that he was acting so *normal*, as though nothing had been said between them, fuelled her fevered imagination like nothing else could have done.

He was on her mind to an extraordinary degree, even though she was as involved as always with Rosa, taking her to pick fruit in Evelyn's garden and drawing pictures of flowers, while Evelyn studiously gave them both little lessons on their names and origins.

She found herself waiting for his debrief call, which duly came just before Rosa was to be settled for the night. He chatted to her while Izzy faffed and tried to subdue a rush of heady excitement and, when he did ask to be put on the line with her, she had to breathe deeply and count to ten before she could speak in a normal voice.

'Yes, everything's just great… We had a really busy day… Went to Evelyn's for tea… Rosa ate all her dinner… Oh, I'm sorry to hear that Bella is going to be in a bit longer than expected. Yes, see you tomorrow… Oh, you'll be back late? Never mind, have a safe trip…'

Afterwards, she replayed the conversation in her head and wondered whether there was anything to read between the lines. Had he completely forgotten about that kiss? About what he had said afterwards? He was a man of the world…maybe he was accustomed to that level of sophisticated, nonchalant flirting that didn't necessarily go anywhere. She'd reassured him that a repeat performance wouldn't be on the cards, so why was she so let down at the notion that he was simply doing as asked?

The more she thought about him telling her that he hadn't been able to resist that kiss, the more she burned with the forbidden desire to take things further between them.

It contravened all her resolutions never to get wrapped up with the wrong man again. Gabriel Ricci could not be *more wrong*. And yet...

The following day dragged. The skies were overcast but there was a dense humidity in the air that made both Rosa and her lethargic.

They had a light lunch and then, at a little after five, when at last the humidity was dying down a bit, Izzy suggested the pool. They had yet to go swimming, partly because the swimming pool, spectacular though it was, had lost it novelty when compared to Evelyn's orchard and exploring her garden. Rosa had grown up with swimming pools and all the other accoutrements of extreme wealth. It was the simple stuff that intrigued her.

With Gabriel not due until well past the witching hour, they both got into their swimsuits, pulled out a few pool toys from the extravagant changing suite built under a canopy of trees by the side and splashed around for a while, playing silly games.

Rosa could swim like a fish. Izzy pretended she couldn't. They laughed and chatted, and it occurred to Izzy that she was discovering a whole lot about Rosa's life with her mother, things that made her wonder how on earth Gabriel could have fallen for the woman, who sounded monstrously selfish.

Post-divorce, he might admit that she was fond of

playing games and used her daughter as a convenient pawn, but there must have been a time when he had been smitten, or else why would he have married her?

And yet she heard tales of Rosa being left to her own devices when there was no nanny around…of Rosa having to make herself scarce when her mother had her boyfriends over…of Rosa being removed from school without warning to go on inappropriate holidays or else being dumped with friends, awkwardly aware that at times she wasn't entirely wanted.

Most damaging of all, as far as Izzy was concerned, was the revelation that Bianca had warned her daughter to keep quiet about what happened on the home front *or else*. The pull to stay for the sake of Rosa, never mind Evelyn, was a powerful force in its own right.

In fairness, Rosa seemed blithely unperturbed, but surely, deep down, she was? Izzy knew from her own painful experiences just how fast and far a disjointed background could travel, screwing up your life for years to come.

The sky had darkened without Izzy noticing and it was only when there was the sharp crack of thunder overhead that she grabbed Rosa and began making a sprint for the house.

The heavens opened. Thunder rumbled, and the rain pelted down with such ferocity that by the time they hit the side door they were drenched.

She didn't have time do anything with her towel. She didn't have time to fling on her T-shirt. Nor did she have time to see anything in front of her because she was one hundred percent focused on both she and Rosa making it back through that side door into the kitchen without slipping on the suddenly treacherous paving.

So colliding slap, bang into an immovable object holding the kitchen door open was a shock, and she recoiled back in confused panic.

It took a few seconds of crazy blinking before she realised that the immovable object was Gabriel. He stepped back, hoisted Rosa off her feet and carried her into the kitchen and, voice high, Izzy couldn't help demanding what the heck he was doing there.

She was shivering with sudden cold, angry that he had surprised her, angry that she had been thinking about him non-stop, and angry that he clearly hadn't been thinking about her because there was not the remotest hint of *anything* when he slowly turned round to look at her.

He looked cool, collected and inscrutable as he glanced at her while whipping a towel from one of the drawers and clumsily wrapping it around Rosa, who had curled up against him like an insect burrowing for safety.

'Have you forgotten?' he asked wryly. 'This happens to be my house. I'm going to take Rosa up.' He paused, expression veiled. 'You should change, get out of those wet things. We can debrief later, once Rosa is settled.'

'I think I'll have an early night, if you don't mind.' Izzy knew that she was overreacting to the shock of seeing him when she hadn't expected to and to her own stupid thoughts about what he had said, what they had done and how quickly he had moved past it all while she had continued mentally to chew it all over like a dog with a bone. She was *piqued*. Pathetic.

'Of course.' He was already moving off, his pristine suit wet from Rosa dripping all over him. 'In that case, I'll see you in the morning.'

CHAPTER SIX

SHE COULDN'T SLEEP. What started as darkening skies, a rumble of thunder and a sudden downpour developed into a full-blown storm as the night wore on.

Izzy had closed all windows yet the force of the rain battering against them made her wonder whether the next sound she heard would be the shattering of glass.

Plus, she was starving.

She'd vanished up to her suite the evening before, head held high, smarting from the way she had allowed that man to climb into her head. That was all well and good but now, here she was, at a little after two in the morning, and the rumbling of her tummy was doing a great job of overpowering the sound of the rain pelting down.

Wide awake, she eased herself off her bed and wondered whether she should call Evelyn and find out if the older woman was okay. Was this sort of dramatic weather *a thing* in these parts of America? Would she be sleeping peacefully through the commotion because she was used to it? Would a phone call in the early hours of the morning to check she was okay have the opposite result, sending her into a state of blind panic?

In the end, she decided not to call. She would head

down to the kitchen and get herself something to eat and something hot to drink. Why not? She was starving and she wasn't going to get back to sleep any time soon.

Despite the storm raging outside, it wasn't cold inside the house. She didn't possess a dressing gown and, rather than go to the bother of putting on jeans and a T-shirt for a midnight raid on the fridge, she crept downstairs in her pyjamas. Although her 'pyjamas' actually consisted of a pair of tiny shorts festooned with cartoon characters and a sleeveless vest which she had bought years ago from the boy's section of a department store in London.

She didn't bother with bedroom slippers and tiptoed like a thief in the night. The vast house was in complete darkness, and it took a little while for her eyes to adjust, but she was familiar with the layout now and working her way down to the kitchen wasn't a problem.

She imagined her mother doing this very thing when she'd been a kid but then she realised that the house would have been much smaller. The rush of nostalgia she had hoped to feel when she had embarked on this trip to Napa Valley hadn't materialised to the degree she had hoped and now, against all odds, she had come to associate this place with Gabriel and Rosa. Their story had eclipsed her mother's presence.

Their story ran the risk of eclipsing *everything*, including the very reason she was here, under this roof. Saving the cottage had taken a back seat as she had become involved with Rosa. What was Gabriel going to do? He never mentioned it, aside from that one and only time when he had informed her that the man Evelyn had spotted on the grounds had been hired a while back to inspect the outlying property.

Was he still thinking about whether to buy or not? To chuck Evelyn out on her ears with a pat on her back and a guilt-salvaging cheque with which to find herself somewhere else? Was he just conveniently using her to help with Rosa? Was stringing her along with vague promises that were never going materialise simply his way of getting her on board while he was nanny-less? He was ruthless, but how ruthless was he?

And had he actually meant it when he'd said that he found her attractive? Beyond temptation? Or had she simply been giving off some weird pheromones at the time which had prompted him to kiss her because he was a red-blooded male? Men, as it was well known, weren't fussy when it came to kissing women who wanted to be kissed.

All those thoughts were whirring round in her head as she peered into the fridge in search of food. She didn't hear a thing and she would have been clueless if the lights hadn't been slammed on, causing her to jerk back, utterly losing her balance which was unfortunate when she was holding a bottle of milk in one hand and a jar of jam in the other.

Both were catapulted into the air and crashed to the ground in a flurry of splintered glass, oozing red jam and a spreading white lake of milk.

In the middle of the chaos, Izzy did her best to struggle to her feet while holding on to the last vestige of her dignity.

Gabriel.

Bare-chested and in a pair of pale-grey jogging bottoms.

'What the hell?'

Izzy wanted to wail. Instead, she glared. She was

marooned in the middle of splintered glass, wet from spilled milk and utterly mortified.

'Don't move, for God's sake.' He left the kitchen at speed to return seconds later in a pair of loafers.

Izzy hadn't budged. She could scarcely breathe, far less get her leaden limbs to work.

When she thought it couldn't get worse, it did, as he stepped onto the glass and scooped her up in an easy movement while she prayed for the ground to open up and swallow her.

She looped her arms around his neck and was instantly flooded with all those taboo thoughts that had plagued her during the night.

The feel of him… The scent of him…

She stifled a moan, closed her eyes, aware of him carrying her out of the kitchen, out into the hall and then up the winding staircase. But, instead of finding herself back in the relative safety of her bedroom when she next opened her eyes, she found that he had taken her to his suite.

Outside, the storm continued to rage. He had switched on a light by the bed and pools of shadow obscured the room. She could see enough to note just how relentlessly masculine it was. No excess furniture and everything concealed behind smooth, glossy, handle-less doors that banked one side of the wall. White on white with strips of walnut wood here and there. A wooden floor and a long floating shelf on which were three computers, two shut, one blinking. She could see an *en suite* bathroom through an open door. His room was roughly three times the size of hers, massive and minimalist.

'Don't stand,' he ordered, pre-empting her where she had been deposited by the window on a tan leather chair.

Izzy hugged herself. 'I want to go back to my bedroom.'

'I don't care what you want. I'm going to examine your legs in case you have any glass splinters anywhere.'

'I don't.'

'Bella is in hospital. Fancy joining her there with an infected leg because you're so damned stubborn?'

'I would know if I had a shard of glass sticking out of my thigh!' She feverishly followed him with her eyes as he disappeared into the bathroom and resurfaced with a black tin, squatting in front of her.

And then he began to examine her feet, very gently, feeling them, then her legs, his fingers smooth and cool against her skin, stirring her body into hot, shameful response.

Her heart was thundering and her mouth was dry.

'I was so quiet,' she whispered, fascinated by the sight of him kneeling in front of her.

'I have an alarm by my bed,' he murmured. 'It detects if anyone is moving in the house late at night and pin-points what room they're in.'

'You thought I was a burglar.'

'I live in an expensive house,' Gabriel murmured, still inspecting her, his voice low and soft as he worked his way up her thighs. 'Many have suggested I have bodyguards.'

'Oh.'

'I've never cared for the infringement that would bring to my personal freedom.' He glanced up at her and their eyes tangled for a couple of heart-stopping seconds. 'Besides, I'm skilled when it comes to fighting. Why did you go downstairs?'

'I was hungry,' Izzy whispered.

'You should have eaten something with me instead of running away upstairs.'

'I wasn't running away.'

'Weren't you?'

Her breathing hitched in her throat. 'I… I wasn't expecting you earlier today…' she croaked. 'I thought you would be returning…later. You said…'

'I cut short a couple of meetings to return earlier.'

'Why? Rosa was perfectly fine here. I told you so when you called.'

Was he aware that he was still stroking her thigh, even though his dark eyes were fixed to her face with an intensity that made her all hot and bothered?

'Maybe my unscheduled arrival wasn't entirely about Rosa…'

'What do you mean?'

'You were on my mind.' He levered himself up and stood in front of her for a few seconds, towering, sending her thoughts into crazy meltdown.

The thrill of danger was like a feather trailing over her skin.

'I was?' she asked breathlessly.

'Does that surprise you?'

'You barely noticed me when Rosa and I ran out of the rain.' Stupid, *stupid*. Why on earth had she said that? Why had she let him glimpse that weakness in her?

Because he had said what he had… Because he had opened that door and invited her to walk through…

'Is that why you ran away? Did you want me to

sweep you off your feet and carry you to my bedroom so that I could ravish you?'

'Of course not.' She felt her face flaming and her body was tingling, buzzing, as if she'd been plugged into a socket. He'd stooped back down so that he was at her eye level.

She wanted this man so much she was giddy with it. And the way he was looking at her… She half-closed her eyes and reached out and stroked the side of his face, and adrenaline rushed through her body in a tidal wave.

'No glass anywhere.' He lifted her up and she gave a startled yelp, but then her fingers were linking behind his neck, and she *wanted* this. 'But I should keep checking…just to make sure. And you're a little damp from that spilt milk. You should get out of those clothes, don't you think?'

'I should,' Izzy muttered against his chest.

He would be her first and, when she thought of giving her virginity to this man, every nerve in her body tingled with barely suppressed excitement.

She'd launched herself into a relationship with Jefferson and had thought, *expected*, that he would be *the one*. He'd been so attentive, so much fun, had taught her how to surf and teased her when she'd kept falling into the sea. And yet, much as she'd been attracted to him—because he *was* attractive, with that blond, blond hair—she hadn't felt like this, hadn't felt this helpless *yearning* that seemed so out of her control. She'd wanted to wait, had wanted to take a little time, get to know him properly.

Had part of her secretly suspected what had become obvious over time? That he wasn't the good-natured, thoughtful, carefree man she'd thought he was? Gabriel had teased so many confidences out of her without really trying, and yet to Jefferson she had been a closed book, skirting over the details of her life, maybe knowing that if she turned those pages too slowly he would soon become bored.

His tolerance had declined rapidly when she'd refused to sleep with him. At first, he'd been brilliant about it, but within a month she'd seen the sulky tightening of his mouth, and then the requests for cash had begun to creep in.

He was waiting for a cheque from his last job…could she lend him a couple of hundred for his rent? Of course he'd pay her back… And could he maybe have a few hundred more…? There was a surfboard he was desperate to get hold of…

And some underlying guilt that she hadn't jumped into bed with him had made her meet those demands, modest enough at first, until finally he'd produced a sketchy outline of a company he wanted to set up. A few boats…advertising costs…half a million would get things going and there'd be no looking back…

Izzy had fled, her pride in tatters, her ego far more bruised than her heart, although she was only now beginning to recognise that.

Thank God she hadn't jumped into bed with him. The thought of it made her feel sick. Yet, here she was, ready to jump into bed with a man who had made no attempts to butter her up with promises of a relationship. He was offering her sex, without even the benefit of some fancy wrapping, and the offer was irresistible and she just didn't get it.

She looked at him from under her lashes as he gently

settled her on his bed and then drew back and looked at her.

'You sure about this?' he asked huskily.

Gabriel hadn't lied when he'd told her that she'd been on his mind. When he'd flown to Chicago, for the first time in his life the adrenaline rush of completing a deal that would add to his already staggering portfolio had failed to deliver its usual kick.

He hadn't been able to focus and it had driven him nuts. Since when had a woman come between him and his work? The answer to that was *never*.

Was it because this was not the normal progression when it came to his love life? Or was it because there was an ulterior motive underlying the situation? Had that given the routine boy-meets-girl, boy-beds-girl situation an added edge? Surely it couldn't be a simple case of wanting someone so badly you couldn't get them out of your head?

He had rejected that possibility and instead focused on the fact that from Izzy lay a direct path to his being able to exert some leverage over his rapacious and vindictive ex-wife.

He'd been keen to return to the vineyards, not just for Rosa, but because he was intensely practical, and if a plan had to put into action then the sooner things kicked off, the better. *That*, he concluded, had been the impetus behind his hurried return.

He had returned to a storm and as he had stood there at the door, ready to race outside, Izzy had come blindly running towards him, every scrap of her given over to protecting his daughter, making sure she was kept as safe as possible.

Something inside him had twisted. He didn't know what but it was a fleeting sensation of strange discomfort mixed with a melting warmth.

They'd been swimming and she'd been in an extremely modest black bikini that had still managed to do the utmost for her slender, gazelle-like body.

He'd taken Rosa, stepped back, temporarily blindsided by a rush of primal desire, and then…

Here she was. He couldn't think straight when his mind zoomed back to finding her in the kitchen… her peachy bottom sticking out as she'd peered into the fridge. Small pyjamas, without a hint of seductive *anything*, yet the most erotic get-up he had ever seen. Somehow he'd always gone for the woman in obvious designer gear but his tastes in women's fashion seemed to be drastically changing.

He wasn't sure what he would do if she had a change of mind but she smiled now, looked away then just as quickly looked back at him, her huge eyes oddly hesitant.

He smiled back, stepped out of his jogging bottoms and watched her mouth open with such blatant fascination that he was tickled pink.

Rich trust-fund babe she might be—and, God knew, all the sexual expertise that went with a life lived in the fast lane, whatever her appearances to the contrary— but, hell, wasn't there something just so damned *refreshing* about her?

Watching him watching her was the most sensual, erotic experience Izzy had ever had. She wriggled and, on cue, he joined her on the bed and she felt the brush of his erection against her thigh.

He was big, *really* big, and a shiver of nerves raced

through her. But no way was she going to admit to being a virgin. He didn't think she was, and if he knew then he would run a mile. Something inside her told her that his casual invitation to have sex held an implicit assumption that they were on the same page when it came to coming together and then moving on, just a couple of ships passing in the night.

She trembled as he edged his fingers under her vest and gently began tugging it up until she felt the cool air on her breasts. Her eyes were closed and she was aware of his breath against her skin, warm and seductive.

Then he kissed her and she opened her eyes. This time the kiss was slow, sweet and leisurely and she arched up, yielding to it as their tongues meshed and his hands coiled into her hair.

Her breasts were pushed against his chest and her nipples were achingly sensitive as they grazed the dark hair on his torso. She was so wet, so turned on, too turned on to be nervous. But she knew that when that moment came she would have to grit her teeth not to reveal just how inexperienced she was.

'You're so beautiful,' he whispered into her ear and she smiled and wriggled.

'So are you.'

Gabriel burst out laughing and his dark eyes were amused when he drew back and looked at her for a few moments. 'That's very direct of you.' He smiled a slow, curling smile.

'I hate playing games.'

Gabriel didn't reply but he felt a twinge of guilt. He wanted information from her. Did that come with the label of playing games with her because he wanted to

gain her confidence? No. If he hadn't been so damned
attracted to her, then yes, but as it stood they were both
doing what came naturally to them, and if he ended up
where he wanted to be then that would be a fantastic
additional bonus.

At the end of the day, he decided, no one was holding a gun to anyone's head and demanding state secrets.

'What are you thinking?' Izzy brushed his jaw and
felt the roughness of stubble.

'I'm thinking that sex and chat don't go hand in
hand,' he growled. With which he reached down,
hooked one finger under her shorts and took them off
in one smooth movement, along with her underwear.

Silky-soft thighs, slender as a colt's. Her breasts were
small and pert, her nipples pink discs begging to be licked.

Gabriel slowly moved down, trailing caresses along
her neck, tasting her skin, then he settled on one of her
breasts and sucked, drawing it into his mouth while simultaneously nibbling her stiffened nipple.

He looked at her. Her long, unruly hair was spread
in a blonde tangle across his pillow, her mouth was
parted, her nostrils flared and the tremble in her body
was a massive turn-on.

He continued to suckle at her breast, letting his hand
drift downwards over her flat stomach, feeling as she
sucked in a sharp breath. Then down lower, over the jut
of her hips and between her legs, going nowhere in particular, just stroking, caressing and ruffling her downy
hair with the tips of his fingers.

Izzy could feel her whole body relaxing. What he was
doing…

She saw his dark head moving at her breast and she

moaned softly. She was barely aware of parting her legs, inviting those teasing fingers to do more, to find the spot that was throbbing, yearning to be touched.

He moved down, and when he settled between her legs she automatically stiffened, her first urge to snap her legs together, because this was an intimacy too far. But even as she weakly tried, he placed his hands on her inner thighs, holding them apart, and then his tongue darted between the soft folds of her womanhood to find the swelling bud. Over and over he teased it until she went mad, until she could hold off no longer and she came explosively against his questing tongue.

That complete abandon shocked her and she lay still, slowly coming down from her high, but then feeling her senses begin to respond even as he remained where he was, gently blowing on her, then kissing away the last of the shudders that had racked her body.

She groaned, lifted her legs a little, shivered and looked down at him buried between her thighs. The urge to tell him that she was a virgin was strong, but stronger still was the urgent need for him to continue, not to pull away in disappointment or shock.

The burden of her inexperience struck her. How should she pleasure him? If she touched him, surely he would see her awkwardness?

She tentatively wriggled away from caresses that threatened to spike to another orgasm. She wanted him in her, dreaded it yet yearned for it. She didn't want to reach another climax against his mouth. Never had her virginity felt more of an albatross round her neck.

She knelt and inched closer to him. With her free hand, she reached to feel the weight of him and felt a heady rush of delight when he groaned in instant response. As she took him between her hands and did what felt natural, and when he covered her hand with his own, guiding her to a steady rhythm, she fell into a groove, breathing fast, melting inside as her body heated up at the feel of him.

She kissed his chest, nibbled a flat, brown nipple and grew hotter and wetter.

Gabriel could barely hang on to his self-control. He was always the one in charge. He called the shots when it came to love-making but now, for the first time, someone else was taking him to places that were new and unexplored.

The gentle teasing of her mouth on his chest, on his nipples, was exquisite. The softness of her touch on his throbbing penis was driving him insane. The turn-on of her shy caress was overpowering.

He clasped the back of her neck, fingers tangling in her hair, and drew her back so that he could kiss her.

'I…have…never…' he confessed brokenly, barely recognising his voice, 'Wanted any woman as much as I…want you now…'

His kiss drove her back against the pillows and he continued to kiss her even as his hand blindly sought her wetness, delving to feel it slippery against his fingers.

He broke off to don protection, which took a matter of seconds yet seemed to drag as long as a lifetime, and as the cool air settled on her Izzy felt a rush of nervous panic.

She flinched back just a fraction as he settled over her, his big, powerful body a vision of strength and muscle. He nudged her entrance and she held her breath, waiting for his entry, praying it wouldn't hurt.

'Be gentle,' she gasped as he pushed deeper. She wanted so much to grit her teeth and find a way through her nerves and the pain she expected, and she was now realising that it had been naïve to assume that a man of his experience would be fooled.

She cried out as he plunged in deeply. The pain was sharp and her eyes were closed, squeezed tightly as he stilled, looking at her. She could sense the glint of his questioning eyes on her face and she refused to meet those questions head-on.

'Izzy,' he moaned huskily.

'Please don't stop,' she whispered.

'I must.'

'No!' Her eyes flew open and she looked at him fiercely. Both her hands reached to cover his taut buttocks, urging him on.

'You should have told me.'

'Please stop talking,' Izzy all but begged. 'I want this. I want *you.*'

She shifted, her body as supple as an eel's, encouraging him to keep going, not to leave her like this, awash with frustration and disappointment.

It seemed vitally important that this beautiful, ruthless and utterly inappropriate man hold her hand and take her through the door that had been opened.

She pulled his head down, arched up and kissed him while he was still inside her and, when he groaned and began to move, she knew that he couldn't *not*.

The nerves had dissipated. The burst of pain she had felt had subsided to a dull, throbbing ache but that was eclipsed by something else as he skilfully moved in her,

How could he do that? How could he angle his body *just so*? How could he make her forget that this was her first time?

He filled her, taking it slow then moving faster, slow and easy one minute, ever deeper the next, until he had developed a tempo that began carrying her away.

He found the spot inside her with expert accuracy and as he pushed against it, over and over, a sensation of soaring began to rise inside her and she succumbed to it, loving the pleasure he was giving her and the pleasure she knew she was giving him.

Her orgasm was shattering, unexpected in its intensity and coming in waves. Izzy heard herself sob a wrenching response just as he arched back, stiffened and had one final plunge that took him over the edge.

He collapsed onto her, but only for a few seconds, then he shifted immediately to move onto his side. He propped himself up on one elbow, and she said without looking at him, 'I don't want to talk about it.'

'That's not an option, I'm afraid.'

'I'm sorry.' Izzy could feel her eyes beginning to well up. Could there be a more crushing anti-climax to what had been the most wonderful experience of her entire life?

'Jesus, Izzy. Look at me.'

She glared at him. 'Why does it matter whether I was a virgin or not?'

'Because if I'd known,' Gabriel grated, 'I wouldn't have…made love to you.'

'Why not? You didn't force me into doing anything!'

'That's not the point, *tesoro*.'

'Then what is?'

'You don't know me, Izzy. I'm…' He sifted his fingers through his tousled hair and met her eyes steadily, seriously. 'I'm not capable of committing to any kind of relationship with you. You've been hurt by some bastard in all sorts of ways and you're inexperienced… You're probably searching for a replacement, someone to fill whatever void has been left inside you by some loser you're better off without.'

Gabriel couldn't remember ever having dug so deep into someone's motivations and psyche. Even as his marriage had been falling apart, he had guiltily acknowledged that he should have asked far more questions, expressed more curiosity, verbalised more. Instead, he had weathered the defensive aggression of his soon-to-be ex, seeking only to get on top of the practical issues.

A virgin! He couldn't credit it, but then he thought of the way she blushed despite her stubbornness and her fighting spirit. He had written off that crazy notion as existing only in his mind because the facts spoke for themselves. She was young, beautiful and rich and those attributes lent themselves to a pattern.

He'd been wrong.

Where he had before justified to himself how their mutual attraction could play into his hands, because all was fair in love and war, he was now assailed with a barrage of misgivings.

They had made love, and there was nothing he could do about that, but his conscience was telling him that he should get out now. Get out because she was vulnerable. Trust-fund babe she very well might be, but the usual attributes appeared to have passed her by.

'Don't you *dare* try to analyse me,' Izzy hissed. Her

voice wobbled. 'You don't know what I'm thinking. You don't know what's going through my head.'

'Izzy…'

'Don't you *dare* "Izzy" me.'

'I don't want to be responsible for hurting you,' Gabriel confessed in a roughened undertone.

'What makes you think you could ever hurt me?' she asked. He didn't want soft and fluffy and he didn't want the girl with the broken heart. It wasn't what he was used to and, if nothing else, pride now stiffened her backbone. No way was she going to allow him to feel sorry for her. She'd spent weeks feeling sorry for herself. She didn't need someone else adding to the pity tally.

'Explain.'

'You're not my type,' she told him bluntly, and when he half-smiled she glared. 'You have such an over-sized ego, Gabriel Ricci! You're attractive but that still doesn't mean that you're my type.' He lowered his eyes, sheathing his expression, but she was pretty sure that the wretched man didn't believe a word she was saying and her pride stiffened just a little bit more.

'I'm not drawn to business men. I like men who are a little more relaxed when it comes to living life. Jefferson turned out to be a creep, but that's life. You're a good-looking guy, Gabriel, and I suppose you know it, but there's a big difference between being physically attracted to someone and seeing them as relationship material. You're not relationship material, and I would have guessed that without you having to tell me.' She paused, looking at him steadily, while her rebellious mind busied itself with stupid, pointless thoughts.

What would it be like to have the heart of this dan-

*gerous, sexy, impossible man? Was he so cold, so ruth-
less, so driven because he had never stopped loving an
ex-wife who now made his life hell, from the sounds of
it? Had that been his one big love? Had that first cut
been the deepest?*

'We made love because I wanted it as well,' she said.
'And I thought it was great. I'm not interested in a relationship with you and I wish you had just…let things be,
Gabriel. One night of pure pleasure without the drama
afterwards.' She clenched her jaw until it ached. 'Instead, you had to make a big deal of it. Okay, so you
think it was a mistake. Fine.'

She began to shuffle off the bed, taking the sheet
with her. 'I'll be on my way. I'm sorry about Rosa, I
know she'll be disappointed, but I don't think I can
hang around here trying to make sure I get out of your
way because you're turned off by me.' She could have
added that Rosa, already the innocent victim of so much
instability in her life, hardly needed more thrust upon
her. To leave sooner would be a million times better for
his daughter than if she were to leave later.

She wanted so much to try and persuade him to just
stop pressuring Evelyn to sell up. She had seen this as
an opportunity to wear down his inexorable need to own
more at the expense of someone else. But she hadn't
been able to withstand the chemistry between them
and now everything was ruined. He would surely proceed with his plans. He couldn't chuck Evelyn out but
he could simply wear her down until she acquiesced.
Weren't there many ways to skin a cat, after all? He'd
wanted someone else, not her. He'd seen the packaging
and liked what he saw, but what was inside the wrap-

ping paper wasn't what he thought he'd ordered, and now it was time to return to sender.

The sting of hurt was overwhelming. She chewed her lip and ungracefully continued to shuffle away, but she felt the clamp of his hand on her arm and she froze immediately.

'What the hell, Izzy? You think I *don't* fancy you?'

'I think I'm not what you signed up for. Which is the same thing, as far as I'm concerned.'

She tried to tug away from him but he drew her back against him and held her close, arms around her, even though she did her best to pummel her way free.

'You've given me the most precious gift any woman could give a man.' He spoke gruffly, his mouth buried against her neck, her hair falling across him soft and silky. 'I am not worthy of it. I may have got my words wrong, but don't think for an instant that what we just shared wasn't as amazing for me as it was for you.'

'You don't have to lie to spare my feelings,' Izzy whispered.

'Lie? Feel me, *amore*, touch me, and you'll find out fast enough just how much I fancy you...'

The fight drained out of her. Sitting here, breathing him in, he filled her. She recognised her weakness and accepted it.

CHAPTER SEVEN

GABRIEL LOOKED AT his daughter and Izzy, heads together, one white-blonde, the other raven-dark.

They were counting fish, which wasn't difficult, because the three of them had managed to catch the grand
total of two fish over a period of several hours. They
were at a trout farm, owned and run by the same family for a million years. Their poles and bait had been
provided and they had been taken to the beautiful, well-
stocked pond and left to do their thing. When they were
ready, the fish would be cleaned by one of the owners
and they would grill it on site and eat it with the massive picnic that had been prepared by his housekeeper.

With Rosa in tow, Gabriel's activities had led him
to places hitherto unexplored. The sanitised early-eve-
ning meals out in expensive New York restaurants—
with the occasional trip to the zoo thrown in when he
took a break from work, which had been rare—were
gone. In their place was a selection of fun activities
meticulously researched by Izzy and enthusiastically
seconded by Rosa.

He had not been allowed to renege on any of these
activities because, Izzy had said four days earlier, Bella
would be back soon enough and their routine would

settle into place, so why not take advantage of the window of opportunity?

Bella would be returning over his dead body.

He continued to look thoughtfully at the pair of them, utterly absorbed in what they were doing, as close as conspirators plotting.

He hadn't asked Izzy anything. Hadn't engineered the conversation in any direction. He had backed off because they were lovers now and, while she certainly played it cool, made it clear that she wasn't in it for anything long term, he was still uneasy with the notion of outright exploiting their situation.

For once, his motto 'the end justifies the means' didn't seem entirely appropriate. A conscience he'd been unaware of had made itself felt.

That said, she had talked, soft, lazy and drowsy when good sex had blurred the edges and lowered any qualms she might have had when it came to confiding. In between the titbits about how she and Rosa spent their time when he was working—the home baking, the den making and the paper-boat racing—he had learnt some rather interesting facts about his daughter's life when he wasn't around.

Bianca seemingly was around far less than she made out. There were lots of trips abroad. He had already got one of his people to tabulate just when those trips had occurred, for how long and with whom?

School was an institution randomly adhered to, with Rosa being removed for things as trivial as manicures and pedicures. What six-year-old needs a manicure? He had barely been able to contain his fury. As with the trips abroad, he had compiled a dossier on all those pointless visits.

No wonder Bella had settled into home schooling. Rosa would need it, judging from her sketchy class attendance.

There had also been men back at the house and, whilst Gabriel did not expect his ex-wife to be a paragon of celibate virtue, he wondered at just how cavalier she was when it came to inviting them back. This last item he had found out from Rosa, who had casually chatted about some man having lunch there.

It had taken every iota of willpower not to get on the phone and lay all his information at his dear ex-wife's door. However, he would play a waiting game. He would garner his facts and he would plan his manoeuvres. There was nothing to be gained from undue haste.

And, in the meantime, his conscience was clear. On every front, he had played it fair and square. He hadn't prised information from Izzy, hadn't asked questions and had been upfront so that, when the time came for them to bid farewell, it would be done without room for accusations about promises made but not delivered.

On the subject of the cottage? The topic had been raised in a roundabout manner just the once and he had skilfully diverted the conversation because, really, business was business. Maybe he would take her on a sightseeing tour of some of the more desirable places in the valley, open her eyes to where life could be perfectly liveable for a woman in her late seventies.

Right now, though…

On so many levels, things were going much better than he could ever have anticipated. He began moving towards them. One week, he decided, and he would have to move on. He would start the ball rolling by telling Bianca that Bella's services would no longer be required and should she throw a hissy fit... Well, this time round she might find that she couldn't hold a man to ransom when he'd stockpiled sufficient ammunition.

Izzy discovered that she was becoming adept at putting off thinking about when the end of this strange relationship with Gabriel was going to come.

She had agreed to be Bella's replacement in good faith. She had seen it as a way of inserting herself into his routine, finding opportunities to persuade him that he must not buy the land to increase his holdings, must not pull the house out from under Evelyn's feet. On site, she'd reasoned, she would be able to work away at him, dismantle his plans bit by bit, or at least *try*.

But they had become lovers a week ago and since then she had broached the subject of the cottage once, and he had had nothing to say on the subject. He had shrugged, told her something vague about tallying up the costs of ditching the project, waffled on for a couple of minutes about the difficulties of stopping the tide once the barriers have been raised and then promptly changed the subject.

And she had let him because she had fallen under his spell. The minutes, the hours, the days... She was drifting on a cloud and she didn't want to spoil things by bringing reality into the equation.

She'd thought that he would continue to devote his time to his work but she had been surprised at the alacrity with which he'd conceded when she had sternly told him that he needed to come with her and Rosa to all the stuff she'd lined up.

Bella would be back soon enough, she'd said, and

he'd looked at her without saying anything for a while, then lowered those fabulous eyes of his and agreed.

Since then, they'd been to a medieval-themed castle winery that had all the atmosphere of a sorcerer's castle with its moat and drawbridge and towers and ramparts, and a torture chamber that Rosa had adored. They'd been ice-skating at a rink which was open all year round, and they'd been apple-picking and sampled home-made ice-cream from a legendary ice-cream shop in Sebastopol.

Everything in this part of the world felt lazy, and the vastness of the scenery helped her feel as though she was living in an alien landscape, in a sort of dream world.

It disturbed her that she didn't want any of it to end.

She gazed up at the house from where she was standing by the pool. It was a little after ten-thirty and for the first time they had been out to dinner, having Evelyn over for Rosa for the evening.

Izzy was still in her finery. Gabriel had nipped upstairs to check on Rosa, having delivered Evelyn back to her cottage.

'Let's have a nightcap by the pool,' he'd suggested. 'Rosa will be safely asleep, and we could even have a swim. There's nothing more invigorating than having a swim at the end of a muggy day.'

Izzy strolled to one of the chairs by the side of the pool, sat down and drew her knees up to clasp her arms around them. When she tried to chart the progression of her feelings for Gabriel, she got lost along the way. How could her seething antipathy have turned into something that held her fiercely captive? How could *lust* have morphed into real feeling? Izzy didn't want to put a name to what that feeling was, but it hovered on the periphery like a flash of something caught out of the corner of the eye, gone before the brain had time to register it.

She found him exciting. Arrogant, infuriating but *exciting*. Even before she'd taken the job of helping with Rosa, even when she'd been gritting her teeth and wanting to *hit* him for the anxiety he was causing Evelyn, there had still been something about him that had begun to suck her in, something intense that made the hairs on the back of her neck stand on end.

She disapproved of him, yet she was drawn to him like a moth to a flame.

He wasn't her type, yet her body curved to his like a flower bending to bask in the warmth of the sun.

Nothing about what she felt made sense yet even now, sitting here, thinking logically about what was happening in her life, she still couldn't control the shimmer and sizzle of anticipation when she thought of him joining her out here and then, later, lying in bed with her, taking her.

She heard the soft pad of his feet and smiled, her body already heating up, as though she'd suddenly been plugged into a socket and the switch turned on.

'Penny for them…'

'I was just thinking what a lovely meal that was.' Izzy would never tell him what was going through her head. Far safer to stick to the uncontentious. 'Made a change going out.'

'It did.' He paused, swerving round to tug her to her feet and gather her in his arms. He didn't kiss her immediately, though, just gazed down, their eyes meeting as he brushed a strand of blonde hair from her face.

She'd dressed up for the evening. Had actually had to go out and buy something.

'I like the dress, by the way,' he murmured, hands on the small of her back gently nudging her against him. 'Thin straps, long zipper down the back… It's a dress made to be removed without too much fuss.'

He was in a pair of black trousers and a white shirt and he'd cuffed the sleeves to the elbows.

He couldn't have looked sexier.

She wound her arms round his neck and drew her to him, reaching up to kiss him, luxuriating in the mesh of their tongues and the pulse of his hardness against the flimsy silk of the dress.

'Swim?'

'Can't be bothered to go and get my swimsuit,' Izzy confessed.

'Who's talking about swimsuits?' He grinned, drew back and tugged down the straps of the dress, unzipping the zipper with seamless ease.

'Gabriel, *no*!'

'Why not?'

'Because…'

'There's no one here to see,' he murmured, cupping one small breast and rubbing the pad of his thumb over her nipple. 'These grounds are completely private, and the access gate to the back here is locked. Rosa is fast asleep. There's just the two of us…and I want you so much. I wanted you through that entire tasting menu. Thought it was never going to end.'

Izzy laughed softly. The dress had caught at the waist. She began undoing the buttons of his shirt but then her patience ran out and she tugged it free of the waistband and pushed her hands underneath to feel his flat nipples and the sprinkling of dark hair on his chest.

He tore off the shirt, ripping the bottom two buttons in his haste, and she followed suit with the dress.

Bit by bit, they somehow managed to get rid of their clothing while making unsteady progress towards the back of the sprawling patio with its trellised roof zigzagged with tumbling flowers.

The wooden outdoor furniture was low, sleek and comfortable, made for stretching out on and relaxing under the shade on a balmy Californian day, the glorious infinity pool within sight.

At this time in the evening, poolside lights just illuminated the pool. The water was still and silvery, reflecting the light from the almost-full moon. The sky was velvet black and dotted with stars and the air was beautifully warm. Izzy could almost hear the soft rustle of the vines stretching for acres all around them. The silence was broken only by their breathing as they settled onto one of the long outdoor sofas.

He manoeuvred her so that she was half-lying, half-sitting, her feet on the ground, legs bent at the knees, and he sat between them and gently blew on the darker blonde curls there.

Izzy sighed and squirmed into a less awkward position, her whole body eagerly waiting for him to slide his tongue between the folds of her womanhood, to find the bud of her core and tease it until she was hurtling towards an orgasm.

He knew just when to draw back, when to switch his caress to the soft skin of her inner thigh, giving her time to slowly ease away from an orgasm, to climb down from her fevered high.

His dark hair was springy between her fingers. In her mind, the contours of his beautiful face were as familiar to her as her own. She could have traced his body blindfolded and knew that that body was his.

She grunted as he wound his way up along her naked body to settle his mouth on her nipple, swirling his tongue over it until she was going mad with wanting more.

'Protection,' Gabriel groaned. 'Where is it when you need it? We're going to have to have some fun without it…'

They did. She took him between her hands, into her mouth, held the weight of him as she slowly, rhythmically stroked him until he had to pull her away to give himself time to find some self-control and then, in the end, he couldn't hold off and he spilled over.

He explored every inch of her burning body with his mouth, his tongue and his fingers, teasing and tormenting until she gave a spasm against his fingers, writhing and arching back, missing the deep thrust of penetration but relishing the waves of pleasure his mouth and fingers could give her.

Afterwards they continued to lie on the sofa for a while, chatting, still naked, their bodies shimmering under the moonlight.

The moment felt fragile and Izzy wanted to hold it tight for ever. In an instant, it would be gone and they would part ways. She felt her stomach tighten and there was a sick giddiness inside her when she thought about them walking away in separate directions.

She wanted to cling but couldn't.

Had she done the unthinkable? Had she fallen for this inappropriate stranger? Her skin felt clammy. *This* was the feeling that had been hovering on the edge of her mind, as wispy as a tendril of smoke curling in the sky from a conflagration below, and just as dangerous.

'When is Bella due to return?' She broke the silence and began shifting to get to her feet, suddenly restless at the disturbing thoughts swirling through her head.

The air suddenly felt cool. She was retrieving her dropped garments when he stood and caught her from behind, hands at her waist, tugging her back against him so that she was pressed with her back to his stomach. Skin against skin, their bodies were still hot and damp from making love.

'What about that swim?'

'I'm not sure I'm in the mood,' Izzy said, heart beating fast and hard inside her as a series of conclusions formed in her head.

Love? How could she have fallen in love with this man? Hadn't she told herself that it was just mutual attraction? How could her body have disobeyed her head?

'It's really late.' She hesitated, suddenly anxious to have some idea as to where this was all going. It was one thing to be philosophical about enjoying what she had and living in the moment but it was quite another putting those noble ideas into practice.

Right now, all she could think of was a place in the very near future that inevitably would be painful.

'And you still haven't mentioned Bella,' she reminded him casually, prising away from his clasp and, without looking at him, flinging the dress over her and sticking on her underwear.

He slung on his trousers as she began walking away and stumbled a bit behind her before catching her by the arm.

'What's wrong?'

'Nothing.'

'Really?'

'You don't know me as well as you think you do,' Izzy said with an edge in her voice. 'Nothing's wrong. I'm just…tired, that's all. I don't want to have a midnight swim. Is that a crime?'

'She won't be.'

'Sorry?' Izzy turned around reluctantly. She didn't want to look at him. The minute she clapped eyes on him, all her willpower evaporated, and right now she didn't want evaporating willpower. If she had to get her act together, then she would have to start thinking about getting it together now. There was no point pretending to herself that she could handle the situation and take what was on offer while the offer was there.

'Bella. She won't be returning.'

'Why not?'

'Don't look so shocked.' Gabriel grinned, took her hand and began leading the way back to the house.

'Is…is she okay? I mean, I should probably have shown more concern but…'

'Oh, she's fine. In fact, due to leave hospital tomorrow.'

'Then, why—?'

'I sacked her.'

'You *sacked* her? But I thought… I thought that… isn't she related to your ex-wife?'

Gabriel shrugged. 'That doesn't confer lifelong immunity to being sacked.' His voice was flat and hard. 'When I see you with Rosa, I realise just how far Bella fell short of the ideal.'

He'd *sacked* Bella! Suddenly, the threat of what they

had ending didn't feel quite so imminent. Cravenly, she realised that a respite would give her a bit more time to think.

'So, have you…found a replacement?' She watched as he pushed open the patio doors that led to a huge utility room beyond the kitchen. It sparkled in a way very few utility rooms did. This particular one, done up to the very highest standard, housed appliances that were all hidden away behind glossy grey doors. Even the shoes, boots and other paraphernalia of outdoor use had their own special cupboard which was tidied daily by a member of staff.

Izzy hovered and finally allowed her eyes to settle on him.

He looked tousled, his dark hair every which way. He hadn't bothered with the shirt, which he had obviously left dumped on the ground where they had been, and the top button of his trousers was undone. He was barefoot. The black loafers were doubtless with the shirt and both would be dutifully tidied away the following day by the same smiling girl who kept the utility room shiny and spotless.

She knew she looked as rumpled as he did. Her hair was a tangle down her back and she was likewise barefoot, although she had her shoes in one hand.

'It's not something that can be rushed,' Gabriel murmured.

'She must be upset to have been told that she would no longer be required, especially as she's still recovering from surgery.'

'I offered her a year's worth of pay. Whatever feelings of despondency she might have had were thankfully short-lived.'

They were moving out of the utility room, opening the door to the kitchen. The house was more or less in darkness. Upstairs, lights on the wide landing were on, but down here they emerged into a pitch-black kitchen.

They didn't see the figure opening the kitchen door just as they were exiting the adjoining utility room.

Izzy was far too busy projecting all manner of unlikely possibilities that might be attached to his pronouncement. *Was this a way of ensuring that she stuck around for a bit longer? He hadn't said a word about a future between them, but if there was no replacement nanny on the scene then didn't that imply that he was happy for things to carry on as they were? And, if that was the case, then could there be the slimmest chance that, like her, he had become more involved in their relationship than he had anticipated—even if that might be something he would not want to admit?*

Looking down at Izzy's bent head, Gabriel was wondering what she was thinking. She gone into a funk earlier and he had no idea why. He didn't do women in a funk but this time it had jarred. He'd wanted to find out why.

Had the Bella situation been playing on her mind? It was the first time she'd mentioned the other woman. Was she uneasy about the prospect of an indeterminate stay at the house? Typically, he had taken it as a given that she would have no objection to sticking around for as long as he wanted her to, but now it occurred to him that he might have misjudged the situation. How, he wondered, would he react if she told him that she was on her way out?

When Gabriel considered that option, it surprised him just how unwelcome her departure would be. Surely he was no longer reliant on her for any information she might be able to pass on? When he had telephoned Bianca three days previously to tell her that Bella's services would no longer be required, he had coldly put her straight the second she had begun to launch a counter attack.

'Accept it,' he had informed his ex-wife, 'Or I'll play hard ball and you won't like it.'

And, when she had begun to go down the usual route of reminding him of all his shortcomings as a parent, he had softly imparted a few words of wisdom of his own and she had shut up. For the first time since the divorce, he had the weaponry with which to fight her and he intended to make full use of it.

Both preoccupied, Izzy and Gabriel only woke to the realisation that someone was in the kitchen when the lights were switched on, flooding the massive space with blinding fluorescent light.

And there she was.

Gabriel had said very little about his ex-wife, aside from her skill at manipulating the custody order. For a man as proud, as ruthless and as sharp as Gabriel, Izzy had seen it as a testament to his bone-deep integrity that he had refrained from setting the dogs loose on her to get what he wanted with his daughter. He had stepped back to avoid Rosa unwittingly being dragged into a row that wasn't her concern and that had been admirable.

Personally, she didn't think the woman had a leg to stand on, given everything Rosa had let slip over the time they had spent together.

At any rate, he hadn't described what Bianca looked like, but straight away Izzy knew that this was his ex.

Five-foot-nine of sizzling, raven-haired, voluptuous beauty stood in the doorway of the kitchen with an expression that could have slain Medusa.

Izzy automatically took a step back, using Gabriel as a shield.

'Bianca,' he said, gathering himself with what Izzy considered formidable self-control. 'What the hell are you doing here?' His voice was glacial and Izzy shivered.

Bianca, on the other hand, looked far from cowed. She took a couple of aggressive steps towards him. Her black eyes were positively spitting fury.

'What do you think, Gabriel? You tell me that you're sacking my nanny and you expect me to nod and agree without a fight? I flew straight back and rushed here to demand an explanation!'

She moved with panther-like grace to look at Izzy through narrowed eyes and this time her expression was one of triumph. 'And I see that nothing has changed with you, Gabriel.' She folded her arms and continued to stare at Izzy. 'I hope you're not getting any ideas, my dear,' she said. 'But, if you are, I should point out that my darling ex-husband is only interested in short-term prospects.'

She turned to Gabriel while Izzy tentatively eyed the kitchen door and toyed with the idea of making a run for it. 'This one is a change for you, isn't she? Nondescript little creature. And bringing her back here? With my daughter sleeping upstairs? Not such a good idea, Gabriel.' She wagged her finger. Izzy held on to her temper through gritted teeth. This wasn't her fight and she wasn't going to get involved, whatever the bait thrown at her.

She thought that this might be what it felt like to be trapped on a battlefield with opposing sides firing cannonballs overhead.

'You think you can threaten me while you continue to womanise with every cheap floozy who happens to take your fancy? I don't think so!'

Finally, Gabriel moved and there was something menacing in his lack of urgency. A simple half-turn towards Izzy, a couple of steps towards her, and then he rested his arm across her shoulders.

What the heck was going on here?

Izzy was mesmerised by Bianca, so beautiful, so larger than life, so flamboyantly exotic, so unashamedly *furious*. A hissing, spitting cobra with deadly venom. She barely noticed the very slight squeeze Gabriel applied to her shoulder.

'You're a disgrace, Gabriel!'

'And you, Bianca, are not welcome in this house. I should have made sure to get the key from you a long time ago, but as I didn't I'll rectify the oversight now.' He held out his hand. Incredibly, it was as steady as a rock. Had the man *no* nerves at all? Izzy thought.

Izzy saw the flash of doubt replace the fury and the triumph on the other woman's face.

'I deserve to have a key so that I can check and see just what is going on behind my back. My daughter is my primary concern. I *knew* that coming here, *surprising you*, would be a good idea. I could have waited until morning, but no, I *knew* from the very second you decided to sack Bella without running it by me that you were up to something. I *knew* that if I showed up here at night I would catch you red-handed. You disgust me, Gabriel Ricci. Well, I can only say that my lawyer will be *very* interested to hear about what goes on when the lights are off and my daughter is asleep and you are in charge.'

'Bring it on, Bianca,' Gabriel said with silky softness. 'My fiancée and I would love nothing better than to rectify whatever misguided impressions you may care to divulge.'

'Fiancée? *Fiancée*, Gabriel?' But there was a sudden ashen pallor beneath the rich, olive skin.

'You know where the door is. Leave. And just remember, Bianca…you have been warned.'

CHAPTER EIGHT

THE KEY WAS flung on the ground. Gabriel retrieved it just as he heard the resounding slam of the heavy front door.

He could feel Izzy's perplexed eyes on him but for once there were no ready answers in his head for what had just taken place.

'I can only apologise for that.' He turned to look at her but maintained his distance, watching her carefully. He loathed scenes and, had he had the faintest inkling that Bianca would be descending and on the warpath, he would have taken appropriate diversionary measures.

Of course, he should have expected nothing less. Sacking Bella, her treasured go-between, would have been a red rag to a bull and it was no surprise that she had made sure to arrive at night. As far as Bianca was concerned, it would have been perfect timing to find him with a woman. He had put a dent in her theoretically unassailable armour and it stood to reason that she would want to rebuild her defences as fast as possible.

It was ironic that finding him with Izzy, finding him with Izzy in a compromising situation, had been sheer luck on her part. The truth was that he had never, not once, brought any woman back to his house when Rosa was with him. The very thought was distasteful.

But Bianca was not to know that and now, here he was, stuck between a rock and a hard place.

He could smell the musky scent of spent passion on himself and could see the same thing in Izzy in her wildly tousled hair, her swollen lips and hectic skin, not to mention the casual disarray of her clothes.

There was no doubt in his mind that Bianca would not have missed a single one of those telling signs of two people who had just made love.

'Does your ex-wife make a habit of surprising you in the middle of the night, Gabriel?'

'Do you want a drink? I think I need something strong and stiff. A whisky.'

'I have no intention of being caught up in whatever marital disagreements you might be having with your ex.' Izzy folded her arms and looked at him coldly. 'And, no, I do not want a drink.'

Izzy, still smarting from the insults that had casually been flung at her, could barely move. Her body was stiff, her head was throbbing and she feared that if she tried to take a step forward she would crash to the ground in a heap of broken bits.

Not his usual type...a nondescript little thing...a cheap floozy...

She was angry, humiliated and mortified but most of all she was *hurt*.

Had she just been a convenient plaything for him? Did his tastes lie with types like Bianca—volatile raven-haired beauties with big hair, big breasts and lots of jewellery? For her surprise visit, she had worn a tight red dress, black heels and full make-up. Didn't they say that men tended to run to type, always drawn to versions of the same woman? Had she just been a novelty toy for him to enjoy because they happened to be sharing the same space and she'd made herself available to him?

Lost her virginity to him.

She felt the prick of tears and looked away quickly, but not fast enough, because he had his arms around her before she could think of taking evasive measures.

'How dare you involve me in your drama?' she whispered shakily. 'How dare you imply that we have that sort of relationship because you wanted to get your ex-wife off your back? How *dare* you?'

She pushed him hard and stood back, breathing heavily, looking at him and wishing more than anything that she could hate him. But there he stood and underneath the usually formidably controlled exterior she could see the man who had been shaken, caught off-guard, a prisoner of his love for his daughter which had stopped him from taking control of the situation in a way she knew he had probably wanted to.

There'd been something so enormously *human* about him just then that she could feel her silly heart begin to soften, which just made her even madder.

'You're furious,' Gabriel said, voice barely audible, 'And I don't blame you.' He moved restlessly, raking his fingers through his hair, unable to quite meet her searching, dismayed gaze. 'You're right, of course. I involved you in my personal drama and I had no right to do that. The only excuse I have at my disposal is that I acted purely on impulse. Highly unusual for me, I admit, but then…' He sighed, seemed to consider getting himself that drink, thought better of it and instead took both her hands in his and held her, resisting her efforts to pull away.

'I don't want you to touch me,' she said, but there seemed little point in trying to detach from his iron grip.

'Aside from involving you in something that is not your concern,' he continued, the sincerity in his deep, sexy voice keeping her pinned to the spot, 'I want to apologise for the fact that she insulted you. I would have laid into her, but my darling ex-wife can be explosive when the mood takes her, and I was simply not in the mood for thrown crockery and shrieking that could wake the dead, never mind Rosa. That's the last thing I want to subject my daughter to.

'I've had experiences of that behaviour in the past and there was no way I wanted a repeat performance. She can get...unpredictable when riled. Physical. It's something that has always been at the back of my mind in my dealings with her. If I rile her, how much would she take her frustration and anger out on Rosa? I avoid courting any situation that could...lead to any unfortunate situations. Like most kids, Rosa is loyal. She would never say anything to me. I live with the reality that it is best to avoid inciting potential unpleasantness.'

He paused and said with rough honesty, 'The truth is, between you and Bianca, there is an ocean of difference.'

Izzy did not want to be tempted into hearing what he had to say. 'I don't want excuses and I don't want lies. I think it's time for me to get back to Hawaii and finish the job I started. My brother's been patient but he won't be patient for ever. I've done what I could for Evelyn, and my heart breaks for her, but if you can't be persuaded then there's nothing left I can do.'

'I… I don't want you to go.'

'And I don't care what you want.'

'I can't stop you, Izzy, but…'

'But what, Gabriel?'

'This isn't a conversation to have standing up. Let's go into the sitting room.'

'I'm tired, Gabriel. I just want to go to my bedroom and go to sleep.'

'Please…'

It was so unusual to hear this strong, proud man plead that she hesitated, then nodded without smiling and followed him into one of the many sitting rooms on the ground floor.

Like the majority of the rooms in this wing of the mansion, the view was of the vast rows of vines, bearing the grapes that yielded the fine wines that graced so many tables up and down the country. Gabriel moved to snap shut the heavy cream curtains then he hesitated and looked to where she was perched formally on one of the sofas.

Finally, he walked towards her and sat close, so that their knees were touching.

Izzy stiffened. With every ounce of willpower inside her, she wanted to ignore the strain etched in his face, but it was hard. He had climbed under her skin, crept into her heart and she felt that she was now conditioned to reach towards him instead of drawing away. And what he had said about his ex-wife and Rosa…how could she fail to be moved?

Gabriel could feel the tension in her. Could he blame her? Not at all. His fury when he thought of Bianca showing up in his house, availing herself of a key she should not have had, was overpowering.

And when he thought of her standing there, addressing Izzy with contempt, he wanted to punch something. He hadn't been lying when he'd said that he knew what sort of scenes his ex was capable of and neither had he been exaggerating when he'd told Izzy that he had endured Rosa being caught in the middle of warfare, baffled and terrified by Bianca in the midst of one of her scenes.

Never again.

He'd remained silent but Izzy deserved more than his silence now.

'I should never have married Bianca,' he confessed, fumbling his way, because discussing feelings and emotions had never been his thing. 'But I did. I suppose part of the attraction was the fact that our backgrounds were so different.'

'How do you mean?'

'I may be able to buy the world now,' he said drily, dark eyes keenly watching the delicate bloom of colour in her cheeks, 'But I came from the wrong side of the tracks. Bianca comes from Italian royalty and at first I found it amusing to be pursued by her. I would have broken up with her, but she fell pregnant, and naturally there was no way I could walk away. We married, but it proved to be a calamitous mistake from day one. By the time Rosa was born, it was clear that everything was unravelling at pace.'

'I'm sorry.' She thought that if the word 'royalty' could be used to define anyone it should be him and not his screaming ex-wife, which just went to show that nobility and dignity could thrive anywhere and in anyone. She itched to question him further about his childhood but remained silent, fighting the temptation to sink right back into him.

Gabriel shrugged and looked at her. 'Why? None of this is your concern, as you made clear.'

Izzy reddened.

'She will use this against me,' Gabriel told her bluntly. 'You leave now, and she will see it as a passport to make things as uncomfortable for me as she can because she will deduce that you were what she expected you to be—a one-night stand, something seedy I allowed to happen while I was in charge of Rosa.'

'We don't live in Victorian times,' Izzy pointed out flatly. 'People actually do continue to have lives post-divorce without hiding those lives away from their kids.'

'It's not so simple for me. At any rate, that's one reason why I would rather you stay. It's selfish, and asking much, but for my daughter I would do anything.' He paused and then said, flushing darkly, 'I would also miss you if you choose to go.'

'You would *miss* me?' Izzy scoffed. Their eyes met and she held his dark gaze with difficulty. It was hard maintaining her tough stance. Was this what love did to you? she floundered desperately. What was the point of it if it turned you into a rag doll, at the mercy of someone you wanted to walk away from? Gabriel didn't love her. That should have been her cue to turn her back and leave after that uncomfortable scene, but she was still nailed to the spot, and when she thought about walking away she quailed inside.

'I would miss you, Izzy.' He looked at her in silence for a few moments. 'Can I offer you a deal?'

He would miss her. There was a simplicity to that statement that chipped away at her weak defences.

He didn't love her but there was something there. She felt it. Surely it couldn't be just her imagination?

'A deal?' Her mind was still busy with the prospect of the void opening at her feet, because go she would have to. Wouldn't she?

'Stay…just until I sort various things out with Bianca… and I will guarantee the cottage.'

'Come again?'

'I have things in place to finally deal with Bianca, to put us on an even footing. She has plans to remove Rosa to Tuscany. She will use whatever means she can to facilitate that, if that's what she decides to do, and she will enjoy the process. Stay and I will guarantee in writing that your friend will be able to end her days where she is in peace. I will cancel all plans to develop the land around the cottage.'

'Why is she so vindictive? You must have felt something for one another at one time…how did it get to the point where you tell me that she'll stop at nothing to even scores with you? What did you do to her?'

Gabriel shifted and frowned, primed to resent the intrusion into his personal life.

With a trace of unease, he acknowledged that she had already crashed through barriers other women had baulked at and hastily retreated from. He wondered when that trend had started and how it was that he hadn't knocked her back sooner. It was what he did…

However, he had to concede that he had already told her so much that clarifying his disastrous marriage added little to the equation. Besides, if he were to get her on board then he would have to meet her halfway when it came to telling her what she wanted to know.

And what was the big deal, anyway? She deserved answers to her very natural curiosity. He trusted her with Rosa. He could trust her with a few incidental details of his past.

'I failed to give her the level of attention she needed,' Gabriel said eventually. He sat back and for a few seconds closed his eyes, then he pressed his thumbs on them in a gesture of extreme weariness. 'Bianca...' he turned to Izzy, thoughtful '...was brought up to expect the world to bow to her and men, in particular, had a duty to put her ahead of everything.'

'And you didn't?'

'Not didn't. *Couldn't.*'

'What do you mean?'

'When you grow up without anything you learn fast that what matters is money,' he said flatly. 'Not because it can buy you this...' He glanced around at the sitting room with its priceless works of art, its expensive furnishings, its cool glass-and-marble décor. 'But because it can buy you respect and freedom. I am untouchable, for want of a better word.'

'You swapped the joy of love for the respect of other people? Strangers?'

'I consider it a fair trade.' He shrugged. 'At any rate she decided that, if she couldn't get the attention she craved from me, then she would look elsewhere. Divorce rapidly followed, and here we are several years later.'

'You would back off from selling the land... Evelyn would be able to relax, knowing that she wouldn't be pressured to sell?'

'You have my word.'

'Despite the fact that it'll mean giving up what you want?'

'I'm at the top of the food chain. I can afford the loss.'

'Then why didn't you offer to do that before?'

'Because I'm not Father Christmas.'

So ruthless, Izzy thought, so cold. Yet so impossibly *human* and so incredibly, compellingly *complex*.

He had dangled the biggest carrot in front of her and she knew that she should resent his blackmail. But then she thought of spending a bit more time with him and she couldn't fight the weakness inside her that *wanted* those crumbs.

He couldn't love, he said. His life experiences had propelled him into locking away his heart and throwing away the key, he said.

But they *had* something. Maybe he had just married the wrong woman…

She impatiently swept that thought out of her head and said coolly, 'I'll have to think about it.'

'This is a once-in-a-lifetime offer,' Gabriel countered. 'I need your decision now.'

'How long would we…?'

'You make it sound as though I'm backing you into a corner where nothing short of a bed of nails awaits. I'm not.' This time, when he looked at her, there was an intimacy in his eyes that had the predictable effect on her disobedient body.

Just like that he could arouse her, fill her head with images of them together naked, his hands on her bare skin, his mouth exploring her in ways that made her cry out with pleasure.

'You're blackmailing me,' she protested weakly.

'I'm giving you options. What's your answer?'

'You still haven't told me how long you think this… er…arrangement will last. What is going to change?'

Gabriel lowered his eyes. Knowledge was power, he thought, musing on all the information he had managed to glean. But that was something he had no intention of imparting. Not least because he had not quite managed to square it with his conscience, however many times he'd tried to justify everything to himself.

With things in motion, he would have a way forward and a timeline, and it would be immensely satisfying. It would take many weeks to get to the final destination, but to get to that vital place where Bianca accepted his authority, in receipt of everything he now had to show her…*days*.

'No more than a fortnight.'

'A fortnight.'

'Like I said, Izzy…' He reached forward to gently trail his finger along her wrist before moving it in tiny circles with devastating effect. 'Two weeks isn't going to be a hardship for me. Will it be for you?'

Izzy tried hard to quell the rising tide of desire inside her. She stared at that brown finger moving against her paler skin and sternly told herself to think *practically*. Two weeks and Evelyn's future would be secured. Was that too great a sacrifice?

No. And he was right. The chemistry between them was undeniable. Two weeks would give her time to adjust to the changes ahead, prepare her for when she had to walk away, go back to Hawaii. Time to pin him down on dates and give herself a vital timeline, she said to herself with the cool logic of someone weighing up the pros and cons and arriving at a decision with thought and good judgement.

'You're right.' Love was something to be hidden away with him. There was no point trying to analyse the whens and whys and how she had managed so completely to fall under his spell. Nor was there any point in telling him that she no longer wanted to be his lover. She did. She still wanted him. He gave her goose bumps and she couldn't think of him, far less look at him, without wanting to touch him.

She knew that she would do what it took for Evelyn to be safe for the rest of her days, and she also knew that it would be no hardship for her either.

But she had to exert some control over the situation. Why should he be the one calling all the shots?

'So you'll stay…a while…?' He smiled a slow, curling smile that threatened to wash away all her resolve.

'A while.' Izzy looked at him with composure. 'I resent being dragged into a situation with your ex-wife, but I do care about Rosa very much, and wouldn't want to see her hurt in any way if it's true what you've said about Bianca.'

'You have my word that the woman would stop at nothing to get her own back at me. Believe me, Izzy, there's no way under the sun I would ever involve you or anyone else in my private life if I had a choice.'

Well, doesn't that say it all? Izzy thought. Left to his own devices, this would only have been about sex, but fate had decided to intervene, and here he was, having to share a sliver of his past with her, grudgingly and resentfully.

Had she ever thought that she would willingly hand her heart over to a man who wasn't interested in love? Who was happy to admit that he had no intention of ever forming any serious and committed relationship with anyone? Especially after Jefferson and the devastating sense of betrayal she had felt at the time. And yet she had, and she could no more make sense of herself than she could figure out how to build a rocket and fly to the moon.

'And I care even more about Evelyn. Her safety and security means the world to me. If I'm to go ahead with this arrangement, then I want your agreement in writing, signed and witnessed by the appropriate parties.'

'You don't trust me?'

'Maybe in this short space of time I've learnt from the master that trust is a commodity not to be taken for granted.' She met his eyes squarely and he scowled in return, withdrawing his hand, leaving behind a coolness she hated. She clasped her hands together and kept her eyes pinned to his handsome face.

Did he have the right to dish out homilies about trusting no one…because *trust* was a hindrance when the only thing you cared about was making money so that the rest of the world could bow at your feet…while expecting *her* to trust everything he said as the gospel truth?

The galling thing was that she *did* trust him, absolutely and completely. He was as good as his word, and she had the grace to blush at what she had just imparted, even though it was just part and parcel of approaching the situation in as detached a manner as possible.

'Of course,' Gabriel countered politely. 'I'll have everything signed and above board. No room for me taking advantage of you.'

'That's not what I meant.'

'No?'

'I also need to call my brother. He's been patient with me taking time out here to try and sort Evelyn's affairs but he's only going to be patient for so long. I'm going to phone him tomorrow and tell him that I'll be back in Hawaii in exactly two weeks' time.' Keen to break the sudden tension, and smiling hesitantly as she reached out for the hand that had just left hers, she added, 'Max isn't the most patient person on the planet.'

Gabriel shrugged. 'That's fair enough,' he agreed, matching her conciliatory smile with one of his own. 'It's late. Let's go upstairs.'

They made love. Again. It was late, and they were tired, but the bed was a soothing haven after hours spent in what seemed to Izzy some kind of parallel universe.

The following morning, Izzy took Rosa into town for ice-cream, and when she returned a little before lunch a lawyer was there and papers had been drawn up for signature.

Gabriel had taken her at her word. She'd demanded everything be done by the book, and he was adhering to that request to the letter.

She signed the papers, Rosa having been dispatched to watch television.

The lawyer was a formally dressed middle-aged man, and everything had been prepared meticulously and explained to her in even more scrupulous detail.

To one side, Gabriel watched, having scrawled his signature on the papers. Flustered and hot after a morning spent in town, Izzy was very much aware of his towering presence behind her.

This felt so formal. They might be lovers, she thought in self-defence, but that didn't mean he owed her anything. If things didn't work out between he and his ex-wife, whatever those *things* might be, then who was to say he wouldn't try to justify reneging on his word?

He never would. But she clung to that very sensible deduction as, finally, the last page was signed and she went to return the pen to the lawyer.

'Not so fast.'

Izzy looked at Gabriel, bemused, and he nodded to the lawyer who produced two sheets of paper, impeccably typed and formatted as the rest had been.

'What's that?' she asked, surprised.

'The issue of trust cuts both ways,' he said drily. 'You want to ensure my promise is legally binding and I, likewise, want to ensure that your promise is legally binding as well…'

Izzy read the document. It was brief. A fortnight bound to his side with no leeway for a change of heart.

Of course. Why not? But for him, there were different motivations. Whilst she had insisted on all the dots and crosses being in the right place, because she had been desperate to assume the mantle of someone detached dealing with an unexpected development in a business-like manner, *he* would have done the same because he was not attached to her in any way, aside from the physical.

Whilst she was pretending to be in charge, he wasn't pretending anything at all. They might be lovers, but a deal was a deal, and she suspected that even if she hadn't insisted on anything being signed *he* would not have been quite so trusting.

She signed, but her eyes were stinging.

Had the lawyer noticed anything? What must he make of this peculiar arrangement? He was obviously well-trained, because his expression betrayed nothing as he gathered the various papers, exchanged a few pleasantries and then left, shown to the front door by Gabriel while Izzy waited in the sitting room.

Why did it hurt so much that he'd made her sign a piece of paper? Was she so naïve to believe that there would be one rule for her and another for him? It felt as though something jarring had been introduced between them, and she wondered how she would be able to relax with him if she knew, at the back of her mind, that he didn't trust her. Yet hadn't her own actions suggested the very same thing to him?

She didn't notice Gabriel back at the door. She was trying to talk herself into an upbeat frame of mind.

Gabriel stilled for a few seconds, looking at her staring through the bay window, half-turned away. Her hands were balled into fists and her body language shrieked unhappiness.

He knew why.

He'd asked her to sign a piece of paper, just as she had asked him to, but his request had cut her to the quick. If he hadn't been as in control of his life as he was, then he might have been tempted to think that her demand for transparency from him was equally cutting, but he decided that any response along those lines was beneath him.

Still, her posture punctured his usual formidable cool and he was tempted to make amends in some way or another.

He scowled, because since when was it in his nature to placate where placating was not necessary? He cleared his throat and strolled towards her.

'Happy?' he asked, circling around so that she was compelled to look at him. How could she look so enticing and so utterly seductive when she was wearing no more than some faded dungarees with a white vest underneath and flip-flops, and had her hair tied back in a pony tail, face bare of all make-up? She was so endearingly fresh-faced, so lacking in artifice. He recalled that first time, finding out that she was a virgin, and the drive to make her smile again was like the physical twist of something sharp inside him.

His reaction bewildered him but he didn't stop to analyse why.

She shrugged and offered him a weak smile. 'Yep. All signed. Evelyn will be overjoyed to find out that she can stay in the cottage. She puts on a brave front but she's had so many sleepless nights…' Her voice tapered off and her eyes skittered away from his. 'I should go and see about fixing Rosa some lunch.'

'Rosa can wait a couple of minutes,' Gabriel told her gruffly. He raked his fingers through his hair and fidgeted. 'You *did* ask for everything to be legally documented,' he pointed out.

'I did. Yes.'

'So why do you look as though the tooth fairy forgot to leave a quarter under the pillow?'

'Do I? I'm sorry.' She tried on a smile for size. 'I'm really happy that everything's sorted.'

'I'm sorry. I should not have asked you to sign that piece of paper.'

* * *

Izzy's eyes flew to his. Her heart skipped a beat because this was not what she had expected. Apologies didn't come easy to a guy like Gabriel and the roughened undertone to his voice said it all. He was uncomfortable saying sorry and the apology was all the more heartfelt for that.

'I was hurt,' Izzy confessed simply. 'And I know I shouldn't have been. I asked you to make sure everything was legal so why shouldn't you do the same with me?'

'Because,' Gabriel told her heavily, 'The situation wasn't the same at all. You needed clarity on something that had to be legally binding with no room for a change of heart, and you were quite right to have insisted on that. I am a businessman, after all. I have learnt to take nothing for granted. Whereas…'

He looked away for a few seconds then returned his dark gaze to her face. 'Whereas there was no such necessity from me. There was no need for you to sign anything because you are not committed to doing anything for me that goes against your conscience or puts you in any position you feel is uncomfortable.'

Gabriel realised, with surprise, that whilst he'd presumed all to be fair in love and war, whilst he should feel no compunction about asking her to stick around until he sorted Bianca, having abandoned his lucrative deal to get her on board, he actually did feel ashamed. Buying her compliance shouldn't make him feel ever so slightly soiled, but it did. Money, it would seem, couldn't buy whatever you wanted after all.

'You just had to ask,' Izzy told him gently. 'I hate the thought of Rosa being used as a pawn because your ex-wife has an axe to grind. I would have agreed to stay on for a couple of weeks either way. I'm not heartless.'

'No. You're anything but.' He smiled. 'Kiss and make up?'

Izzy's heart soared. Relief that peace between them had been restored was overwhelming. 'Kiss and make up,' she agreed.

For now…

But the present would soon become the future and then…the kisses would come to an end.

The clock was ticking. She knew it and she knew that he did as well…

CHAPTER NINE

'I HAVE SOME NEWS.' Izzy smiled drowsily and twirled the stem of the wine glass in her hand.

It was a warm night. Above them, the sky was black velvet, studded with a million stars. Here, in the gazebo Gabriel had arranged the evening before—because he was sick of eating indoors and neither of them thought it was fair to impose on Evelyn to babysit—she felt like royalty.

This likely had something to do with the huge Egyptian cushions on which they were sitting, not to mention the silver cutlery, the crystal wine-glasses and the fine bone-China plates on which the remains of their main course were awaiting collection by the waiter hired for the evening. They were having a selection of finger foods prepared by one of the local chefs and the very best Sauvignon from the grapes of Gabriel's vineyard. On the ground, four over-sized lanterns provided pools of mellow light and there were strings of fairy lights entwined on the sides of the gazebo.

It was breathtakingly romantic, although when she'd mentioned that earlier Gabriel had laughed and said he'd commissioned the thing to appear at a designated time, not chosen it himself.

Still…

The past five days had been dreamy. It was almost as if this weird deal had opened up another door between them…had given them permission for what they had to deepen.

At least, that was what Izzy cared to think. She loved him and keenly noticed every small gesture he made, every sideways glance, every passing smile.

And, now that he had explained about Bianca, she felt that there was a bond between them, even though he'd never recognise anything of the sort. He wouldn't. It wasn't his way. When it came to anything to do with feelings or emotions, he resolutely took the same line. Whilst she was sure he firmly believed the stories he told himself about not being able to feel, surely there was something there, something strong and binding?

Izzy knew that she was treading on dangerous ground just thinking like that but she couldn't help herself.

'What's that?'

'My brother is getting married. I spoke to him this morning. I could scarcely believe it but he's marrying my friend Mia.'

'When's the big day?' Gabriel asked, stifling a yawn, and Izzy nudged him with her toe. He couldn't possibly fall asleep. It was way too beautiful out here.

'In a month's time. They're going to go to London to have a look at places to buy just outside it—he said that Mia isn't interested in the frantic pace of big city life. And they're going to divide their time between Hawaii and England.'

'Interesting.'

Izzy laughed languidly. He was half-lying, propping

himself up. He'd complained about the low seating arrangement in the gazebo but had burst out laughing when she'd told him not to be boring. Tapas wasn't meant to be eaten at a table sitting upright on uncomfortable chairs.

He'd kissed her long and slowly until she'd been trembling all over and half-wishing that they were near a bed instead of under the night skies.

While she had gone all out and was wearing a floaty, flowery silk dress with thin straps and sandals, the very opposite of anything she'd normally consider wearing, he was in a pair of faded jeans, a T-shirt and some loafers.

The waiter emerged from the shadows to remove the plates and reappeared minutes later with a silver platter groaning under the weight of tiny desserts, exquisitely made and begging to be eaten.

'I shall have to email Mia to get all the gory details,' Izzy went on, slipping down so that she could nestle in the crook of his arm, leaving the desserts for a while. He was staring out towards the dark sky and so was she. His house was within sight, just, but it still felt as though they were the only two people in the world.

'I'm picturing a ten-page email.' His voice was low and amused. 'Might be a better idea to call...'

'There *would* be a lot of questions,' Izzy agreed, grinning. 'You're right about a phone call. I wonder if James knows? I guess he must... I'll have to find out.'

'I want to make love to you right here, right now. How does that sound to you?' Gabriel murmured, angling his big body so that he could kiss her.

'Is sex all you ever think about?' Izzy teased, but she curved against him, angling back so that she could trail little kisses against his neck as she slipped her hand underneath his T-shirt, thrilling to the feel of solid, packed muscle. 'Besides, we can't do anything out here. Don't forget, there's a very attentive waiter in residence.'

And remember the last time we were surprised in a state of disarray, she was almost tempted to add. She didn't think her blood pressure could stand anyone else catching her *in flagrante delicto*, so to speak.

'I'm paying for that attentive waiter,' Gabriel drawled. 'He'll do whatever I tell him to do.'

'Yes, but what on earth would he think?'

'Yes,' Gabriel mimicked, half-laughing. 'But why on earth would you care?'

He gave the waiter instructions that they were not to be disturbed under any circumstances, short of his daughter waking up or the house burning down.

He pushed aside the tray with the tasty titbits. He pushed the silver wine cooler to one side and then he tenderly semi-undressed her, instinctively seeming to know that she would feel more comfortable if she weren't in a state of complete undress.

There was something exquisitely thoughtful about that, a subconscious act of consideration that warmed her heart.

Their sex was stupendous. With him she had dropped all her inhibitions—had even gone on the pill so that neither of them had to worry about an unexpected accident—but she was still shy when it came to nudity and he had clocked that without her ever having to say.

He slipped the straps of her dress down and methodically undid all twelve pearl buttons down the front so that he could suckle on her breasts, swirling his tongue across her nipples as she moaned softly, eyes closed, her hand behind his dark head.

Around them, the breeze whispered through the acres of vines, and the shadows of little flying insects were exaggerated around the lanterns and fairy lights.

They made love quietly. When his hand slipped under her panties to sink into her wetness, she felt her muscles contract, and small ripples of pleasure grew longer and fiercer, from ripples to waves, until she was so close to coming that she had to squeeze shut her legs and focus on just hanging on for a bit longer.

He didn't strip off his T-shirt but he shoved his jeans down, unzipping them unsteadily, kicking them off. Then he tugged off her panties and came inside, filling her, stretching her until she was soaring and clasping him tightly against her.

Their bodies were slick with perspiration and their grunts of satisfaction were muted, which added to a certain sizzling excitement. They were two teenagers making out in the back of a car, even though Izzy had never had that experience first-hand, so she could only surmise.

Afterwards, sated, they lay back. Izzy wriggled her dress back on, he climbed into his jeans and then he drew her towards him and haphazardly began pointing out various constellations, some with silly names, obviously made up to make her giggle.

She talked to him about Max and growing up. She'd dipped into that conversation on a few occasions now, revealing a little more about herself with each foray.

He asked her about her brothers, and she laughed and told him that she'd always been closer to James, who was relaxed, easygoing and instantly charming in a way Max had never been.

'Although,' she said pensively, 'Who knows how he's changed since he's fallen in love and is full of the joys of getting married?' She paused and then said cautiously, 'You could come to the wedding with me. If you like.'

Silence greeted this and Izzy could have kicked herself. Everything had been going so well.

'Just a thought,' she added hastily. 'Crazy, considering I'll be well gone by then! We will both have moved on.'

Gabriel didn't have to see her face to know exactly what was going on in her head. Was it so far-fetched? Here they were, having a great time—why should they be compelled to limit their enjoyment to a two-week period? Things were in place with regard to Bianca. He had consulted a top lawyer, handing over all the evidence at his disposal. It seemed that he would have no problem in levelling the playing field, if not taking it over completely, fencing it off and putting up a sign that trespassers, in the form of his dearest ex-wife, would be prosecuted. Her parenting was borderline negligent and he had the proof to present.

Izzy didn't want to tread on any toes by presuming anything and he really liked that about her. She was funny, smart, touchingly disingenuous, forthright and she had never, not once, overstepped the mark.

Not once had she asked anything of him that she knew he would be unwilling to give, do or say.

'I could think about it...'

* * *

He tucked her neatly against him and stroked her cheek with his finger. Izzy felt a surge of pure bliss.

'Really?'

'Really,' Gabriel murmured huskily. 'Why not?'

'Well…this charade has a timeline, remember? Two weeks. We're well into week one. Max and Mia won't be getting married for another month.'

'There are exceptions to everything,' Gabriel returned silkily. 'Timelines included. I'm enjoying this—I'm enjoying *you*—so why should I limit myself to a two-week curfew?'

Izzy snuggled against him, heart soaring. That small victory felt huge. Life had become a rollercoaster ride and right now she was at the height of the arc, swooping into the heavens and loving the euphoria.

Soon after, they tidied themselves up and headed back into the house. The catering staff would clear up behind them. The tiny desserts hadn't been touched, but she'd been too distracted to remember them.

It had been the perfect evening.

She hadn't been expecting it and the mere fact that he had done something so wildly impulsive had appealed to her romantic heart in ways she could scarcely vocalise, even to herself. It was all the more impressive because it was the sort of thing she would never have associated with him. He was so coolly logical, so fond of keeping his emotional distance… The gesture had felt strangely significant, even though she fought hard to bank down that impression.

And now…he'd agreed to attend Max and Mia's wedding with her. For someone who was resolutely proud of his inability to love, surely a wedding should be the last event he would agree to attend?

But they would be together, still an item, no more time limit on their relationship. That elevated it from being a business arrangement, which had felt so strange, to something entirely different and she couldn't help but want to savour the difference.

Was she being an idiot? Probably, she mused happily, but since when was it a crime to be an idiot?

They hit the house and both went up to check on Rosa, with Izzy hanging back by the door, half-watching him as he leant down to kiss his daughter and gently pull the covers back over her, half-thinking about how everything had changed for her in such a short space of time.

She waited for him, hovering, kissed him once he'd half-shut Rosa's door and then turned away to head back to her own bedroom suite.

'The night's not over yet.' He tugged her to him, hooked his arm behind her back and kissed her long and deeply, his tongue meshing with hers and instantly making her body forget that they had only just made love, that she should be sated and ready to sleep.

They made it to his bedroom, semi-entwined, and were already stripping off as the door shut behind them. He pressed her against the door, pinning her with his mouth and his hands, his knee nudging between her legs, opening them, pressing against her crotch until she was whimpering and as weak as a rag doll.

The wispy summer dress, only just back on, was stripped off in under a minute and she wrenched off her panties as he did the same with his clothes.

Neither had bothered to switch on the light but the

bank of white floor-to-ceiling shutters were open and the breeze sifting through was cool.

They staggered naked, wrapped up in one another, barely making progress until he hefted her off her feet and strode towards the bed.

She was halfway to coming and so was he when he entered her in one deep, powerful thrust. She felt his release just as hers swept her away, wrenching a long, guttural cry from her lips and leaving her utterly and wonderfully shattered afterwards.

The fierceness of this love-making…the decadent night time picnic under a starry sky…his husky admission that he no more wanted this to end than she did… was all adding up to something that felt very much like love. For a few perilous seconds, she gave herself over to imagining what it would feel like for this relationship to veer off on a tangent he might not anticipate into a world for which he had no road map.

Lazily, she felt herself dozing off, but not for long, because he ran her a bath and it was another forty minutes before she yawned and sleepily kissed him on the mouth.

'Don't go.' Standing by the door, he buried his face in her hair. Her arms were wrapped round him. He pulled back and looked down at her, and in the shadows his face was an arrangement of beautiful angles. 'Stay the night…'

Later, Izzy was to think that habit was the enemy of caution. That first night together heralded the beginning of nights spent together.

A routine was established. Gabriel reluctantly returned to his work, having spent several days doing all manner of family-orientated activities. The three of them would breakfast together, usually outside, and then he would disappear, leaving Rosa and her to busy themselves, which they very happily did. They explored the vineyards, went on day trips and shopped in the small, pretty town.

They often went to visit Evelyn, who had a renewed bounce to her step now that the hangman's noose had been removed from around her neck. Often, she and Rosa would lose themselves in planting something or other, with Evelyn meticulously explaining everything about whatever plant they happened to be handling. Izzy would sit in one of the deck chairs in Evelyn's back garden, her thoughts at last turning to the job she had left behind.

She would have to go back but she wanted to know that the parameters of her role had changed. No longer would she be dealing with the business side of things, the very side she was so qualified to deal with, given her degree. Max had emailed her suggestions as to what her responsibilities might be, and she had tweaked a few areas, but was pleased to know that the creativity that had lain buried for so many years would be allowed free rein.

She would design the layout of the hotel and the cottages which would be nestled amongst the trees. She would be responsible for sourcing everything that went into making them unique, from wall hangings to artists who could produce the murals and furniture made from the various local woods she envisaged for some of the spaces. With the hotel no longer to be luxury five-star but luxury eco, she envisaged a completely different bias to her job, one she was very much looking forward to bringing to fruition.

And how would Gabriel slot in?

Izzy didn't spend time thinking about the details. She was happy to accept the fact that they now shared something, a bond that would bypass whatever inconveniences might rear their irritating heads. After all, didn't they say that where there was a will, there was a way?

And it felt like they were a team, the three of them. She, Gabriel and Rosa...

Gabriel stopped work at six without fail, if not earlier, and engaged with this daughter in a way Izzy admired. The business with Bianca had been satisfactorily sorted. He didn't go into details, merely informing her when she asked that his ex had finally had a taste of the medicine she had been so keen to dish out before.

And they made love. Spectacular, wonderful love that more and more persuaded her that the chemistry between them ran so much deeper than he probably thought. Yes, shimmering on less rosy horizons lurked the uncomfortable reality that for him, whilst not for her, chemistry might be something quite detached from anything else. After all, had he ever, even in the throes of passion, mentioned *love*? Wasn't it always easy to believe what you wanted to believe? The pictures and possibilities she had conjured could be oh, so different from the ones he had, and she knew that somewhere deep inside her she was scared to find out.

She was absently watching Evelyn and Rosa meticulously patting down earth into bright-blue flowerpots when she heard the ping of her phone.

And there it was.

The timely reminder that the very minute you began

to take things for granted, to allow yourself to enjoy life and nurture expectations that your enjoyment might actually last, fate stepped in to shatter the daydream.

It was no more than a short text but from the very last person on earth she expected to hear from.

Why was Bianca texting her? Why did she want to meet up? What the heck could the other woman have to say to her? She would be in town, the other woman said, and she thought it would be mutually beneficial for them to have a chat. *How could either of them have anything to say to one another that could be mutually beneficial?*

Should she say something to Gabriel?

A place was suggested.

Izzy was shaking ever so slightly as she shoved her phone back into the rucksack she took with her everywhere.

Why would she bother Gabriel with this nonsense? It was ten in the morning. He would be sequestered in his office, working, and would be there all day until he broke off in the early evening. It was his routine. Lunch was brought to him, barely causing a ripple in his working day. What would be the point in disturbing him?

Two o'clock was suggested. It would be easy enough to leave Rosa with Evelyn.

Izzy only hesitated for a few seconds, then she extracted the phone and texted back.

Okay.

The meeting place surprised Izzy because it wasn't the fanciest place in town. After a mere five minutes' acquaintance, she suspected the other woman was really only comfortable somewhere expensive and pretentious, where wall-to-wall waiter service was on tap at the click of an imperious finger.

This was more of a café, busy and pretty, nestling alongside a collection of shops and boutiques, all of which lazed under a portico interrupted by a series of jade-green columns.

The city of Napa, Izzy had discovered, was made for picture-perfect snapshots, with the impressionistic backdrop of hazy, lavender hills in the distance as far as the eye could see.

It was warm and sunny, and the pavements were busy. Izzy had dressed smart-casually. She'd ditched the jeans in favour of a pair of trousers and a short-sleeved blouse, which was neatly tucked into the waistband, and some tan sandals.

Bianca was unmissable in the café. Eyes down as she scrolled through her phone, she was in a tight peacock-blue mini-dress, precariously high heels and a wealth of jewellery.

Proceed with caution, Izzy thought as she took a deep breath and headed towards the table.

She had to clear her throat before the other woman glanced up, and even then she made a show of blinking in puzzlement, as though startled by the appearance of a perfect stranger at her table.

'You came, my dear. I had my doubts.'

'I haven't got long, Bianca.' Izzy slipped into the chair and adjusted it slightly so that she was a few inches further away from Bianca.

'And I wouldn't dream of keeping you. Perhaps you need to hurry back to play at being the dutiful girlfriend to my ex-husband?'

Izzy reddened but was saved from a response by the appearance of a pretty young waitress.

'A coffee... No, nothing to eat.'

The sooner she got this over and done with, the better.

'So...' Bianca leaned forward in a waft of expensive perfume and her expression was hard. 'I am assuming Gabriel has kept you in the loop about his...recent attacks on me? No?'

'What point are you going to make, Bianca? I really can't sit around here playing games with you.'

'The point I am making, my dear little thing, is that you really shouldn't trust my ex-husband. You might be engaged, although I don't see a ring on your finger, but it won't last.'

'I don't have to sit here and listen to this.'

'But you do, dear child, because I only have your wellbeing at heart.'

'Thank you for that.' Izzy smiled sweetly, gearing up to get to her feet and leave as fast as she could. 'I'll treasure it for ever.'

Bianca's coal-black eyes glittered with menace and she reached out to circle Izzy's wrist with her fingers.

Dismayed, Izzy froze, her cornflower blue eyes widening. Inbred politeness compelled her to stay put, but her heart was beating like a sledgehammer and her head was throbbing.

'Gabriel has suddenly come by a great deal of information about my movements,' she hissed. 'About my whereabouts. He had always made a stupidly big deal about making sure to keep Rosa out of our private battles, and I can attest to this because Bella has been my trusted confidante for many years.'

'You mean *spy*? And would you mind releasing me? I don't want to have to create a scene.' Izzy could think of nothing worse, but the threat worked, because Bianca removed her hand and smiled a small, vicious smile.

'Gabriel will have obtained his information from someone, my dear. I have looked at the paperwork and all the relevant dates and it would seem that a little birdie has been whispering all sorts of things in his ear while Bella has been away. All sorts of things he has duly noted and had followed up by a team of investigators. I believe my saintly ex will be able to say, with his hand on his heart, that he learned nothing from Rosa—because someone else has been feeding him information.'

Colour was slowly draining from Izzy's face. *Pillow talk*. And not even specifically pillow talk. Just talk. Mixed in with the laughter, the anecdotes, the stories of her life and the winding tales of what she and Rosa got up to when he wasn't around… Yes, there had been asides…things said to her about Bianca and her unusual style of parenting.

She couldn't put her finger on exactly what had been said but she knew that Rosa had said stuff, head bent as she concentrated on drawing a flower or doing a piece of homework or just sitting alongside her as they played on her games console. She'd talked about the way she often skipped school to go somewhere frivolous with her mother…or was told to disappear because one of Bianca's *friends* might be turning up for a *sleepover*.

'Well!' Bianca reached for the clutch bag on the table, withdrew some bills and left them by her coffee cup. 'Just something to think about, my dear.' She stood up but then immediately leant over and whispered in Izzy's ear. 'As soon as Gabriel has everything he wants, he'll wave goodbye. He used you, dear, and believe me, I *hate* to be the one to have to tell you this. I was going to visit Rosa, but tell her I won't be making it today. So lovely to have this chat. We should do it again some time!'

In a state of shock, Izzy watched Bianca's sashaying departure from the coffee shop.

She couldn't recall making it back to the house. Her head was in a spin. She'd had no idea what she'd expected when she'd agreed to meet the other woman but she should have known that it wouldn't have been fun or relaxing. She'd just been inside a lion's den and she felt nauseous at the revelations Bianca had laid at her door.

Had she been used? She tried to think back, to follow the pattern of their relationship so that she could discover the answer to that question, but the harder she tried, the more confused and upset she became.

The meeting had lasted only minutes. She let herself quietly into the house. She would fetch Rosa later but for now…

She made her way to the far wing of the house, straight to the sprawling space where Gabriel worked. It had everything, from a dedicated work space to a vast sitting area and, of course, a luxurious bathroom suite. A billionaire's home office.

She didn't knock. She pushed open the door, walked right in and, not caring that he was on a call, said, 'I think we need to have a talk.'

This was the first time Izzy had walked into his office without knocking. Gabriel concluded his conference call immediately, then he sat back in his leather chair and looked at her, head tilted to one side, for once not knowing what the hell was going on.

And into that very brief silence Izzy said without inflexion in her voice at all, 'Guess who I just met for coffee?'

Gabriel's eyes narrowed and he watched as she moved forward to subside into the chair in front of him. She was flushed and her bright-blue eyes were shiny, glittering. She'd roped her long hair back into a loose braid and it hung over her shoulder.

He began joining the dots.

'What did she say to you?' he asked, without bothering to beat around the bush.

Bianca had been cornered and had done what she did best—she'd gone for the jugular. In this instance, however, the jugular did not belong to him.

His face revealed nothing, but it was an effort, because inside red-hot fury at his ex-wife was running through his veins like molten lava.

Thanks to what he had learnt, to the people he had commissioned to provide the proof he needed of her negligent parenting, he had his ex on the run. And it was at just the right point in time, because he had discovered she hadn't been bluffing when she had told him about her intention to remove Rosa from the US and take her back to Tuscany, which she had summarily decided was her 'natural home'.

Bianca's mother had got herself involved with a younger man, it would seem, and Bianca had no intention of allowing her inheritance to fall into the wrong hands. Filial duty had suddenly morphed into daughterly love.

With those plans in disarray, it was little wonder she had decided to wreak whatever revenge she could, making sure to keep far away from him. He suspected the nature of the retribution and his blood ran cold.

'How could you, Gabriel?' Izzy whispered.

'Tell me what it is I am supposed to have done.'

'You know what!' She sprang to her feet, as though suddenly unable to remain still, and paced the room in jerky steps before spinning round to look at him with hostile accusation. 'You *used* me. You pretended… You made me think… All because you wanted me to tell you what Rosa said to me.'

He lowered his eyes, shielding his expression. When he raised them to look at her, he knew his face was shuttered, revealing nothing.

'I didn't use you, Izzy. You're looking at signposts but misreading the signs.'

'What does *that* mean?'

'You should calm down.'

'Don't you *dare* tell me to calm down. You used me to get what you wanted and I *hate* you for that!'

Gabriel felt himself flush as all the chickens came home to roost, except…had he used her? No, he hadn't. He had been the passive recipient of useful information and why was anything wrong with that? She'd taken what Bianca had said and was twisting it into something that sat like something ugly and sharp on his conscience.

He clamped down hard on any inappropriate feelings of guilt. She said that he'd 'made her think…' Made her think *what*? That he *loved* her? Was that the conclusion of that unfinished sentence?

Had he taken his eye off the ball? Encouraged her

to have feelings for him? Even though she must surely know, because he had been utterly upfront that he wasn't in it for the long term.

And now she was here, hurling accusations at him, screaming, shouting and tearful.

Was this what he wanted, needed? No. He'd never had time for demanding women with chaotic feelings that needed to be nurtured. He'd learnt the hard way that the only thing that mattered was the cold logic of making money. He'd been lazy and now it was time to say goodbye.

Something inside twisted. He ignored it. Control over lust...*that* was the bottom line...and if he'd forgotten that for a while, then it was time he remembered.

He stood up and moved towards her, paused to meet her fierce blue eyes.

'Don't get on the moral high ground with me,' he said darkly. 'Your friend is sitting pretty in her cottage. No more pressuring Evelyn to sell her home. Some might say that *that* is what using is all about.'

'It's just not the same, Gabriel.'

'Explain the difference.'

'If you can't see it for yourself—' her voice was subdued and she was already half-turning towards the door '—then you never will. Tell Rosa goodbye from me. She's with Evelyn.'

She walked out without looking back.

CHAPTER TEN

GABRIEL WEARILY RUBBED his eyes, swivelled his chair and stared out of the window of his office.

The view was somewhat different from the one he had had a fortnight ago. No symmetrical, gently swaying vines marching into a distant lavender-hued horizon... No charming local town with a pace of life as slow and steady as a snail's progress across the grass... No pleasing sight of a flat, blue infinity pool waiting to soothe at the end of a hot day.

No very many things, come to think of it.

No Izzy sharing his bed every night... No hearing the sound of her laughter... No walking with Rosa tucked between them asking a million questions... No unwinding at the end of the day with a glass of wine and the soothing backdrop of Izzy's soft voice.

No, that particular bubble had burst, and of course it had always been going to burst.

He was back in New York. The view from the skyscraper that housed his offices looked down at matchstick-sized crowds scuttling frantically across gridlocked streets with everything buried beneath the haze of exhaust fumes and pollution.

Or so it seemed. Everything had changed for him

with Rosa, and he told himself that that was the main thing.

Currently, she was with Bianca in Tuscany for two weeks, with a nanny of his choice in attendance. When she returned to America, she would be with him. He was now the one holding all the trump cards. Bianca had had no choice but to cave in to his demands, not that she had fought too hard. She was going to decamp to Tuscany because the threat of losing the family fortune to a greedy, gold-digging toy boy was far more imperative a calling than sticking around in America so that custody could be more fairly shared.

She would see Rosa for a fortnight during the summer holidays, for ten days over Easter and they would split Christmas—unless she tried bending the rules, at which point, Gabriel had told her, he would slam into her like a freight train.

All was good. All was fine. And this…

He stood up, strolled to the floor-to-ceiling panes of glass that fortified his office, turning it into a glass-house, and looked down twenty storeys to the streets below, thin and pulsing like thread veins. *This* was reality. *This* was what he had trained himself to appreciate. *This* was his life blood.

He and Izzy were not going to share space indefinitely. That had never been an option. It was staggering enough that she had shared his bedroom at all. None of his mistresses ever had, nor had he ever been tempted to issue any invitations.

And yet…

She was gone but she still filled his head. She'd left his bed and yet he still reached for her in the morning when he opened his eyes. Everywhere felt silent without her laughter filling the space between them. He closed his eyes and saw her face and his heart ached.

Forget about reality and bubbles that had to burst... Forget about pride and not having to justify himself to anyone. He hadn't been ready to let her go and, sitting here now, he finally admitted what he'd subconsciously been thinking for so long...

He might never be able to let her go.

Izzy sat back on her haunches and gazed at the mural she was in the process of creating. It was stiflingly hot inside the first of the cabanas to have been fully built based on the ideas she had had for the hotel, ideas which Max had put into place, as he had said he would.

Air conditioning was due to be installed when the remaining cabanas were all constructed, which would not be for another three months. Until then, she would work away in the heat, taking time out every so often to step outside and grab what little breeze there was.

Izzy didn't mind. She welcomed the stifling discomfort. It was more bearable than her inner torment, which was with her all the time, from the very moment she opened her eyes to the moment she closed them.

In theory, life was looking very good for her on all other fronts bar the emotional one. Max was in London at the moment, but they had had the most rewarding week together before he'd left. They'd actually talked and listened to one another. He'd sat next to Mia, his arm slung casually over her shoulder. Izzy had never seen anyone so much in love and her heart had twisted because, against all odds, he was living the dream she wanted so desperately for herself.

But it didn't erase the fact that she hadn't heard a

word from Gabriel. She had closed the door behind her nearly a fortnight ago, and with that, she had closed a door to him and to Rosa…closed a window that had begun to feel like a dream. She could almost believe none of it had ever happened were it not for her memories, which were as sharp and as cruel as shards of glass inside her.

She was relying heavily on the cliché that time healed all.

Her mind was a million miles away, so when she heard *his* voice behind her, she didn't register that anyone had spoken at all until, a little louder, the voice said, 'I like it. Could I commission you to paint one for me?'

Very slowly, Izzy stood up and turned around. Her heart was racing and, even as her brain recognised that distinctive deep, dark drawl, her impulse was to deny the obvious.

Her memory hadn't done him justice. He was even more devastatingly drop-dead gorgeous than she remembered. He wore cool, grey linen trousers, loafers, a faded grey polo-shirt… He looked urbane and elegant— as though the temperature wasn't in the high eighties.

While she was the opposite, with her short overalls daubed with paint, her hair tied up in something that was somewhat of a bun but not quite. Even her flip-flops had drops of paint on them. She was a mess.

'What are you doing here?'

'What do you think? I've come to see you.'

'Why?'

'Will you come with me so that we can talk? I have a chauffeur waiting outside.'

'What do we have to talk about, Gabriel?'

'Everything.'

'No. We don't.' She was furious because she could feel the prick of tears behind her eyes. Just looking at him opened up a well of sadness inside her. 'We're finished and it's much better if it's a clean break.'

'Is that what you want? A clean break?'

When she didn't answer, he looked away then strolled towards the mural, staring at it, his back to her.

'How do you think it felt for me to know that the stuff I'd said to you in confidence had gone into building a case against your ex?' Izzy asked, a wrenched accusation. 'You may think that's okay, because it was all for the sake of Rosa, but it didn't feel okay to me. I have *feelings*, and if you don't get that then forget it.'

'I hurt you.' He turned round to look at her, his movements for once lacking their usual assuredness.

'Yes. You did. And don't you *dare* tell me that there was anything cold or calculating about me sleeping with you because I was keen to help Evelyn. Don't even think of implying that it was some kind of trade off! It wasn't like that and it never could be. Not for me.'

'I know it wasn't.'

'And don't even think of trying to get me back into your bed again because you've decided you don't want a clean break.' She didn't want to look at him at all, but was still driven to stare, and she hated herself for her weakness.

'You're right,' Gabriel said huskily in a low, barely audible voice. 'I don't want a clean break. I don't want any break at all. I just…want you.'

'Too bad!' She spun round on her heels and half-raced out of the cabana. It was still scorching hot at a little after four and a combination of a need to flee and pure instinct drove her to run through the trees, brushing past the foliage that was in the process of being trimmed back, out past the main hotel and down towards the beach, which was empty.

He would follow her. She knew he would. She wanted it so badly, wanted *him* despite everything, and yet she was desperate to escape his stranglehold.

She didn't want him to talk her into doing anything her head would say no to and she feared her own weakness when it came to him.

She stopped dead to stare at the open ocean for a few seconds, to feel the soothing caress of the sea breeze cooling her down. Then she sat on the sand, drew up her knees to her chin and continued to look out at the deep-blue water with its white lacy spume where the waves rose and broke in a jagged pattern.

She felt his presence, saw his shadow over her and tensed up as he sat next to her, staring out, his body language mirroring hers.

'I didn't…use you,' he said haltingly, not looking at her. 'I just wasn't open. You talked, I listened and, instead of telling you how much you were doing to help me do the best for my daughter, I kept silent, because silence has always been my best friend. Rosa took to you, confided in you. I'd always promised that I would never put her in the middle, never make her feel as though she was taking sides in a situation not of her making. But she chatted to you and, instead of being honest with you, I wasn't. I should have trusted you. I should have communicated better but I just didn't have those skills. At least, I didn't think I did.'

'I hate you,' Izzy whispered. She brushed a tear off her cheek and was barely aware of doing so.

'This is who I am,' he said huskily. 'I grew up on

the wrong side of the tracks and it was ingrained in
me that my strength was my ability to remain focused.
I think...' He sighed. 'I think when my marriage fell
apart I woke up to the reality that love, and everything
else that went with it, wasn't something I was capable of
experiencing. Those were things sacrificed somewhere
along the line. It was a sacrifice I accepted. I had my
daughter. It was enough. And then you came along.'

'Don't do this. Don't lie to me.'

'I wouldn't. I couldn't.' He paused and Izzy sneaked
a glance at him to find that he was staring off in the distance, as thoughtful as she had ever seen him.

'I slept with you that very first time, and if only
I'd known just how much the foundations of my life
would change afterwards... No, scratch that. I *met* you
that very first time—so different from anyone I'd ever
known. God, I told myself that you were just another
privileged kid, that underneath the sweet and innocent veneer lay someone who would be accustomed
to getting just want she wanted. On every count, I was
wrong.'

He turned to her and looked at her gravely. 'That's
why I couldn't use you although, yes, for better or for
worse, I did use the information that came my way. I
never asked you to confide in me...but you did, and I
was grateful because, in a strange way, you gave me
my daughter. I don't want you to feel you have to forgive me, Izzy. I just want you to know that I fell in love
with you and, if I hurt you, then from now to the end of
time you have my apologies.'

He didn't touch her but their eyes met and the breath
hitched in her throat.

Was he leading her up the garden path? This was a

man who had just admitted that he was more than capable of using someone, that he had considered using her. Was this a ruse, something introduced to get her off-guard? Was there something else he wanted from her?

She didn't want to trust him but she could feel a singing in her veins.

'You're not in love with me,' she said, confused.

'I am. It's not something I ever expected, and I guess that's why I didn't recognise the signs. You shared my bed and I couldn't conceive of anything else. I trusted you with Rosa…let you open my eyes to what it felt like to stop being a businessman and instead to be just a dad. But trust was something that was so alien to me that I couldn't easily believe in it.'

'You never said before… You never let me know…'

'It crept up on me, Izzy. Like I said, I showed all the symptoms but chose to ignore them.' He reached to stroke the side of her face with his finger. She shivered and closed her eyes briefly.

'I don't want to believe you,' she said honestly and he smiled.

'Why not?'

'Because then I might wake up and realise that this has all been a dream.' She knew what it felt like to be giddy with happiness. 'I fell in love with you and I was so scared that it would all fall apart. I trusted Jefferson and that was a train crash. Did I dare trust you? Trust myself? If only I'd known how you felt then I might have been brave enough to tell you how *I* felt…'

'Or,' he said with wry honesty, 'You might have hit a brick wall. I closed myself off after Bianca and that detachment became my default position when it came to women. I figured it worked for me, gave me the uncluttered life I wanted. I didn't stop to ask myself what was lost in the process, but in the end you showed me.'

'I love you so much…' Her eyes shone. Nothing else mattered. This very moment was something to be held close and treasured, no more questions asked.

'I came here, Izzy, to ask you to marry me. I wanted to bring a ring…wanted to do something dramatic… but I was scared stiff that you'd turn me down. And if you turn me down, I'm not sure what I'll do. The truth is that it's more than love—it's need as well. I've spent my life insulating myself against the background I came from. I equated power and money with freedom and self-determination, and between those opposite poles there was nothing. Life, before you came along, was black and white. You turned it to Technicolor and that's why I want you by my side for ever. So will you, Izzy? Will you marry me?'

Izzy smiled and said two words to last a lifetime. 'I will.'

* * * * *

PREGNANT WITH HIS MAJESTY'S HEIR

ANNIE WEST

Aurélie and Lucien's story is for all of you
who (like me) love a Cinderella story.
Happy reading!

CHAPTER ONE

HE'D BARELY MOVED. The man whose face would make a sculptor weep and women stare.

More than stare. A couple of young, confident women had ventured across the restaurant, all shiny smiles and eager body language, only to return to their table disappointed.

The man with the wide shoulders, brooding expression and stunning amber eyes beneath night-dark hair wasn't in the mood for company.

He wasn't surly and he'd been perfectly polite to Aurélie, more polite than a lot of customers, but when he wasn't speaking with her, his face settled into stark lines. Even the way he was backed into that corner alcove for two, with his broad back against the ancient stone wall, seemed somehow defensive. As if ready to repel unwanted intrusion.

His face would be arresting at any time with those powerful, spare lines and generous mouth. But something about his sombre air and the pleat of a frown on his forehead caught Aurélie's attention. The way the frown intensified when his phone vibrated on the table. The way he refused to pick it up, spending the evening staring into space from under dark eyebrows or, occasionally, watching Aurélie as she wended through the tables.

It wasn't a busy night. So late in winter Annecy's tourist numbers had dropped. This town near the French Alps would attract them again as the weather warmed.

Aurélie told herself that was why her attention kept returning to Mr Tall, Dark and Handsome, because he was by far the most fascinating patron in the half empty restaurant.

She was honest enough to admit to a frisson of excitement as he'd followed her to his table. She'd been hyper-aware of his tall frame behind her and the intoxicating scent of the outdoors and warm male spice that tantalised when he passed her to take his seat.

Her awareness was grounded in intense attraction.

And something more. The conviction that something was wrong.

It was there in the whitened grip of his fingers around his drink. In the single-minded way he'd downed the first glass of wine as if he needed it badly. Yet now he seemed to have forgotten all about the drink in his hand. It was as if a dark cloud hovered over that corner, despite the dazzling effect of those stunning eyes and the couple of brief smiles he'd given her.

What would it be like if his smile reached his eyes?

Aurélie forced down a shiver of speculation as she cleared a table. The two Spanish guys had drunk their way through the meal and were ready to party. One still hadn't given up his determined flirtation. As she leaned forward, he lifted his hand as if reaching for her bottom. Instantly Aurélie tipped the plate she held. Another centimetre and he'd wear gooey cheese from leftover raclette. Meeting her stare, he raised his palm in apology.

From the corner of her eye she saw the man in the corner stiffen and put down his glass. Earlier, when the young Spaniard had first tried to touch her, the stranger had started to rise as if to intervene.

But she didn't need help. A few friendly but pointed words in Spanish reminded them that she wasn't on the menu. On the way to the kitchen she gave the man in the corner a discreet smile of acknowledgement. He responded with the tiniest tilt of his head.

Something caught hard in Aurélie's chest at the knowledge that he was watching out for her. She wasn't used to gallantry or protectiveness.

That had to be why her eyes kept seeking him out.

That and his aura of tightly restrained emotion. She felt

it like a zap of energy whenever she approached his table. More so when those fiercely bright eyes locked on her, sending a shimmer of heat through her.

Or maybe she was projecting her own feelings onto him.

Her life was at a turning point. Opportunity lay ahead, but it had come at a cost. Stoically she told herself it was better to know than merely to suspect as she'd done for years. Yet it was hard having her suspicion proved true. That no matter how hard she tried she wasn't special enough to matter to those closest to her. She was on her own. Her family had finally stopped pretending otherwise.

Aurélie blinked and smiled at a customer looking to pay, ignoring the hollow ache behind her ribs. She refused to wallow in self-pity. She'd do what she'd always done, put her head down and work hard.

The difference was that now she had a real opportunity for change. This time she'd grab it with both hands and make the most of it. It was time she stopped playing safe and took a chance.

Lucien watched the waitress beam at a customer, her smile lighting up her face. There was a radiance about the woman that kept drawing his gaze and dragging his thoughts from the well of darkness that encompassed him.

It wasn't just her dimple-cheeked grin as she swapped comments with customers in at least four different languages. Or the vibrant red hair, pulled back in a bouncing ponytail that gleamed like jewels and firelight.

His eyes followed her quick, supple movements, a mix of grace and strength as she manoeuvred through the tables carrying laden plates. Then there was her easy humour. Even when that drunken lout tried to grope her, she'd used humour underscored by steel to put the guy in his place yet leave him smiling.

And sometimes, as if to remind Lucien that he wasn't completely cut off from the rest of the world, her eyes would catch on his. The effect was startling. Each time warmth began to trickle painfully through his frozen being.

Since the news had reached him this morning it felt as if a wall of ice separated him from the rest of the world. Lucien knew it was shock and when it wore off everything would be far too real.

Strangely, when she met his eyes, *that* connection felt real. She looked at him and he imagined he saw acceptance and understanding. A warmth that, despite his need to be alone with his grief, beckoned invitingly.

What he didn't see was the voracious eagerness those other women had shown when they'd come to his table uninvited. As if he'd make their raucous girls' night out complete.

Lucien couldn't imagine ever wanting to party again.

Not when his world was a yawning maw of hurt.

He frowned into his glass, swirling the liquid then downing it in one, heat spilling down his throat. Yet still he was chilled to the marrow. He'd thought alcohol might dampen the biting ache but it had no effect.

He kept imagining Justin, his car smashed by the impact. And when he couldn't stand that, his brain conjured images of the trip they'd made here years ago. Justin had been ecstatic with his incognito escape. Lucien's memories of that time were filled with the sound of his cousin's laughter. At the simple joys of camping. At paragliding or sailing on the lake or drinking beer by a barbecue like two ordinary guys.

That was why Lucien had found himself turning off the *autoroute* and heading for this town in eastern France that was only marginally on the way to Vallort. They'd wanted him to fly straight there but he'd insisted on driving himself. Tomorrow would be time enough to face his grim responsibilities.

Tonight he needed to be alone with his memories.

First Uncle Joseph, the only father he'd ever known,

had succumbed to what had at first seemed a mild illness. Then, less than twenty-four hours later, Justin, as close as any brother. Had his reflexes been impaired by grief over his father?

They were the last of Lucien's family.

He dragged in a breath laden with lacerating ice shards, despite the heat of the room. With it came skewering pain, lancing his chest, so sharp his lungs froze and the edges of his vision blackened.

Lucien lurched to his feet.

He needed to get out of here.

It was snowing when Aurélie left the restaurant. Soft plump flakes drifted across her cheeks and settled on her dark sleeves, making her smile. All around was silence, as if everyone else was tucked up snug and warm and she was the only one to witness the light fall.

Hugging her old coat closer, she stepped across the cobblestones towards the shallow river flowing through the heart of the old town. The Palais de l'Île was illuminated, its ancient stonework picturesque on its island in the centre of the river.

Would she miss this place when she left? Would she—

Movement at the corner of her vision made her turn. A tall form melded with an old wall but wasn't part of it.

In her pocket Aurélie's hand closed around her keys, threading them between clenched fingers. She'd always felt safe here even after a late finish, but it paid to be cautious.

She was turning away, deciding to take the long way to her tiny flat, when something about that shadowy figure made her pause.

He, for it was definitely he, looked familiar.

For three heartbeats she stood there, not sure why she hesitated, till her eyes adjusted to the gloom and she recognised him.

'*Monsieur?* Are you all right?'

It was him, the solitary customer who'd awakened her curiosity.

Aurélie realised he was coatless, wearing only jeans and a pullover. From the way the finely knitted fabric clung to him she'd wondered earlier if it might be cashmere. Certainly it was expensive. But it wasn't warm enough for standing out in the snow. How long had he been here? He'd left almost an hour ago. Snow had settled on his shoulders and dark hair.

She frowned. He could certainly afford a coat given the generous tip he'd left.

Aurélie took a step closer and saw a ripple pass through him. Like someone waking from sleep. Or someone on the verge of hypothermia?

'It's you.' His deep voice had a roughened quality she didn't recall from earlier. There was no threat in it. Instead it sounded rusty, as if his vocal cords had seized up.

'What are you doing here?' she probed.

Waiting for you.

She could imagine the young Spaniard saying that, grinning lasciviously.

'Just…thinking.' She heard him swallow. 'I needed some fresh air to…' His words petered out.

'To think.' She nodded briskly, telling herself she wasn't disappointed that he wasn't waiting for her.

Occasionally in the past a customer had, misinterpreting her professional friendliness for something else. Why was it that tonight she almost wished this man had?

Because tonight her professional smiles hid an awful emptiness. Because she felt alone, rebuffed, even betrayed by her family.

Because this man made her feel something powerful and different. As if they knew each other, despite being strangers.

Aurélie slammed a lid on such frivolous thoughts. Frivolity had no place in her life.

'You can't think here. You'll freeze,' she said briskly, taking another step closer.

His eyes were fixed on her but something about his expression told her his thoughts were elsewhere.

'Where's your coat?'

He shrugged. 'In the car, I suppose.'

'Which is where?'

He nodded towards the lake in the distance. 'In the underground car park.'

'Okay then, where are you staying tonight?'

'Staying?' Then, as if surfacing from deep water, he shook his head and drew a deep breath. 'I'm not sure. I was going to drive on after dinner but I had no real plans.'

'You've been drinking. You can't drive any further tonight in case you cause an accident.'

His reaction shocked her. A great shudder ran through him and he put out a hand to the wall beside him as if needing its support. He said something under his breath that Aurélie couldn't catch but she didn't miss the note of searing anguish.

She'd been right. Something was wrong.

Closing the gap between them she briefly touched his hand. Ice-cold. This close she saw the way he shook.

'Are you sick?'

'No. Just cold.' He sounded surprised and she wondered if he even realised how long he'd stood out here.

'Have you taken drugs?'

'Of course not!' He straightened away from the wall, suddenly taller and more alert. 'I don't do drugs.' His voice was more normal too, as if he'd surfaced from whatever place his thoughts had led him.

Aurélie weighed her options, knowing her friends would tell her not to do what she was going to. That *she'd* advise any friend in similar circumstances to walk away. Yet she couldn't. Not tonight. Not with him.

It was inexplicable but she knew this was right.

'Come with me.' She turned on her heel.

'Where?'

'To my place.'

CHAPTER TWO

'You can have a hot drink and warm up and we'll find you a safe place to stay.'

Lucien forced his stiff legs to work and followed her quick steps down the narrow pedestrian street.

He wasn't used to taking orders. Usually he was the one giving them. Tonight though, his heart was full of grief. His mind was buffeted by the complete derailment of his life. By the problems awaiting him in Vallort. It was simpler to let this woman issue her instructions.

Yes, a hot drink. He hadn't realised how cold he was. He couldn't feel his feet and his cheeks and ears felt frozen.

Yes, a place to stay. Dimly he realised he needed that. Somewhere quiet where he could be anonymous. It would be his last quiet, anonymous night. Suddenly that seemed incredibly precious.

From this point on there'd be no anonymity, at least in his home country. Certainly no chances to head off with friends after work for a party.

As for working late in his office… Lucien drew a sharp breath. No doubt he'd spend many nights working late but it wouldn't be at his architect's desk and it wouldn't be on any of the projects he'd planned.

All that would be denied him.

He grimaced, catching the direction of his thoughts.

How could he feel self-pity when Justin could feel nothing at all? When, in a couple of days, Justin and his father would be laid side by side in the family vault.

'Are you sure you don't need a doctor?' She'd stopped before a battered wooden door, the meagre light from a wall sconce making her hair glow.

'Quite sure.' Lucien made an attempt to escape his circling thoughts and focus. He frowned down at her. 'You don't know me. Do you think it safe to invite strangers home?' Her eyebrows arched as she stared up at him. 'Sorry. I don't mean to sound like your father.'

He didn't like the idea of someone taking advantage of her. Through the welter of old memories a new one surfaced, of that young tourist trying to grope her. Lucien's jaw tightened.

Her laugh was short and bitter. 'You don't sound at all like my father.'

Instinct nudged Lucien, telling him there was more to her words than was obvious, but already she was opening the door.

'Don't worry, I'm not inviting you here to have my wicked way with you.' Her words were sharp but her eyes slid from his. It struck him that she'd misinterpreted his concern as a jibe at her morals. 'I just don't want to come out tomorrow to find you frozen in a doorway. So, if you're coming, hurry up.'

No mistaking the snap in her words. Lucien silently cursed his clumsy tongue. The last thing he'd intended was to insult her. He liked her. And right now she felt like his only anchor to a sane and better world.

A couple of minutes later he stood in a tiny living space with the smallest excuse for a kitchen he'd ever seen tucked at one end.

She threw out an arm to one of two doorways and he felt a pang of disappointment that she didn't meet his eyes. He wanted her cautious with other men but not, he discovered, with him. 'That's the bathroom. There's a clean towel on the shelf. Help yourself to a shower to warm up while I make us hot drinks.'

'Thank you. You're very kind. I appreciate it.'

Lucien paused, willing her to turn. Finally she did and he saw wariness and a bruised look in her brown eyes. Had he hurt her? Tonight he felt clumsy, lost between the present and the past, having trouble expressing himself. It took a monumental effort to conjure a smile of thanks. His taut facial muscles protested, but he saw her expression ease a little.

She nodded towards the bathroom. 'And pass out your pullover. I'll put it near the radiator to dry.'

It was only then Lucien realised he was wet as well as cold. In the warmth of this tiny space his clothes clung uncomfortably, the wool itching his skin.

'I'll give it to you now.' He hauled the wet wool up and over his head and held it out to her. 'Thanks.'

Then he took the couple of strides to the bathroom, telling himself he'd feel more himself when dry and warm.

Aurélie blinked as the bathroom door closed. Minutes later she heard the shower start up and realised he'd have to bend to fit under the spray. The flat was tiny and he dwarfed it. He was well over six feet tall.

And beautifully built.

Her thoughts strayed to his lean yet powerful-looking body. The play of muscles as he shrugged off his pullover then strolled away, loose-limbed and straight-shouldered. Aurélie's gaze had dropped to his perfectly rounded backside in black jeans and her mouth had dried.

No, it had dried when he smiled. Those amber eyes had warmed, crinkling at the corners, and she'd felt it like a punch to the middle.

As if no man had ever smiled at her before.

Never a man like that.

She wasn't sure what made him different.

Her mouth tugged into a rueful curve. Nothing apart from stunning looks, an aura of magnetism and a smile that transformed his face despite the lines of strain. And that air of brooding distraction that teased her curiosity.

Whatever it was, it made Aurélie realise with a sudden

jab how isolated she was, despite her busy schedule and her plans for the future.

Even surrounded by family she'd felt unloved.

Now they'd gone and she realised she was actually *lonely*.

She had friends but they weren't very close since Auré-lie had always been too busy juggling the demands of work and her family to enjoy a very active social life.

Was that why she'd taken pity on a stranger and risked bringing him here? So that, for the time it took him to fin-ish a hot drink and warm up, she wouldn't be alone?

Aurélie stiffened. She wasn't so needy.

She looked down at the damp black wool, heavy in her hands. Her fingers twitched, registering residual body heat and that slight yet heady fragrance of masculine skin.

Nostrils flaring, she stalked across to the radiator and hung it over a nearby rail.

The drinks were ready when he emerged.

'That was terrific. Thank you, Ms…?'

'Aurélie.' She stirred his drink rather than stare at that honed body. 'I'm sorry I don't have a shirt to fit you, but your pullover should be dry soon.' As for his damp trou-sers, there was no way she was offering to dry those too. He needed to be at least semi-clothed.

'Thank you, Aurélie.' His deep voice turned her name into a lilting caress and a tiny shiver raced through her. 'I'm Lucien.'

She nodded and passed him a steaming mug, feeling crowded since he took up all the space, or at least all the oxygen in the room.

'Hot chocolate?' He sniffed the drink.

'I never have coffee at night. It takes me ages to unwind after a shift. Please—' she gestured to the small, lumpy sofa '—take a seat.' Because it was easier to think with some distance between them. She'd stay here, leaning against the benchtop.

'You play chess?' He gestured to the board on the crate

that served as a coffee table. 'How about a game while I wait for my pullover to dry?'

Aurélie's gaze flickered from his sculpted profile to his bare chest with its fascinating dusting of dark hair. Chess would give her something to concentrate on rather than gawking at his body. Finally she nodded.

It didn't work as well as she'd hoped. Sitting close to him was distracting and Lucien beat her easily. But Aurélie found it surprisingly comfortable, sharing the night quiet with him. Her residual discomfort at rashly inviting a stranger here died as they spoke desultorily about chess and then about games they'd played as kids.

She learned he loved to ski and that he'd grown up in the mountains, though, judging by his faint accent, not in France. Aurélie chose not to query him more closely. What was the point? He'd be gone soon. Tomorrow he'd be just a memory. Besides, he seemed so self-contained that any direct questions would feel like an intrusion on his privacy.

He heard about her love of music, that she'd wanted to play the piano but sang instead. Aurélie made that sound like a choice, not mentioning there'd been no money for music lessons.

When he suggested a second game she agreed, surprised when she won to discover how long they'd been playing. She felt relaxed with Lucien. Except for that tiny current of awareness running deep into the core of her body. He might be good company but he was still the most attractive man she'd ever met.

'Congratulations,' he murmured. 'There are flashes of real brilliance in your game.'

'Why, thank you.' Her smile died as she saw his hands clasped, white-knuckled between his knees. His mouth was a crooked line. 'Lucien, what's wrong?'

The man was in pain, no doubt about it.

'Nothing. You just reminded me of someone.' His jaw clenched so hard it was a wonder the bone didn't splinter.

'Another chess player?'

He nodded and she watched him swallow, his Adam's apple jerking against the strong line of his throat.

It was none of her business. Whatever bothered him wasn't something she could solve. Yet Aurélie read stark misery on that proud face and felt its echo within her.

'Do you want to talk about it?'

He raised his head then, his eyes so bright they seemed to catch all the light in the room and drive it deep inside her where a confusion of emotions—pity, regret and the desire to comfort him—melded.

'Thanks.' His voice was a raw whisper. 'But it's too late. He's dead.'

'I'm sorry.' Aurélie knew about grief. Even after all these years, she remembered the loss of her mother, the pain so keen it defied belief. And then the long, lonely days that followed.

Aurélie couldn't bear to watch the way anguish etched his features. She leaned towards him then made herself stop.

'Someone close to you.' It was a statement, not a question, but he answered anyway.

'My cousin, but we were brought up like brothers.'

Aurélie's heart rolled over in her chest. How would she feel if one of her little brothers died? They'd grown up taking her for granted, as her father and stepmother did, relying on her rather than loving her. But still she cared for them. She'd be devastated to lose them.

'Sorry,' he murmured. 'You don't need this.'

'It's fine. Grief takes a long time. How long has it been?'

His mouth dragged up at one side in a grimace. His eyes met hers and again that blast of connection hit her like a drill bored right into her soul.

'I found out this morning.'

'Oh, Lucien!' Her heart wrung for him. He must feel raw inside.

Aurélie rose and took a seat beside him on the sofa. Tentatively she touched the back of his hand with her fingertips. She didn't want to intrude but there were times when human contact was important. This seemed one.

His skin was hot and his fist was clenched so hard it shook. She tried to ignore the sizzle of energy that shot through her from the point of contact, instead breathing deep and concentrating on him.

'I wish I could say something that would make a difference.'

He shook his head, a stray lock of espresso-dark hair falling across his brow. It made his sculpted features look almost boyish as he turned to look at her.

'You've already done so much. You brought me back. For a while there I felt completely lost.'

Beneath her fingertips his hand turned, palm up, and he laced his fingers with hers. Another ripple of sensation, stronger this time, shimmied up her arm. It spread warmth through her chest and lower, right down into the depths of her being.

What was this? She'd never felt anything like it.

'You feel it too.' His eyes held hers.

Aurélie felt trapped, caught by his bright gaze and disorientated by something within her that urged her to hold tight and not let go.

'Sorry?'

'This.' His hand squeezed hers and her breathing turned fluttery.

Aurélie stared back, overwhelmed by the need to stay connected. By a response to this man—this *stranger*—that was beyond anything she'd experienced.

'I don't understand you.' An instinct for self-preservation prompted the words.

For a second longer she felt it, the thrill of contact, his flesh against hers, his stunning eyes holding hers, then he moved. Her hand fell to the red upholstery and the blaze inside died a little as he turned away. Not only turned but surged to his feet.

'You're right. I shouldn't have… That was a mistake.' He raised his arm and forked his hand through his hair, pushing it back off his brow. Aurélie watched the mesmerising shift and play of his oblique muscles and others she couldn't name as he moved.

Moved away.

Her heart hammered to a stop so abruptly she felt sick, then it started up again, fast and erratic.

'What are you doing?' Aurélie was on her feet.

He didn't look at her. He wore that closed expression she'd seen in the restaurant and out on the street.

'Thanks for your hospitality, Aurélie. I appreciate it. Now it's time I left.'

'You can't go.' Her voice rose. 'It's not safe to drive and you haven't got a place to stay.' Why hadn't she made that a priority?

He shrugged and reached for his pullover. 'I'll sleep in the car. I have to leave now.'

Aurélie stood in front of him, forcing him to look at her. When he did, the impact of that glittering stare almost rocked her back on her feet. Yet it was nothing to the urgent emotions within.

'Why?'

He paused, hands fisting in the dark wool, his bare chest rising sharply on a ragged breath.

'Because I want you, Aurélie.'

He dragged in another breath that rasped loud in the silence while his words demolished something inside her.

'I've wanted you from the first moment you smiled and led me to my table. I watched you walk in front of me— your scent, the sway of your hips, the perfect curves of your backside…even the damned swing of your ponytail beckoned me.' His voice ground low, hitting a husky note that dragged through her like fingers raking velvet.

Lucien swallowed and she watched the movement, read urgency and mouth-drying hunger in the jerky action. It mirrored her own response to his words, his nearness. Her throat was parched, her heartbeat jagged and she felt strung out with anticipation.

Hadn't she spent the evening fascinated? *Wanting?* Trying to pretend that she didn't? Telling herself it was mere charity that led her to invite him here when from the first she'd been driven by another compulsion entirely?

'I thought I could control it. Be civilised and grateful and walk away. I *will* be all those things,' he added through clenched teeth, 'but I have to go *now*.'

Her hand closed on his bare arm and he went rigid, his breath like the hiss of water on molten metal. Surprisingly soft hair tickled her palm. She felt corded muscle and heat and again that singing, soaring sense of rightness.

'I feel it too.'

'What?' Finally he swung his head to look at her.

'I feel it. The connection. The…need.' Aurélie swallowed against the emotions constricting her throat. 'I don't understand it. I don't usually…'

She shook her head, bewildered by the strength of her feelings. Then, blessed relief, his other hand cupped her face, his touch fortifying and reassuring.

'I don't usually either.'

His expression was dead serious, despite the sexual tension twanging between them.

Aurélie lifted her chin. 'I hadn't realised how alone I felt until tonight. When you came…' She paused, trying to find the words.

'When I came, what, Aurélie?'

She could listen to him saying her name for ever, in that smoke and suede voice that undid her every time.

'I can't explain.'

His thumb brushed her cheek, slowing to swipe her bottom lip. She shivered. It felt as if a fine wire tightened between her mouth and her breasts.

'Like there's a link between us?' he murmured.

'As if I recognised you, knew you, though you're a complete stranger.' It was a relief to admit it, however crazy it sounded. Her hand tightened on his arm. She revelled in the connection, as if claiming him.

'I feel the same.' He shook his head, his expression grave. 'I don't want to leave, Aurélie. I want to be with you. Spend the night making love to you.'

Relief was a sigh of breath as her lungs emptied then refilled.

'Yes.' A smile trembled on her lips. 'I want that too.'

Lightning flashed in his eyes and surely a jagged bolt struck her too. She felt the heat solder her feet to the floor.

'Aurélie.' He shook his head as if he couldn't quite believe it. 'You know I'm passing through. I won't be back—'

'Shh.' Her finger on his lips stopped his words. 'I know this is only for tonight.' She hesitated a second then added, 'I'm leaving here too. I don't think I'll return.'

It was the first time she'd said it out loud. It felt like crossing into unknown territory.

Whereas, remarkably, planning to have sex with a man she'd met just hours ago felt perfectly normal.

She needed this, needed Lucien with a force she couldn't comprehend yet couldn't doubt. Whatever the reason, this felt real and right.

For once she'd do something for herself, not because it was demanded by others. Just as, later, she'd move from the only town she'd known and begin the new life she'd dreamed about.

For one slow, delicious moment their gazes held and time stood still. Then Lucien bent his head and his mouth brushed hers, soft as a drifting snowflake, teasing her lips. Aurélie looped her arms around his neck and rose on tiptoe, responding, inviting, urging.

A second later her body was plastered against his, pulled close by strong arms lashing her to him. Lucien delved into her mouth and she welcomed him, stroking tongue against tongue, feeling a churning hollow ache low in her body as their kiss moved from tantalising to erotically charged in seconds.

His naked torso, the solidity of those hard thighs against her own, the absolute certainty of their kiss, as if they weren't strangers but lovers who'd been apart too long and came together instinctively—all made her long for more.

Aurélie had no recollection of moving to the bedroom. But stripping Lucien, *that* was clear in her mind. The sound of his zip louder than her drumming heartbeat. The drag of fabric down his hips to pool at his bare feet. The phenomenal heat of his lower body. That glimpse in the half-dark of his erection that made every feminine part of her soften in readiness.

His hands on her clothes were deft yet gentle. Her ears echoed with whispered words of praise as he eased off her shirt, kissing the bare flesh of her shoulder with a desperation she felt with every snatched breath.

Briefly she considered suggesting they take this slow, wondering if her limited experience might be a handicap. But the idea dissolved as his naked body touched hers. She didn't care about lack of technique when he lowered himself beside her, flesh against searing flesh.

Maybe it was Lucien who made this seem inevitable and perfect. Maybe it was a feminine instinct she'd barely been aware of previously. But there was no fumbling, no uncertainty.

Instead of covering her body with his, Lucien explored her with hands and mouth, learning what she liked. Which was everything, including the slide of his strong body down hers, making her pulse thrum and her breath catch. He worshipped her breasts with his mouth and watching him loosened something inside her, making her shudder with the need for release.

But she wasn't submissive. She was curious about his body, pleased when he let her push him onto his back so she could explore.

He was perfectly formed, taut, silky skin over muscle and bone, and she wanted to feast on him. Lucien gasped when she bit his earlobe and trailed her fingers across his hipbone. She moved lower, discovering the taste and texture of him. When she licked his nipple he muttered something gruff and unintelligible into her hair as his whole body trembled.

Aurélie took him in her hand, fascinated by the combination of velvet softness over iron-hard arousal. Trailing touches gave way to deliberate caresses, a tighter grip that made him sigh and his hand close over hers, guiding her. She loved giving him pleasure, watching his big form grow rigid. She was bending to take him in her mouth when he hauled her up his body, his hand between her legs turning her protest into a sigh of delight.

They didn't speak beyond fractured gasps or groans of pleasure and encouragement. Through it all ran a sense of rightness, that their coming together was as natural as spring following long, cold winter.

Aurélie blossomed beneath his touch and his tenderness. When, finally, Lucien sheathed himself and settled between her thighs, his gaze holding hers as their bodies merged, it was so easy it felt like coming home.

Home to a wonderful place where every yearning was satisfied.

For long moments neither moved.

Then, abruptly, it was too much, the need for completion too overwhelming.

Lucien moved and she rose to meet him, soles planted on the mattress as she lifted into his caress. Murmuring words of encouragement, he slid his hand beneath her, bringing them into even closer alignment. Control shattered. Their movements quickened, his thrusts taking him deeper than she'd thought possible as she clung to his wide shoulders.

Her brain scrambled, bombarded by so many sensations. The one constant was that amber gaze, holding her safe, as his body took her higher and higher till their climax engulfed them simultaneously.

Passion escalated from glorious to sublime. The world fell away and they became the whole universe, hearts beating in unison, mouths fused, bodies clinging as rapture stormed in, shattering them and then reforming them again.

Her body, her mind, and even her soul, basked in glory. And through it all she held Lucien close, needing him but wanting to protect him too.

Lucien's heart raced, his whole body wrung out from ecstasy, yet despite the exhaustion he felt triumph and gratitude to the woman already fast asleep in his arms.

He should sleep too. They'd spent the whole night making love, tenderly then urgently, then with laughter and finally now, as grey dawn lightened the sky, with a silent, hungry passion that scoured him to the bone.

Because their night together could only be that, a solitary night.

It seemed preposterous when, with Aurélie, the woman whose surname he didn't know and never would, he'd discovered more than solace from grief. He'd found, somehow, the part of himself that had gone missing when he'd heard of Justin's death. He wasn't healed. His grief was too big for that, but Aurélie had given something of herself, or perhaps they'd created something miraculous together, that filled the gaping hole in his heart. At least enough for him to face what must be faced.

He smiled against her hair, inhaling her delicate floral scent, enjoying the way her unbound curls tickled his skin.

Or maybe his imagination was running riot because he'd just had the best sex of his life.

His smile flattened. No. It was more than that. It had been more than that from the moment he'd seen her. Sexual attraction was easy to identify. What he couldn't name was the other thing between them. It drew them like old friends reuniting or lovers together again after a long absence.

He huffed out a breath, half hoping Aurélie would wake. But she was out for the count. While he'd spent the evening brooding over his troubles, she'd been on her feet for hours, working.

Lucien recalled the touch of her hands on his body. They weren't soft hands, though they spun magic easily, whether tender or demanding. This was a woman who worked hard, not some pampered socialite.

His own hand slid down the amazing curves of her body, from her ribs to the tight sweep in to her waist then up her hip, lingering there as she shifted in her sleep and murmured something he couldn't catch.

It struck him that he'd give a lot to be able to do this again. Every night in fact. Imagine coming home to Aurélie. To those big brown eyes that seemed to understand so much. To her pragmatic, understated sympathy. To her warmth and generosity, her passion and...

Lucien slammed an iron door on his thoughts.

It couldn't be.

Even thinking about it could only bring regret and pain.

Softly he pressed one last kiss to the side of her neck, heard her sigh and felt her tiny wriggle against him, as if even in sleep she needed to be close.

He knew the feeling.

Slowly, determined not to wake her, he withdrew his arm from under her and slid out of the bed.

It took enormous willpower to dress and turn away. He paused in the minuscule living room, switching off the light they'd left burning all night.

As he did, his gaze went to the chess board. A pawn had dropped to the floor, probably when they'd kissed. It was

hard and cold in his hand and for a moment Lucien felt again
the desperation that had risen inside him yesterday, along
with the grief of loss. He'd felt like a pawn, being shuffled
around some cosmic chess board without the right to choose
his own direction. His future was being mapped out for him
by forces beyond his control.

This morning, as he placed the small piece on the board,
his gaze swept to another piece, taller and distinctive.

He breathed out slowly, feeling his chest swell and fall.
Now he felt the calm of acceptance. There was no use fight-
ing fate. He had a duty to perform and he wouldn't shirk.
Both his cousin and his uncle would have expected it of him.
More, he knew in his heart that he'd never live with himself
if he didn't do this, even if it felt like nothing but sacrifice.

He allowed himself one last look over his shoulder, heart
squeezing at the picture of pale limbs and tumbled bright
hair. Aurélie would only be a memory in his new life.

Lucien opened the door and quietly left.

CHAPTER THREE

A couple of months later Aurélie looked at the shabby back-pack at her feet and wished she'd done the sensible thing and checked into a hostel as planned.

She'd had it worked out. Find somewhere cheap to stay. Have a hot shower after the long bus trip and change into the set of good clothes she'd bought.

But there were roadworks in the capital and the bus had taken a detour through the picturesque old town with its quaint buildings and arched lanes. When it stopped right before the Vallort royal palace it had seemed like providence and Aurélie had taken that as a positive sign.

Besides, today was one of the days part of the royal palace was open to the public. It was already late, due to delays on the journey. If she found a hostel and returned here she might be too late to get in.

So here she was, sitting on a gilt chair in the corner of a grand reception room, being stared at by a granite-faced guard. He and another staff member had told her multiple times that there was no point waiting. But wait she did, feeling totally out of place and more than a little daunted.

She'd tried before, via phone and email, but had been fobbed off. Speaking to a VIP who didn't want to talk to you or who hadn't told their staff to allow contact from you was impossible.

Aurélie leaned back in the uncomfortable chair and pretended interest in the frescoed ceiling which, according to the guidebook, was a masterpiece of baroque art.

Above her on the painted surface stood a figure draped in ermine, some grand King of Vallort, surrounded by courtiers and family. She scrutinised his face but, in his wig and regalia and wearing that expression of serene arrogance, he bore little resemblance to the man she'd come to see. Around him fat cherubs strung garlands and elegant women who wore nothing but fabric improbably draped around their hips looked on approvingly. Maybe they were goddesses. No one seemed to notice their state of undress.

Aurélie folded her arms and told herself if they didn't mind being here half naked she surely couldn't feel underdressed in faded jeans, boots and her favourite red turtleneck pullover. It was just that she was nervous, her heart beating high in her throat.

She wished she'd found time to change into her dress and heels. Her foot tapped nervously and a churning in her stomach spoke of fear.

Fear that, after coming all this way, she'd be fobbed off. Fear that there was no way of getting a private message to—

'Ms Balland?' A thin man in an impeccably cut suit emerged from a door in the gilded panelling.

Aurélie shot to her feet. 'Yes, that's me.'

'I'm sorry to keep you waiting. But I'm afraid your request is impossible. People don't walk into the palace unannounced and demand an appointment.'

'Request. I *requested* an appointment.'

'Nevertheless…'

'Believe me, if I'd been able to make an appointment in the normal way, I would have. I tried and every time was told it's impossible.' She heard her voice waver on the last word and swallowed hard. She wouldn't be put off this time.

The man smiled as if sympathising, but his eyes remained watchful. 'If you'd like to tell me why you believe you need this interview—'

'No!' Her voice rose and the security guard stirred as if expecting her to run amok. She took a deep breath, searching for calm, despite the unease feathering her spine and the queasy cramp of her belly.

'In that case, I'm afraid I can't assist you. But—' his

raised hand forestalled her protest '—if you leave a note
I'll see it's delivered.'

Aurélie was already shaking her head before he stopped
talking. Any note would be opened and vetted by staff. 'This
is a private matter.'

'Ah.'

To her surprise that one syllable sounded almost understanding. She looked at the bureaucrat, only to find he
wasn't watching her face but her hand, pressed low to her
abdomen. Hastily Aurélie moved her arm to her side, heat
flooding her cheeks as his gaze snapped to hers.

Suddenly, instead of feeling desperate and annoyed at
the hurdles she faced, Aurélie felt vulnerable. And even
more nervous.

Her breath came in shallow gasps. The cherubs above
her seemed to tilt and she realised the chocolate bar she'd
had on the bus was no substitute for a proper breakfast.
Or lunch.

To her surprise the man said, 'Perhaps this one time I
might venture to make an exception. Come with me, please.'

From the corner of her vision she saw the security guard's
eyes widen. Then the grey-suited man scooped up her pack
and led her into a part of the palace the public never saw.

Aurélie finally had what she needed—the chance of a
face-to-face meeting.

Why did that make her feel as if she'd burned her bridges?

Lucien ignored the vibration of his phone in his pocket.
Again.

Instead he watched Ilsa walk up the aisle towards him,
as beautiful as ever in high heeled boots, tailored trousers
and a top of muted gold that matched her hair. Late afternoon light angled through the cathedral's stained-glass
windows, so that as she reached him she was bathed in
jewel colours.

She met his stare and smiled briefly. Ilsa, the girl he'd

known years before, had grown into a lovely woman. Poised, elegant and good-natured. No wonder Justin had been happy to make her his bride in a dynastic marriage.

Lucien wished he could be more enthusiastic now he'd reluctantly stepped into his cousin's shoes. For with Justin's death, Lucien had stepped not only into his shoes but his crown and all his obligations.

Including the promise to marry the Princess of Altbourg.

Surprisingly it was only Ilsa who'd questioned his willingness. Not because she'd loved Justin, but because she knew Lucien hadn't been raised, like Justin, to expect a marriage of convenience. She'd been one of the few who fully understood the seismic shift in his life, catapulted from private citizen to King in a single day. The only others who truly recognised that were Felix, his royal secretary, and a few close friends.

Lucien breathed deep, aware of the air shuddering into his tight lungs. Of his rigid spine and shoulders, the ache at the base of his skull.

'Excellent,' said the archbishop to Ilsa. 'Then your father will place your hand in His Majesty's.'

They stood together before the old man as he went through the ceremony, describing each detail, ensuring they understood not only the process but its significance.

As if they didn't both already know!

Everything was riding on this marriage. It would join their two countries. Another step on the road to finalising plans that had been in the making for almost twenty years. A step towards an exclusive economic and trade zone between their nations. A symbol of hope and renewal to a country still reeling from the loss of two much-loved royals.

It would change Lucien's life for ever.

There would be no divorce, no separation if he and Ilsa couldn't make their relationship work. It would work because they'd *make* it work. It was expected, necessary.

Lucien drew in a slow breath, inhaling the pungent scent of lilies massed beside the altar. A shiver rolled up his spine to curl around his neck.

The over-rich perfume reminded him of the double funeral here two months ago. Justin's coffin and Uncle Joseph's had rested where Lucien stood now. There'd been hothouse lilies then too, arrangements of foliage and flowers. Green and white for the royal house of Vallort.

'Your Majesty?'

He blinked and realised the archbishop was waiting for him. Beside him Ilsa wore a hint of a frown.

'I'm sorry. Would you mind repeating that?'

'I said, at that point you'll be able to kiss your bride.'

Lucien nodded. 'Good. I see. And then?'

The clergyman hurried on to describe the rest of the procedure. Leaving Lucien to ponder how doing what he knew to be right, because it was his duty, could feel so wrong.

He tried to imagine kissing the woman beside him and couldn't. As for taking her to bed…

His lungs clamped.

No matter how beautiful his fiancée, and how necessary this marriage, when he thought of being naked with a woman it was a woman with fiery hair and fascinating brown eyes.

Lucien was no fool. He knew these were natural reservations about a cold-blooded marriage of convenience. Until now his love-life had been anything but cold-blooded.

As for the way his thoughts kept returning to Aurélie, it was probably because she'd been there when he needed someone. When his world turned inside out and he'd felt helpless in the vortex of loss.

At last the archbishop finished and it was time to walk down the aisle. Once they reached the cathedral's massive doors the rehearsal would be over.

He couldn't wait. With a brief smile for his bride-to-be

he hooked her hand over his arm and led her away, telling himself his qualms about marriage would settle.

In the shadows something caught his eye. Felix, his private secretary, stood there, face unreadable.

Yet his stance, his very stillness, communicated a warning. Lucien had weathered the challenges of the past two months fairly well but he always felt he barely juggled the multitude of royal demands. Now he sensed a problem, his nape tingling in presentiment.

They reached the front of the cathedral and Felix approached. The archbishop had followed them and Ilsa turned to him, listening to him reminisce about the last royal wedding held here.

'Felix.' Lucien beckoned. 'What is it?'

'Something you need to know about immediately.' Felix's voice dropped and Lucien saw his gaze flicker to their companions. 'You have a visitor. I thought it best not to leave her in the palace's public rooms. The fewer who know about her the better.'

'There's a woman to see me?' He caught Ilsa's curious glance and lowered his voice. 'I don't see the problem.'

Felix had been Uncle Joseph's secretary. Lucien had never seen him flustered or unable to deal with a problem.

'I couldn't leave her alone in an office with so many confidential records, but I didn't want to bring anyone in to stay with her in case they learned too much about her.' Felix cleared his throat. 'The young woman refuses to state her business. She says it's strictly for your ears only.'

Lucien raised his brows. Growing up in the country's ruling family he knew they attracted their share of cranks and fantasists.

'Surely you can deal with her.'

Felix shook his head. 'You need to see her.' He drew a slow breath and leaned closer. 'If I'm not mistaken her health is…fragile. I brought her through the private passage and she's waiting in the anteroom.'

'She's *here*?'

Lucien shot a look towards a dark corner of the building. There was a small chamber, usually locked, and beyond that a private passage the royal family used to cross between the cathedral and the palace next door. As he looked the carved wooden door cracked open and he glimpsed a figure wearing dark trousers and a vibrant red top.

'Her name is—'

'Aurélie!' The name shot from Lucien like a bullet from a gun. His breath jammed in his lungs while his heart hammered.

The archbishop turned, and Ilsa too. The door swung shut, blocking out the woman who'd stood there. Lucien had only seen her for a second but couldn't mistake her, even if her hair looked muted in the dark shadows.

His heart pounded and the skin around his nape grew tight. 'What do you mean, she's unwell?'

Felix flashed him a warning glance then turned to answer a question from the archbishop.

'Lucien? What's wrong?' Ilsa moved closer, curious.

Lucien forced down his confusion and shock. 'I'm sorry, Ilsa. I didn't mean to startle you. Felix has an unexpected visitor he wants me to see. That's all.'

As he spoke, Lucien felt another frisson of warning. This time it skated the full length of his spine. Aurélie had understood that they'd only ever share a single night. What brought her here?

He put his hand to his fiancée's elbow, steering her towards the main entrance. 'What time is your appointment? Your car will be waiting.'

She surveyed him with clear eyes. He saw she was curious but Ilsa was too polite to probe. She glanced at her elegant gold watch. 'You're right. It's time I left.'

Minutes later, with Ilsa on her way to meet friends, and Felix steering the archbishop away with questions about the wedding, Lucien made for the royal antechamber.

* * *

Aurélie felt sick.

A different sort of sickness to the nausea she'd felt in the gilded palace. The royal secretary had offered her coffee and her stomach had rebelled at the smell. She'd only just made it to the bathroom in time, chalking up the experience to her first ever bout of morning sickness.

What a time to begin!

The. Worst. Possible. Time.

She'd felt shuddery and weak, and worried that he'd guessed the reason for her illness.

She gnawed her lip and paced the small room.

What she felt now wasn't morning sickness; this was distress.

Because she'd seen Lucien with his bride-to-be. Rehearsing their wedding.

The first time she'd peeped out of the door she'd seen the pair of them hand in hand before the altar. Lucien handsome in a dark suit and his fiancée stunningly beautiful with her poise, her gold hair and couture clothes.

Aurélie's palm slipped across her flat abdomen as if in reassurance that everything was okay.

But nothing was okay. Everything was topsy-turvy.

It had taken such courage to come here, seeking out Lucien. She hadn't expected to barge in on his wedding rehearsal!

Gingerly she sank onto a hard-backed chair as her knees began to wobble.

The last weeks had been one shock after another. She'd told herself everything would be okay. Billions of women faced pregnancy at some point.

But many of those had a supportive partner or family.

Aurélie had neither.

More, she was finally on the verge of achieving her dream of attending university. A goal fostered all those years ago by her mother who'd encouraged her to dream big. Now that looked like being put on hold, again. How could she move to the city, support herself and study full-time? Once the baby arrived…

The door swung open and there he was.

Lucien. Her one-night lover.

He looked different. Had he lost weight? Maybe it was seeing him in the exquisitely tailored suit, complete with mirror gloss shoes and a perfectly knotted crimson tie. His hair, which had been just a little over-long before—tempting her to run her fingers through it—was impeccably styled.

He looked like what he was. No longer her sexy stranger but the King of Vallort.

That had been another shock. She'd set about searching online for him, expecting it would be like looking for a needle in a haystack. Instead she'd had immediate success.

If you called it a success to discover the man you'd slept with was a king. And that he was about to marry another woman.

Aurélie got to her feet. 'Your Majesty.'

Something passed across his face. A ripple of emotion gone so quickly she couldn't identify it.

'It *is* you.' He didn't approach, but stood inside the door.

That was the instant Aurélie realised part of her, the part that had listened to fairy tales at her mother's knee, had imagined him striding across the small room and sweeping her into his arms.

Not that she expected a happy ever after. She was no Cinderella.

But they'd shared so much that night. The experience had been a shining beacon in a drab world of disappointment and dull, grey mundanity.

Now she realised the glow she felt whenever she recalled that night was one-sided. Judging by his grim mouth and furrowed brow, Lucien didn't share her fond memories. His jawline was sharply defined and his eyes…she couldn't re-member his eyes looking so cold. Even when she'd found him half-frozen on the street. Then he'd looked blank and bewildered. Now he simply looked hard.

'Why are you here, Aurélie? What do you want?'

And hello to you too!

Okay, so a warm welcome wasn't on the cards. But did he need to sound so brusque?

Disappointment merged with outrage. Clearly her memories of their night together were rose-tinted. This was the real Lucien. The one she remembered was a mirage.

'I came to see you.' She found her hands twisting together in front of her and put them behind her back so he couldn't see them. 'We need to talk.'

'Are you all right? Felix thought you weren't well.'

Did that mean Lucien cared after all? Yet she didn't feel that warmth of connection that had made that night so amazing.

Her breath eased out in a disappointed sigh.

'I'm fine.' Except that her life wasn't her own any more. Nor was her body. As for her long-delayed plans, they were dying before her eyes.

I'm scared. I'm totally out of my depth.

But looking up into that stern face, Aurélie would never admit that. Not to this man who was more a stranger than the Lucien she'd known in Annecy.

'Then why are you here? And now of all times?' That was when she heard it, a trace of anger.

She lifted her chin, refusing to let his temper daunt her. Her father and stepmother had treated her like a slave, hurling abuse if she didn't anticipate their needs. She would *not* be bullied by this man too.

'I didn't plan to arrive when you were…' Her throat constricted and she waved a hand in the direction of the aisle where he'd walked with his oh-so-suitable fiancée. 'Rehearsing for your wedding.'

One dark eyebrow arched and she was treated to a stare as supercilious as any she'd ever seen.

It was on the tip of her tongue to tell him she wasn't awed by royalty. France was a staunch republic and had guillotined one king.

'No?' The single syllable carried a weight of distrust.

'No!' She took a slow breath and sought calm. 'Can we sit?' She looked around at the couple of hard wooden chairs.

'I prefer to stand. I don't have much time. I'm needed elsewhere.'

It was probably true. Yet it sounded like a personal insult. As if she were some footnote in his personal history that he'd rather forget.

Which meant she probably had her answer already. It had been pointless coming here. But she needed to be certain.

Aurélie drew a deep breath. Telling herself it didn't matter that this man was royal. That she wasn't daunted by his fancy clothes or the fact she looked washed out and travel-weary in old jeans.

'I came all this way because something's happened.'

She faltered to a stop, horrified at how emotional she felt, sharing her news with an uncaring stranger. She swiped her tongue around her dry lips and forced herself to continue.

'I'm pregnant, Lucien. You're going to be a father.'

CHAPTER FOUR

LUCIEN HEARD THE words but couldn't process them.

Usually he was a quick thinker. In his architectural practice he coped easily with change, whether the result of difficult clients, challenging sites or his own inspiration. In the last couple of months he'd risen to one challenge after another, shedding his old life and acquiring responsibility for a kingdom.

Today he felt mired, his reactions slow.

Because the last time he'd set foot in here it had been to bury his family? Because he felt trapped in a nightmare?

But this was no dream. Aurélie was real.

Hungrily he ate up the sight of her with her vibrant hair and all that remembered softness beneath the bright red pullover. She was a burst of flame and heat in a world of chill bleakness.

He wanted to reach out and touch her. Haul her to him and keep her close, like a talisman, a reminder that there was light in the world.

'A father?' He shook his head.

Lucien understood the words but applying them to himself seemed impossible. It had been just one night.

One memorable night.

Brutally, he cut short the memories. He couldn't go there. Not when he had a fiancée, a whole nation, depending on him.

'You're sure?'

Lucien searched her face, finally noting her tension and her pallor. Initially all he'd registered was her miraculous presence. Then the bright colour she wore and that gorgeous hair.

And a tide of something that felt almost like relief, running hot through his belly.

The mouth he remembered as lush and soft flattened into a crooked line. 'You think I'd go to the trouble of locating you and come all this way if it wasn't true?'

'No.' It was there in her face. Aurélie wasn't lying.

An invisible fist punched him in the ribs, winding him.

Now Felix's words made sense. Beneath that feistiness she looked fragile. That hint of vulnerability scraped at his protective instincts.

'Sit down, please.' He gestured to the chair behind her.

'I thought you were in a rush?'

Lucien hadn't seen that proud, argumentative angle to her jaw before. Stupid to find it attractive, given the gravity of their situation. Yet he felt a tug of pleasure, deep in his belly, at the sight of her flashing stare and up-tilted chin.

Or maybe it was relief in recognising she wasn't as weak as he'd feared.

'You look like a strong breeze would knock you over. Sit, Aurélie. This is no time for pride.'

Lucien took a chair at right angles to hers. He saw pique war with weariness before she subsided onto the seat.

'Talk to me.'

She frowned. 'I've told you. I'm going to have a baby. There's nothing else to tell you.'

Of course there was. Lucien wanted to hear how she'd found out. How she felt about it. How she was faring.

Except she was right. He wasn't simply Lucien, talking to a one-time lover. He was a king faced with news that could wreak havoc in his kingdom. Like it or not he had other priorities he couldn't ignore.

'Have you been to a doctor? Had a test?'

'Yes and yes. I'm two months pregnant and so far everything is going normally.'

His gaze dropped to her bright red pullover. There was no sign of a bulge. But maybe it was too early for that. Lucien knew next to nothing about pregnant women.

Or babies.

Like a brick thrown through plate glass, reality smashed into him. In seven months there was going to be a living, breathing baby. A squirming, squalling bundle needing care and love. Not just in seven months but in all the years that followed.

Lucien sat back, his spine colliding with unyielding wood, his breath escaping in a whoosh of air.

'What's so funny?'

'Funny?' Then he realised his mouth had curled up at the edges. It must look to her like a smile but in fact it was a grimace of shock.

Was there anything else fate could throw at him?

He'd lost his family. The only people he truly loved in the world. He'd been forced to give up the career he'd worked so hard at and reinvent himself as a royal. He'd even agreed to take on a wife he didn't love in a marriage he didn't want.

Now it seemed he was going to be a father.

He shook his head. He doubted Aurélie would sympathise. She had her own problems.

'Nothing at all.' He drew a slow breath and fixed his gaze on hers. 'You say it's my baby?'

Her response was instant, as if a bolt of lightning shot through her. She stiffened, nostrils flaring and eyes narrowing. The hands in her lap clenched hard. 'I wouldn't be here if there was any doubt.'

It confirmed Lucien's instincts about her.

Yet, it pained him to admit it, his new position changed things.

Lucien the private individual might be satisfied with Aurélie's word, but now he was Lucien the leader of a nation, and he had a duty to be careful. Especially as he recalled his cousin Justin fielding two separate paternity claims from women who'd liked the idea of becoming Queen. One had been a complete stranger who'd never met Justin.

The other an ex-lover whose baby was conceived months after they'd split.

'So you won't object to investigators looking into your recent past, to check for other lovers?'

Her warm brown eyes turned chilly and her skin seemed to shrink back against her bones, making her look starkly fragile.

'I do object but I suspect I have no choice if that's what you plan to do.'

Guilt eddied inside. But no matter his personal inclinations, Lucien had to do this. If he didn't, others would. He didn't want anyone else interrogating Aurélie.

'And you'll agree to a paternity test?'

She shot to her feet, pacing across the small space then spinning on the ball of her foot and stalking back to stand before him, hands on hips and breasts heaving as she struggled to contain her emotions.

She looked magnificent. An embodiment of pure energy. And, he admitted, spontaneous sexuality. A few strands of her glorious hair had escaped to frame her face. Her pallor was banished by a flush of what he guessed was fury and her eyes sparkled.

Lucien curled his hands into fists on his thighs as temptation assailed him. He wanted to touch her, try to connect with all that sizzle and snapping electricity.

'You're calling me a liar?'

Slowly he rose, still battling the urge to reach for her. To warm himself with her glowing heat. To wrap his arms around her, seeking that sense of wondrous peace she'd given him.

Lucien shook his head. 'Put yourself in my position, Aurélie.' His voice bottomed out on her name, as if saying it scraped his senses raw. 'I'm a king. My children will stand in line to inherit a throne. I owe it to my people to be sure about this.'

Before his eyes she seemed to shrink in on herself. Her

hands lifted to rub up and down her arms, as if warming herself against a sudden chill. Lucien hated that she felt that way because of him. Her spontaneity and generous warmth were so precious.

'And to your fiancée,' she reminded him.

Lucien's jaws clamped.

Ilsa. As if he needed reminding. How was he supposed to explain this to his bride-to-be?

For a moment he let himself wonder if this could be sufficient reason to cancel the royal wedding.

But this deal was bigger than either of them. It was about the future of their countries. Plans for this royal match were an unstoppable juggernaut. Even an unexpected baby wouldn't undo that.

'I won't do anything that might endanger the baby.' Aurélie folded her arms across her chest. 'If there's any risk at all to its health then you'll have to wait till after it's born to do your test.'

'Agreed.' Lucien knew nothing about how paternity tests worked but that was fair enough. He couldn't ask Aurélie to risk the baby's well-being.

'I didn't come to make trouble.' Her gaze held his and this time the glacial chill was absent. 'I thought you had a right to know you're going to be a father.'

Her mouth crimped at the corners and pain sliced through Lucien. He'd barely had time to consider how much of a burden Aurélie was carrying.

'I understand.'

He didn't, of course. He was still processing her news, but it took no imagination to understand that however big a shock this was to him it must be more for the woman carrying his child.

His child.

Emotion sideswiped him. Aurélie was most likely carrying his baby. Once more his gaze swooped down to that flat belly behind the bright wool. He remembered kissing her there. The soft cushion of her skin fragrant beneath his cheek.

Arousal juddered through him, instantaneous and shockingly real, yanking him out of this cool little chamber and straight back to her bed.

'Please sit down, Aurélie. I meant it when I said you look unsteady on your feet.'

Slowly she subsided onto the hard chair. It struck him that he should take her somewhere more comfortable. Somewhere warm and cosy. But this place had one huge benefit. They'd be uninterrupted.

'What *did* you expect in coming here?' He knew it had been no small feat. How had she got past the royal minders to Felix?

'Sorry?'

'You said I had the right to know about the baby. But what are your plans? What do you want, Aurélie?'

'You *do* think I came here to...what? Extort money from you?'

'I mean, do you want to keep the child?'

'Oh!' Her eyes rounded and one slim hand slid across her abdomen. It was such an inherently protective gesture and it told him so much about Aurélie.

Relief feathered the back of his neck. No matter how many complications a termination would remove.

'Yes, I think so.'

Think so? He sat straighter, every sense on alert. 'You're considering a termination?'

She shook her head and met his stare, her chin again taking on that determined cast. 'I know it might be simpler. Neither of us planned on a child. But I don't want a termination.' She paused and he felt the weight of her regard like a touch. 'It's crazy. I've never felt particularly maternal and I've already spent enough time looking after little kids. But, despite the burden, I don't feel comfortable just...ending this.'

'You see this baby as a burden?' It shouldn't surprise him. He wasn't the one who'd have to carry it then give birth to it, yet Lucien wanted his baby to be wanted. What future could it have with a woman who only grudgingly accepted it?

'Of course it's a burden.' Her eyes flashed. 'It might be a miracle and if the mothers I know are to be believed, it could be the most wonderful thing in my life. But nothing is that straightforward. I have plans...*had* plans...and they don't include a child.' She spread her hands. 'I still need to think that through.'

'What sort of plans?' A man? Was that what she meant?

'To study. I've dreamed for so long about going to university and I won a place too. But I already had to defer my studies once to help my family.' She looked down at her hands, now pleating the edge of her pullover. 'It's important to me to better myself. It's what kept me going through... things. But how can I study and support myself and look after a child too? I'll be giving birth around the time the academic year starts.'

Her words reminded him how little he knew of Aurélie. Of her upbringing, her dreams and how it was that she'd spent time looking after young children.

'What about family support?'

Her mouth twisted. 'I'm on my own.'

No mistaking the finality of her tone.

'Then you came here so I can support you.'

Her head rocked back. 'I came here because I respected your need to know. I was acting responsibly. But now you mention it, would it be so wrong to expect my child's father to help out in caring for it?'

Lucien thought of all the press coverage there'd been of his engagement and approaching wedding. He thought of the huge disparity between his wealth, even before he'd inherited the throne, and a waitress's wages. Of her tiny apartment tucked in the eaves of an old building and his luxurious lifestyle.

Of course she'd come to him.

'So,' he murmured, 'after coming all this way, I assume you have a figure in mind?'

CHAPTER FIVE

AURÉLIE BENT AT the waist, hunching protectively as Lucien's words hit. They were bites against soft flesh, a tearing ache through her middle.

Her eyes snapped wide open and she saw her shock reflected back on his face, as if he too were taken aback by what he'd said.

He'd accused her of putting a price on her baby's head, coming to extort payment.

'Aurélie, that didn't come out right.'

She stumbled to her feet, ignoring his words. They seemed to come from a long distance, indistinguishable over the roaring blood in her ears.

Her lips twisted as the sour tang of disillusionment filled her mouth.

She'd thought better of Lucien. She'd imagined...

That was the problem. She'd imagined too much. He was simply a man who'd had no-strings-attached sex with her. Everything she thought she knew about him was suspect.

All she knew for sure was what he did and said. Today that wasn't edifying.

Aurélie swung round and wrenched open the door to the passage she'd followed from the palace.

An arm shot out in front of her, blocking her way.

She stared at the hand anchored on the doorjamb and remembered those long fingers caressing her, making her body thrum in pleasure.

Frantically she dragged in a deep breath, only to find it scented with something that reminded her of mountain forests and the sultry heat of sex.

'Wait, Aurélie. We need to talk.'

She surveyed the fine suit fabric of his sleeve in a designer shade of charcoal. The pristine white cuff, secured with a heavy cufflink. The watch that must have cost more than she'd earn as a waitress in a decade.

Everything reinforced the yawning gap between them. They were no longer equals. No matter what she did or said, Lucien would believe she wanted his money.

She should stay and negotiate a settlement because the baby would need it, given her meagre savings. But the voice of logic was drowned by pain.

Aurélie shuddered. 'We've talked.'

She needed somewhere to lick her wounds and think about what to do next.

Quickly she ducked, scooting under his imprisoning arm and into the flagstoned passage. Her breathing was raw, her lungs aching as she almost ran. From just behind came the sound of footsteps.

'Aurélie, please! At least slow down. These flagstones are uneven. You don't want to trip and injure yourself or the baby.'

That stopped her mid-stride. She flung her arm out to the panelled wall for support and drew a shuddering breath. In the light from the high windows she saw the worn stones were uneven.

It wasn't like her to panic, yet she felt that skittering sensation, the urge to flee.

Because she'd hoped Lucien would live up to the idea of him she'd built in her imagination. If he wasn't real then she was more alone than ever.

Aurélie dropped her hand from the wall.

She was stronger than that. She'd learned self-reliance long ago. She'd cope, no matter how overwhelming everything seemed.

Slowly she stepped forward, concentrating on putting one foot in front of the other, all the way back to the grand baroque palace where she'd felt so utterly out of place. But it wouldn't be for long. She'd grab her pack and go. She'd find a hostel for the night and tomorrow she'd leave.

A veneer of calm cloaked her as she walked. Even the sound of measured steps following didn't bother her. At least he didn't try to stop her. He must realise she'd had enough.

Through a massive panelled door that thankfully opened easily then right, left and right to the office where she'd left her pack.

All was quiet, even those following footsteps were muted as they passed onto golden-toned wooden floors then thick carpet.

Aurélie pushed open the final door with relief. She'd get her pack and…

Another door opened and there was the secretary, carrying a cafetière. The coffee aroma hit, rich and pungent. She spun on her heel, trying to hold down a rising tide of nausea.

Aurélie blundered into a hard body. Hard and warm. Hands gripped her elbows and she was encompassed by comforting heat. But not comforting enough to stop the sickness.

The secretary spoke from behind her. 'Let her go, Lucien. She's unwell.'

Thankfully those hands released her and she staggered to the now familiar bathroom. She barely had time to snick the lock before she was retching, succumbing to morning sickness.

Fifteen minutes later, Aurélie smoothed her hair, pulling it back into a fresh ponytail. She wished she had lipstick to give her face more colour, but she'd left her purse with her backpack.

What did it matter how she looked when she was leaving? There was no one here she wanted to impress. Yet she felt gauche. This was the second time she'd retreated to be comprehensively ill. She felt washed out and it was an effort to hide her weakness.

What happened to morning sickness being in the morning? She thought of tomorrow's bus ride back to France and winced. It could be very uncomfortable indeed.

Pulling her spine straight, she entered the office. The secretary wasn't there, nor, thankfully was his coffee.

Aurélie would almost rather have faced that when her gaze caught on an intense amber stare that feathered memories through her mind and her body. As if she only had to meet Lucien's gaze to be swept back into the sensual world they'd shared.

She snapped her gaze towards the view of an inner courtyard beyond the desk.

'Do you feel any better?' Lucien sounded concerned. He probably wasn't used to women running from him.

'Thanks. I'm good.' For now. She had no idea if this afternoon's experience was typical of what she could expect. The thought was daunting. 'I need to collect my luggage.'

She looked to where she'd last seen it but Lucien gestured to another door. 'This way.'

Aurélie hesitated. She didn't want to prolong conversation with a man who thought she'd come to take his money. Indignation vied with tiredness.

She entered another office, larger, luxurious, yet clearly a place for serious work. There might be a floor-to-ceiling bookcase on one wall, and comfortable-looking leather sofas either side of a lovely crackling fire, but the mail trays on that big desk were full, and the ergonomic keyboard and sleek computer were all business.

'Please take a seat.'

She shook her head. 'I want my luggage. Then I'll go.'

From the corner of her eye she caught Lucien's frustrated movement, raking his fingers through that impeccably cut dark hair.

'Please, Aurélie. Hear me out for five minutes. Then I promise I won't stand in your way.'

Belatedly she realised where she was. At the heart of the

palace in the King's study. Who else would have an office three times the size of her flat?

She stiffened, ready to refuse. But what would that gain? Besides, Lucien wasn't ordering. He was asking.

Aurélie crossed the beautiful antique carpet and took the corner of a sofa by the fire. It felt like sinking into an embrace and she wondered how she'd find the energy to pull her weary bones away from such comfort and the fire's welcome heat.

It was only after she settled that she saw the plate of cracker biscuits on a side table with a glass of water.

'Firstly, I apologise.' He didn't sit but stood facing her, frowning. 'I insulted you and that wasn't called for. My choice of words was unfortunate.'

'You didn't realise what you were saying?' Aurélie didn't hide her sneer.

'I mean I thought it likely you'd need help. I didn't mean to sound accusing.'

He put his hand on the carved mantelpiece which, she realised, was a work of art, decorated with mountain deer and ibexes. A second later he dropped his arm and shoved his hands in his pockets, clearly ill at ease.

'But you're right.' His eyes met hers. 'If we were still just Aurélie and Lucien my reaction would be different.' His chest rose on a slow breath. 'But I'm not simply Lucien. I'm a monarch with a country depending on me. A fiancée due to marry me in a month.'

'And people want things from you.' Aurélie's voice sounded flat, matching her disappointment.

It was fine to feel insulted that he questioned her motives. Yet she could see his side of things. Not enough to ignore the insult, but enough to try to view this without emotion.

'It's fairer to say I have obligations to others. And I'm still learning to accommodate those.' His mouth tightened and Aurélie remembered how distressed he'd been that night in Annecy, filled with grief.

It was only later, when she'd identified him through press reports, that she'd learned how much Lucien had lost. First his uncle, King of Vallort, who'd raised him like a son after Lucien's parents died during his infancy. Then, a mere day later, in a terrible twist of fate, Lucien's cousin, the heir to the throne, had died when a rockfall hit his car on a private road outside the city.

In two days Lucien had lost his closest family.

He'd had to give up his architectural business and come home to Vallort. Taking the throne he'd never expected to inherit must feel like stepping into dead men's shoes. Men who, presumably, had been dear to him.

Looking at his clouded eyes and taut features, Aurélie knew she should cut him some slack. A man in his position would have to check the child was his. Naturally he'd wonder how much she wanted from him.

Yet distress lingered. Aurélie folded her arms across her chest, trying to hold it in.

'I'm not here to cause a scandal. I don't want to blackmail you or sell my story to the press.'

Lucien nodded. 'But you need my help.'

Did she? Aurélie knew that, come what may, she'd manage. She had too much fighting spirit not to do her best for this baby. Yet doing it on her own would be tough.

'How do *you* feel about the baby, Lucien?'

'Me?' His eyebrows rose as if the question took him by surprise. Had he been too caught up thinking about consequences to consider his feelings? Maybe he didn't have any. Maybe he only saw this unborn child as a problem to be dealt with.

A chill frosted Aurélie's bones, despite the nearby fire. She hunched against the deep cushions.

'You're going to be a father. You must feel something.' This time saying those words had the strangest effect, making it suddenly real. As if the evidence of her own body and the doctor's confirmation weren't enough. An image wavered in Aurélie's mind, of Lucien holding a baby close, his shoulders curved protectively around it. But she couldn't make out his expression. Was he looking tenderly at his child or wishing himself far away?

'I feel…' He paused and reached for the mantelpiece. Firelight cast his features into gold and shadows, highlighting grooves beside his mouth and the strong angle of his jaw. His shoulders rose in a fluid shrug. 'Stunned. Excited.' He paused. 'Nervous.'

He fixed her with a stare as bright as the flames and Aurélie felt relief and warmth pour through her. He wasn't unaffected. The weight pressing down on her lifted a little.

'In awe that you're carrying a new life inside you.' His gaze dropped to her midriff and again she felt it like a caress on bare skin. The sensation didn't seem maternal but sexual, snatching her breath. Desire for Lucien was *not* what she needed.

'Incredibly aware that I know nothing about raising babies.'

Aurélie almost said that was okay because she had experience. But that might imply she thought they'd raise their child together. Nothing was more unlikely.

Yet she had to know.

'Do you want to be involved? As a father?' That was why she'd come. To find out.

Lucien moved so swiftly he took her by surprise. One minute he was standing on the other side of the fireplace, looking brooding and thoughtful, the next he was hunkered before her, his hand capturing hers.

Aurélie concentrated on steadying her breathing, hoping her runaway pulse would ease before he noticed how he affected her. He shouldn't, not now, but—

'Of course! This is my *child*.' He paused and she saw a flicker of expression on his face that might even have been awe. His fingers tightened around hers. 'I'd never turn my back on my child, my family.'

She remembered those headlines about the double tragedy in Vallort. How Lucien had lost his remaining family.

Was that why he was so eager to marry his beautiful Princess? To start making a new one as soon as possible?

Was he in love?

Aurélie ignored the ache behind her ribs. It was none of her business.

Except it would be, if she shared her child with Lucien and his other children from a royal marriage. She tried to imagine ferrying their child between the palace and her flat in Annecy and failed. Besides, she wouldn't be there. She'd have to find a place more suited to raising a child. In her home town? Or would she find a way, somehow, to attend university?

It was too much to think about now. She felt so weary and so disturbed by this man who felt no qualms about holding her hand and invading her space.

Aurélie told herself she didn't want to feel his warmth or inhale that teasing hint of male skin scent. Yet she didn't disengage her hand.

'So, we'll have to work out a way for you to be involved.'

Because the traditional solution, marrying to provide a home for the child they were expecting, was out of the question. He was a king and she was a waitress. There was no question of a match between them, even without his aristocratic bride waiting in the wings.

'We'll find a way.' His hand squeezed hers. 'But not now. You're tired and you've had enough stress for one day.'

He drew her to her feet and Aurélie didn't resist. It was a welcome novelty to have someone concerned for her instead of expecting her to look after them.

She didn't even object when he kept hold of her hand, telling herself she simply found comfort in the touch of another person, after weeks of feeling incredibly alone, worrying how she was going to manage.

At least the nausea had subsided. Her knees were shaky but she'd be fine.

'I'll get my luggage and find a room for the night.' A glance at the window told her it was getting late. She had an impression of looming mountains shrouded in cloud. Spring in this Alpine kingdom was slow coming.

'It's taken care of. Come.' He stepped away, releasing her hand, and she bit down an instinctive objection. Not at someone booking a room, but because her hand felt empty without his.

That was a bad sign.

She followed him, rubbing her palms together, trying to obliterate the sense memory of his touch.

Five minutes later she was lost. Surely it didn't take this long to reach the palace entrance?

Lucien pushed open a door and invited her to precede him. Aurélie stopped in a high-ceilinged room, her breath catching.

It was glorious. The walls were cream but the curtains and upholstery on the antique furniture was a fresh lemon shade that made the heart lift. Vases filled with yellow primroses, snowdrops and blue forget-me-nots gave the elegant room a welcoming feel. Beyond the window was a view of charming old buildings in a range of pastel colours and, rising beyond them, the dark blue slope of a mountain.

'Lucien?'

She turned. His gaze fixed on hers. That stare was so intense the blood in her arteries slowed to a ponderous, thrumming pulse.

Then he moved into the room and the spell broke.

'You need somewhere to stay. The palace has hundreds of rooms so it makes sense to stay here. Your luggage is in your room.' He gestured towards an open door which she assumed led to a bedroom.

Stay under Lucien's roof? In the palace?

His fiancée won't like this.

Aurélie felt sorry for the woman. For all of them. What a mess!

'Tomorrow we'll talk again, discuss some options.'

Slowly she nodded.

'I've organised a doctor to visit you tomorrow too. I know you've had someone confirm the pregnancy, but you should get that morning sickness checked. You seem very fragile.'

Aurélie didn't know whether to be warmed by his concern or worried that she looked so bad.

'Okay.' Truth be told, she'd be glad to talk to someone about the sudden nausea. She knew lots of women suffered with it but hadn't realised how debilitating it could be.

No doubt the doctor would talk to her about a paternity test and how safe it would be for the foetus. She could be sure it would all be very discreet. Presumably that was why Lucien had arranged for her to stay here.

The warmth she'd felt at his thoughtfulness faded.

'Excellent. I'll leave you to rest. A maid will be here soon to draw a bath or do whatever else you need. Tell her what you'd like and dinner will be brought.'

Aurélie nodded, fully understanding, at last, Lucien's generosity. She'd stay in the palace, where she'd have no chance to talk to anyone or arouse curiosity about her reason for visiting Vallort.

Because if that became known there would be a huge scandal.

CHAPTER SIX

'ILSA, I NEED to talk with you about the woman at the cathedral.'

His fiancée's blue gaze met his across the coffee table. 'Is she your girlfriend?'

'No.' Why did it feel like a betrayal to Aurélie to discuss that night? Ilsa was his fiancée. He owed her the truth. 'But we spent a night together.'

She showed no shock. Had she guessed? He'd seen her curious gaze on Aurélie this afternoon.

'Recently?' In other words—after their betrothal?

'Two months ago. The day I heard about Justin.' He paused, scraping his voice from where it stuck to the back of his throat. He'd stepped into his cousin's life, his home and duties, even his engagement, but sometimes even now the pang of loss threatened to undo Lucien. 'I was on my way back here when she and I met. Before our engagement. I didn't set out to betray you.'

Slowly Ilsa nodded. 'I didn't think you would, but this is a dynastic marriage, not a love match.' Her gaze didn't waver. 'So you're not in love with her?'

The word caught him by surprise.

He enjoyed the company of women but he'd never been in love.

His only experience of love wasn't romantic. It was what he'd shared with his aunt and uncle, who'd been like parents, and Justin, as close as any brother could be.

Now he'd discovered how much love cost. An outsider might envy him, inheriting a kingdom and a glamorous bride. Yet Lucien had lived in shadow and pain since the news had broken.

Except once, he realised in shock. One bright spot

when the pain hadn't gone away, but receded enough to be bearable.

With Aurélie…

'You can't fall in love in a night.' He swallowed hard. 'But you can make a baby.'

'Ah.' Ilsa put down her teacup and leaned back against the seat. 'I see. That…complicates things.'

Lucien felt a surge of relief that his fiancée wasn't the sort to indulge in recriminations.

'It does.' With Aurélie's news, everything had altered. *Again.* Once more his world rocked on its axis.

He tried once more to imagine his child, maybe with dark hair, or his height. But his brain refused to cooperate.

Yet he had no difficulty picturing Aurélie round with his child, glowing and maternal. He could even imagine her holding a swaddled baby, but further than that his imagination wouldn't go.

'And she…?'

'Aurélie.'

'Aurélie is going to have the baby?' Ilsa's tone was even, but Lucien saw her tension.

'She is, though she's not sure she's ready to be a mother.' As he didn't feel ready to be a father.

'And you want to be involved? Do you want to marry her?'

Lucien's mouth tightened. He didn't want to marry anyone. But he couldn't say that to Ilsa.

He'd been forced into their engagement by the weight of expectation. The match between the Princess of Altbourg and the King of Vallort had been long planned. The fact that there was a new king hadn't altered those plans.

As for marrying Aurélie… Lucien barely knew her.

Yet the moment he'd seen her today he'd felt that whump of sensation in his chest. The flare of heat he remembered from their night together. It was still there.

But it wasn't love. That was impossible on such a short acquaintance. It was physical attraction.

Lucien unclenched his hands and spread his fingers over his thighs.

The fact that he didn't feel any such reaction to his attractive fiancée told its own story. This royal marriage wasn't about sexual compatibility but duty.

Yet surely he had an obligation to his child? And if he were to imagine spending long winter nights sharing a bed with anyone, his thoughts strayed to—

Lucien pulled himself up. He didn't have the luxury of acting like a private citizen.

'I'm an engaged man and there's no easy way out of our wedding, is there, Ilsa?'

He watched her closely, alert to any sign that she too felt discomfort at what was expected of them. But Ilsa said nothing, silently reinforcing his words. They were both trapped. Lucien's mouth tightened.

'Aurélie and I have nothing in common except the baby she's going to have in seven months.'

Ilsa leaned forward. 'But you want to be involved with the child?'

He inclined his head. 'I'm sorry, Ilsa. I know I'm bringing trouble your way. There'll be gossip and scandal. But I can't walk away from my child.'

Lucien drew a deep breath and felt his tight lungs ease. Despite the consequences, this was one thing he knew for sure. One thing that felt *right*.

'The baby is my responsibility. I have a duty to be involved. I *want* to be involved.'

Lucien knew how important family was. His aunt and uncle had welcomed him into theirs when he was orphaned. He wouldn't be the man he was today but for them. His life could have been so different if he'd been fostered by someone unable to love him like a son.

'I could never shun my own child.'

'I understand.' Perhaps she did. Ilsa knew his history. Besides, she seemed a compassionate woman.

He reached for his coffee and took a sip, to discover it was cold. He put it down, remembering Aurélie's reaction when she'd smelled coffee.

Lucien stiffened, aware his thoughts had strayed. Though Ilsa seemed lost in her own thoughts too.

'The issue,' he said slowly, 'is what to do now.' Being engaged to one woman while having a baby with another would be complicated at the best of times. When he was a newly minted king trying to manage national and international expectations of a royal wedding...

'You say Aurélie doesn't feel ready for motherhood?'

He frowned. 'It's come as a surprise. She had other plans.'

'I'm not disapproving, Lucien, just making sure.' After a moment she sat forward, her forehead crinkling. 'Because I have an idea...'

Morning sun streaming through the windows washed Lucien in warm light as he crossed the sitting room. He wore another perfectly tailored suit. The sunlight caressed his chiselled jaw and the slight furrow along his brow, at odds with his smile of greeting.

Aurélie shifted restlessly on the sofa. Once Lucien had made her feel wonderful. Now his towering presence in the suite where she'd spent the night made her nervous.

Not because he was royal.

Because, despite telling herself yesterday's response to him was due to tiredness and stress, she still felt his sexual pull. Her hormones stirred.

He doesn't want you here. You're a problem to fix.

Her chest squeezed. She felt bereft, knowing they were no longer equals. She yearned for the man he'd been two months ago. An amazing, generous lover who'd made her feel cherished.

'How are you feeling today, Aurélie?'

'Better, thank you. I've been very comfortable.'

That was an out-and-out lie. She'd occupied a grand half-tester bed in a room filled with antiques that looked as if they belonged in a museum. Years before she'd visited the palace at Versailles on an excursion and this place had a similar feel. Aurélie hadn't dared touch the furnishings, afraid she'd damage something priceless. She felt overawed.

At least she'd managed to keep her breakfast down and, despite her imposing surroundings, felt more rested than she had in weeks. She'd been working extra shifts, saving as much as possible for the future. An early night had been a welcome luxury.

'Excellent.' Lucien sat opposite her, his long legs stretched out. He looked relaxed in this stultifying opulence. As if ornately frescoed ceilings, gilt-edged furniture and the do-not-touch air of refinement didn't intimidate him. 'I was worried about you.'

Aurélie's heart jumped. 'You were?'

Their eyes met and she felt a little stab of sensation. It ran straight through her middle, warming her deep, deep inside. She stared into eyes the colour of amber and imagined heat there.

Imagined. To Lucien she was an unwanted complication. What they'd shared in Annecy was over, for him at least.

He frowned. 'You doubt it?'

'I…no.' Of course Lucien cared. He wasn't an ogre. Even if he hadn't been at his best yesterday.

'I asked the doctor to check on you today.'

'She's already been.' Aurélie had been glad to see a female doctor. Had Lucien arranged that specifically? 'She says I'm doing well.'

'And that you need rest.'

Slowly she nodded. 'She said I should try to avoid stress.'

Lucien's eyebrows rose and a wry smile curved his

mouth. For a second it felt as if they shared silent camaraderie. As if stress could be avoided in these circumstances!

An answering smile tugged Aurélie's lips. The moment strung out between them, neither moving. It could only have lasted seconds yet to Aurélie's fertile imagination it seemed as if neither wanted to shatter the connection.

Her thoughts moved to what else she'd discussed with the doctor. The non-invasive paternity test using blood drawn from the mother and a mouth swab from the father. Learning there would be no danger to the baby, Aurélie had asked the doctor to take blood from her arm right away. The sooner Lucien knew the baby was his, the better.

Yet the thought of needing to prove her child's paternity brought her back to reality. This wasn't the sort of relationship she wanted with a man. Where was the trust?

But you're not beginning a relationship with Lucien.

'It would be best if you stayed here.'

'Sorry?'

'I'd like you to stay, as my guest, till you feel better. And till we agree on what we'll do about the baby.'

That was the nub of it—the baby. Lucien might be caring but she wasn't his main concern. What was?

The baby they'd made?

Avoiding scandal?

Pleasing his fiancée?

Aurélie's mouth dried and nausea stirred. She reached for her glass of water, taking a sip, telling herself the sudden discomfort could be dealt with by mind over matter.

'You're sure you're all right?' Lucien leaned in, elbows on his knees.

Aurélie smiled, willing her mouth not to wobble. See, she was fine.

'Yes. Nothing to worry about.' She took another sip of water.

Lucien sat back and she had the impression of energy fiercely leashed. He was waiting for something.

'You came to talk to me.'

'It can wait till you're feeling better. I can see you're not quite yourself.'

Aurélie couldn't help it. She laughed, the sound half amused, half bitter.

'You might have a long wait. I haven't felt normal for a long time.' Even before the morning sickness there'd been a sense of unreality as she'd tried to come to grips with news of her pregnancy. 'I've got seven months to go.'

Then the changes would really begin. Aurélie would be a single mother. The only thing she knew for sure about the future was that she and Lucien wouldn't be playing happy families together.

He scowled. 'The doctor said you'd be sick for the rest of your pregnancy?'

Aurélie stared at his outraged expression. Stupidly, that warmed her lonely heart. 'No. She said it happens very occasionally but it's highly unlikely. She's given me some tips for managing it.' She glanced at the plate of biscuits beside her glass. Smaller, more frequent snacks had been one suggestion.

'You need looking after.'

'I'm not an invalid.' Aurélie wasn't sure whether she was trying to convince Lucien or herself. She'd been shocked at how bad she'd felt yesterday, but the doctor had suggested overwork, travel and stress might be factors. 'What did you want to discuss?'

As if she didn't know. Her fingers tightened on her glass.

'The future. Our child.'

Our child.

Surely it was pregnancy hormones that made those two words sound intimate. As if she and Lucien were embarking on this together, like a couple.

'Does your fiancée know?'

He nodded. 'I told her last night.'

Aurélie's eyes rounded. 'And you still want me to stay

here? That doesn't seem right.' How must the Princess feel, learning her husband-to-be was about to become a father with another woman?

It struck her that *she* was the 'other woman' in this triangle.

Her breath became a hiss of shock and she rubbed her forehead with her fingertips. This was such a mess.

'Aurélie, it's okay.' Lucien half rose as if to touch her but she shrank back in her seat.

She didn't want his touch. Yesterday had proved that she was anything but immune to him. He'd taken her hand and ignited a longing that she couldn't— wouldn't—allow herself to feel. Her only hope was to keep her distance.

Warily she watched him frown then sink back into his seat. His jaw clenched and a tiny muscle worked there as if tension rode him hard. Aurélie wanted to reach for him, feel the clasp of his hand. Instead she stiffened her spine.

'Ilsa is reasonable. Fortunately she's not prone to panic or outrage.'

His mouth curved in a tight smile and Aurélie felt pain jab her ribs. Surely that wasn't a stab of jealousy?

'You mean she doesn't *mind* that you've got a pregnant ex-lover?' The words emerged sharply, like an accusation, and she pressed her lips together. She shook her head. 'Sorry. I didn't mean to sound—'

'Ilsa is a remarkable woman,' he said stonily and Aurélie felt about an inch tall.

What was wrong with her? The Princess hadn't done anything to her. Aurélie had never expected a permanent relationship with Lucien, even before she'd realised his royal status.

'I'm sure she is.' That spike of discomfort jabbed again. Aurélie told herself indigestion was a well-known symptom of pregnancy. She was *not* envious. She wasn't looking for Prince Charming.

Lucien scrutinised her and Aurélie once more felt that

prickly sensation sweep across her skin. Like an electrical charge that made the hairs on her arms stand up. She had the uncomfortable idea that he read her jumbled emotions whereas she had no idea what went on in his head. His expression was unreadable.

'Ours isn't a love match.'

Aurélie opened her mouth to ask if that meant they wouldn't be faithful, then, horrified, snapped it shut. It was no business of hers.

So why did she feel a rush of relief?

'I explained we'd been together before she and I became engaged.'

Aurélie nodded. When she'd discovered who Lucien was she'd been horrified to learn he was engaged, wondering if she'd been a passing amusement for a man already tied to another woman.

It hadn't fitted with what she knew of him but she wouldn't have been the first woman fooled by a guy. It had been a relief when she'd discovered their engagement happened after he'd returned to Vallort.

'The engagement still stands? She hasn't been frightened off?' Aurélie watched for some clue to his feelings.

Lucien shook his head and Aurélie felt something within her dip.

'Too much rides on our marriage for us to back out. Negotiations between our countries have taken years.'

That didn't sound like a good basis for a marriage but what did she know? When she was little she'd had a romantic view of love and marriage, inherited from her mother. Watching her father marry a scant six months after her mother's death, and to a woman like her stepmother, had dashed Aurélie's illusions. Her cosy belief that her father had unwaveringly loved his first wife was long gone.

Reality had cured Aurélie of romantic dreams.

'I see.' She nodded as if she really did understand how two people could marry for reasons that had nothing to do with personal preference. But perhaps that *was* a factor. Princess Ilsa was beautiful. Maybe Lucien *wanted* to marry her. Maybe they were lovers.

That sick feeling stirred anew in her stomach.

'Meanwhile we need to decide what to do about the baby.' As if it were an item to be ticked off an agenda.

Aurélie's hackles rose and she bit down a retort. She was being too sensitive.

Her hand slipped across her stomach in a gesture that was as much about comfort as protectiveness. Silently she vowed, again, to do the very best for her child.

'You've had an idea about that, have you, Lucien?' It felt bold and a little provocative, using his first name now that he was a monarch, but it made her feel more in control.

He shrugged, but the set of those wide shoulders betrayed tension.

'There are several options.' Their eyes met and she felt he tried to gauge her mood. 'Especially since you said you weren't thrilled at the prospect of being a mother.'

'I…' She shook her head. There was no point feeling defensive or guilty. It was true.

She wanted the best for her baby. Yet she felt trapped, knowing it would change her life.

Aurélie had spent years as the primary carer of her younger half-brothers. She'd even postponed her studies when her father and stepmother played the guilt card, saying they'd never cope without her help while the last two were so young.

Was it any wonder she felt cornered, knowing what raising a child involved? Aurélie told herself she wouldn't turn bitter or resentful that her child would prevent her achieving her dream of study and a better future when she'd finally come so close to achieving it.

Yet doubt niggled that maybe she *would* grow bitter. That scared her. She wanted her child to have love and positivity in its life. Not constant complaints and blame, as Aurélie had experienced after her mother had died. Nor the scrimping for money that made life tough when there wasn't enough love.

'I said yesterday that I want to be an involved father. That hasn't changed.'

Something inside eased at his words. 'I'm glad. It will be better for our baby.'

Abruptly Lucien's gaze dropped to her mouth, making Aurélie hyper-aware of the way her lips shaped the words. Warmth trickled through her as she looked into eyes like flame and felt that flicker of connection again.

She sucked in air. 'What are you thinking? Visits to France? Sharing care?'

'Both those are possible.' Lucien hooked his finger around his tie and loosened it. 'There's a third option too.'

'There is?' Aurélie had been around the issue so many times but hadn't come up with an alternative, apart from the obvious—bringing up the baby alone.

'Yes.' He paused, eyes watchful. 'If you don't want to raise the child, Ilsa and I could adopt it, make it our legal heir and bring it up in Vallort.'

CHAPTER SEVEN

'YOU *WHAT*?' SHE couldn't have heard right. Except she had. 'You want me to give my baby to you and your…wife—' a knot in her throat threatened to choke her '—and walk away?'

Aurélie shot to her feet to stand, trembling. Looking down at the man who surveyed her with watchful eyes.

Gone was the latent hint of nausea. Gone the fog that impeded her thoughts when she tried to imagine the future.

Instead, she saw everything with crystalline clarity. King Lucien and Queen Ilsa, beautiful, charismatic and gracious, waving from a royal balcony to an adoring crowd, holding *her* baby.

A toddler, taking its first steps across a polished palace floor into the arms of its smiling blonde mother.

A little girl, her fiery hair tamed into neat plaits, being sent away to an exclusive boarding school where she'd learn all the things expected of an aristocrat.

The images flashed through Aurélie's mind in an instant, alarmingly vivid. Pain banded her chest and she realised she'd forgotten to breathe. She inhaled quickly, dragging air deep into her lungs. Yet still her pulse thundered.

'Aurélie.' She blinked, focusing on that deep voice, and saw Lucien on his feet. 'Please be calm and hear me out.'

'Calm?' She heard her voice turn shrill and swallowed.

'No one's asking you to walk away from your child.'

'That's how it sounds.'

The result was a sharp insight into her feelings for her unborn child. She'd thought herself tired of playing mother to her half-brothers and shouldering the maternal responsibilities her stepmother wouldn't. She might be frustrated and, yes, sad that once more her own plans for the future were disrupted. But she couldn't imagine turning her back on her baby and not seeing it again.

The idea constricted her breathing all over again.

'I'm sorry. I didn't mean to upset you. I should have explained better.'

'Oh, I understand.' Aurélie wrapped her arms around her middle in a gesture that was half protective, half defiant. 'Adopting my baby and raising it without me is pretty clear.'

Lucien stepped into her personal space, filling her field of vision, forcing her to focus on him and not the images in her head. Was that concern she read in his face?

'Adopting the baby so that it has every protection under our law and every right to inherit. That's a positive, surely?'

Aurélie blinked, running through his words. She wasn't worried about inheritance; she was still coming to grips with adoption. 'Your wife would be its mother, not me.'

A shuddering began deep inside. Again she was stunned by how much the idea hurt.

Warmth closed around her upper arm. She felt the weight of Lucien's hand. Her nostrils flared as she caught a hint of scent, male flesh and mountain forests that dragged her back to that night in Annecy.

Her mouth tightened at the corners as she bit back words. Whether to demand he release her or ask him to hold her close, she didn't know. Being near Lucien aroused feelings that yanked her in opposing directions and made her feel totally vulnerable.

Because he isn't and never could be yours. He has a fiancée. A beautiful, glamorous fiancée who belongs in this world of royalty and privilege. A woman who's everything you're not.

'No one is going to take your child from you. This is just an option to consider.'

She wished she could believe him.

Once she'd believed in her father, trusted him, and that

trust had been misplaced. He wasn't the man she'd once thought him.

'You can let me go now.' Maybe then she could think. How was it that his touch, his proximity, addled her thoughts?

For a heartbeat longer he held her, his bright gaze snaring hers. He was so close his slow exhalation stroked her cheeks, sending a quiver of need humming through her.

Abruptly he stepped back, frowning, his hand falling. Yet to her disordered mind even that felt like a caress. As if he didn't want to let go, his fingers clinging as long as possible.

Fury rose at her capacity for self-delusion. Lucien was more than over her. He'd moved on to a woman he wanted in his life permanently. Aurélie had been okay for a one-night stand but that was all.

At least anger didn't make her weak.

'If you adopt the baby your wife will be its mother. You'll bring it up here and I'll never see it.' An aching emptiness carved through her middle.

Lucien shook his head. 'I can see you're upset, Aurélie, and I understand the idea must seem shocking. But give us some credit. You said you weren't sure you wanted to raise the child. This *suggestion*—' he emphasised the word '—arose from that possibility. It provides legal security, and a single stable home if you choose to give it up. Neither of us would stop you visiting whenever you want.'

But she'd be an outsider. An occasional visitor. Not a parent.

'It's only one option,' he added.

'But it's the one you want.'

He shrugged, his hands spreading. 'How about we sit down to discuss it? You still look far too pale.'

Aurélie disliked being an object of pity, or knowing she looked unwell. At the same time, Lucien's concern felt special. When she'd lived with her family, no one had worried about her well-being. She'd been the one to look after everyone else. Even when she'd been exhausted from overwork there'd always been someone demanding more.

She took her seat and watched him do the same.

'Aurélie, whatever we do has to suit all of us. This option would give our baby legal protection. It would mean that he or she would grow up in Vallort, used to palace life, which is vital if he or she is to have a royal role. But neither I nor Ilsa would bar you from contact.'

'You really think your fiancée would agree to bring up someone else's baby?'

'She's already said she would.'

Stupid to feel betrayed that he'd discussed this with the Princess. She wanted to say that this baby was her personal business—hers and Lucien's. But that would be childish. There were wider implications, even if it did feel as if she were already being replaced by another woman.

Aurélie fought to repress raging misery and think logically. Instead of smarting because Lucien had discussed her private business, she should be impressed at his honesty. Some men would conceal an illegitimate child, especially when they were marrying someone else.

'She's trying to please you. She'll feel different when you have children together. Won't she want her children to take precedence in inheriting?'

Lucien shook his head, his gaze leaving hers as if his thoughts were on the Princess, not her. 'No. She's more than happy to do this.'

Which seemed unusual. Surely a royal princess would be concerned about precedence in the line of succession?

Lucien continued before she could press the point. 'I believe she'd be a good mother. Ilsa is kind and sensible.'

Was it Aurélie's overactive imagination or did that sound like faint praise? Surely a man should be more enthusiastic about the woman he was about to marry?

Not that there was anything wrong with kind and sensible. They were important qualities in a mother.

Aurélie told herself she was clutching at straws, trying to pretend Lucien didn't care for his princess bride. How pathetic was that?

'Your idea is that you and… Ilsa—' silly how tough it was to say her name '—would raise one big happy family? With my baby and any others you have brought up together?'

Lucien caught the doubt in her voice. More—cynicism.

'You don't believe I'm serious? Why would I lie?'

He'd known this discussion would be difficult. Naturally Aurélie had strong feelings about her child. Yet he wasn't used to people questioning his word. He sat straighter, jaw tightening.

Lucien had felt unprepared to become King, but he knew his duty and did it to the best of his ability. Now he felt stuck in a quagmire; whichever direction he went there were complications. Surely Aurélie could see he was trying to find a solution for all of them? That he was doing his best in difficult circumstances?

She must know he'd never deliberately hurt her.

Managing the fallout from this would be diabolically difficult but he was trying to protect Aurélie and the child.

Brown eyes fixed on his and the expression in them sliced the edge off his annoyance. It wasn't the look of someone being deliberately offensive. He saw sadness there. Sadness and disquiet. It stifled his indignation.

'I don't think you're lying. But you don't have any idea what the future might hold for this ideal family unit you imagine.' Aurélie's voice grew huskier and he had the strangest sensation, as if her words raked through him.

'And you do? You think you can see into the future?'

Her shoulders lifted in a tight shrug. 'I can tell you stepchildren aren't always welcome. Or welcome only on certain terms.'

Everything, from Aurélie's tone to her expression and

tense body language, told him she meant it. And that this wasn't only about their unborn child. The air seemed to thicken as she spoke. The way she sat higher indicated defensiveness. He leaned forward, sensing this was vital.

'You need to explain.'

Her eyes flashed. Impatience? Anger? But Lucien refused to put words into her mouth. He waited.

Finally she continued, her voice clipped. 'I thought it was obvious. Not all stepchildren are loved like the rest of the family. Love, approval, even a place in the family home can be conditional on...' she paused and waved one hand '...good behaviour.'

'You think we'd discipline this child more harshly than any others?' Lucien was still coming to grips with the reality of *this* baby, let alone others.

'It's not just about discipline but belonging.' He watched her hands clasp, fingers knotting as she moved to the very edge of the sofa. 'Being cared for rather than being seen as a burden or another pair of hands to help with chores.'

Something shifted in Lucien's chest. They'd gone from talking about theoretical future children to something quite specific.

'Is that what happened to you?'

Aurélie's eyes held his for a long moment. Then she turned towards the window.

'Weren't you welcome in your family?' Lucien saw her mouth tighten and regretted the need to push. But he had to know. For the sake of the child they were going to have. And because he wanted to understand Aurélie.

The suffering he'd glimpsed on her face affected him. He didn't like seeing the resignation that came with long-standing, deep-seated pain. He forced himself to sit still, pushing his hands into his trouser pockets instead of rising and taking a seat beside her.

She shrugged again. 'My mother died when I was seven. Within months my father married again.' Her mouth turned down. 'My stepmother wasn't cruel and didn't beat me. But from the day of their marriage I never felt loved. Not by my father or my stepmother.'

Grave brown eyes met his. Instead of seeking sympathy, that stare felt challenging.

'I have three younger half-brothers, so I know about being part of a blended family. But my reality was different to your theory.' Her nostrils flared in distaste.

'You weren't happy?' That was obvious.

'I'd been loved, you see. My mother truly loved me.' Her lips curved in a wistful smile that faded almost before it formed. 'So I felt the loss when it wasn't there.' She shrugged and looked at her pleating fingers. 'Lots of older siblings look after the younger ones, so I wasn't special in that. But I was never allowed to feel part of the family like before. I was the unpaid help, the one to do all the chores and take the blame when things went wrong.'

Lucien frowned. 'What about your father?'

'He took his cue from my stepmother. I was treated like a servant, abused if all the work wasn't done. Ignored otherwise. The boys picked up their attitude.'

Distaste soured Lucien's mouth. He was about to say that her brothers should have learned better. But Aurélie continued.

'I'm not afraid of hard work. But when it's clear your value is *only* because of that, not because of any intrinsic worth of your own, family doesn't mean the same.' Her mouth twisted. 'I delayed starting university because they said they needed me, that they couldn't manage without me. But three months ago, when my father inherited a small-holding on the other side of the country, they packed up and left without even asking if I wanted to go too.'

He was horrified. 'I'm sorry, Aurélie.'

'It doesn't matter. It's in the past.'

Was it? She still bore scars from her family's treatment. How much of her cheerful, friendly demeanour in the restaurant was real and how much a façade? Or, if not a façade, merely one side of a complex whole?

Lucien would give a lot to meet her so-called family and give them a piece of his mind.

He wanted to comfort her, draw her close and tell her she *was* special. That she deserved to be cherished.

But he didn't have the right.

The knowledge was a slam of pain that reverberated through his chest and down to his churning belly.

'Of course it matters.' He watched her eyes widen and her mouth gape in surprise. 'Every child deserves love and support. I know that more than most, which is why I swear to you that, however we decide to bring up our baby, I'll do my best for it, and for you.'

'I… Good.'

She nodded, a jerky movement that made him wonder if she wasn't used to people supporting her. Surely, even if her family had failed her, she'd had friends, lovers—someone to fill that gap?

'I come to this from the opposite side,' he said.

'Sorry?'

'I didn't have step-parents but I was adopted. You know the story?'

'I read that your parents died when you were a baby.'

Lucien nodded. 'I don't remember them. All I knew was my adoptive family, my aunt, uncle and cousin. I knew they weren't my birth parents and that Justin was my cousin, not my brother.' He ignored the gravel roughness that tinged his voice as he mentioned them. 'But I never felt anything but loved. Justin and I received the same care and discipline. I never, for one moment, felt I didn't belong.'

'You were very lucky.' A gentle smile lightened Aurélie's features and Lucien felt another pang at the yearning he read there.

'I was.' His mouth curved in a crooked smile. All that he did now, accepting the throne and an arranged marriage, was tied to the love his family had given him. The desire not to let them down but to shoulder the responsibilities they'd left him and live up to expectations.

Though he'd never wanted a royal future. More than ever, it felt like a trap he couldn't escape.

'So.' She exhaled on the word. 'You're serious about this?'

'It's a good option. If you decide you don't want to bring up our baby.'

It struck Lucien forcibly that in other circumstances he'd offer to live with Aurélie to raise their baby together. Shotgun weddings might be old-fashioned but he preferred the idea of his child being born to his wife and having his name.

If he were still an architect and able to please himself, that was what he'd do.

It was easy to imagine being with Aurélie and their baby. Telling her about his day and asking about hers. Spending each night with her in his arms, her bright hair a halo on the pillow, those soft brown eyes welcoming him when he sank into her body and—

'But surely…' Her words dragged him to the present. 'Surely it's not so easy? You can't keep this secret.'

'Of course not.'

'But what about public opinion? And the press? If anyone discovers the baby is mine and not…your wife's, won't there be scandal?'

His lips curved in a tight smile. 'Of course it will be newsworthy.' Royalty might have its perks but it had its downside too. Press interest being part of that.

'There will be a flurry of interest whatever we do.' Lucien saw her eyes widen in horror and was glad he'd downplayed the inevitable fallout. 'But I'll help you. My staff will work with you. You won't be alone.'

Yet what if she decided to go it alone, returning to France as a single mother? Even with his support it would be tough.

'Surely adopting our baby, making it your heir, would create scandal in Vallort? Would people accept it?'

Lucien's mouth firmed. She was right. It wouldn't be a ripple of interest; it would be a furore. But he'd accepted the burden of kingship and was determined that, in this at least, tradition would bend to *his* demands.

'I told you I'll acknowledge my child. I won't walk away from that. This baby is my family, my flesh and blood. Nothing will make me turn my back on it.'

No matter what it cost him.

He breathed deep, turning his thoughts from the inevitable fallout to the worried woman before him. She looked drawn by strain.

'I've given you enough to think about. I'll leave you to rest.' Lucien stood. 'At the very least you should stay here until we agree what to do.'

The thought of her leaving, drifting off to some hotel where there was no one to look after her or, worse, getting on a bus back home, sent a shiver of dismay down his spine.

He needed her here. Because they had decisions to make. But mainly because she needed rest and care.

No matter what his secretary or anyone else said about keeping his pregnant ex-lover under the same roof as his visiting fiancée. What mattered most was here in this room. His unborn child and a woman who, whether she realised it or not, needed him.

Her chin lifted and their eyes met. Again he felt that disturbing frisson of response shudder through his body.

'I'll stay for now.'

Lucien wanted to push for more but he read obstinacy as well as tiredness in that pretty face.

He nodded. That would have to do for the moment.

CHAPTER EIGHT

AURÉLIE LOOKED DOWN the pedestrian street towards the sun-lit mountains. In the last three days spring had arrived in Vallort. She felt its warmth and smelled it on the air.

Which made a nice change now her sense of smell seemed so heightened. Walking past a café and inhaling the rich coffee aroma made her nauseous, as did cigarette smoke.

She sat on a bench beside a planter box of budding flow-ers. In a few days it would be full of blooms.

Would she be here then?

She had to make a decision. Soon.

For her baby's sake and her own.

A woman could get used to living in luxury. More wor-ryingly, seeing Lucien every day, however briefly, under-mined her resolve to ignore her attraction. It tugged stronger than ever, despite discovering his royal identity.

Despite discovering he was almost married.

She sucked in a ragged breath and buried her hands in her pockets. It wasn't like her to dither over a decision. But she'd never faced one like this.

As well as suggesting adoption, Lucien offered money to support her through her pregnancy and beyond, whether or not she kept the baby. She could find a place near the university while she studied psychology. Lucien was gen-erous. She'd have enough to cover childcare. But did she want that? Someone else caring for her baby while she studied?

Was she crazy to hesitate? She could achieve her goal of a university qualification and keep her child. But, even with support, Aurélie had no illusions that being a single mother would be easy.

Would her baby thrive better living with Lucien and Ilsa? Everything within her had rebelled at the idea. Until Ilsa had sought her out.

Instead of a cool, distant woman she could dislike, Aurélie had discovered the Princess to be genuine and likeable. Ilsa had disarmed her by admitting she thought Aurélie might be offended by the suggestion they adopt her child. She was right. Aurélie had been offended and hurt. Then Ilsa explained she'd recently received medical advice that, though she wasn't infertile, she had a condition which made pregnancy more difficult.

'Lucien didn't tell you, did he?' she'd asked and Aurélie had shaken her head.

'I thought not.' The Princess had stared at her stunning sapphire engagement ring. 'He's a decent man. He knows it's something I prefer to keep private.'

'I won't tell a soul,' Aurélie had assured her.

Ilsa had nodded. 'But you deserve to know.' She'd paused. 'I wouldn't marry Lucien if I were barren, because he needs heirs. But conceiving won't necessarily be easy. Which means if we *did* adopt your baby it would be a blessing, not a burden.' Her gaze had caught Aurélie's. 'The decision is yours, but I want you to know that. If you imagined I'd resent the child, you couldn't be more wrong.'

Aurélie sighed and stretched out her feet on the cobblestones. Where did that leave her?

Lucien had even suggested she enrol at university in Vallort so they could both be near their child.

Most men in his position would try to hide a child born in such circumstances, and its mother. But whenever Aurélie mentioned the scandal Lucien would face, adopting the baby or simply acknowledging it, he turned stubborn. He'd given up his own life to become King, he said, and the world would have to take him and his family as they were.

His family.

Aurélie strove not to read too much into that word. Yet it

weakened her defences against him. She sensed that, whatever happened, Lucien would stand by their child. What more could she ask?

He and his fiancée were incredibly accommodating. Yet she couldn't bring herself to agree to adoption. At the same time the idea of being a single mother with no family support was scary. Her mouth flattened as she imagined asking for help from her father or stepmother. That would be futile.

Tired of her circling thoughts, she got up and strolled down the street. A drift of music reached her and she saw buskers in the distance, collecting a smiling crowd.

On both sides old buildings housed beautiful shops that vied with each other to create tempting window displays. From a patisserie with a display of mouth-watering pastries and cakes to boutiques of fabulous fashion and exclusive leather goods that reminded her Vallort was a wealthy, if small nation.

Yet the city had an attractive quaintness. Outside each shop the cobblestone pavement contained a mosaic of white stones. There was a mosaic design of glasses set in the cobbles outside an optician's. A stiletto heel in front of a shoe shop. Crossed skis on the ground outside a ski store and a scatter of coins outside a bank.

She smiled, lingering before a shop full of handmade wooden toys, for which Vallort was famous. Then a bookstore with a display of bright children's books.

Aurélie imagined reading to her son or daughter before bed, as her mother had read to her every night.

Did she want to miss out on that? On holding her baby and watching it grow?

On the other hand, if she gave it up, it would be heir to a kingdom. Lucien had explained that her child would inherit if adopted or born in wedlock. It would have everything money could buy. Was she selfish to hesitate?

To her horror, tears pricked her eyes. No matter what she

decided, she'd wonder if she'd done right. All she could do was go with her heart.

Aurélie spun round and turned towards the palace.

'So, I've decided.' Aurélie frowned and looked at the fire crackling in the grate. The light played across her face, highlighting the intriguing curves and hollows of her features and the tension imprinted there. 'I'll keep the baby with me and go back to France. But you can see it whenever you want. Later on, he or she can come to stay with you for holidays or…' Her voice petered out.

Lucien pulled his gaze away as pain sliced his belly. Was that feeling of loss, the sharp stab through his gut, because he wouldn't get to raise his child? Because he'd be a long-distance parent?

Or because Aurélie was leaving?

But that was a good thing. The alternative, of her living close enough to see regularly, would be a mistake.

He tried to be a decent man. He was doing his duty by his country. Yet no bridegroom, even in an arranged marriage, should promise his life to one woman when he felt like *this* about another.

Suddenly he was on his feet, pacing the sitting room and back to the mantelpiece, staring down into the orange tongues of flame.

Aurélie's timing was terrible. He was about to escort Ilsa to an official dinner. There was no time for proper discussion. Had Aurélie known that? Had she chosen her moment deliberately?

'I'm sorry. I guess you're disappointed.' Aurélie rose and moved towards him. In well-worn jeans and a figure-hugging long-sleeved black top, she looked far too sexy. Her hair was a bright, glowing halo and her downturned pout drew his hungry gaze.

As she approached Lucien stiffened then saw her reg-

ister the movement. She pulled up short. Did he imagine a
bruised look of distress in her eyes?

'I know it seems mad not to accept your offer. I'm de-
nying our child the right to inherit all this.' She waved her
arm wide. 'But when it came to the crunch, I can't leave it
here. It's my child. I want to know it, love it, care for it. I
want it to know and love me too.'

Lucien's mouth twisted.

Did she think he didn't want that?

He'd lost his family, not once but twice. First as a baby
when his parents had died in an accident and then more recently with the deaths of his aunt, uncle and cousin. At least
Aurélie had family, even if they weren't close.

He had no one. He'd try to care for Ilsa. But, despite
their mutual respect, he doubted there'd ever be a deep connection.

That wasn't Aurélie's fault. They were in an impossible
situation. One of them had to lose. Yet that didn't stop the
hollow ache of emptiness.

'It's probably just as well.' His voice emerged like gravel
from his constricted throat. 'I don't know anything about
babies.'

But he could learn. It surprised him how much he wanted
to learn. How much, as the days passed and the baby's ex-
istence became more real, he looked forward to being part
of its life.

He forced a lighter tone. 'When he's older he can visit.'

But was that any way to build a relationship? Occasional
visits when the child was old enough to travel? Surely the
parental bond began earlier. Didn't he owe it to his baby to
be there from the beginning?

Lucien dragged his fingers through his hair, torn by conflicting emotions. The need to respect her wishes versus
the need to act, to stop Aurélie from making what felt like
a huge mistake.

'You might change your mind about that. Once you're

married...' she paused '...visits from an illegitimate child could be an embarrassment.'

Lucien didn't pause to think. He took a single long pace that brought him right into her personal space, his hands gripping her slender arms through soft cotton sleeves.

'Don't even *think* of going there!' He dragged in a deep breath then realised his error when the scent of lilacs filtered to his brain. He recalled that delicious perfume from his night in her bed. 'If you think I'd let public opinion keep me from my child you're totally wrong. Do you understand?'

His fingers tightened on her arms and he leaned closer, needing to be sure there were no doubts about this. 'I won't have you pretending you know how I feel about this baby, or deciding I don't want to see it.' Lucien heard the grim note in his voice and sucked in a deep breath.

'I will be part of this child's life from the beginning. Get used to it, Aurélie. Don't try to fob me off or pretend to anyone ever, *especially* to our child, that I don't care.'

His jaw ached with tension and his heart thundered high against his ribs.

He didn't like what she'd decided. He wanted to force her hand. But he couldn't let her set up barriers between him and their child.

'I'd never do that.' Her eyes looked huge as she tilted her face up. 'Honestly.' Her palm pressed to her chest as if her heart beat hard like his. 'If you really want to be involved—'

'I do. How many times do I have to say it?'

Her lips flattened and her earnest gaze searched his. 'There's a difference between your legitimate, adopted heir and an illegitimate—'

'Don't!' he snarled, control slipping. 'Don't label our child that way. Especially as you're the one making it so.' He would have adopted their baby, made it legitimate. Lucien saw her eyes widen and snagged a deep breath. 'I will love this child whether it has my name or not.'

He might have been born into a family with a proud royal

lineage, but a person was a person, their value not limited by lines on a paper.

The knowledge that Aurélie, and no doubt others, expected him to treat this child differently struck his pride and his budding paternal instincts.

'I'm sorry.' Her hand lifted to splay against his shirt front. Lucien felt instant warmth as if her touch imprinted a brand on his flesh. Heat sank deep within him, past flesh to bones. 'I know you care.' She paused and when she spoke again he had to bend his head to catch her words. 'My emotions are all over the place and trying to decide what to do for the best has been so tough.'

She blinked and Lucien saw her eyes glisten, over-bright. Her bottom lip trembled before she clamped it with pearly teeth.

A curious sensation rose within him. Tenderness and a compulsion to shield her.

He reached out and brushed back a curl of burnished hair that had escaped her ponytail. It was silky smooth and he found his hand anchoring in her hair instead of letting go.

'It will work out, you'll see,' he murmured, as much to himself as her. 'Between us this child will be loved and well cared for.'

She nodded and offered him a trusting smile of piercing sweetness.

Lucien's breath caught. Everything stilled as he looked deep into Aurélie's eyes. The world narrowed to nothing but her and him, this moment, and the craving he battled to contain.

His fingers tightened around satiny hair. The weight of her palm on his chest seemed heavier by the moment. He needed to step back, he knew that, but knowing and acting were separate things. Especially with the addictive scent of spring flowers and warm woman teasing his nostrils.

'Aurélie…' His voice was a murmured rumble, cut

off when another sound intruded. He looked up, past her shoulder.

There, her hand on the now open door, stood his fiancée.

'Hello, Aurélie, Lucien.' Ilsa's voice broke the spell.

Aurélie stiffened, her heart jamming high in her throat. Had she been leaning up towards Lucien or had he been bending to her?

For a second longer her fingers clutched the pristine white of his formal shirt, feeling his body heat seep into hers. Then, with a gasp of horror, she stepped back.

Lucien's eyes were unreadable but her own thoughts fed her guilt.

They'd started out discussing their baby. They'd argued and somehow ended up close enough for her to feel the thud of his heart and the urgent need to be closer. She'd remembered the taste of his kiss and wished she could relive it one final time.

Until Ilsa spoke.

Aurélie licked her lips, realising her mouth was bone-dry. Lucien's gaze flickered on the movement and electricity zapped through her, puckering nipples and drawing her flesh tight.

She shuddered and they both stepped back.

She didn't hear Ilsa approach over the thrumming of blood in her ears. But when she turned, the Princess was there, gorgeous in a dress of sky-blue silk. She wore bright blue gems at her ears and throat.

As Aurélie watched, Lucien turned to his fiancée. 'Ilsa. We were discussing the baby. Aurélie has decided against us adopting.'

Ilsa's gaze caught hers and Aurélie found herself holding her breath. Because she liked the woman and guessed she'd be disappointed by the decision?

Or because of the swamping guilt? She'd been caught leaning into Lucien, silently begging for his kiss.

Heat flamed her cheeks. Surely she'd never come on to another woman's man? What had she been thinking?

Besides, look at this pair. They were perfect together.

Her gaze skated from Ilsa to Lucien, his formal evening-wear emphasising his lean, dark handsomeness and rangy athletic frame. Even the golden glow of his skin against the snowy shirt seemed to reinforce the difference between him and ordinary people like her.

Seeing them together, ready for their royal event, made a mockery of Aurélie's crazy dreams. Here she was in jeans and a T-shirt top, while they… They looked exactly what they were. Inhabitants of a rarefied world she could never be part of.

It was as well she'd decided to go. Any other option would be impossible.

Ilsa spoke. 'Aurélie, we need to—'

She didn't want to hear any more. Not while her pulse still pounded in anticipation of Lucien's mouth on hers. 'I'm sorry. I can't discuss this any more now. I'm very tired.'

She hurried to the door, filled with guilt and shame. To-morrow, early, she'd go home.

For everyone's sake, especially her own, she couldn't stay here any longer.

CHAPTER NINE

'WHAT DO YOU MEAN, I can't leave?'

Lucien's assistant winced as Aurélie's voice hit a high note. She strove to calm herself.

She was stressed. Sleep had been impossible last night. She'd spent hours tossing and turning, burning with regret as she relived the moment she'd been caught by Lucien's fiancée, trying to kiss him. For, no matter how she evaded the truth, that was what she'd been doing. *Willing* him to lean in and take her mouth.

She shivered at the memory.

As a result, she'd fallen asleep around dawn and woken so late that the meal she'd just finished in her room was lunch rather than breakfast.

She'd hoped to be on a bus out of the country this morning.

'His Majesty wants to see you. He asked that you do him the courtesy of waiting here.' For the first time since she'd met the royal secretary he looked almost disapproving. 'If you wouldn't mind waiting, Ms Balland? The King won't be long. He's had a very busy morning.'

Naturally. He had a country to run.

As for her desire to leave immediately... What had she been thinking? She mightn't want to face him and she hoped Ilsa wouldn't be with him, but Aurélie owed him a goodbye. And thanks for his hospitality. Besides, they had to make arrangements for the baby.

'Of course.' She summoned a smile. 'There are things we need to discuss.'

She looked at her backpack by the door. 'I don't suppose you know if there are any buses leaving for France in the afternoon, do you? I haven't been able to get online to check.'

Last night she'd taken refuge in a long soak in the sunken bathtub, trying to relax. Unfortunately, she'd dropped her phone, seeing it crack on the marble then plunge into the water.

'You haven't been online?'

'No. My phone is damaged. Does that mean you don't know about buses?' She frowned as she took in his arrested expression. Maybe people in palaces didn't catch buses.

'I'm afraid I don't, but I'll find out for you.'

He withdrew from her sitting room, leaving her with her thoughts. She hadn't woken to nausea and, despite feeling miserable, had more energy than she'd had in days.

Because she'd made a decision? Because she was making a clean break, distancing herself from Lucien?

She didn't want to think about that. It might be the right thing to do, but it felt terrible. Which was ridiculous. She barely knew the man she was already missing.

With a *hmph* of self-disgust she opened her pack, took out the textbook she'd brought and settled to wait.

When she didn't respond to his knock, Lucien opened the door.

Aurélie was curled up in the corner of the sofa, eyes closed, a book open on her knees.

Lucien paused, his heart skipping as he took her in.

Given the high-octane tension gripping the palace, it seemed impossible that she slept.

Seeing her relaxed, her hair spilling across the cushions, reminded him of the morning he'd left her in bed. He'd had to force himself to leave. The temptation to stay and deny the demands of the real world had been so strong.

Now the real world intruded with a vengeance.

His mouth tightened as he thought of this morning's work. The long discussions with Ilsa and others last night and today. The press release and its instantaneous results. The road in front of the palace jammed with royal-watchers.

And here was Aurélie, oblivious. With her soft curls escaping her ponytail, wearing jeans and a shirt of vibrant purple, her socks striped in different shades of purple, she looked about eighteen.

And innocent.

His gaze dipped to her abdomen where, even in sleep, one palm rested protectively.

Back in his office, dealing with one official after another, he'd had a moment of doubt. Most considered his actions crazy. But standing here, watching the woman who carried his unborn child, he knew with a deep certainty that he'd made the right decision.

Interestingly, both Ilsa and his secretary agreed, though the latter hadn't said so explicitly. He, like the rest of Lucien's personal staff, was too busy dealing with the ramifications of this morning's announcement.

Lucien walked to the sofa and lifted the book from Aurélie's legs before it slid to the floor. Psychology. Was that what she wanted to study?

He imagined she'd be good at it. He remembered her interest in other people at the restaurant. Her ability to read character and respond in a way that left customers smiling and, in one case, defused potential trouble.

'Lucien?' Her voice was husky with sleep, running up his spine like the brush of velvet.

He smiled at her, enjoying the warmth in her unguarded eyes and the supple twist of her slim body as she stretched. For this moment it felt again as if they shared that remarkable unspoken communion.

Till her eyebrows snapped down and she sat up, mouth flattening. 'You wanted to see me.'

It sounded like an accusation. He remembered being told she was ready to leave for the bus station. Did she really think she'd walk away from him so easily?

'Yes. We have things to discuss.' He gestured to the backpack propped by the wall. 'Is that all your luggage?'

She nodded.

'Good. We'll talk on the way.' Because after the tense night and fraught morning he'd had, Lucien was ready to get out. 'I need fresh air.'

Huge eyes met his with an expression that made his stomach drop away. 'You're driving me to the bus station?'

She ripped off the band securing her hair back and for a second she looked like an angel painted by some old master. All big eyes, glorious hair and translucent skin. Then she yanked her hair back and tied it in her usual ponytail.

Lucien wanted to tell her to leave it loose. No doubt she'd object and they had more important matters to negotiate.

'You wanted to leave the palace, didn't you?'

She nodded. Did he imagine she looked disappointed? Maybe she wasn't so eager to leave after all.

'I'll take you somewhere quiet where we can settle the details.' The palace was buzzing with excitement and speculation and he'd had enough. There'd be no real escape from public curiosity after this morning, but even half an hour's respite would be welcome.

Aurélie nodded jerkily and reached for her boots. Moments later she was on her feet. Lucien swung her pack over his shoulder, stifling her protest with a look, then shepherded her out.

They took a secret exit from the palace, driving an unmarked dark blue sports car and emerging from a tunnel known only to a few palace intimates. They emerged a block behind the official back entrance.

Just as well. Even here there were more cars than usual. According to Security, the throng of onlookers at the palace perimeter was now three deep.

Lucien sighed and concentrated on manoeuvring through the busy streets. He didn't regret what he'd done. But there were still obstacles to be overcome.

Including the obstinacy of this woman.

For fifteen minutes Aurélie was silent, then as he nosed the car towards an exit from the city, she spoke. 'Where are we going? This can't be the way to the bus stop.'

'No, we're going to my place.'

She spun round towards him. 'Your place? Don't you live in the palace?'

Lucien took another off ramp, heading not towards the highway that ringed the city, but another road that led through green farmland towards the head of the valley.

'Sometimes.' He felt the corners of his mouth tuck in. 'I've stayed there since returning to Vallort because it's convenient, given the huge amount of work to be done.' And because he hadn't wanted to face the drive to his family home, up the winding road where Justin had met his death. A deep-seated shudder racked him and he tightened his grip on the wheel.

'But I don't think of it as home.' It was magnificent, ideal for royal events, but its grandiose formality made it a showpiece not a home. 'Much of the palace is used for government administration. There's a museum in one wing and some of the larger spaces are available for public events like concerts and conferences.' He paused, slowing to take a narrow bridge. 'Usually the royal family stays there for major functions or to host international VIPs.'

'Like Princess Ilsa?'

'Exactly.'

'I should talk to her. Explain about last night.'

Lucien turned to see Aurélie frowning at a massive waterfall dropping down a cliff on the other side of the valley.

'There's no need. Ilsa and I have spoken about that.'

Aurélie turned to catch his gaze, her expression worried. 'She understood? About what she saw? I didn't mean to—'

'She understood completely.' Lucien felt again that dragging weight of shame and relief in his gut.

Ilsa had known exactly what she'd seen when she'd

opened the door on them last night. It had made their later discussion much easier, though Lucien had never felt so uncomfortable in his life.

He hadn't actually kissed Aurélie and he'd told himself he'd have pulled back before it came to that. But it had been a relief not to have to pretend indifference any more. It had been tearing him apart.

Lucien had never been indifferent to Aurélie, though he'd tried for Ilsa's sake. Last night any thought of dissembling had been ripped away.

Even now, after a sleepless night and hours fraught with diplomatic difficulties, Lucien was glad.

'Nevertheless, I should talk to her.'

'She's gone.'

'Gone?'

Lucien felt Aurélie's gaze as he swung the car round a curve at the end of a tranquil lake and took a turn that headed into deep forest.

'She left for Altbourg this morning. I drove her to the airport.'

They'd parted amicably. Remarkably so, in the circumstances. But he suspected Ilsa had her own reasons for supporting him as he faced this watershed moment.

'Oh.'

Lucien's mouth twisted wryly. He'd been told Aurélie hadn't heard today's news. He suspected she'd have a lot more to say when she did.

'I'd hate to think I hurt her. I like her. She's very nice.'

'She is.'

Aurélie said no more. Which was good as Lucien had other matters on his mind as he guided the car around a hairpin bend then accelerated on the upward climb. His whole being, body and mind, tensed and the skin between his shoulder blades prickled.

It was the first time he'd driven this way since his return to Vallort.

He knew this road like the back of his hand.

But then so had Justin.

Aurélie subsided into silence. She felt terrible about last night. No matter what she tried to convince herself, she *had* wanted to kiss Lucien. She'd wanted to melt into his embrace and feel his mouth on hers.

Heat scored her cheeks as she thought of Princess Ilsa and how Aurélie had wronged her, trying to seduce her fiancé.

Mouth compressing, she focused on her surroundings. How far were they travelling? She should have asked but had been too caught up in their conversation.

She tried to summon annoyance that Lucien was taking her out of the city when she had a bus to catch. But they needed to talk about future arrangements. She had no doubt he'd have someone help get her on a bus when they'd finished. Besides, she was curious to see Lucien's home.

And, the dangerous thought hovered, maybe despite her determination, she wasn't eager to say her final goodbyes.

Aurélie watched the rock wall of a cutting slide by as the low-slung car purred around another bend then surged forward on the straight. The view was spectacular. She looked out of the far window to a perfect vista of green valley dotted with traditional wooden farm buildings and beyond that the foothills of snow-capped mountains. But what caught her eye was Lucien's profile. His expression was grim, his brow furrowed and jaw locked.

'Is everything all right?' she asked as they rounded another curve and a couple of workmen came into view. A truck was parked in a layby and they seemed to be inspecting a retaining wall.

Lucien expelled his breath in a sigh. He slowed the car and lowered the window. One of the men raised an arm in greeting. Lucien responded, calling out something in a language she didn't know. The workers nodded. Then the car inched forward.

Aurélie saw an ugly bare patch above the new retaining wall, barren of vegetation. Turning, she noticed a break in the treetops below them on the other side of the road.

'Has there been an avalanche?'

'It's okay.' Lucien's voice held an unfamiliar rough note. 'The whole mountainside has been surveyed and the necessary work completed.'

Aurélie nodded. 'That's good. You wouldn't want to have an…' Her words stopped as she recalled the press report about his cousin. A rockfall after storms and heavy rain on the road from his residence.

She gasped as the implication sank in.

Lucien's hands tightened on the wheel. 'It's safe now. I wouldn't risk you or the baby.' Still that deep voice didn't sound like his. Her heart squeezed as she recognised pain.

'Are you all right, driving here?'

Briefly his eyes met hers and she felt a jangle of sensation in her midriff.

'You know about Justin?'

Aurélie nodded. 'I read about the accident.'

Lucien turned back to the road, manoeuvring the powerful car with ease. 'It should never have happened. They knew that area needed attention. There'd been a small slip the month before. But I'm told he was distracted by my uncle's failing health, even when warned of the danger, and didn't order the necessary work.' Aurélie heard strain in his tone and read tension in his powerful frame. 'I'm having every mountain road in Vallort surveyed and upgraded where necessary.'

Aurélie's heart wrung at the ache in his thickened voice. She reached out and lightly touched his upper arm. 'I'm so sorry, Lucien. I know he meant a lot to you.'

She remembered his terrible blankness the night they'd

met, as if, trapped in the depths of grief, the world no longer made sense.

'Thank you.' Then, before she had time to say more, they rounded another curve and pulled up in a wide levelled space with the valley on one side, the mountain on the other and dead ahead the most wondrous building she'd ever seen.

It looked like a castle from a storybook. She half expected to see some medieval princess or a knight in armour emerge from the entrance. Or a fairy godmother.

'You *live* here?'

From this angle the castle looked taller than it was wide. It was built of pale stone and sprouted a forest of towers with conical roofs. Curiously, the tops of some towers were whitewashed and half-timbered, softening the effect of grim stone. Afternoon sun shone on mullioned windows and on roof tiles of a deep, rich green that, in this moment of whimsy, made Aurélie think of dragon scales. From the tallest tower flew the royal green and white banner of Vallort.

She'd left the real world and entered a fairy story.

'This is where I grew up.'

Aurélie shook her head. 'I can't imagine it.' It was a far cry from the cramped rented home where she'd been raised. 'You live here?'

She turned to see Lucien's face grow mask-like.

'I will now. It was time to leave the city.'

That was right. He'd said he hadn't been living here. Aurélie surveyed his taut features and thought of that ugly slashing scar on the mountainside below. Was that why? Had there been too many memories here?

It was none of her business but she felt tenderness well up. Without stopping to think she touched his arm, feeling the rigid strength of his biceps.

'Welcome home.'

He jerked his head around from contemplating the castle. Those remarkable eyes flared brighter as they captured hers and something tugged deep within. Not just the sexual tension that always simmered around this man, but something more profound. Her hand settled on his arm, fingers gently squeezing.

'Thank you, Aurélie.' He covered her hand with his.

Again it wasn't a sexually charged gesture, though the warmth of his touch sent heat shimmering through her. This was about comfort given and acknowledged and it felt utterly natural.

Aurélie refused to consider whether she had the right to comfort him. Soon she'd be leaving. Time enough for regrets then. She sucked in a quick breath at the sudden ache filling her chest.

Lucien turned back towards the castle. 'It was a good place to grow up. There are lots of happy memories.' His lips curved. 'Justin and I had a ball, playing here. It's a paradise for kids.'

Aurélie flinched and pulled her hand away.

She guessed he hadn't said it deliberately but Lucien's words reminded her that she was depriving her child of so much, choosing to raise it alone, rather than here as part of the royal family.

'You wanted to talk.' Her voice sounded flat. Which she supposed was better than revealing the tumult of her conflicting emotions.

'Yes, come inside.'

The building was everything she'd expected from the outer view, and more. Its ancient origins were clear to see but blended with modern comfort.

Built around a large central courtyard, the place was actually circular. They entered through a vaulted hall that looked as if it could host a banquet for a couple of hundred. The massive fireplaces were so big she could have stood up in them. Huge, beautiful tapestries lined the walls and above them was an incredible display of old weapons.

They were greeted by an older couple who Lucien explained ran the castle, with help. But they were more than staff, Aurélie decided when she saw the housekeeper blink back tears as she welcomed Lucien and heard the warmth in their voices as they exchanged greetings.

'What was that you were speaking?' she asked as she and Lucien made their way up a broad, handsomely carved staircase.

'The ancient language of the mountains. It's one of our national languages, along with French and German. It's spoken mainly in the country areas though there's a bit of a revival in the city. This way.' He opened a panelled door and stood back.

Aurélie walked in then stopped, eyes widening and jaw dropping. After a couple of moments she stepped forward, drawn by the vista.

'This is incredible,' she whispered. The ceiling was high and the whole wall before her, from knee level up, was a vast expanse of glass facing out over the valley to the mountains on the other side. It was so beautiful it stole her breath.

She reached the window and experienced a moment's vertigo. Below her was a sheer drop into a chasm where white water sprayed and swirled on its way down to a waterfall. Sunlight caught droplets of moisture on the air, creating a miniature rainbow that reinforced her earlier sense that this was a fantastic, magical place.

'You like it?'

'I haven't got the words. It's amazing.' She turned to see Lucien beside her, a smile turning his face from solemn to irresistibly attractive.

She sucked in a fortifying breath and made herself turn back to the view. 'I thought it would be dark and gloomy inside.'

'Some parts are, since it was originally built for defence. Fortunately, some of my predecessors decided to renovate. Most of the rooms away from the front have large windows. We also have decent heating and a couple of lifts so you don't have to climb endless staircases unless you want to.'

Dragging her attention from the view, she surveyed the big sitting room with its plump upholstered sofas, gleaming wood and beautiful carpets that looked like ones she'd seen in museums. There was an enormous bookcase on one wall, filled with paperbacks as well as more serious-looking tomes, and bowls of spring flowers on small tables. The effect was of restrained luxury but, above all, comfort.

Something inside her eased. She didn't feel intimidated here as she had in the gilded palace. This was a home, not a showpiece. Even if it was inside the most fabulous fairy tale castle.

Her gaze settled on the polished dark wood of a grand piano, sporting an array of photos in silver frames. Aurélie wanted to investigate, guessing they were family portraits. Would there be photos of Lucien as a child? Of his family?

But she wasn't here to explore. He wanted to discuss arrangements for their baby.

'Please take a seat,' he said as the housekeeper entered with a tray.

Settling into the corner of a cosy sofa, Aurélie was relieved to discover the tray held a pot of tea along with home-made biscuits and cake, but no coffee. Had Lucien warned his staff?

He waited till they were both seated and she'd had a sip of tea before speaking. 'We've got important things to decide, Aurélie.'

'I know.' It had been stupid to think of leaving without seeing him. But she'd been spooked by the strength of her reaction to him, how close she'd come last night to doing something regrettable. Even now, her body hummed with tension, with need. 'We have to agree to some arrangements.'

'Especially as circumstances have changed.'

'They have?' Reading his serious expression, Aurélie guessed it wasn't good news. She stiffened, her mind racing. 'Is something wrong? Did my blood test show a problem with the baby?' She put down her tea and braced her hands on the edge of her seat, heart pounding.

'No, nothing like that. As far as I know, the baby is fine.'

Aurélie sank back, catching her breath. The baby was fine. That was all that mattered.

The moment of intense fear simplified everything, revealing the bond she already felt with her child. She *was* doing the right thing, choosing to raise it.

'What *has* changed is my status.'

'You're not King any more?' She frowned and his mouth curved in a wry smile that tugged a cord deep inside her.

Desperation beat at her. Aurélie could no longer deny her weakness for this man. She barely knew him yet it felt as if she knew everything she needed to, and liked it all.

She needed to leave *soon*. Her fingers tightened on the seat beneath her. Being near him was pure torment.

'It would take a lot for that to change. Apart from anything else, I'm the last of my line.' He paused, his smile fading, and Aurélie wondered if his thoughts had strayed to his dead cousin. She recalled Lucien's expression as they'd passed the scene of the rockfall. He was still grieving.

'No, what's changed is that I'm no longer engaged. Ilsa and I agreed last night to end our betrothal.'

Aurélie opened her mouth then closed it again. Finally she spoke, her dry mouth making her voice husky. 'Because of me? Because of what happened last night?'

'That was the catalyst. But the truth is, neither of us was eager to marry.'

Aurélie felt about an inch tall. Her cheeks burned.

Yet at the same time she felt like rejoicing.

'I'm so sorry. I—'

'There's no need to apologise. Ilsa and I were relieved to end it.'

Aurélie stared, wondering if that were true. Did he really believe that? He and the Princess were so well-matched. Besides that, she'd never met a man more magnetically attractive than Lucien. He had charisma as well as good looks, a depth of character that appealed as much as his charm. Had Ilsa *really* wanted to end the engagement or had she felt forced to?

'But it was all arranged! Everyone was preparing for the wedding.'

He inclined his head. As he did the light from the windows shifted, or maybe she just saw him more clearly, registering the signs of weariness around his eyes and mouth.

'Yes. It's taking some organising.'

'But the Princess's family! Won't they be upset?' Surely breaking off the betrothal at this late date would cause offence? Plus the two countries were on the verge of new financial and economic arrangements. Wasn't this the worst possible timing?

'There are some issues.' Lucien's voice, as much as his expression, confirmed her thoughts. 'But our decision was mutual. Ilsa and I agreed the marriage wouldn't be in our best interests and, as a result, not in our countries' interests.'

He wrapped his hand around the back of his neck as if to ease some stiffness there. Aurélie wondered if it was due to stress. 'There's some diplomatic fallout and a whole lot of media interest, but we'll get through it.'

'I'm so sorry.' She wanted to reach out to him but forced herself to sit still. 'I feel responsible.'

Lucien shrugged. 'Let's face it. Whatever arrangement we made about our baby was bound to be problematic, with me married to Ilsa. At least this simplifies things.'

Aurélie was busy telling herself there was nothing momentous about the way Lucien said *our baby*, yet she couldn't deny her shiver of delight at his words.

'I suppose it does.' Two parents instead of three made decision-making easier. And though she liked Ilsa, Aurélie wasn't keen on her child having a stepmother.

Though that would come one day, when Lucien chose another royal bride.

'Of course it does.' Lucien leaned forward, his eyes snaring hers. 'Now I'm free I can do what I should have from the start. Marry me, Aurélie, and we'll bring up our baby together.'

CHAPTER TEN

'YOU CAN'T BE SERIOUS!'

Lucien stared into Aurélie's dazed eyes and reminded himself to be patient. She hadn't been expecting this. Yet he'd expected more enthusiasm.

Disappointment stirred. He'd seen the desire in her eyes last night. He'd read her body language. She'd wanted him then, as she'd wanted him before. That couldn't have changed in one night.

But was attraction, even the profound desire they shared, enough? Royal life was a privilege but a burden too. Would the prospect of it scare her into saying no?

Lucien couldn't accept that. Not if he was to look after Aurélie and their baby as they deserved.

'Never more serious. Now there's nothing stopping us from taking the obvious step that's best for our child. Marry and raise it together.'

Aurélie's mouth opened and closed but no sound emerged. Her eyes grew enormous.

'But we... We're not...' She shook her head and slumped back in her seat.

Anyone would think he'd given her bad news instead of inviting her to marry him. Disquiet niggled his belly.

She looked at him as if he'd grown a second head. As if his proposal were preposterous. As if she denied what was between them.

Lucien thought of the women who'd insinuated themselves into his life, or downright pushed their way in, and that was while he had no expectation of inheriting a throne. The number who'd been eager to try persuading him into a long-term relationship.

Was this some sort of cosmic justice that the only woman he'd ever proposed to didn't want him?

The knowledge grated, harsh and raw, shredding his pride and bringing something close to hurt.

With Ilsa he'd inherited a fiancée. There'd been no proposal, no choice. This time he'd acted of his own volition, trying to do what was right by the baby, and by Aurélie, yet she looked as if he'd insulted her.

Lucien's jaw clenched and his body stiffened.

Nothing in his experience with the opposite sex had prepared him for rejection.

He watched her shoot to her feet, step away then stop. As if she didn't know what to do with herself.

Lucien knew the feeling. He was a jumble of emotions he preferred not to analyse. He forced a calm voice as he got up to stand before her.

'We *are* an item, Aurélie. There's a bond between us nothing can erase. We're lovers, and we're having a baby.'

'Ex-lovers.' The word shot out.

Her instantaneous repudiation felt like a physical blow.

All this time he'd struggled to do his duty by his country and his family's memory, and by Ilsa. He'd fought but been unable to banish his response to Aurélie.

He'd been through hell in the past day, bearing the brunt of Altbourg's disapproval at the broken engagement, the threat of severed diplomatic and economic ties, and the outrage of his own councillors. Thankfully the worst was over and, with Ilsa's help, relations with her country would be smoothed out.

Lucien had stood firm because finally he had the chance to do the *right* thing. He knew in his bones that marrying Aurélie and raising their child together was his future.

'It's not over between us, Aurélie. You know it.' He moved closer, invading her space. He drew in her distinctive lilac scent and felt something unfurl inside him.

Yet the stubborn woman shook her head, her mouth a mutinous line. 'It's over, Lucien. That was two months ago.'

'Two months and four days.'

He'd tried not to count them. He'd had plenty to fill his time, taking a crown and a fiancée. Maybe that was part of why he hadn't been able to erase Aurélie from his thoughts. Remembering their night together had been a bright flame during the long, burdened days and nights.

She looked shocked that he knew the number of days. Even so her chin rose. 'It's finished and—'

'Liar.' He closed his hands around her upper arms.

Instead of wrenching free or demanding that he released her, after one swift inhale Aurélie's muscles loosened. Lucien saw her bottom lip tremble and remembered the taste of her, rich and seductive.

Triumph burst through him in a rush of molten heat.

'It's not finished, is it, Aurélie?'

Oh, no. Not anywhere near it.

This time, the bond between them didn't feel like weakness. Its potency resonated through him.

The long wait was over.

Lucien slid an arm around Aurélie's waist and pulled her in. Heat to heat. Body to body. So close he saw the jittering pulse at her throat and felt her exhalation against his throat.

He waited, unmoving.

Giving her time to pull back?

Not likely! He felt a tremor rip through her and knew it for excitement. The same excitement he felt, holding her again.

No, he gave her time to admit she felt it too, the magnetic pull between them.

Still she avoided his eyes. 'We shouldn't. We can't...'

Lucien had spent the last two months hemmed in by restrictions and expectations. By everything he was supposed to do and not supposed to do, including who he was expected to marry. He'd had enough. Last night he'd ripped free, creating an international incident in the process. He had no intention of letting Aurélie play coy now.

'We *can* and we definitely *will*. That's a promise.'

He turned her head up, forcing her to meet his gaze. She didn't try to pull away. Instead her pupils dilated and her lips parted and Lucien felt his soul sing as he tilted his head down and took her mouth.

Yes. This.

One touch of lips on lips and it was like flame to tinder-dry kindling. Lucien almost heard the whoosh of ignition as restraint exploded and their mouths clung.

He moved, angling his head for better access, and found her already shifting to accommodate him.

His arm tightened around her waist, hauling her up against him. His other hand was in her hair, relearning the silky texture, tugging free the band that held it back, so a froth of soft waves tickled him.

Lucien's eyes shut, the better to concentrate on searing delight.

Aurélie's hands went to his shoulders, clinging as if to ensure he didn't let her go. She had nothing to worry about. He had no intention of stopping.

Lucien kissed her deeply, lapping up the taste of her, exulting in the ravenous demands of her tongue tangling with his. Swallowing the little humming sounds of appreciation and encouragement she made.

She was so enthusiastic, so attuned to him, he was already hard.

So much for her pretence she didn't want him. She pressed her lithe body up against his as if nothing mattered but the need to touch and be touched.

His arm dropped from her waist so he could cup her buttocks and pull her closer.

It was as if he'd flicked a switch. Aurélie bucked her hips against him and Lucien saw stars as all the blood rushed to his groin. She ground her lower body against him, emitting a sound somewhere between a groan and a purr. That felt so good. So incredibly good he needed more. Now!

Breathing ragged, hands soldered to her eager body, he opened his eyes enough to scan the room.

Right behind her was a sofa. Long enough to take his tall frame and roomy enough for the pair of them.

But Lucien wanted more than a quick tumble before someone bustled in to collect the tray. He wanted Aurélie, all of her, and he wanted privacy.

Still with his mouth locked on Aurélie's, he bent, sliding his arms around her, and hoisted her up against his chest.

'What are you—?'

'What do you think? I'm taking you to bed.'

She didn't utter a word of protest. Instead her eyes took on a glow that matched the fire in his belly.

At last she'd given up on denial. The clutch of her fingers around the back of his neck betrayed urgency. Her breasts rose and fell quickly as if she couldn't suck in enough oxygen. He knew the feeling. His lungs laboured, not from effort but anticipation.

He was heading for the staircase to his private suite when he heard a sound behind him. A sharp rap on the outer door and the sound of someone clearing their throat.

Silently Lucien cursed. Every muscle stiffened and his jaw gritted. How often in childhood had he heard that sound? Inevitably it had been Henri, the family's ultra-discreet major-domo, come to inform the King of some urgent interruption that would drag Uncle Joseph, groaning, away from his family and back to work.

Lucien knew he could trust implicitly in Henri's discretion. He also knew that he'd never interrupt unless it was vital. He was incredibly protective of the royal family's privacy. In some ways he was like a family member.

Lucien had hoped to carve out a few hours of privacy with Aurélie, but he'd been kidding himself. Today he'd dropped a grenade into the well-oiled machinery of government and international diplomacy and the consequences had been cataclysmic.

Soon, though. Soon he'd have Aurélie to himself. He vowed it.

The knock came again.

With a superhuman effort he turned and lowered Aurélie so she stood beside him. He wrapped his arm around her, holding her close when she wobbled. He pressed his lips to her hair, whispering words of reassurance.

'Yes, Henri?' he called.

The door opened and Henri appeared, his gaze fixed on the tea tray at the end of the sofa rather than the room's occupants.

'I'm sorry to interrupt, Your Majesty. It's the Prime Minister. He says he needs to meet you again urgently. He's offered to drive up to the castle—'

'No!' That was something Lucien had learned from his uncle. To keep official meetings away from home. To preserve some sort of private life.

Lucien looked down at Aurélie's bright hair and felt again that clench of hungry possessiveness. And some emotion he guessed stemmed from the fact she carried his baby.

If they were going to have a private family life, he needed to safeguard it, beginning now. Of course he'd spend hours of his so-called private time doing official paperwork, but he wouldn't turn their home into a meeting place for government officials.

It struck Lucien that the castle *was* home, no matter how reluctant he'd been to return.

The first time driving past the spot where Justin died had been tough, but here, in the place where he'd spent so many happy years, he felt only comfort.

And anticipation. He squeezed Aurélie's waist and her eyes met his. Immediately heat reignited in his belly, and he silently cursed the Prime Minister, even though he was doing his job.

'Ask my secretary to set up a meeting in the palace—' he glanced at his watch '—in an hour.'

'Very good, Your Majesty.'

What had just happened?

With dazed eyes Aurélie looked from the withdrawing butler to Lucien's serious expression.

Inevitably her gaze slid to his mouth, to those lips that had taken her to the edge of paradise.

What a kiss!

She'd been putty in his hands, not just acquiescent but collaborating in her own seduction.

Because Lucien had insisted it wasn't over between them.

Because he knew to the day how long they'd been apart. Her stupid heart had dipped and shivered when she heard that. It had seemed impossibly romantic.

He had the power to undo her defences with a look, aside from the caress of his lips and that hungry, confident way he'd hauled her to him as if she was his.

But none of that meant she belonged here! She didn't. She never would, no matter what her wayward body felt.

She stepped back, only to discover his arm still around her waist.

'Where are you going?' he murmured and Aurélie hated herself for loving the deep gravel note of his voice, as if his body hadn't yet accepted the news that sex wasn't on the agenda.

'I can't stay here.' She didn't try to break his hold, knowing it was futile. Instead she jerked her chin higher and met his stare with what she hoped was cool confidence. 'I don't belong.'

'I want you here, which means you belong. No one else has a say in that.'

'Not even me?' Aurélie wished she could shake free of the fog engulfing her. It was hard to think because Lucien had kissed her and said he wanted her.

But then he kissed like a fallen angel, with all the skills of a born sensualist and the ruthless determination of a man used to getting his own way.

'You're being deliberately obtuse. Of course you have a say. That's why you're here, so we can talk. Among other things.'

One look from under heavy eyelids, one suggestive comment and her body fired with longing. Flames licked through her veins, flaring in deep-seated places that made her shift and look away.

Aurélie moved back, out of his hold. 'Now who's being obtuse? You're a king. You meet with the Prime Minister! I'm a waitress. I'll never belong here.'

'You have something against royalty?'

'It's not that.' He was deliberately misunderstanding. 'You can't be serious about us…marrying.' There. She'd said it. 'It's preposterous.'

His dark eyebrows furrowed into a deep V. 'You don't believe in equality? You think you're less than me because of who our parents were?'

'It's not about being less or more. It's about being…' she searched for the right word '…incompatible. I don't belong in this rarefied world.'

Blazing amber eyes held hers. 'I never thought you such a snob, Aurélie. Next you'll be saying our child doesn't belong here.'

'That's different—'

'Of course it's not. It's all about what we want and what we believe. And what we choose to teach our child.' He paused. 'As for being incompatible, we've just proved that's a lie.'

Aurélie closed her eyes, summoning patience. 'I don't mean I think you're a better person than me. I mean I don't have the background, the knowledge, to live as a princess.'

'Queen, not a princess,' he murmured and she could have clouted him.

'You're not taking this seriously!'

'Oh, believe me, Aurélie. I've never been more so.'

That rocked her back on her heels, especially when she read the expression in those glittering eyes. He might taunt and tease, but he was in earnest.

'Can't you see that our marrying would be a recipe for disaster? Your people expect you to marry royalty. Someone who can hold their own with diplomats and politicians and royals.'

'Have the two royals you've met been so terribly daunting?'

'Of course not.' He was trying to distract her. 'But I don't know anything about royal etiquette. I've never worn a full-length dress, much less a tiara, or exchanged chitchat with VIPs.'

Lucien tilted his head as if trying to see into her head. 'That's what worries you? Talking to VIPs and wearing fancy clothes?'

Aurélie folded her arms in frustration. 'Those are examples. You can't deny we come from different worlds. It would be…ridiculous.'

'On the contrary, we come from the same world.' He stepped closer, stealing all the oxygen in the room and making her gasp. 'As a couple we're anything but ridiculous. Exciting, yes. Amazing. Sublime even.'

She huffed out an impatient breath. 'You're talking about sex. Not a relationship.'

'I'm talking about both.' He paused and shrugged. 'Okay, so I'm guessing about the relationship because we haven't had much of a chance at one. But I know when I'm with you I feel grounded, not in a heavy way, but as if everything is in the right place for once.'

Aurélie stared. Lucien was the ruler of a country. He had wealth, charm and an obstinate willpower that threatened to bulldoze her into a ridiculous situation. Yet all she could think of was how happy she was to hear he felt the same.

Unless they were empty words.

'You can imagine me at a royal soirée, chatting with the great and the good?'

'I can imagine it very well. Though I have to disappoint you by observing that just because someone's a VIP, it doesn't make them good.' He smiled and went on before she could interrupt. 'You'd be the belle of the ball. Everyone would want to talk with you and I'd have my hands full fending off the men.'

Aurélie's breath hitched. It was crazy but the picture he painted, of Lucien guarding her possessively from male interest, was too appealing.

'You've got the people skills to make a fine diplomatic hostess. Not to mention your language abilities.'

She gawped at him. 'How would you know what abilities I've got?'

A smile curved his lips, making him look far too attractive. 'I sat for hours in that restaurant. You did a lot more than serve food. You negotiated and advised. You averted some nasty scenes with that tourist when he came on too strong. Somehow you let him down firmly but gently enough that he was still happy. You were kind to the young woman eating alone who looked miserable, and you dealt with both rowdy groups celebrating and families with difficult kids as if nothing fazed you.'

Aurélie stared. She knew he'd watched her, as she'd watched him, drawn by a force stronger than anything she'd known. Yet she'd never imagined him observing quite so clearly.

'You make it sound like I did something important.' She shook her head. 'It's just my job.'

He laughed. 'You have no idea, have you? I wish half our diplomats had your people skills. And what about your languages? I counted four that night.'

Aurélie took a half step back. It felt as if she was being assessed for a job.

That was exactly what he *was* doing! For if she married
him she'd take on the job of being royal, which was terri-
fying. Yet, at the same time, having Lucien break it down
into a matter of learnable skills made it seem slightly less
daunting. Slightly more…possible.

'What languages do you speak?'

'Other than French? I'm fluent in German and English.'
She'd loved learning them at school, for the insight it gave
her into other places and people. When she'd started wait-
ressing they were useful during the tourist season. 'I have
basic Spanish and a few words of Russian.'

He nodded, as if approving. 'You're better than me. I
could never get my head around Russian.'

'There's more to being royal than talking with people.'

'Actually, it's a large part of the job. So is listening. I remember you being a good listener that night we spent together, even if you don't want to listen to me now.'

'What's the point? It would never work.'

'On the contrary.' His jaw firmed and that trace of lazy
amusement disappeared. 'We'll make it work. For our baby's sake. You want the best possible future for our child,
don't you? We can give it a stable home, a loving family
and a bright future. What more could it need?'

He was right.

The knowledge slammed into her, cutting off her protests. Everything he said was true. She was still adjusting
to the idea of a baby, yet Aurélie knew what she wanted for
it: love, security and a bright future.

There was just one problem. It might be the best for her
child, but what about her?

She'd be the odd one out, accepted only because of her
baby. She'd never fit in.

But you're used to not belonging, aren't you?

The memory of how disposable she'd been to her own
family scoured deep, like sharp fingernails drawing blood.

She couldn't expect to find love in such a marriage. Lucien only considered it for the sake of the baby.

Her mouth turned down and she wrapped her arms around herself, holding in the sadness welling up in her.

'I won't be railroaded.'

Lucien watched her with narrowed eyes. Aurélie had the feeling he read her fears and doubts. She prayed he had no idea how vulnerable she was to his arguments.

Of course he knows! You were about to have sex with him.

'Did I mention you could still do your psychology degree here in Vallort?'

Aurélie's eyes widened. 'There'd be no time. Not with royal duties and a baby.' Yet her heart beat faster at the idea.

'We'll carve out time since it's important to you.'

Lucien made it sound so simple. Maybe, with his help, it could be, lots of work and challenging, but achievable.

Did he realise how he tempted her?

'I need time to think.'

'Of course. Your luggage has been brought in. You'll stay as my guest till we agree.'

His tone made her shiver despite the room's warmth. It was the way he said *agree*, like a veiled threat, as if her one option was to change her mind and accept.

Aurélie told herself Lucien wasn't a bully. But there was something in his stance, and the implacable glitter of his eyes, that made him look not like a modern man but a warrior of old. The sort who might have defended this castle wearing a suit of armour and wielding one of those long battle swords she'd seen downstairs.

'And if I prefer to stay in the city?'

He was already shaking his head.

'You're saying I have no choice? What if I leave?'

'You'd find that difficult. Taxis can't come up here without permission and the estate boundary is patrolled.'

'I'm not your prisoner!'

'No, you're my guest.' He paused and Aurélie felt her pulse beat high in her throat as she saw again that bright, hard gleam in his eyes. Proprietorial, that was how it looked. As if she belonged to him.

She wanted to rail at him, tell him he had no right to keep her here.

Yet part of her revelled in that fierce possessiveness. Because it matched her feelings for him.

That was the secret that above all she had to hide.

'Now, if you'll excuse me, I must go.' He raised her hand to his lips, his open-mouthed kiss sending a rush of longing through her, weakening her knees and making her heart pound. Then he was gone, leaving her prey to turbulent emotion.

CHAPTER ELEVEN

AURÉLIE DIDN'T SEE Lucien again that day or the next. He sent his apologies, saying affairs of state kept him busy but he'd see her soon. Leaving her frustrated.

Yet, having watched the news, Aurélie understood he wasn't avoiding her. The broken royal engagement had rocked the country and, it seemed, the whole of Europe. Speculation was rife on the cause of the split but Lucien and Princess Ilsa refused to make a public statement.

No wonder the Prime Minister had been desperate to see Lucien. There was talk of a rift between the two nations and plans for a joint economic zone disintegrating. Aurélie felt sick, knowing she was at the heart of it all.

She told herself that was why she couldn't settle to sleep on her second night in the castle. Despite her long walk through the woods, and the delicious dinner, and even a mug of hot chocolate before bed.

Finally she gave up trying to sleep and in desperation dragged on yoga pants and a T-shirt. Stretches and gentle yoga might help relieve her tension.

It was almost midnight when she heard footsteps outside her room. Surely even Lucien's motherly housekeeper wouldn't be on duty now. She'd discreetly fussed over Aurélie since she'd discovered her retching in the bathroom this morning. Aurélie had been embarrassed, but the woman's practical kindness and encouraging smiles had finally put her at ease. So much so that Aurélie feared she'd miss being looked after when she left.

A soft knock sounded.

'Come in.'

The door opened and her breath stopped as Lucien stepped in.

From her position on the floor he looked bigger and more imposing than ever. At her eye level tailored trousers outlined rock-hard thighs. He'd taken off his jacket and tie, wearing a pale shirt with the sleeves rolled up to reveal strong forearms dusted with dark hair.

Her pulse beat hard, so hard it was a wonder he didn't hear it.

'Lucien.' Was that her voice, wispy and breathless?

'Aurélie. I expected you to be asleep.'

'You came to check?' She rose as he approached.

He stopped, fingers flexing at his sides, and she recalled the last time he'd touched her. How it had felt, wrapped in his embrace.

Eventually she remembered to breathe and his gaze lowered, tracing the T-shirt that clung to her suddenly heaving breasts. Slowly his attention moved lower. Her thin yoga pants seemed somehow negligible, as if that scorching gaze saw right through them.

Aurélie felt the crackle of heat igniting deep inside. She pushed her shoulders back, telling herself she needed to look in control. Or was she recklessly responding to the interest darkening his eyes?

'My room is at the top of the tower, above this. I saw the light under your door.'

Crazy that the thought of him sleeping just above her should feel intimate. Crazier still to feel arousal like a jag of lightning sear through her.

They weren't even in touching distance, yet the fine hairs on her arms rose as her skin prickled in awareness. Her mouth dried and she swallowed hard. In the stillness of night it felt as if no one else existed. Just them.

Aurélie tried to claw her way back to sanity. 'Have you been working all this time? You look tired.' She forced herself to focus on the signs of weariness on his handsome face. Concern knotted her stomach. 'You can't keep working such long hours.'

If he's been working all this time. Maybe he was out with someone who doesn't argue all the time.

She winced, ashamed at the thought, knowing it stemmed from her own experience, rather than anything to do with Lucien. For she suspected her father hadn't been faithful to her mother during her last illness.

Lucien wasn't like her father. In fact he couldn't be more different. She admired his honesty and sense of duty. He had more self-respect, more decency than to dally with another woman while he waited for her answer.

Lucien's mouth quirked up in a constrained smile that made her even more aware of the tension zinging between them. 'Worried about me, Aurélie? Careful, you sound almost like a wife.'

For some reason the jibe didn't hurt. What did was seeing the shadows beneath his eyes and the tight lines bracketing his mouth.

They might disagree on the future, but Lucien was doing his best by the baby and, she admitted, by her. He was dealing with nuclear-grade fallout as a result. She was worried about her future and her baby's. He had a nation to consider on top of that.

'I'm serious, Lucien.' She took a step towards him then halted. Any closer and she'd be tempted to touch, despite what her conscience said.

His shoulders lifted and seemed to spread wider, making her aware of the primal male strength behind that casual movement. 'It's been a busy couple of days. Things will get easier now.'

'Now? What's happened?'

For a second he hesitated, leaving Aurélie to wonder if he'd rather not share the details.

'The King of Altbourg has weighed in. At first he was shocked and disinclined to honour the diplomatic and economic arrangements we'd agreed on. Until Ilsa and I had a frank discussion with him.'

Aurélie felt her eyes widen. How frank had that discussion been? Did it include mentioning her pregnancy?

'Fortunately he loves his daughter. Once he knew she genuinely wanted out of a relationship that couldn't go anywhere, he became extremely understanding.' Another shrug. 'He and his government want this new economic zone as much as we do.'

'So it's over? Everything's okay?'

Aurélie felt the weight of guilt slide from her. She hadn't done anything wrong, but she'd blamed herself.

'As far as our governments are concerned, yes.'

'You're remarkable.' At his raised eyebrows she continued. 'I didn't think you'd be able to negotiate a settlement. You talk about your inexperience as King but it seems to me Vallort is lucky to have you.'

His mouth twisted ruefully. 'It's not quite so simple. The press fallout will continue. But I don't live my life to accommodate the media.'

Aurélie had fretted about that. She'd seen how the media hounded royalty. If she stayed here, or even if she didn't, the press would be part of her life, and her child's.

'Aurélie? What is it?'

She was shocked at how easily he read her disquiet.

'I'm thinking about the stories they'll write when they find out about us.'

Lucien's gaze dropped and she realised her hand lay against her still-flat abdomen.

'If you marry me I can protect you.'

Aurélie huffed out a laugh. 'Hasn't it occurred to you that saddling yourself with me could be the worst thing from a PR point of view?'

Lucien moved closer, so close she had to lift her chin to meet his stare. 'Absolutely not.'

Then he did something that shocked her into silence. He fitted his big hand over hers where it lay against her belly.

He splayed his fingers and his hot touch branded her. Like a pledge of allegiance and protection.

Or was that crazy, wishful thinking?

'Whatever anyone says, Aurélie, we've created a miracle. I intend to stand by you and our child for the rest of our lives.'

The words reverberated in the silent room, echoing not just in her ears but in the desolate places inside that had felt empty since her mother died. In all the intervening years no one had cared enough to take time and really notice her the way Lucien did, much less put her first.

It was powerful, wonderful and utterly overwhelming. Unexpected heat pricked her eyes.

'Aurélie?' Concern puckered his forehead. 'Are you okay? What have I said?'

Her smile felt ridiculously tremulous but she didn't care as she turned her hand, capturing his heat and solidity as she threaded her fingers with his.

'Something wonderful. What you said…' She shook her head. 'It sounds pathetic but I'm not used to anyone caring.'

Their eyes locked and Aurélie felt a great swoop and rise of emotion. It was so strong it caught her at the knees, making her legs tremble. Convulsively she clutched Lucien's hand.

'I care, Aurélie. Never doubt it.' His whispered words trailed like a silken caress, wrapping around her fast-beating heart.

It should have been impossible to feel so much for this man. Logic said there'd been no time to form a strong bond, or to know him properly.

Instinct, bone-deep and unwavering, disagreed.

In this moment she realised that wherever she went in the future, whatever she did, there'd always be this attachment. Even though his prime concern was their unborn child, not her.

There was more, she discovered anew as his thumb

brushed hers and a ripple of sexual awareness coursed through her.

Did he feel it too?

Suddenly Lucien's concerned stare turned into something different. Beneath those dark eyebrows his amber eyes lit like flame. She felt the heat of that look down in her core and higher, where her breasts drew tight.

'I haven't stopped wanting you since that night.'

His words cut through the charged atmosphere, making her suck in a sharp breath.

She shook her head. 'You were engaged to Ilsa, remember?'

'Oh, I remember.' If anything that fiery gaze grew hotter and Aurélie felt the blood rise under her skin, scorching her breasts, throat and cheeks. 'There was never anything between Ilsa and me except a formal agreement. I admire and like the woman but I never *wanted* her. We never…' He shot Aurélie a searing look from under lowered brows. 'We didn't even kiss. Neither of us was in a hurry to marry. That was just the schedule arranged when she was supposed to marry my cousin.'

Aurélie wondered what it would be like, expected to wed and produce heirs to order. She'd imagined such dynastic arrangements had died out years before.

'But the Princess is beautiful. You must have desired her.' As soon as the words escaped she cringed inwardly. Did she sound as needy as she felt, seeking further affirmation?

'You'd think so, wouldn't you?'

He pulled back the hand that covered hers and Aurélie felt a piercing moment of regret. She'd shattered their precious closeness with her tactless questions.

Lucien drew himself up to his full, imposing height. 'In the last six months I've been so busy with work, first as an architect and now here as King, that I haven't been with any woman except you.' He paused as if letting her absorb his words. 'In that time the *only* woman I've imagined in my bed is you, Aurélie. No one else.'

Her breath hissed on a stunned breath. It seemed impossible, yet everything within her urged her to believe.

'There's only one woman I want, Aurélie.' His words throbbed with a need that matched the primal pull and drag inside her own body.

Yet he made no move to meet her halfway.

She breathed deep, inhaling that tantalising male scent of clean skin, fresh air and spice.

'Then what's holding you back?'

He knew she wanted him. She hadn't let out a peep of complaint yesterday when he'd swept her into his arms to take her to bed. Yet now, frustratingly, she sensed a barrier between them.

His frown deepened. 'I'm trying not to take anything for granted. Because if I touch you again, there'll be no stopping. No time for second thoughts.' Lucien drew a breath that made his chest expand.

Aurélie had never heard or seen anything as powerfully arousing as Lucien, standing before her, warning he'd reached the limit of self-control. He made her feel confident and strong. Made her feel wanted and cherished. Even if it was only sex. She didn't make the mistake of thinking the attraction Lucien felt was more than physical.

But at this minute that didn't matter.

She stepped up and planted her palm on his shirt, pressing against the solid muscle that protected his drumming heart.

For a second he stood still, then he took her other hand and pressed her palm against him, right where the hard ridge of his erection tested the limit of his tailoring. His eyes narrowed as he watched her, waiting for her reaction.

Desire crested as she curled her hand against him. Aurélie's inner muscles clenched and other muscles softened.

Liquid heat spilled between her legs as her skin drew tight and her nipples puckered.

Lucien shuddered when she moved her hand against him. A pulse throbbed as he clenched his jaw.

She opened her mouth to say his name but the word stalled on her tongue as he moved his big hand between her thighs, cupping her hard.

Her reaction was instantaneous, a jerky buck forward into his touch. A clenching of fingers, one hand tearing at his shirt, the other at his trousers.

Aurélie heard an unfamiliar shushing sound and belatedly realised it was her breath, chugging into constricted lungs.

A second later there was no air between them. Their mouths fused, lips and tongues sliding together, seeking, urging, demanding. It was every bit as glorious as she remembered.

Before she could undo his clothes, Lucien pulled her T-shirt high, urging her arms up so he could slide it free. Air kissed her bare flesh as he dragged her bra off.

Another *shush* of breath. This time Lucien's, as he looked down at her. Aurélie's breasts felt heavy, tingling with the weight of his stare.

He swallowed hard. Seconds later he knelt before her, feasting on her breast, kneading the other till she cried out and arched back as sparks of fire showered inside her.

Aurélie shivered, her legs unsteady, only able to stand because of her grip on Lucien. One hand dug into his shoulder and the other held his head to her. She didn't ever want to let him go.

She shivered voluptuously as the fire inside whirled to a conflagration that threatened to consume her.

'No more.' It was a raw gasp and he didn't hear. Aurélie had to push at those hard shoulders till he withdrew just enough to survey her with eyes that looked blank with heat.

'Please.' She fumbled at his collar. 'I need you inside me.'

She felt the heavy pound of her heart against her ribs, heard the rasp of rough breathing. Moments later Lucien was rolling the last of her clothes down her hips to her thighs. His eyes held hers, even as he shoved the clingy material down to her ankles and she stepped free.

Aurélie had only managed to undo a couple of his shirt buttons. Lucien was more efficient. He simply gripped the open neck of his shirt and pulled. Seconds later he tossed the torn cotton to the floor and rose before her, kicking off his shoes and stripping his socks. He straightened and she had a perfect view of his sculpted torso. She heard the hiss of his zip, the sound of his trousers landing on the floor as she leaned in and kissed his bare chest.

Heaven!

Almost as heavenly as his arms wrapping around her, drawing her close so they touched all the way down their bodies.

Her breath came in sharp little bursts that didn't fill her lungs. Lucien was against her, naked and wanting, and it was better even than she'd imagined. She remembered the bliss of their night together but this was different. This was urgent and desperate, as if two months apart had turned attraction into need, desire into craving.

Lucien wrapped his arms around her, lifting her off her feet. Seconds later he sank down onto the edge of the bed with her cradled close, her knees splaying on either side of his hips so she sat astride him, breasts to chest, his erection hard against her abdomen. She wriggled and he gasped out an oath under his breath.

Warm hands on her hips urged her up onto her knees, her breasts sliding against his chest. Aurélie's eyes shut as she battled the overload of exquisite sensations. But not for long. This was too good to miss a second.

When she opened them Lucien's bright gaze snared hers. For a second neither moved. She felt his heavy pulse, the humid waft of his breath on her lips, the intense heat of his hard body.

The sense of fulfilment as if her body and even her soul had been waiting for this moment.

As his fingers tightened on her hips she slowly sank, this time nudging the head of his erection. For a microsecond they both stopped breathing, until staying still was no longer an option.

Aurélie slid down, centimetre by slow centimetre until it felt as if Lucien was lodged right at her heart. The feeling was wondrous. So wondrous she shuddered at the twin sensations of his eyes eating her up and his body completing hers.

He might let her set the pace but she sensed what it cost him to exert such tight control. His big body was taut and trembling with the effort of restraint. That in turn made the moment more piquant, her own response more acute.

'More,' Lucien demanded in a deliciously deep voice that growled across her bare flesh.

Aurélie was about to say that he already filled her completely, when his hand covered her breast, kneading and gently squeezing. She gasped, arching back, eyes closed, as a ripple of ecstasy took her.

She was so close. She wasn't sure she could move.

Except Lucien was right. She wanted more too.

Anchoring herself on his shoulders, she rose, luxuriating in the slide of their bodies, then sank again, a little harder, a little faster.

Then again and again.

Inside the fire built to a conflagration that threatened to consume her. She told herself she couldn't give in to it yet. They'd only just started and—

Thought died as he slid his thumb down through damp curls to press that sensitive nub at the centre of her sex.

There was a roaring sound, as if the world caught alight.

She saw flames reflected in Lucien's eyes as they reached up to engulf her.

Aurélie was swept in a tornado of fire and light. And pleasure, such pleasure.

She heard a high, keening sound, felt the rush of blood and the power as they arched together. Then came something she'd never experienced before, since in the past they'd used condoms. Lucien's deep groan of release heralded his body's quickening and his seed pulsed into her.

It felt…profound.

She and Lucien had already made a baby so this feeling that they shared something unique didn't make sense.

Yet as she collapsed against his shoulder, riding the jerky motions of his powerful body, Aurélie smiled. It felt as if she and Lucien experienced the most profound link a man and woman could. A link that was physical, but so much more too. A link that bound them irrevocably.

CHAPTER TWELVE

LUCIEN WOKE TO a feeling of calm and well-being. There was no buzz in his brain, reminding him of the people relying on him, the work he had to do, his schedule and expectations.

Instead there was warmth and...cosiness.

He stretched, arching his back, and instantly stopped as he registered the warm, feminine body in his embrace. One arm was stretched beneath Aurélie and the other wrapped around the curve of her waist. He lay on his side, spooned behind her. That fresh hint of flowers teased his nostrils and when he bent closer, soft curls caressed his mouth.

He inhaled deeply, unable to resist.

Memories flooded of last night. Of the incredible rapture he'd found with her. The release and sense of utter rightness had confirmed he and Ilsa had done the right thing, ending their betrothal.

Aurélie even made him feel better about the way he tackled the task of kingship. Her words about Vallort being lucky to have him might have been naïve but they'd been a welcome change after months fretting that he wasn't ready for the role.

With her everything was simpler, despite the complications in the outside world.

Lucien felt once more that stillness, as of time stopping, while they were together. As if they were somewhere unaffected by the world rushing past.

He'd experienced it the night they'd met. She'd grounded him when the depth of his grief overwhelmed him.

He felt that sensation again now. He had no name for it. Could only assume it was a blend of super-charged attraction melded with understanding. Now that bond was strengthened by their child.

That had to explain the intensity of what they'd shared last night. The explosive ecstasy. When he'd finally come back to himself it felt as if he'd broken apart and the pieces had been put back together to make a new Lucien. Someone familiar but not quite the same as before.

Renewed. That was how he'd felt. Still felt.

These last couple of months had been an emotional strain and an enormous challenge. He'd grown up with the royal family, knew how it functioned, but had never expected to step into Justin's shoes.

Leading a nation racked by the deaths of not one but two beloved figures, proving himself and coming to grips with new responsibilities, had been his total focus.

Now that focus had shifted.

He stifled a grin, acknowledging his hard-on pressed against Aurélie's soft derrière. Imagining the ecstasy of losing himself in her lush warmth. But she was sleeping and she needed rest. He'd seen how stressed she was and how weary. Morning sickness had taken its toll.

With Aurélie desire was a constant. It had tortured him through the days when he was still caught in a dynastic betrothal but lusted after this gorgeous redhead. It had almost undone him when he'd tried to use logic to persuade her to stay.

Lucien tried and failed to repress the need to slide his erection against her warm curves. He bit his lip, forcing back a sigh of raw pleasure.

'You're awake.'

Lucien's eyes snapped open, taking in the pale light of dawn. 'Sorry,' he murmured. 'I didn't mean to wake you.' But now she was awake he fitted her more closely against him, fanning out his fingers across the silky skin of her abdomen. Excitement shot through him. His child was in there. Tiny, vulnerable, but alive.

His grin widened. This time it had nothing to do with

sex. Or not as much, he corrected, as Aurélie moved, hips twitching in a shuffle that teased his tight groin.

'I've been awake for a while.'

Lucien's grin faded as he tried to read her tone. Was it pensive? Distracted? Had she lain there thinking through her list of objections to marriage?

His mouth firmed. Whatever it took, Aurélie would marry him, and soon.

'How are you feeling?' He glanced past the undrawn curtains to where the sky pinkened around the peak on the opposite side of the valley. 'Any morning sickness?'

She shook her head, her hair tickling him. 'Not at all, surprisingly. Not yet, anyway.'

Lucien heard a world of weariness in her tone. Despite the dictates of his body, it reminded him of how tough things were for her at the moment.

Reluctantly he lifted his hand from her warm flesh. 'I'll go and let you catch up on sleep.' He clenched his jaw, preparing to move away, despite an internal howl of protest.

Her hand on his stopped him. She planted his palm on her hip as she twisted a little, looking over her shoulder.

The movement of her buttocks against his erection made the breath hiss between his gritted teeth. Her rich brown gaze met his and it was as if it had a direct line to his libido. Try as he might, he couldn't prevent the throb of his arousal against her.

Aurélie's lips twitched. 'You're a morning person.'

He shrugged. His throat dried with the effort it took to hold still. If her lush body wasn't temptation enough, that almost-smile shredded his resolve to give her space.

'So am I. Usually.'

He nodded. 'I understand.' Even if she wasn't nauseous, she was probably fragile in the morning. She wouldn't want...

His heart hit his ribs as she pulled his hand up to cover

her breast. Automatically his fingers closed around her ripe curves. Riper, surely, than before?

Lucien nuzzled her neck, brushing away wavy locks, then gently bit down at the spot where her shoulder curved up to her neck.

'Ah!' She arched, her derrière pushing back hard. Pleasure scudded through him.

'You like that?' He sounded smug and didn't care. He liked it when Aurélie forgot to argue and throw up obstructions. When she was responsive and downright needy. 'When we're married we can do this as often as you like. And more, much more.'

Gently he pinched her nipple, feeling her shudder of response and the rolling wave of excitement that made her undulate against him. He pushed his knee up high between her legs. Her choked moan was music to his ears.

'*When*, not *if*?' she gasped. 'You take a lot for granted.'

'You know it's the best option.' He kissed her neck, breathing in the scent of spring and needy woman. 'Best for our baby.' He slid his hand to her belly, feeling that surge of excitement over his child growing there. 'Best for us too, Aurélie. I promise you won't regret it.'

On the words he moved his hand to the downy hair at the juncture of her thighs, slipping through damp folds to the slick heat at her core.

A shudder erupted. From her or him? Either way, feeling her readiness for sex, hearing her laboured breaths, made him harder than ever.

Yet Lucien understood the art of negotiation. Reluctantly he lifted his hand and withdrew his knee from between her thighs. It was torture, since Aurélie wasn't the only one straining for completion.

'Lucien!' She grabbed his hand and pulled it towards her, but her strength was no match for his. 'Why did you stop?' It sounded like a sob.

'I'm waiting for you to say yes.'

'You *know* I want you!' She sounded petulant. Lucien imagined her pouting mouth and, despite his determination to make her wait, couldn't stop the tilt of his hips that brought him into delicious friction with her bare rump.

'Yes to marriage, Aurélie.'

She stilled. He heard her sigh. He was tempted to use his hands and mouth to tease her into submission but this was important. Instead he waited, willing her to see sense.

'I...'

'Yes?' He couldn't help himself; he planted his hand at her waist, his fingers spanning her ribcage, sliding along smooth, warm skin.

'It would be disastrous. A huge scandal.'

'I didn't take you for a coward, Aurélie. I don't care about scandal. I care about you and the baby. About us.'

He waited, throat dry and pulse too fast.

Then she sighed. 'On one condition.'

Even now she didn't make this simple. How easy he'd had it with previous lovers, who'd agreed with whatever he wanted. But that was one of the things that set Aurélie apart. She was her own woman. He liked that. Most of the time.

'Name it.'

'We don't announce it yet. I need time to prepare.'

'Agreed.' He knew, better than most, how taxing the transition to royalty could be. For Aurélie, brought up in another country, not knowing Vallort or him very well, it was much more difficult. She was right, the fallout when the press discovered he was marrying his pregnant lover—

'Then yes.'

She didn't sound like a woman who'd agreed to the deal of a lifetime. Wealth, status, hot sex, a stable home for their child...

Lucien leaned over her shoulder, turning her face up with his fingers. Their eyes met and emotion smacked him low in the belly. Aurélie didn't look feisty or argumentative. She looked lost, those big eyes anxious in her pale face.

Tenderness welled up within him. A need to reassure. He wanted to tell her he'd stand by her through whatever came, but didn't want to dwell on anything that would increase her doubts. For she was right, there were tough times ahead.

'Thank you, Aurélie. You honour me.'

Her crooked smile carved a trench through his gut. She still had doubts and he hated seeing her worried.

'Then distract me from what I've agreed to. Make love to me, Lucien.'

As if he needed urging.

He made to pull away and settle above her, but she shook her head. 'Like this.'

Lucien pressed his mouth to her shoulder. 'Any way you want, Aurélie.'

'Is that a promise?' Laughter lurked in her eyes. And was that excitement? The sombre mood dissipated as abruptly as it had descended.

'Count on it.' Slowly, he settled against her back, thigh between her legs, parting them. He nudged the slick folds waiting for him. Thinking about it blasted his willpower to smithereens. Especially as, before he could do it himself, her slim hand was there, guiding him, and he had to bite back a growl of warning.

Was it the feel of their almost joined bodies that threatened to send him over the edge? Or the new understanding they shared? Even simply watching the erotic excitement flush Aurélie's skin made this special.

Whatever the reason, taking this slow was going to be more difficult than ever. They'd barely started but Lucien knew this for the best sex of his life. So far.

Slowly, every muscle straining at the effort at control, he pushed up into honeyed heat.

Aurélie's eyelashes fluttered and her mouth opened on a sigh of satisfaction that spurred him on. Inching forward, drawing out the sensations, Lucien felt the enormity of the moment. Joining himself with the woman who'd be his mate for life.

'More.' She licked her lips and he pushed the rest of the way in a hard, uncontrolled thrust, stars exploding across his vision.

Lucien shut his eyes, searching for restraint. Maybe if he focused on the new laws waiting for his consent... Or the intricacies of the new trade deal.

It was no good. They were both too close. He felt Aurélie's excitement in the tiny rotations of her pelvis as she pressed back against him, heard it in her tantalising moan of pleasure.

He brushed his hand across her peaked nipples, enjoying her jerk of response and capitalising on it with another easy thrust. Then temptation triumphed. Vowing to take it slow next time, he cupped her sex then slid his finger across—

'Lucien!'

That was all it took.

Hand pressing hard on his, as if afraid he'd stop caressing her, or perhaps needing to cling on, Aurélie shattered. He felt the tremors build in force, her muscles drawing hard, milking him till he exploded in stunning climax.

The waves of ecstasy went on and on.

When Lucien's brain rejoined his body he realised that, like every time last night and on that night months ago, it felt as if he'd just experienced the most stunning sexual experience of his life. Yet each time it got better. His mind boggled at the possibilities.

As their sated bodies sank together in the remnants of bliss, he congratulated himself. Marriage to Aurélie might provoke gossip and even scandal. But the compensations would be spectacular.

When Aurélie woke the bed was empty. There was a dent in the other pillow and the sheets were rumpled, though the bedcover had been pulled up neatly to her shoulders.

As if Lucien had straightened the bedding so she was warm and cosy. She stretched, her body instantly reminding her that last night had been no ordinary night. She and Lucien had had sex multiple times and each time it had felt as if he'd opened a door to heaven.

She smiled as she shuffled higher in the bed, plumping up the pillows.

A sudden swooping dive in her stomach sliced through her rose-tinted thoughts. Aurélie breathed slowly out through her mouth, trying not to move too much as she reached for the glass of water on her bedside table. Her stomach roiled as she took a small sip. She waited, trying to assess if the morning sickness would increase or lessen. Another cautious sip.

She was congratulating herself that it appeared to be easing when a rolling tide of nausea rose higher. She slammed the glass down and thrust back the covers, hurrying across the carpet to the lavish en suite bathroom.

So much for her post-coital glow. The woman staring at her from the mirror had parchment-pale skin and a bruised look under her eyes. Her hair was wild and so were her eyes as she fought the inevitable.

Fought and lost.

Seconds later she was hunched, retching over the toilet, wishing she hadn't eaten last night because then she'd have nothing to bring up. Her arms shook and her eyes watered at each violent spasm. Even her skin was taut and clammy. All she could do was hang on and ride the wave of misery.

Then, out of nowhere, warmth encompassed her shivering body. Callused fingers pulled her hair back, anchoring it behind her ears, and she gave an unsteady nod of thanks.

Lucien. The heat of his hard-packed muscles and the tenderness of his skimming touch were so familiar.

She had a moment to wish he hadn't found her like this.

When they'd been in bed together she'd felt like a sex goddess. Now she had all the charm of a dishrag. Then another bout of sickness hit and pride disappeared. She was simply grateful for his support, one arm carefully bracing her while with the other he blotted her forehead with a damp cloth.

When the wave passed she leant back against him, letting him take her weight. Silently he wiped her face, the dampness reviving her enough to open her eyes.

'Thank you. I think it's over now.'

'You want to get up?'

Aurélie nodded, telling herself that in another second she'd have the energy to rise.

Before she could try, Lucien tossed the washcloth into the basin and scooped her up against him. For a second the world tilted and she gasped, fearing the worst. But, as if he read her thoughts, Lucien stood still, waiting till she nodded before taking her back to the bed.

Installed there, catching the V of concern furrowing his brow, she felt self-conscious.

'Sorry. That can't have been nice for you.'

'You're apologising for your morning sickness?' He sat beside her and reached for her hand, threading his fingers through hers. 'I'm just glad I could help. It's rotten that you have to go through this on top of the shock of finding yourself pregnant.'

Aurélie shot him a startled look.

'What's wrong?'

It should worry her that Lucien read her so easily, but she couldn't bring herself to stress about it now. He was right. She still felt too fragile.

'Nothing. It's...' She paused and shrugged. 'Whenever my stepmother was sick during pregnancy my father made a point of leaving the house. He didn't like to be around illness.' It had been left to Aurélie to do whatever was necessary to help her stepmother and look after the boys. It had become a habit over the years till she'd become the one responsible for all the household chores. Her stepmother had got used to relying on Aurélie and never bothered teaching her sons to share the workload. 'I'm not used to men who are so…domesticated.'

Or to anyone caring for *her*. Most of her life she'd felt almost invisible, taken for granted like a piece of furniture. Aurélie couldn't remember the last time anyone in her family had noticed her enough to consider what *she* needed, much less supported her.

Lucien's mouth hooked up, turning his frown into a wry, far too attractive smile. 'You make me sound like a tabby cat.'

'Hardly.' Her gaze dropped to the wide straight line of his shoulders, skating across to the open top button of his pristine business shirt and lower to that hard torso she could snuggle against all day. Lucien had all the power and lethal athleticism of a predatory big cat, despite the way he made her purr.

'Aurélie, you're carrying all the burden of this baby right now. The least I can do is help where I can.' His stare held hers and she felt something inside ease and soften. 'Speaking of which, I went to get you biscuits and ginger tea. I'm told ginger is good to prevent nausea. And you need to keep up your fluids.'

His words settled behind her breastbone, snug and comforting, and she drew a deep, unfettered breath. Was she really so besotted, so needy, that Lucien's practical concern affected her?

It seemed so. She felt again that abrupt spike of emotion and vulnerability she'd experienced before when he was kind.

Lucien reached for the tray he'd put beside the bed. Had the doctor recommended this or had Lucien taken time to enquire about possible remedies?

Either way, that melting sensation quickened at the sight of him pouring a small cup of fragrant, pale liquid with as much concentration as if he were handling a rare antique.

His expression was serious as he held it out to her and watched her take a sip. Aurélie held her breath, wondering if she'd be making another undignified bolt to the bathroom, but this time her stomach didn't rebel.

'Lovely,' she sighed. And it was. Not just the tea, but the way he made her feel.

Cherished. Again that word sprang into her mind. Though she understood Lucien was making the best of a bad situation. Last night, in the throes of passion, she could be excused thinking he really cared. But now, in the light of day, she couldn't let herself be swept away by foolish imaginings.

She was taking another sip when Lucien spoke.

'About your stipulation. About needing more time before we announce our wedding.' He paused as if waiting to make sure he had her attention. 'We need to agree a time-line. There's a lot to organise.'

Aurélie nodded, ignoring the dragging sensation inside. *Disappointment.*

Naturally Lucien needed a timeline. Their marriage would be as practical as his arrangement with Ilsa. They were doing this for the sake of their baby and to secure the royal succession. The feeling of being cherished evaporated.

'I want to be married well before the baby arrives.'

Again she nodded, feeling like a puppet whose strings were being pulled by a master. Of course he wanted to marry before the birth. He wanted a legitimate heir.

Because he was royal and such things mattered.

'If we keep it very simple and small…' Aurélie stopped as Lucien shook his head.

'Simple and small won't be possible.' As if reading her horror he went on quickly. 'We can tailor it as much as possible to suit your preferences, but this won't be a hole-and-corner event. We need to show the world that you're a suitable consort. And we need to give the people of Vallort a chance to share the celebration.' His expression changed, a flicker of something that looked like pain dimming his eyes. 'Something joyous after all the grief.'

Aurélie swallowed, forcing down her automatic protest. She'd been about to fight him on this. The thought of a big wedding full of pomp, with her at its centre, an imposter pretending to be a royal princess, made her nauseous. And that had nothing to do with morning sickness.

Everyone would see this was a sham, that *she* was a sham.

But that haunted look in Lucien's eyes stopped her. Aurélie forced herself to take another sip of tea. It didn't taste as good as before.

'A royal wedding takes lots of planning.'

'You mean you don't want to wait to announce our engagement.' Her voice sounded as dull as the leaden weight sitting in her stomach.

'I agreed to give you time, Aurélie.' He paused, mouth compressing. 'But there are limits.'

'Have you thought about what you're asking me to do?' Her voice rose unsteadily and she clamped her teeth on her bottom lip, not liking the thready note of panic she heard.

'I have.' His gaze held hers and, surprisingly, she felt that tremor of distress settle. 'Don't forget I've come into this role unexpectedly too.'

'But you were brought up royal, even if you never expected to inherit. You know how it all works.' She lifted her chin to indicate their surroundings. 'You grew up in a castle! I grew up in a cramped flat in a working-class neighbourhood.'

He covered the hand that wasn't holding the teacup. Absurdly, Lucien's touch eased her jittery pulse. When she had spare time to think on that, Aurélie knew it would be yet another thing to disturb her.

'Which means I can help you. I've made a list of people who can bring you up to speed on what you need to know.'

Aurélie reached across to put her cup down, her mouth

firming. She imagined a schedule of tutors trying and failing to turn a commoner into a queen. Would she have to practise deportment, walking with a heavy book on her head? Learn to curtsey? Have a crash course in politics?

She moistened dry lips, about to tell him it was too overwhelming.

'Isn't it worth it, for the sake of our child?'

Aurélie sagged back against her pillows. Mere days ago she'd planned on returning to France and raising this baby alone. She told herself that was still possible.

Except it wasn't.

Not because she wanted her child to inherit a throne. Not because she wanted to be Queen. But because she recognised Lucien's care for this baby and understood he would love it too. That was too precious to ignore.

Lucien was determined and that would make a huge difference to their baby. It would have a father who fought for it in every way that counted.

Unlike her father. Who'd ignored her, except as an unpaid drudge.

If they married she'd secure a family for her child, the chance to study as she'd dreamed, plus she'd be with Lucien...

'Aurélie?'

Her breath faltered as she met Lucien's probing stare. Reluctantly she answered. 'Yes, it's worth it.'

Was that relief that made his shoulders drop while hers tightened?

'Give me three weeks before you make the announcement. They say the first twelve are when there's most danger of complications.' She stopped, trying not to think about the possibility of miscarriage.

'Three weeks then.' Lucien smiled and raised her hand to kiss it. But strangely Aurélie felt no shiver of sensual awareness. Because all his delight was for the baby. This wedding was to secure its birthright.

She should be used to it now. Since her mother died, she'd never been more than a convenience to anyone. She'd never been treasured or loved. Never valued for herself.

Aurélie set her jaw and told herself it didn't matter.

Lucien was marrying her for their baby's sake and she was doing the same. That was what counted.

She ignored the crumbling feeling inside. As if the futile imaginings she'd begun to spin around this man during last night's passion cracked and disintegrated.

CHAPTER THIRTEEN

'HIS MAJESTY IS on the phone, mademoiselle.'

The housekeeper waited in the doorway as Aurélie approached from the woodland path, quickening her step.

In the five days since she'd arrived at the castle her morning sickness had become just that, hitting her only in the morning. She'd got into the habit of heading out for a walk mid-morning, enjoying the clear air and fairyland beauty of green dells and deep forest. The weather had improved, the sun shining and the temperature rising.

Aurélie had a full afternoon ahead, with a tutor coming to teach her about the government, administration and politics of Vallort. Maybe he'd had to cancel...

She was fascinated by Lucien's country, but studying to become a queen left her unsettled and doubtful.

'Thank you.'

The housekeeper smiled as she handed over the phone and disappeared inside the castle.

A *castle*. Aurélie was staying in a castle. She was the King's lover and would be mother of a future monarch. Yet again the unreality of her situation sideswiped her.

'Aurélie? Are you there?'

There it was. The deep-seated sizzle that came whenever she heard Lucien's voice. She'd hoped it would abate—the strange magic when she heard his voice purr the syllables of her name. But still she was in thrall. Five days as Lucien's lover, sharing his bed, and the cosy evening hours when they shut the world out, and the magic ensnared her more strongly than ever.

'I'm here, Lucien.' Aurélie turned to look down the valley to the city where he was.

She didn't have time for magic. If she wasn't careful she'd

start imagining there was more between them than sexual attraction and an unplanned pregnancy.

'What is it? You sound different. Are you okay?'

The man was too perceptive. Of course she wasn't okay. She was too fond of him, too caught up in what he made her feel. Things could only end in tears if she let herself believe he cared for her as anything other than his baby's mother.

'I'm fine. I've been for a walk and feel better for it.'

'You're not sick?' Concern tinged his voice and she couldn't stop a flare of delight that he cared.

Because you're carrying his child. Remember?

'No, I'm okay.' She paused, realising how unusual it was for him to call during work hours. 'What is it, Lucien? Is everything all right there?'

This week had been tough on him, though Lucien refused to burden her with details. When he arrived home each evening, there was no mistaking the strain he tried to mask.

Fortunately they found ways to relieve that strain...

'You're worried about me?'

Aurélie couldn't tell if that was hope in his voice or curiosity. But it wouldn't do to let him know exactly how much she felt for him. As it was, parting each day was ridiculously difficult.

Because of pregnancy hormones or something else?

'You have an enormous workload and you're facing tremendous pressure.'

Yet just yesterday he'd carved out a couple of hours to take her to a charming mountain inn for lunch. What made the date special wasn't a romantic rendezvous, but that he'd invited his closest friends to meet her, introducing her as 'special to me' but not mentioning her pregnancy.

Aurélie was stunned by his generosity, drawing her firmly into that warm, intimate circle with no caveats, just open-hearted acceptance.

As if she *were* special.

Her own circle of friends had broken when some had

moved away and others had grown distant as she'd devoted herself to longer hours working at home and the restaurant.

Aurélie had been nervous yesterday, expecting a backlash over the broken engagement. But Lucien's friends had been welcoming. There'd been no judgement, though she guessed they were curious. They'd set her at ease and she'd enjoyed herself enormously.

'Don't worry about me, Aurélie. It's nothing I can't handle. You concentrate on resting.' It was a familiar refrain, as if her bouts of sickness really worried him.

'You only want me to rest so I'm ready to learn about politics and parliamentary processes.'

He huffed a laugh that rippled like sunshine over her skin. 'That's only for one afternoon. Surely you can spare the time. Besides, I was ringing to tell you I've arranged something a lot more appealing. A couple of things, actually.'

Aurélie's hand tightened on the receiver. 'I don't need treats, Lucien. I totally get that this is stuff I need to understand if I stay here.'

Silence lengthened. She'd snapped the words out like an ungrateful harridan. She'd said *if* she stayed, though she'd already agreed to marry him.

Yet every time she thought of the future Lucien planned she felt nervous and worried.

'I'm sorry, Lucien. I'm a little...'

Out of my depth?

Petrified I'm falling in love with you?

Aurélie drew in a slow breath. 'What did you want to tell me?'

'You'll have two more visitors this afternoon.' His tone was unreadable and for some reason that was worse than hearing anger or disappointment. 'A stylist will visit straight after lunch with a selection of clothes for you to choose from. I want you to feel comfortable that you have something appropriate for any occasion.'

Aurélie was about to object, then stopped. He was right. She had only a handful of outfits here. Even if she had access to all her clothes she had nothing suitable to wear in royal circles.

'No complaints?'

Her mouth twisted ruefully. 'You know me too well.'

'I know you're independent and you don't like being beholden, but—'

'It's okay, Lucien. I can see the wisdom of having the right clothes.'

Though accepting them felt a step closer to the future that felt so unreal. She'd already agreed, yet she baulked at the idea. Surely his people would never accept her. Aurélie bit her lip and dragged her gaze from the city in the distance to the calming green of the forest.

'And the other thing you've arranged?'

If it was deportment classes she'd just have to grin and bear it.

'You have a half hour lesson at five-thirty with a piano tutor.'

'Sorry?' She couldn't have heard right.

'You said you'd always wanted to learn the piano.' He paused and when he spoke again his voice dragged low across her senses. 'I thought it might make the crash course on being a royal easier if you had something fun to look forward to, like music lessons.'

Aurélie opened her mouth then closed it again. She blinked as the forest greens blurred.

'I...' She swallowed hard, a sharp knot of emotion scraping her throat then raking down into her chest. 'Thank you, Lucien, that's...' Her throat closed again.

'Aurélie?' His voice sharpened. 'I thought you'd be happy.'

She pressed a hand to her breastbone, trying to hold in the riot of feelings. Her heart hammered and her chest felt too full.

'I am…happy. Thank you. That's very thoughtful.' She swallowed. 'I need to go now. Sorry.'

Disconnecting the call, she leaned against the doorway, overwhelmed. Hadn't she known from the first that Lucien made her feel too much?

This confirmed it. His gift of piano lessons was thoughtful and well meant. It was the nicest thing anyone had done for her in…well, as long as she could recall. Not since her mother had anyone taken time to do anything special for her.

The fact that Lucien remembered her desire to play the piano, that he'd thought about it in the midst of the pressures he faced and then acted on it, because he wanted to make her happy…

Beneath her palm her heart thundered.

Through the tall trees, beams of sunlight shone; she was transfixed by their brightness.

That was how she felt inside. Burning bright.

Because she couldn't pretend any longer. She'd fallen in love with Lucien. His kindness as much as his passion undid her.

Somehow she had to work out a way to marry him, have his baby and live with him, play the part of his Queen, and never betray her feelings for him.

'His Majesty said you like bright colours,' the stylist said, smiling, as she wheeled in several racks of clothes.

Which proved again that Lucien paid attention. Aurélie's heart gave a fluttery thump, like it had when he'd told her about the piano lessons. Ridiculous to feel wobbly inside. Simply because he'd noticed *her*, thought about her preferences.

It made her feel *cared for*. Something she wasn't used to.

Aurélie loved colour, including some yellows and deep pinks that redheads were supposedly not meant to wear. Yet she was surprised he'd paid attention. Or surprised he'd remembered to mention the fact. She'd imagined him telling his secretary to make sure she had suitable clothes and then turning back to other business.

The stylist pulled the cover off the first rack and Aurélie sucked in a stunned breath.

The light caught jewel colours that gleamed rich and inviting, wonderful dresses that even she could tell were haute couture.

She couldn't resist reaching out to finger the sleeve of a jade-green dress, its silk as fine as a butterfly's wing. The slippery satin of an evening gown in deep amethyst. A halter-neck in an amber shade that reminded her of Lucien's eyes.

'It helped that I knew about your fabulous colouring.' The woman smiled as she uncovered another rack. This one was filled with trousers and jackets, including a long, stylish coat of cobalt blue wool that Aurélie couldn't take her eyes off.

'Yes, you'd look terrific in that. The fitted style would make the most of your slim figure.'

Aurélie's hand dropped. Not slim for long. How far into her pregnancy would she develop a baby bump?

'I don't need too much. Just a few things for the moment.'

The stylist nodded and smiled but immediately explained that a full wardrobe had been ordered. 'Perhaps if we start on what you're going to need in the next week or two, then see how we go?' She ran an expert eye over Aurélie, then back to the racks. 'Tonight, for instance, you'll want something special.'

'Tonight?'

'For the opening of that new photographic exhibition people are talking about.' Seeing Aurélie's blank look, she went on, curiosity evident. 'I was supposed to tell you to be ready at eight. Apparently there was some problem getting the message to you earlier.'

Probably because Aurélie had hung up on Lucien before he could tell her. Guiltily she bit her lip.

Had he realised she'd felt undone by his kindness, or

did he think her still in a snit over the 'royal' tutorials he'd arranged?

Quickly Aurélie nodded, pretending she'd known about the opening. It must be the one she'd heard about yesterday. One of Lucien's good friends was a professional photographer. His wife, a bank executive, had spoken about this new exhibition and how he'd almost broken his neck climbing a glacier at dawn to get the right shot. By the time they'd finished describing some of his more outrageous adventures in search of the perfect photo, Aurélie had been relaxed and laughing with the rest of them.

Now, though, she faced the prospect of deciding what to wear for a gala opening. She was torn between eagerness at seeing the exhibition and Lucien's friends, and dismay at accompanying him in public. Surely it was too soon after his broken engagement?

'Do you have any suggestions for tonight?'

The stylist put her head to one side. 'Nothing too formal, of course.' She moved away from the full-length dresses and Aurélie relaxed a little. 'But definitely something eye-catching. The opening is a high-profile event. Everyone who's anyone will be there.'

She reached for a cocktail length dress in bright aqua, shimmering with tiny beads.

'It's gorgeous.' Instinctively Aurélie moved closer then stopped herself. 'But I think something not so bright.'

'You'd look a million dollars in this style and the colour against your wonderful hair would turn every head.'

That was what Aurélie was afraid of. 'I think, for tonight, I'd rather not stand out from the crowd.'

She caught speculation in the other woman's eyes, then the stylist nodded her understanding.

'Society events can be a bit overwhelming if you're not used to them.' She didn't glance at Aurélie's jeans and cheap knitted top, but she'd no doubt sized them up in the first seconds of them meeting. 'Okay, something a little less bright, at least for tonight, yes?'

Aurélie's tight shoulders eased a little. 'Yes, that would be perfect.'

'How are you holding up?' Lucien lowered his voice and Aurélie felt it as a velvet caress across her shivery skin. That deep murmur reminded her of making love. Then his voice, roughened with arousal, would make her body sing as much as his touch and his hungry amber stare.

'I'm good.' Her smile was real, not like the fake one she'd put on as they'd arrived at the gallery. 'I'm actually enjoying myself.'

Especially as no one had thrust out an accusing finger, pointing to her as an intruder who didn't belong. Though there *were* plenty of curious looks. The gala opening had attracted a glamorous crowd and Lucien hadn't left her side.

'I'm pleased.' His hand lingered at the small of her back, not quite touching, yet her skin warmed as if from direct contact.

Her heartbeat stilled for a moment as she caught satisfaction in Lucien's eyes and something more. Heat blossomed in her pelvis.

Aurélie heaved a deep breath, fighting excitement at his flagrantly possessive expression. But that only made her breasts rise against the midnight-blue silk of her dress and Lucien's gaze dropped to her bodice. Inevitably her nipples pebbled needily.

'Stop it,' she hissed. 'You're drawing attention to me.'

She'd been unable to resist the dress the stylist had suggested. Aurélie had assumed the darker colour and simple lines would help her blend into the background. She'd reckoned without the fact that standing beside the King meant she could never be in the background. Or that the silk's lustrous shine drew attention to the shape of her body. Had it clung so much when she'd tried it on this afternoon?

The almost grim line of Lucien's mouth turned up in a rueful smile. 'Believe me, Aurélie, you don't need me to draw attention to you. You're doing that all by yourself. You look magnificent.'

She shook her head, trying not to react to his over-the-top praise.

'*Those* are magnificent.' She gestured towards the photographs on the black wall before them. Alpine scenes in deepest winter. 'Your friend is so talented. The light and shade on that frozen waterfall is amazing.'

'I agree. They're some of his best, and he'll be delighted to hear you say it.' His voice dropped. 'But you're changing the subject.'

Aurélie's chin jerked up. 'I don't need flattery, Lucien.'

But when she met his eyes he looked completely serious. 'You don't believe you look magnificent?'

She shot a quick look around and found that for once there was no one standing close. Yet instinctively she moved closer to a photo of tiny meadow flowers surrounding a mirror-surfaced mountain lake.

'So long as I look passable, I'll be happy.' She'd never mixed with people in couture fashion and jewels before. Never run the gauntlet of press photographers. It had been nerve-racking, though Lucien had thoughtfully arranged for them to arrive with the friends they'd met yesterday.

There it was again. Thoughtfulness.

Because he cared?

Or because he didn't want her spooked into changing her mind about staying?

Lucien listened to Aurélie chat with a German count and countess about kayaking.

They'd met in front of a stunning photo of a kayaker descending rapids in full flood. It turned out Aurélie had enjoyed the little kayaking she'd done years before with a friend, enough to unwind when the Count began talking of rapids and Eskimo rolls. Her eyes shone brightly and the tension that had stiffened her shoulders all evening evaporated.

He guessed it would return if she realised she was talking to the CEO of one of Europe's most prosperous banks or that his wife was a senior diplomat.

Lucien knew Aurélie felt out of place with the rich and powerful. If only he could convince her that the job of royalty was as much about protecting and serving ordinary citizens as it was about mingling with VIPs. But that was something she'd have to realise for herself over time.

If only she knew it, her down-to-earth freshness totally suited the Vallort royal family, which, for the last two generations at least, had focused on substance rather than pomp. As a royal, she'd spend as much time interacting with the general public as the privileged.

Another couple joined the group and Lucien watched, delighted, as Aurélie chatted easily. Her vivacity drawing more than one admiring glance. Once she forgot about social barriers and royalty she was fine.

More than fine.

Lucien spoke little and he realised how relaxing it was not to have to carry the whole burden of conversation. How good it felt to have a partner who could contribute and take her share of social interaction.

It wasn't something he'd considered when he'd insisted Aurélie marry him.

But lots of things weren't as he'd imagined then.

His feelings about Aurélie for a start.

It had been easy to decide that marriage was their only option. Because he refused to give up his child—his *family*.

But their relationship wasn't just about duty. Which was some compensation, since the scandal he dealt with now was nothing to the blast of attention they'd get when it was discovered she carried his child.

Nor was it simply protectiveness he felt. Nor even lust, though both were there, strong and easy to recognise.

What he felt for Aurélie…

Looking at her, vibrant and sexy, made his chest ache.

Unlike most women here she wore no jewellery except tiny stud earrings. Her deep blue dress was plain but it packed a punch he felt right to his groin. Whenever he looked at her he imagined his hands following the contours of her luscious body.

She had no need of diamonds or gold to catch the eye. But as soon as he thought of her in jewels, his unruly mind conjured an image of her wearing some of the royal jewels. And nothing else.

His throat dried and his brain blurred so the bustle towards the exit took him by surprise. He looked at his watch. The event was ending.

Lucien drew Aurélie closer. 'Are you tired? If you prefer we could go straight home instead of to supper with the others.' He'd enlisted his friends' assistance to enter and leave together in the hope that any paparazzi wouldn't single Aurélie out for special attention. That would come soon enough but she was understandably skittish about the press.

Brilliant eyes met his as she gave him a stunning smile. The impact would have rocked a lesser man. His hand tightened on her elbow. It would be selfish to hope she'd opt to go straight to bed—

'I'd love to go to supper with your friends.' Aurélie lowered her voice. 'I've had such a lovely night I don't want it to end. I'd forgotten how much I like being with people.'

That reinforced his assessment of her personality. Her warmth as she'd chatted with customers that first night wasn't solely because it was her job. She was genuinely interested in them.

Then her forehead creased. 'Unless you'd rather not. You've had a long day.'

She was worried about *him* being tired? She was the

one carrying their baby. A thought which turned him on as much as it evoked protectiveness. Now her concern was liquid warmth in his already overheated body.

'Oh, I think I've got enough energy for a little more *excitement* tonight.' His voice dropped as he took her hand, running his thumb across the centre of her palm and the sensitive skin of her wrist. Satisfaction surged at her shudder of response.

Her eyes glowed and her lips parted and Lucien cursed himself as a fool for playing this suggestive game as his arousal tightened his trousers.

'Come on, Aurélie. The others are ready.'

The group walked from the gallery half a block to a restaurant tucked into an old hotel renowned for exquisite and innovative food. The evening was convivial and they enjoyed the camaraderie of the group.

It was good to relax with friends, putting aside for a couple of hours the burdens of kingship. And when he draped his arm around the back of Aurélie's chair and she leaned closer he didn't even try to find a definition for the upswell of emotion that flowed hot and strong inside.

Even the photographers in the street failed to destroy his good humour.

And when they reached the castle tower where Aurélie had shared his bed for almost a week, his sense of well-being grew.

'I like your friends,' she said as she unpinned her hair and a froth of fiery waves cascaded around her shoulders.

'I'm glad. They like you too.' He pulled her in and bent his head, burying his face in that mass of lilac-scented waves. Aurélie smelled like spring. Could that be why he craved her so badly? Until she came he'd felt he faced endless winter.

His arms tightened, hauling her close. 'I love your hair.'

He felt a second's surprise at his choice of words. He wasn't a teenage girl who *loved* this or that. But it was true, he did love her hair. And her soft skin. And…

'Really? It's very bright. And I have to work to keep it under control. Pinning it up tonight took ages.'

Lucien drew back enough to meet her dark eyes. 'It's perfect. It's vibrant like you and I love the curls. Do you have to pin it up?'

'It looks tidier that way. More formal.'

He watched her chew her lip, something she hadn't done all evening.

Because they were talking, obliquely, about how royalty looked and she wasn't at ease with the idea of becoming a queen. The change from the confident woman earlier this evening made him pause.

Lucien straightened and slipped his hands down to capture hers, threading their fingers together.

'Start as you mean to go on.'

'Sorry?'

'It's something my uncle used to tell Justin. That when the time came for him to inherit the throne he should start as he meant to go on.' He paused, realising that for the first time he'd spoken of them without that awful catch in his chest. 'He said each new monarch had to forge his own way, make his own rules and be comfortable with his choices. He was all for moulding the job, as he called it, to suit changing circumstances and generations.'

'I don't understand.'

'It's natural you're overwhelmed by the idea of becoming royal. But in my family it's viewed as both an honourable obligation and a job. We're bound by it but each generation makes it their own.' He paused, realising how important this was and that he wasn't explaining clearly.

'For instance, I know you were concerned tonight was too soon to be seen in public with me. But I intend to be your husband. There's nothing to be gained by hiding you away from the press. I'm not ashamed of you or our baby.' Lucien felt his chest rise. 'Vallort, and the press, will grow accustomed to us being together. That's something I won't bend on.'

Aurélie regarded him seriously but Lucien wasn't sure she was convinced.

'If you want to wear your hair loose, do it. If you want to wear one of those cute ponytails—' her eyebrows shot up and he smiled '—then do it.' He shook his head. 'There are some things we can't change—the constitution and the laws of inheritance—but if anything, and I mean *anything* about the way we live our lives as royals bothers you, then tell me and we'll search for a compromise.'

Finally she nodded. 'Thank you. I like the idea of compromise and hearing some of the rules might be elastic. Maybe that way when I make a mistake it won't be a disaster.'

Lucien stroked his hands up to her shoulders, enjoying her sensual shiver. Deliberately he massaged her shoulders, feeling tense muscles loosen.

'We all make mistakes. Ask my staff. I've kept them busy since taking the throne. I still have a lot to learn.'

Her eyebrows rose and to his delight she slanted him a sultry smile. 'In some things. In others you're very proficient, Your Majesty.'

That was when he noticed her nipples thrusting against the silk of her dress. 'Proficient, eh? At what?'

He skimmed his hands down her bodice to cup her breasts. Her breath sighed out and her back arched as she pushed into his touch. Lucien had no idea if her responsiveness was due to pregnancy hormones or a naturally sensuous nature, but he loved Aurélie's eagerness for sex.

Another thing he loved about her.

He might tell himself marriage was the right thing to protect Aurélie and his baby, but he couldn't fool himself that he was motivated purely by duty. His feelings for her were far more complex.

'You know exactly what I mean,' she murmured, licking her lips.

And just like that she turned the tables on him. That pink

tongue against those soft lips. The glorious bounty of her silk-clad breasts in his hands. The perfume of her skin—flowers and female arousal.

His groin hardened, heavy with blood rushing south.

'But practice makes perfect, don't you agree?' He bent to fit his mouth over one pert nipple and sucked hard. Hands clawed at his skull and her pelvis thrust into him.

'I think…' she gasped '…it's time to stop teasing and put your money where your mouth is.'

Lucien swallowed a chuckle of delight and proceeded to strip his lover bare. Then he took them both to a pinnacle of ecstasy that couldn't be, but seemed, even higher and more perfect than the ones they'd reached last night.

Each time with Aurélie seemed better than before.

And it wasn't just sex. Tonight, being in her company, enjoying her enjoyment, had been a delight.

Finally, well past midnight, they slumped together, sated and content. Blissfully unaware of the firestorm about to hit them.

CHAPTER FOURTEEN

LUCIEN STARED AT the headlines in the media report his office had sent through.

He'd known this was going to happen. He'd been prepared. Or he'd thought he was. Yet he felt nauseous.

Was this how Aurélie felt when morning sickness hit?

Aurélie. His mouth firmed and his gut clenched.

For most of his life the press had published positive stories about the Vallort royal family. True, there'd been speculation and shock about his broken engagement. But, if today's press reports were any indication, things had changed. Not so much for him, but for Aurélie.

A cold, hard sensation settled low inside. It was okay for him to talk about standing up to public opinion. Poor Aurélie hadn't asked for this and didn't deserve it.

He'd expected to bear the brunt of any negativity. He'd assumed she'd be painted as an innocent and he a serial seducer.

Which showed he'd never make a journalist.

A surge of rage pummelled him. He wanted to ring the editors and shout at them. Except that would be exactly the wrong thing to do. Instead he'd have to bury his ire and decide how to deal with this. His team had been developing a PR strategy but it needed work.

'You're still here! I thought you'd left.' Aurélie stood in the doorway wearing a new wrap of soft green. She looked like a woodland sprite with her wide eyes, pale skin and glowing hair cascading around her shoulders.

A sexy sprite, with that nipped-in waist and curves his hands itched to touch, even now when he wrestled with incandescent rage.

Lucien shoved the chair back from his desk. 'Something came up that the palace wanted me to see straight away.'

She moved further into his study, a symphony of soft curves and lithe lines that dried his brain despite the urgent need for action.

'Something bad.' It was a statement.

Lucien hesitated. His instinct was to shield her. Especially as it was his fault she faced this. If he'd been an ordinary citizen, not a king... But regrets were useless and Aurélie needed to know.

'There are reports about us.'

'Because we went out last night?' She refrained from saying *I told you so*. He'd been adamant that they shouldn't wait till he announced their engagement for Aurélie to appear in public. That had felt too much as if he were hiding a dirty secret, instead of presenting the woman who'd be his wife.

He spread his hands, palms up. 'And about our lunch the day before.'

'With your friends?' Her brow twitched as if her concern was about the intrusion into his friends' privacy.

'The press has had time to discover your name and nationality. They'll be digging for more now.'

Aurélie clutched the front of her robe with one hand, her chin going up. 'It was inevitable, I suppose.'

Regret was temporarily eclipsed by admiration. His woman had steel in her spine.

Lucien couldn't stop himself. He stepped in, wrapped an arm around her waist, plunged his hand into the thick mass of her glorious hair and kissed her full on the lips. Fire ignited as their lips fused. Their bodies aligned as the kiss deepened and Lucien was tempted to carry her back to bed.

But he couldn't be so selfish. He had to work with his staff to refine their PR strategy. To make things better for her.

Breathing heavily, he drew back enough to meet Aurélie's eyes.

'Is it really that bad?'

'It's not good. I'd suggest staying in the castle today. No one will bother you here.'

'I see.' Her gaze meshed with his. '*That* bad.'

Lucien shrugged, but his shoulders felt stiff. 'It will get better. I'm going now to meet with key staff about our media response.'

'What can I do?'

Once more it hit him that he'd struck gold with this woman. They mightn't see eye to eye on everything but she was resolute and courageous. His baby would have a wonderful mother. His country would have a wonderful queen.

'Why are you smiling? I didn't say anything funny.'

She frowned and Lucien hurried to explain. 'It was a smile of approval, Aurélie.' He stroked the back of his hand down her cheek. Soft as a peach but she had a core of strength he could only admire. 'As for what you can do, rest up this morning. Don't worry about the press for now. You've got tutorials this afternoon and when I come back tonight we'll discuss how we're to deal with this. Okay?'

Slowly she nodded and Lucien felt a tiny bit of the weight lift from his shoulders. By tonight he'd be better placed to discuss concrete options with her.

'Walk me to the car?' He slid her arm through his and smiled when she pressed close.

What he and Aurélie shared might have begun unconventionally but there was something genuine and strong at its heart. They'd make this marriage work, despite what the world said.

Aurélie entered Lucien's study with a sense of trepidation. It was clear he didn't want her viewing the media reports. On the way to the car he'd reiterated that it would be better if she ignored the press today and they'd talk it through tonight.

It must be very bad.

She settled at his desk and lifted the lid of his laptop.

He'd forgotten to shut it down and it opened immediately to a list of media stories. There were lots.

Aurélie hesitated. But she wasn't prying into state secrets. This was about her.

Last night Lucien's confidence in her, his support, had made her feel good about herself. As if, should she wish to, she could do anything she set her mind to. Just as her mother had told her when she was little. Just as she'd told herself time and again, as she'd fought against being ground down by her family's dismissiveness.

Breathing deep, she clicked on the attachment and saw story after story.

The first couple, from the local press in Vallort, were fairly mild. Curiosity over her identity. A couple of photos from last night. Reference to Lucien's broken engagement and speculation over her role in his life.

But then came the rest, from foreign press and social media. A barrage of blaring headlines that hit her like physical blows. A few painted Lucien as a callous playboy.

Ilsa Heartbroken as Lucien Flaunts New Lover!

And there was a photo of Ilsa looking stoic. But most focused on Aurélie. She read them with increasing horror.

Lucien's Red-Hot Redhead!

King Flaunts Mistress!

Tragic Ilsa Ousted by French Floozy!

Bile rose in her throat as the stories grew more and more lurid, with speculation that she'd seduced Lucien out of his betrothal with phenomenal sex. One sordid flight of fancy painted her as a whore who'd connived to get access to a royal fortune.

She slammed the laptop shut. Lucien was right. She didn't want to read this.

It could only get worse when they discovered he planned to marry her. That she carried his child.

Aurélie swallowed, battling nausea.

She was caught. Even if she broke her promise to marry him, the press would follow her. There'd be stories about her child, probably even more cruel ones, if she left Lucien and returned to France. The press would never go away. The stories would continue for years, about the King's child and Lucien's ex-lover.

She looked at her hands, clenched on the laptop.

It made sense to stay.

But that wasn't why she'd remain.

She'd do it *because she loved Lucien*. Had fallen in love with him that first night, no matter how improbable that seemed.

Everything she'd learned about him since—his honesty and sense of duty, his positivity and kindness, his wry sense of humour and camaraderie—just strengthened her feelings. Aurélie didn't want to leave him. She wanted to stay at his side, raising their family.

For good or ill, this was her world now. She lifted her head and took in the spectacular view down the valley to the capital city, ringed by snowy mountains. Her gaze moved around the room to centuries-old carved bookcases filled with a mix of leather-covered books and modern office binders. The decorative plasterwork ceiling and huge antique rug that contrasted with and yet complemented the series of modern photographic studies on one wall.

Lucien had stepped into the Kingship, making his own changes along the way.

Start as you mean to go on.

Aurélie shoved the chair back from his desk, ignoring the laptop, and turned to the door. She had a lot to do before this afternoon's tutorials.

'She's where?' Lucien couldn't believe his ears.

'In the centre of the old town. She walked through the pedestrian zone with a pack of photographers on her heels. Now she's in a bookshop. I've organised some security to be there when she comes out, to keep the press back. But their numbers are growing.'

'A bookshop?' Lucien scowled. 'What was so urgent she had to go out today of all days to buy a book?'

His secretary cleared his throat and offered his phone. 'From what I saw there was no urgency. She took her time.'

Lucien stared at the small screen, the short film clip of Aurélie strolling through the city's most exclusive shopping zone. She looked pale and the high set of her shoulders gave away her tension, but her pace was slow and she took her time window shopping.

His heart rose to his throat and he had to swallow jerkily to find his voice. 'She's gone there deliberately.' Certainty swelled behind his disbelief.

'Then she's a brave woman.'

Lucien nodded, torn between admiration and anger. She shouldn't be doing this alone.

'Organise a car for me. I'll be down in a couple of minutes.' He stood, picking up his own phone and dialling as he reached for his jacket.

He found her in the children's section, apparently engrossed in the book she held. But her head lifted at his footsteps.

'Lucien! What are you doing here?'

'I could ask you the same.' He kept his voice low. 'I told you to stay at the castle.'

Her fine eyebrows rose. 'Was that an order?'

'Of course not. I was trying to protect you.' He'd run the gauntlet of the press clustered outside. His throat clogged as he thought of her facing them alone.

Her expression softened. 'I appreciate it. But I remembered your advice. To start as I mean to go on.' She closed the book with a snap. 'I was afraid if I hid away from them today it would get harder and harder.'

She swallowed and Lucien saw past her raised chin and determined mouth to the upset woman. Distressed because of him.

'Ah, Aurélie.' He lifted his hand to her cheek, stroking gently. 'I'm sorry. This is my fault.'

'Don't be nice to me.' Her mouth wobbled in an approximation of a smile. 'This is tough enough as it is.'

'But you're doing wonderfully. And you look delicious.' It was true. 'That green suits you and I like what you've done to your hair.' He touched a curly strand that feathered her alabaster neck. Her hair was up but not in a rigidly smooth arrangement. Instead it was gathered in a soft-looking knot with a few wispy curls framing her face. 'Sophisticated and sexy.'

Colour streaked her cheeks and her lips twitched. 'I thought it better than a ponytail for this.'

He nodded. 'You look perfect.'

Her mouth turned down. 'Perfect as a king's lover?'

'Perfect for me. And to meet someone important. I spoke to her about you yesterday and planned to take you to see her later. But, in the circumstances, we'll do it now.' He gestured to the book she held. 'Are you buying that?'

Aurélie nodded, picking up another couple of books resting on a low shelf. 'I thought I'd buy my brothers a book each. It didn't have to be done today but...' She shrugged her shoulders.

The brothers who followed their parents in seeing her as a drudge? Aurélie's generosity surprised him.

'You don't have to explain to me.' He paused and met her grave brown eyes. 'I admire you, Aurélie. More than I can say.'

Perfect for me.

Lucien's words carried her through the purchase of the books and out into the cobblestoned square in a haze of excitement and delight. Did he mean it or were they simply words of reassurance?

Common sense decreed the latter, yet the heat of approval in those stunning amber eyes turned her inside out and almost—almost made her believe in miracles. Like the handsome Prince falling for his pregnant commoner Cinderella.

His praise and support lifted her confidence and made her feel good about herself. That had boosted her determination to face the press today.

They were sweeping across the square, reporters trailing them, before she really paid attention to the press scrum. And it was a scrum, even worse than when she'd arrived. The difference was that now there were dark-suited men ensuring they kept their distance.

And Lucien, his hand at her elbow, his tall body solid and reassuring at her side. She tried not to huddle closer, knowing it wasn't the cool breeze that made her want to lean against him.

'Where are we going? Who are we meeting?'

'The only other remaining member of my family. I'd arranged for us to visit her in a few days' time but when I heard you were here, with a press pack in tow, I brought the meeting forward. Remarkably she was free.'

Aurélie had known he must have been informed about her being in the city. He hadn't just happened along. But as they made their way towards an elegant building on the far side of the square, his staff keeping the press at a respectful distance, she realised what she hadn't before. This was a rescue. Lucien had abandoned his schedule to come and protect her.

There was that word again.

He felt protective. Was it madness to hope he might one day feel more?

Perfect for me. His words teased her.

She'd never been perfect for anyone except her mother. It was dangerous to think in those terms. Lucien was a good man, and caring, but he was only making the best of a difficult situation. They were together because she was pregnant. That was all.

The building had huge plate glass windows. On the ground floor she made out acres of display cabinets crammed with delicious treats and beyond that an elegant high-ceilinged room, exquisitely decorated. The patisserie looked as if it belonged in a more gracious age.

'We're going upstairs.' Lucien nodded towards more huge windows and Aurélie caught sight of tables facing out across the square.

'It's very…imposing.'

'It's one of the city's finest restaurants. An ideal place to see and be seen.'

Be seen? Aurélie was hoping to escape public attention for a bit.

A uniformed staff member opened the door with a bow and they headed up a grand crimson-carpeted staircase.

'It feels as opulent as the palace,' she whispered, trying to repress nerves and burgeoning curiosity.

'It's had royal patronage for three centuries. But don't worry, the food is fantastic and the service friendly.' He stopped, passing his coat to a waiter and helping Aurélie out of hers.

Lucien's gaze skimmed her new dress. 'I *do* approve,' he murmured, then looked up. 'Ah, she's already here.'

He ushered her across the spacious room towards a table at the centre window, set apart from the others. It commanded a view of the whole square and up a broad boulevard to the palace.

His fingers squeezed Aurélie's as they stopped before the table, set with damask linen, cut crystal and heavy silverware. A slim woman in a stylish crimson suit surveyed them with shrewd amber eyes. Her hair was white and her hands knobbly with age but her bearing was upright and her aristocratic features firm.

'Aunt Josephine, I'd like you to meet Aurélie Balland. Aurélie, this is my great-aunt, the Grand Duchess Josephine of Vallort.'

Aurélie's heart skipped. Grand Duchess sounded as daunting as King and this old lady's severe stare wasn't welcoming.

Should you curtsey to a grand duchess?

Aurélie decided to treat her as she would anyone else.

'It's lovely to meet you.' She reached out to shake her hand. For an instant she just *knew* she'd done the wrong thing, when that stare turned piercing. Then an arthritic hand lifted and clasped hers in a surprisingly strong grip.

'How do you do?' The old lady turned to Lucien. 'Sit down, do. You'll give me a crick in my neck, looking up so far.'

Instead of being daunted by her complaint, Lucien grinned and bent to kiss her. 'It's good to see you looking so well.'

'And why wouldn't I? Nothing wrong with me, Lucien. I don't have time to be ill.' She paused, frowning, as the waiter approached and murmured something to Lucien.

Lucien shot Aurélie an apologetic look and her heart sank. 'I'm sorry. This will only take a few minutes but I really do need to deal with it.'

The Grand Duchess shooed him away. 'Come back when you can devote your full attention to us. In the meantime we can have a cosy chat.'

The gimlet stare she gave Aurélie looked anything but

cosy, but Aurélie told herself it couldn't be worse than facing the press pack shouting questions. Could it?

'So, you're Lucien's young woman. Like the idea of feathering your nest in a royal palace, eh? I gather it's a far cry from your previous life, waiting tables. I'm not surprised you jumped at the chance to hook Lucien.'

Aurélie jerked back in her seat as if she'd been slapped. She hadn't expected to be welcomed with open arms, but nor had she expected this. Naively, she'd thought the worst she'd have to face today was the clamorous press.

'Actually,' she said, knotting her fingers in her lap and lifting her chin, 'living in a palace, or in this case a castle, isn't my preference. Apart from anything else, I don't like the way people think it gives them the right to judge what goes on inside.'

Not wanting to meet that inimical amber stare that should have been like Lucien's but wasn't, she turned to look outside. There, sure enough, was a huddle of photographers, lenses trained on her. If Lucien had booked this table hoping to show her being welcomed into the royal family that was about to backfire terribly.

'If you're looking for sympathy you won't get any. There's a price to be paid for notoriety.'

Aurélie dragged her gaze back, stifling the urge to get up from the table. Running wouldn't help. Besides, why should the words of one sour old woman hurt her? She'd ignored jibes from her father and stepmother and by now all of Europe thought her some tart.

She sighed. 'So I'm learning. Though, believe it or not, I don't want notoriety. Or riches. Or even a palatial nest.' She clamped her mouth shut, realising it was pointless. The Grand Duchess wasn't disposed to like her.

'But you do want Lucien, don't you?'

Aurélie met those bright eyes and denial died on her tongue. To her chagrin she felt heat flood her cheeks.

'You'll have to try camouflaging that high colour of yours or everyone will know when you're lying.'

Aurélie shook her head. 'I don't lie.'

'You're saying you care for him? Do you love him?' she snapped out, leaning across the table.

'Yes, I do,' Aurélie snapped back.

Her eyes rounded as she realised what she'd admitted. She swivelled her head towards the stairs where Lucien had disappeared but there was no sign of him.

'Ah, now that makes it interesting. Does he know?'

Mutely Aurélie shook her head.

'And yet he wants to marry you.' At Aurélie's stunned look she nodded. 'He told me of his plans. To be honest I couldn't work out why he was so set on marriage. Unless...' Her gaze dropped to Aurélie's waist and Aurélie felt her cheeks burn. Nevertheless she kept her chin up and her mouth closed.

Finally the Grand Duchess spoke. 'You're not as I'd feared, Ms Balland.'

'It would be nice to think that was a good thing. But the way my day's going, that would be too much to expect.'

To her amazement, the old lady gave a sharp crack of laughter that echoed across the room. In her peripheral vision Aurélie registered heads turning.

'It's definitely a good thing. I like you, Ms Balland. I hadn't expected to, but you're everything Lucien said and more.'

Aurélie frowned, wondering what he'd said, and how she'd managed to sway her interrogator.

'I hope you'll forgive my rudeness, my dear. But I have a soft spot for my great-nephew and I'd hate to see him caught by a conniving gold-digger.'

'I'm not—'

'Yes, I can see you're not.'

And to Aurélie's astonishment the Grand Duchess gave

her a smile every bit as charming as Lucien's. It transformed her expression from stern to welcoming.

'You were testing me?'

'Someone has to look out for him. He's so busy taking on a burden that was never supposed to be his, I couldn't be sure he was thinking clearly.'

Those amber eyes flickered and for a moment Aurélie thought she read terrible sadness there. Until the old lady seemed to gather herself.

'It's been a terrible time for your family. I'm sorry for your losses.'

The Grand Duchess nodded abruptly. 'Harder for Lucien though. Much harder. But now he has you. If you can stay the course.' Her eyes narrowed and Aurélie felt she was being sized up. 'Being King is no job for a single man. Lucien needs someone who'll support him. Can you do that?'

'I…' She hadn't thought of Lucien needing support. He'd been the one making everything happen. Managing problems. Protecting her. But she remembered his weariness as he'd dealt with the fallout of his broken engagement and it would only get worse. 'The media doesn't like me.'

'The media? Pish! We don't let those hounds rule our lives. This fuss will eventually pass. I'm talking about someone who'll give him stability, companionship, support.'

'I'd like to help him.' If he'd let her. 'But there's so much I don't know. Rules, politics, etiquette.' Aurélie gathered her courage. 'For instance, should I have curtsied to you?'

'Only if you wanted me to think you were toadying. You've got a good firm handshake, excellent posture and a pleasant smile. More than that, you can think for yourself and you've got courage.' She nodded. 'You'll do. And you can come to me for advice. Good to see you have an eye for colour too.' She gestured to Aurélie's dress. 'Clever of you to wear Vallort green. The press will lap it up and locals will see it as a sign of respect for our country.'

Aurélie didn't have the heart to admit she hadn't realised

the significance of the shade. But looking down the boulevard to the palace she saw the national flag flying proudly, white and the very same green.

Was that why Lucien had been so pleased with the dress? She'd hoped he thought her pretty in it.

But just because they shared spectacular sex didn't mean he was falling for her. She had to remember that.

'You haven't been trying to scare Aurélie off, have you?' Lucien murmured as he slid into the seat beside her, taking her hand in his. Immediately her stiff body softened. He smiled but a slight frown wrinkled his forehead.

'Nonsense. The girl has more gumption than to be frightened by a harmless old lady.'

Aurélie smiled and Lucien snorted with laughter. 'The day you behave like a harmless old lady is the day I start worrying.' Yet he slanted a questioning look at Aurélie.

'We've been having a cosy chat,' she reassured him and caught the Grand Duchess's approving eye.

Remarkably, it seemed she'd discovered an ally. Which was just as well. Aurélie was going to need one.

CHAPTER FIFTEEN

'I CAN'T ACCEPT IT.' Aurélie dragged her eyes from the jewellery box to Lucien, sitting on the edge of the bed.

His straight shoulders looked wider than ever naked. Her pulse quickened as she saw the tiny marks there. Marks she'd just made with her fingernails as they made love.

'You haven't even seen what's inside.' A smile lifted one corner of his mouth and she cursed the familiar melting sensation deep inside.

'It looks expensive. I don't need expensive gifts.'

For a moment Lucien looked almost disappointed. But she put that down to a trick of the light.

'Occasionally a bit of bling is called for. Tonight is one of those nights. Aunt Josephine's parties are very exclusive and very formal. If you don't wear at least *some* jewellery, you'll draw extra attention to yourself.'

Finally Aurélie nodded, accepting the box he pushed into her hands.

The last couple of weeks had been a trial, with so much public curiosity about her. Luckily she'd had the support of Lucien, his friends and even his indomitable and surprisingly likeable great-aunt.

The spiteful stories had eased a little after Princess Ilsa was photographed leaving a party with a notorious billionaire, apparently for a private rendezvous on his luxury yacht. Stories about her being heartbroken over Lucien couldn't survive in the face of what looked like a blatant affair with a hot lover.

Plus the press who'd tried to dig up dirt on Aurélie had come up empty-handed. People from her home town had been generous with praise. Even her family had for a change been positive. Her stepmother had got quite teary about how much they missed her!

Her family had called to wish her well. The boys had been excited and full of questions about life in a castle but her father and stepmother had been subdued. They would never be close. Aurélie told herself she'd concentrate on the new family she was making with Lucien.

'Aurélie?'

She opened the box. Then froze.

'This is for *me*?' Her voice sounded strangled.

It was dazzling. Two rows of lustrous pearls made a choker style necklace. At the front, surrounded by brilliant diamonds, was a huge aqua gem. Yet when it moved in her shaky hand highlights of deeper green, cobalt and even crimson glowed.

'It looks alive.'

'It's an Australian opal. You like it?'

Aurélie swallowed. Like didn't go anywhere near her feelings. 'It's the most beautiful thing I've ever seen.'

She looked up and found Lucien watching with such intensity her breath stuttered. This wasn't simply a kind gesture, like arranging the piano lessons she so enjoyed.

This was the sort of gift a man gave the woman he loved.

Was it possible?

She licked suddenly dry lips and Lucien's attention dropped to her mouth. Her blood sizzled.

'It will look perfect with that aqua dress you've been saving for tonight.'

He'd chosen it because it matched her *dress*?

She'd hoped he'd think *she* was perfect, not her wardrobe. That he'd see not the image she projected but the woman desperate for his love. He'd described her as perfect once, but then too he'd meant appearances.

Aurélie's stomach hollowed as she stifled disappointment. 'It's an expensive gift just to match my dress.'

Their gazes caught and held. Anticipation rose.

'Appearances are important. I know you're still not comfortable at court but wearing this will help you look the part.'

Hope crumbled and Aurélie berated herself for a fool. How could she have thought…?

She looked down at the gems before he could read her distress. This was window dressing to help her look as if she belonged.

'Besides, in two days you'll be twelve weeks pregnant and we'll announce our engagement.' He paused as if awaiting a response. 'Look on it as an early engagement gift. You'll need something special to wear for the official photos.'

Lucien was being thoughtful, ensuring she'd look the part tonight and next week when they officially got engaged.

Even so, a great ache started up in Aurélie's chest. Thoughtful was nice. But it was no substitute for love.

She nodded, stroking the fiery opal rather than meeting Lucien's eyes. There was no point pining for the impossible. Lucien *cared*. That had to be enough. And he wanted her physically.

Maybe that was why she felt so needy. Making love always made her feel emotionally close to him, though for him it was just lust.

'You're right. It will look terrific with the beaded dress.'

'Stand up and I'll put it on you.'

Aurélie slid out of bed and turned so he stood behind her. She looked through the open dressing room door to their reflections in a full-length mirror. Her pale body and messy hair contrasted with Lucien's taller, stronger frame, his golden skin. Her heart dipped as he swept her hair aside, settling the necklace around her throat and fastening the catch.

He was right. Even naked, the piece transformed her into someone else.

Like the sort of woman he'd have chosen for himself if an unexpected pregnancy hadn't forced his hand?

Aurélie swallowed convulsively.

'You're so sexy.' Lucien's voice was a gruff rumble that twisted her insides needily.

For her it wasn't only sex, it was love too. Maybe that was why, despite her turmoil, she found it impossible to resist when he wrapped an arm around her waist and hooked her back against him. His other hand went to her breast. Desire weakened her as she watched him tease her nipple and felt the deft play of his fingers on her flesh. Threads of fire wound through her and she shifted back against his erection.

In the mirror their eyes met, Lucien's glazed with hunger. He looked magnificent. Strongly muscled, handsome and sensual. His heavy-lidded stare was pure invitation.

Need ignited. She wanted *not* to want him. *Not* to love him. But there was no remedy for it.

'I want you, Aurélie.' His arm dropped from her waist and she watched it slide down her still-flat abdomen, into her nest of red curls. She was already wet, muscles clenching around his fingers as he delved then withdrew. Her knees loosened.

This man made her weak. But she wanted to be strong. Strong enough not to care that he didn't love her.

She reached around and grasped him, fingers sliding down his length.

That solid jaw clenched and his neck arched back as he groaned. The sound elicited a thrill of pleasure at her power. It made her feel less helpless, watching the tendons stand proud in his taut throat, feeling the jerky thrust of his body into her hand.

'I need you. Now.' It was a gruff demand. Lucien stepped back, holding her against him as he sat abruptly on the bed.

The hair on his thighs tickled the back of her legs as she sat but her focus was on his jutting arousal behind her.

'Spread your legs.' Aurélie didn't refuse. She wanted this. Large, impatient hands splayed her legs wide so she sat astride him, open to his touch. She gasped as he delved again to her core, teasing till she shivered and her eyelids fluttered.

'Keep your eyes open, Aurélie. Look at us.'

Through the open dressing room door she saw their reflection. She looked utterly wanton, naked and spreading herself to his touch. Her legs were wide across his thighs, his hand teasing her clitoris as she rocked against him. Her inner muscles spasmed at the picture they made, his face looming behind her, taut with primal hunger.

'Lift up, sweetheart, and let me in.'

Aurélie rose then sank slowly, savouring the thick thrust of his erection, piercing deep. She shuddered as he shifted and ripples of arousal spread.

He moved again, urging her up. She rose then fell again, harder this time, and sensation rioted through her. In the mirror she watched his hands cup her breasts as he grazed her neck with his teeth and pinched her nipples. Aurélie jerked forward, needing friction, and his hand was there again, rubbing while he filled her from behind, pushing hard and insistent till everything exploded in a desperate rush to ecstasy.

She heard him shout, felt his teeth on her flesh, his thrusting weight fill her to the limit, and rapture took them both.

An age later he spoke. She was too spent even to open her eyes, just lolled against him, not wanting to move.

'You didn't want to marry for our child's sake, Aurélie, but there are bonuses, don't you agree?'

Her eyes opened then to see herself spread, boneless, across his big frame, his grin one of satiation.

Sex was a bonus, not some spiritual connection. They would marry for their child's sake. Clear and simple.

So much for her pathetic hopes.

Lucien looked across the glittering crowd to his fiancée and fought a frown.

It had been a good night. Josephine's parties were always

terrific, with interesting people and engaging conversation. Aurélie had fitted in beautifully and appeared to enjoy herself. They'd drifted apart after she'd insisted he didn't have to stay by her side all night.

Funny how that had struck a jarring note. He *wanted* to be with her. But seeing her conversing with various guests, her smile engaging, he knew she'd been right. He couldn't be by her side all the time, no matter how much he wanted to be. She needed to forge some relationships of her own.

Yet he'd felt unsettled since they'd left the castle. They'd had stupendous sex and Aurélie had been suitably dazzled by his gift. She wore it now with a strappy beaded dress that caressed her curves and glittered when she moved. She looked a million dollars.

Yet something wasn't right. Despite her smiles this evening. Despite the passion. He thought back to the scene in his bedroom and how, even as they'd shared that awesome climax, he'd felt a change in her. A shift away from him.

It was impossible. Two people couldn't get closer than they'd been. He'd *felt* it, damn it! He'd fought for weeks to break down Aurélie's barriers and thought he'd succeeded. Now he wasn't sure.

The strange thing was that, while he'd tried to dismantle those barriers, she'd sneaked under his guard and made him feel things he hadn't thought possible. He knew the acute ache that came from losing loved ones and had guarded his emotions, wary of feeling too much. He'd been spectacularly unsuccessful.

Tuning out the conversation around him, he narrowed his gaze on his fiancée. She looked pale and there were tiny vertical lines on her brow.

Excusing himself, he crossed the room, his hand sliding around her elbow. She was trembling and instantly leaned into his hold.

'Will you excuse us?' Without waiting for an answer, Lucien led her from the room, his arm around her waist.

'What is it?' he asked when they were alone. 'Morning sickness?'

'No, I—' Her breath hissed and her hand went to her abdomen. 'I need the bathroom.'

Quickly he shepherded her there then paced the corridor, staring at but not seeing the artwork on the walls. Instead he saw the downward tug of Aurélie's lips as if she were in pain.

She'd be okay. Of course she would. Perhaps the finger food hadn't agreed with her. Yet he paced again, too restless to settle. His nape prickled and apprehension blocked his gullet.

Finally the bathroom door cracked open. Lucien was there in two strides. His blood chilled as he read Aurélie's milk-white face.

'Please, I need the hospital.' Her mouth twisted. 'The baby...' She put out a hand and he grabbed it, steadying her.

'It'll be all right,' Lucien murmured, telling himself it *must* be, as his brain clicked through the mechanics of getting her to hospital as soon as possible. Fear stirred but he thrust it down. He didn't have that luxury when Aurélie needed him. 'Everything will be fine, you'll see.'

He pushed the door open, lifted her into his arms and turned towards the entrance.

Soft curls nudged his neck and chin as she shook her head. 'It won't,' came the stifled sob. 'I'm bleeding and there are cramps.' Her voice rose on a gasp of pain and terror.

Lucien's stride faltered and his blood turned icy, then he quickened his step.

'Lucien?' It was Josephine, stepping out from the drawing room, her eyebrows raised.

'Aurélie's unwell,' he said without stopping. 'Ring the hospital. Tell them we're coming. It may be a miscarriage.' His voice cracked.

'An ambulance,' Aurélie whispered, her breath warm

and strangely reassuring against his throat. Nothing bad was going to happen to her. He wouldn't let it.

'It's not far and my car's outside. We'll be there in the time it'd take them to reach us.'

And they were. Fortunately his aunt lived on the side of the city closest to the hospital. As he pulled to a stop at the entrance, emergency staff appeared and within moments Aurélie was being taken inside.

After that events became a blur. Later, all Lucien could remember was the stark fear on Aurélie's face and the need to appear calm, for her sake. Inside he was a wreck. He couldn't believe this was happening. They might lose the baby. Was Aurélie herself safe?

Guilt scorched him. Had this happened because they'd had sex tonight? He hadn't been gentle. He'd been desperate to possess her. Or maybe it was the stress she was under, plus him taking her to the party. Maybe if she'd rested at home instead… Regrets lay heavy on his conscience.

He spoke to staff who were so composed he wanted to rage at them for not taking this emergency seriously. For it *was* an emergency. Bright blood stained Aurélie's dress and her pain was terrible to watch. Lucien did what he could, held her hand, reassured, answered the staff's questions when she wasn't up to it.

There were murmured consultations, tests, more tests, more questions.

Finally, in the early hours, they were alone. Senior staff had been and gone. They'd been grave and couldn't give firm assurances. What they did say, what Lucien clung to, was that Aurélie hadn't miscarried.

Yet.

He swallowed, pain searing his dry throat, and blinked to clear his vision.

'You should go home and get some rest.' Aurélie sounded wrung out.

'I'll stay with you.' Somehow he conjured a smile, pretending that her strained face, as white as her hospital gown, didn't terrify him.

'You need rest too. Who knows what tomorrow will bring?' Her mouth trembled and she swallowed. She looked so pitiful his heart wrung. 'If you go, I'll try to sleep too.'

'Good idea. I'll settle in the corner so I don't disturb you.'

But she shook her head. 'Please, Lucien. I need to be alone for a little while.' Something must have showed on his face because she hurried on. 'You've been marvellous. But I need…space. They'll call you if there's any change.'

She looked so horribly vulnerable. How could he deny her? Finally he nodded.

He leaned over and brushed his mouth against hers, taking heart from the way her lips clung.

'Call me any time. I'll have my phone on.'

Reluctantly he straightened. He had no intention of leaving the hospital but he'd respect her desire for space. Though it felt totally wrong leaving her.

As he reached the door she spoke. 'If the worst happens. If I lose the baby…' He swung around to see her lips form a crooked line of distress. 'There'll be no need to marry.' Her gaze skittered away. 'I'll go straight home to France.'

Her words tore through him like a grenade through unprotected flesh. Shockwaves ricocheted across his bones. His belly hollowed then filled with bone-freezing ice. How could she even *think*…?

Lucien was halfway back to the bed when her upraised hand stopped him.

'Please, don't argue. Not now.'

Lucien stared down into taut features. Saw the rapid rise of her breasts, the clenched-knuckled grip on her sheet.

Everything urged him to protest, persuade, demand. She couldn't go back to France. He wouldn't allow it.

But she was growing more distressed the longer he stood there. And distress couldn't be good for her or the baby. Lucien breathed deep, nostrils flaring. It shouldn't be possible to detect her floral scent over the antiseptic hospital smell yet it was there. Teasing him with all he stood to lose.

It felt as if someone had plucked his still beating heart halfway out of his ribcage. It thundered high in his throat and his skin felt clammy. His hands clenched but he resisted the urge to reach for her.

'Rest now, Aurélie. We'll talk tomorrow.'

He strode from the room.

Only when he was out of sight did he sag back against the corridor wall. He'd thought he'd plumbed the depths months ago, but this…

Lucien had lost everyone he'd ever loved. Now he faced that prospect again.

CHAPTER SIXTEEN

FROM HER HOSPITAL bed Aurélie stared out over the rooftops to the valley beyond. She could even pick out Lucien's castle in the distance.

She blinked and felt her mouth crumple, helpless tears pooling and blurring her vision. She hated feeling so emotional. Despite the doctor's cautious optimism this morning, it was too early to believe everything would be okay.

Her hand crept across her abdomen.

Was her baby safe?

She thought of Lucien last night. His concern. His determination to look after her.

He was worried about the baby.

Their relationship was predicated on her pregnancy. Last night she'd got ridiculously hopeful, thinking that fabulous opal necklace could be a love token.

Because she'd fallen in love with him at first sight she'd hoped for a miracle.

Lucien had set her straight. He wanted her suitably dressed at glamorous functions and for their engagement photos. He didn't want her looking like a waitress, a pregnant working-class woman, but a royal.

As if even the most gorgeous jewellery could turn her into someone she wasn't.

Her mouth twisted. No jewellery would make her into the sort of woman Lucien could love.

Her hopes had finally died last night when he'd left her. Though she'd asked him to.

If he loved her, he'd have stayed.

If he cared about *her*, he'd have been horrified at her decision to leave if she lost the baby. He'd have told her he wanted her, baby or not.

Yet after an initial objection he'd nodded and left.

What had she expected? A vow of undying affection?

She hadn't been testing him. She'd just stated facts.

Hadn't she?

A convulsive sob escaped. It was clear where she stood. Nothing had altered.

To Lucien her value was solely as mother to his child. As an individual she wasn't worth fighting for.

She rubbed her hand across her face, smearing the tears that leaked down her cheeks.

The door opened and a nurse entered. She pretended not to see the tear tracks, instead greeting Aurélie with a smile and telling her she'd come to help her freshen up. 'The castle sent through a bag for you. You'll be much more comfortable wearing your own things.'

Aurélie looked at the designer suitcase, so different to her battered backpack. Lucien's housekeeper had probably filled it with those lovely silk nightgowns the stylist had organised. What she really wanted was the comfort of the baggy old T-shirt she used to sleep in.

She offered the nurse a wobbly smile. She couldn't afford to mope. She had to be strong and hope for the best. That her baby would be okay. Everything else, like Lucien's feelings for her, was secondary.

By the time she was clean, changed and resting back against the pillows, Aurélie was exhausted. But she roused as the nurse congratulated her.

'Sorry? I don't understand.' It couldn't be for the pregnancy, not while they waited to see if she miscarried.

'On your engagement.'

'Engagement?' Aurélie frowned.

'It's in today's paper.' The woman beamed. 'And so romantic. It's good to think of the King finding happiness after so much loss. We're all so excited for you both.'

Aurélie's brain froze. An engagement, announced in the paper?

There'd been a terrible mistake. Lucien had agreed to wait until next week. Given the danger of a miscarriage, surely he'd wait even longer, because there might *be* no baby. Without a baby, there'd be no engagement, no marriage.

Again Aurélie had to blink back tears.

'Now, now.' The nurse took Aurélie's hand, checking her pulse. 'I know it's scary, being here, but you're doing well this morning. Truly. Rest and try not to worry.'

Aurélie conjured a wobbly smile. 'Thank you.'

When the nurse left she curled up on her side and shut her eyes, though sleep would be impossible. How could she not worry when everything was going wrong? How had the press learned their secret? No one had known—

'Aurélie?'

Her eyes snapped open and there was Lucien. Her heart gave a thump of joy and the cramping pain in her chest eased.

The lower part of his face was shadowed with beard growth, emphasising the masculine angles of chin and jaw. Even the concern etched around his eyes only made him look less like a fantasy hero and more like the man she loved.

Till she remembered his concern was all for the baby she carried, not her.

'You're here early.' Her voice was husky. The sound undid him. He could bear most things, but Aurélie hurting…

Lucien crossed to her bedside and pulled up a chair, yet he didn't reach for her. She looked so fragile.

Seeing the change in her made his chest ache. He wanted to haul her into his arms and reassure himself as much as her. He wanted to make things better for her but some things were beyond his control. He wasn't even sure how to reach her when she wore that shuttered look.

But he had to try. More, he had to *succeed*. He refused to consider the alternative, of her shunning him permanently.

'I stayed the night.' Seeing her stunned look he clarified.

'The chairs in the waiting room are surprisingly comfortable.' Or would be if you weren't well over six feet. 'I had someone bring clothes for us both this morning.' He rubbed his stubbly chin. He'd forgotten to ask for a razor.

Her red-rimmed eyes rounded. 'You could have gone to the palace. Someone would have rung if there was a change.'

Lucien shrugged. 'I wanted to be here.'

Not wanted but *needed*. He couldn't stay away.

The staff had got used to him prowling the corridor through the night, checking on Aurélie through the window in the door and demanding updates whenever staff checked on her.

Fortunately the news this morning was more positive. He clung to that.

'I hear you're doing well today. You and the baby.'

Aurélie's gaze slid away. The connection he'd felt from the moment she'd met his eyes frayed.

'We've got a problem.'

'The baby?' He reached out and took her hand. To his horror she flinched.

What was that? He was used to Aurélie melting in his embrace, snuggling up to him, not shrinking away. His fingers tightened, *willing* her to accept his touch. Needing it.

She shook her head, her mouth a tight line.

'What is it, Aurélie? Tell me.' A chill enveloped him. 'Is there some complication? Are *you* in danger?' The doctor hadn't mentioned anything, but a nurse had just been in here. Maybe she'd seen something…

'No, nothing like that. I'm okay.'

Solemn brown eyes met his and his racing heartbeat settled a little. He sank back in his seat, still cradling her hand.

'The press know about our engagement. Did you have a press release ready? That must have been it—'

'That's what's bothering you?'

'Of course!' She frowned. 'It's complicated everything.

What if the baby…?' Her mouth folded in tight at the corners and she swallowed. 'What if I miscarry?'

'Whatever happens I'll be with you, Aurélie. I won't leave you again.'

Lucien silently castigated himself. He should have stayed with Aurélie, despite her protests. She was fretting about things that didn't matter.

'Don't you see?' She sat up straighter, colour whipping her cheeks. 'It complicates everything. With this news the media will be even more full of gossip.'

Lucien surveyed her taut features. Her distress was a danger, surely, to herself and their baby.

'Don't worry about the media, Aurélie. Your safety, and our child's, are more important than any news story.'

For a moment those brown eyes met his with something like hope. Then her mouth crumpled.

'If I lose the baby there'll be no engagement. If only they hadn't found out—'

'They were going to find out soon anyway.' Lucien drew a deep breath and folded his other hand around hers, cradling it in both of his. 'I can't apologise for releasing the news.'

It had been a calculated, deliberate action.

'*You* did it?' Shock etched her features. 'But why?'

Grimly he acknowledged his timing hadn't been ideal, but he'd had no choice. He hoped she'd understand and forgive. He'd gambled everything on that action.

The knowledge of what he stood to lose twisted his stomach in knots. He'd never been so frightened.

After months devoted to duty, to meeting the demands of his country, acting in the way his family would have expected and putting his own desires last, Lucien had rebelled. He'd acted selfishly. Yet he couldn't regret it.

He was no saint. Self-sacrifice had limits.

'Because I was desperate.' He'd feared admitting it but now that didn't matter. All he cared about was Aurélie.

She frowned as if he were a puzzle she couldn't fit together. Not surprising when he hadn't explained. Lucien gathered himself, sitting straighter.

'Last night I was scared.' Terrified would be a better description. Even now he was on edge, hyper-alert. 'When you said you'd leave if you lost the baby, I panicked.'

Aurélie's expression gave nothing away except shock. At least she hadn't pushed him away.

Lucien shook his head. 'That makes it sound like I acted without thinking, and yes, I made a snap decision. But I knew exactly what I was doing when I put through the call.'

'I understand you were worried about the baby, but not why you told the press we were engaged.'

'*Are* engaged.' He paused, heart thundering, waiting for a confirmation that didn't come. He forced himself to continue, despite the glacial chill around his heart. 'Yes, I'm worried about the baby. I don't want to lose it and I worry about how you'd cope if we did. But more than that, I don't want to lose *you*.'

Aurélie's fingers twitched in his hand. 'I don't think there's a big risk to my health from a miscarriage.'

'I mean I don't want you to go back to France. I want you to stay here, with me, no matter what happens with the baby.' He paused, knowing she'd think his action arrogant, whereas in fact he'd been desperate. 'I wanted to force your hand.'

'Why would you want that?' Her fingers curled around his so hard he felt the bite of her short nails.

'Because I want to spend my life with you, of course. I love you, Aurélie.'

There, he'd said it. Revealed what had finally become clear to him.

Lucien surveyed her closely, hope fighting fear.

She didn't smile back.

The chill spread, icing his bones.

'You can't. It's just sex and sharing this baby.'

A dreadful plummeting sensation stole his breath. Was

that all she felt? He'd hoped for more. Surely that way she made love, and it *was* making love, not just slaking physical desire, proved Aurélie felt more.

He gathered his voice. 'That's all you feel for me?'

'I'm talking about *you*. I know you enjoy sex.' She said it briskly as if she'd never felt that phenomenal shared ecstasy, and something gave way inside him. 'The only reason we're together is because I got pregnant. I even had to prove it was yours with a paternity test. You didn't trust my word. Hardly the action of a man in love.'

As she said it, Aurélie knew how unfair that was. Any man in Lucien's situation would want proof. Clearly he now knew the child was his. He was pretending he loved her to keep her and the baby here.

Aurélie blinked and concentrated on not giving in to futile tears.

'There was no paternity test.'

Their gazes locked. She told herself he was deliberately using her weakness for him, trying to cajole her into believing him. But it wouldn't work.

'Of course there was. The doctor took my blood the first morning I was here.'

Lucien looked back from under lowered brows, his bright eyes somehow dimmed. 'Yes. But when she approached me about a DNA swab I refused. It felt wrong. I didn't need a test because I knew you were telling the truth.'

'You knew…?' Aurélie had to be hearing things. 'How could you know?'

Those straight shoulders rose. 'I have no idea. Just like I don't understand how I trusted you that first night or why you took the risk of inviting me into your home when you knew nothing about me.' He looked down at her hand, dwarfed between his. 'From the first there's been something between us that defied logic. Connection. Trust. A link. Whatever it is, it's real and I trust it.'

Lucien breathed deep, his chest expanding mightily, and Aurélie felt her own lungs swell on an in-caught breath. The hair at her nape rose. So often she'd pondered the link she'd felt to a man she barely knew. Now she knew him better she understood she'd fallen in love but—

'You really don't know for sure if this is your baby?'

'Oh, I know, Aurélie. It's ours. Because you say so. You'd never pass off another man's child as mine.'

He lifted her hands to his mouth and kissed first one then the other and tendrils of need blossomed, despite her determination to hold strong.

'I hope with everything I am that our baby survives and we can all grow together as a family. But even if the worst happens, I want you with me, as my wife. Not because I want a queen but because I love you.'

Her heart fluttered as if it was about to burst out of her ribcage and escape.

His expression. The look in his eyes. The hammering pulse at his throat. The way his hands shook as they held hers. All chipped away at her certainty that this was a ruse.

'We only met three months ago—'

'I know. I'm asking a lot of you and I'll understand if you don't feel the same way about me yet, but give me time, Aurélie. Stay with me and—'

'I don't want time.'

Before her blurring eyes Lucien's proud face paled. His serious expression turned sombre, as if he'd heard grievous news.

She hurried on. 'You really love me?' Even now it didn't seem possible.

He swallowed hard then nodded.

'Oh, Lucien!' She pulled one hand free of his death grip and cupped his hard jaw. Beneath the prickle of stubble she felt a muscle work and the frantic beat of his pulse. 'I've been so miserable because I thought you only wanted our child. I wanted you to want so much more.'

The transformation in his face was like a blinding flash of sunlight.

'Tell me.' It was a rough command and Aurélie adored the sound.

'I love you, Lucien. I think I've loved you since—'

Aurélie never finished. His mouth slammed into hers and for a long time there was nothing but the desperate need for reassurance between them both. The shared shock of realising their love was mutual. The frantic joy that made them cling to each other.

As the minutes passed and the panicked need for reassurance eased, their kisses grew tender. Lucien caressed her face, his touch soft as he brushed hair from her cheeks.

She looked into his eyes and now she saw it. Something she hadn't seen since her mother. A light that eclipsed all else.

A light that warmed her right to the core of her being.

Aurélie had come home. She was wanted, truly wanted, not for something she could provide but for herself.

She'd found love.

'I've never been so happy,' she murmured between kisses.

'Nor have I.' Lucien's voice was tender yet serious. Eyes the colour of sunshine and promises smiled down into hers. 'This is only the beginning, my darling. Only the beginning.'

EPILOGUE

'AND SO, MY FRIENDS, I give you our beloved King Lucien. May his next ten years on the throne be as peaceful and successful as his first ten.'

Lucien's chest swelled with pride. Not because of Aurélie's kind words about his first decade as King, but because of *her*.

Seeing her on the royal podium in the vast ballroom, poised and lovely as she addressed the crowd in all three of Vallort's official languages, Lucien wanted to sweep her into his arms. To kiss her with all the wild passion nine and a half years of marriage hadn't dimmed.

A vision in brilliant aqua, in a gleaming sleeveless ball gown, wearing her favourite opal choker necklace and a delicate opal and diamond tiara in her bright hair, she was everything to him.

Almost everything. A small hand twisted in his and he looked down to meet earnest brown eyes beneath copper hair.

'That's you, Papa! King Lucien.' Five-year-old Prince Alex's voice was almost drowned by the swell of sound as the throng repeated Lucien's name in a toast.

'So it is.' Lucien smiled.

'He'll have to go up there to make a speech. You'd better take my hand instead, Alex.' At nine years old, Justin had a royal's upright posture and sense of responsibility. At least at official occasions. The rest of the time he was usually haring around with his friends, getting into mischief. He was also, according to Aurélie, the very image of Lucien.

'Or,' said a third voice, 'we could *all* go and join *Maman*. She might be lonely up there by herself.'

Lucien tried and failed to suppress a smile as he met his

daughter's beguiling gaze. Another redhead like her mother, seven-year-old Chloe knew far too much about how to get her own way. But she was good-natured as well as smart, with a cheeky sense of humour. She was hard to resist.

Lucien looked up to see his wife watching him with raised eyebrows.

'An excellent idea, Chloe,' he said, ushering the children forward. 'We'll all go.'

Seconds later, Lucien stood on the podium with his children before him and his sweetheart at his side. He held her closer than royal tradition dictated. But certain traditions had changed in the last decade.

Among the celebrating crowd he saw not one shocked face that he'd bring his brood to the anniversary ball.

To one side of the room, with a glass of champagne in her hand, sat Great-aunt Josephine, regal in crimson, her eyes sparkling.

'After Papa's speech we can dance, can't we, Papa?'

'One dance only,' Aurélie whispered, 'then it's bedtime.'

His wife might be the one with the psychology degree but Lucien had enough experience as a father and a diplomat to know it was time to begin his speech. Before the complaints began.

He spoke briefly but warmly before inviting the crowd to enjoy the rest of the night.

Lucien danced with his daughter and both boys waltzed with their mother. Justin even persuaded Aunt Josephine onto the floor, to the delight of onlookers.

Finally, Lucien held his beloved wife in his arms, whirling her down the length of the gilded ballroom.

'Have you danced with the new English ambassador yet?' she murmured in his ear. 'She has a soft spot for you.'

Lucien bent his head, inhaling Aurélie's fresh flower scent, the same after all these years. 'I will on one condition.'

'What's that, Your Majesty?' Sultry dark eyes met his and heat shot straight to his groin.

He growled under his breath, 'Don't rush to take off that necklace when we go upstairs.'

Aurélie's eyebrows rose in mock surprise. 'But I can't sleep in it, Lucien.'

He hauled her closer and bent to murmur against her lush mouth, 'It's not sleep I have in mind.'

Then, as he whirled her round the end of the ballroom, her dress flaring out against his legs, Aurélie's laugh pealed out and his heart soared.

They might have fallen for each other in a single night but what they shared grew better and better.

No man looked forward to the future more.

* * * * *

MILLS & BOON

Coming next month

HIS BILLION-DOLLAR TAKEOVER TEMPTATION
Emmy Grayson

"Mr. Cabrera?"

The husky feminine voice slid over his senses and sent a flash of heat over his skin. He took another deliberate sip of his wine before turning his attention to the second woman who had invaded his space this evening.

Her.

The blonde woman he'd locked eyes with before Alejandro's arrival now stood before him. The neckline of her dark blue gown plunged down in a V to the silver ribbon wrapped around her slender waist. From there the dress flowed into a long, billowing skirt that reminded Adrian of the waters of the Mediterranean before a storm.

His eyes drifted back up to her face in a slow, deliberate perusal. Lush silver-blonde curls enhanced her delicate features. Violet eyes stared back at him, and her caramel-colored lips were set in a firm line.

"Yes," he finally responded, his voice cool, showing that, despite the unusually intense effect she was having on him, he was still in control.

She stepped forward and held out her hand, bare except for a simple silver band on her wrist. Adrian grasped her fingers, pleasantly surprised by her firm grip.

"My name is Everleigh Bradford. Congratulations on your Merlot. It's exquisite."

"Thank you." He arched a brow. "While your compliments are appreciated, was it necessary for you to ignore the 'Balcony Closed' sign and invade my privacy?"

Everleigh's chin came up and her eyes flashed with stubborn fire. "Yes."

Intriguing… There were plenty of men who would have cringed at the slightest hint of his disapproval. But not this woman. She stood her ground, shoulders thrown back, lips now set in a determined line.

"You're a busy man, Mr. Cabrera. I need to speak with you on an urgent matter. I'm sorry for breaking the rules, but it was necessary for me to have a moment alone with you."

Her honesty was refreshing. A night with someone as bold and beautiful as Everleigh would more than make up for his past few months of celibacy.

He infused his smile with sensuality as he raked his gaze up and down her slim form once more, this time letting his appreciation for her body show. "I would greatly enjoy a moment alone with you."

Everleigh's cheeks flushed pink. The blush caught Adrian unawares. Was she an innocent or just playing a role? Much as it would disappoint him, she wouldn't be the first to go to such lengths to catch his attention.

"This has nothing to do with sex, Mr. Cabrera."

"Adrian."

Her lips parted. "I… Excuse me?"

"Please call me Adrian."

Those beautifully shaded violet eyes narrowed. "This is a business discussion, Mr. Cabrera. First names are for friends and family."

"We could become friends, Everleigh."

What was wrong with him? He never teased a woman like this. He complimented, touched, seduced… But with this woman he just couldn't help himself.

Perhaps it was the blush. Yes, that had to be it. The delicate coloring that even now crept down her throat toward the rising slopes of her breasts…

"We will never be friends, Mr. Cabrera," Everleigh snapped. "I'm here to discuss your proposed purchase of Fox Vineyards."

"Then let's talk."

Continue reading
HIS BILLION-DOLLAR TAKEOVER TEMPTATION
Emmy Grayson

Available next month
www.millsandboon.co.uk

COMING SOON!

We really hope you enjoyed reading this book.
If you're looking for more romance, be sure to
head to the shops when new books are
available on

Thursday 13th May